# Sacred
# and
# Profane

By Faye Kellerman

*The Ritual Bath*

# FAYE KELLERMAN...

# Sacred
## and
# Profane

ARBOR HOUSE     NEW YORK

Manufactured in the United States of America

10  9  8  7  6  5  4  3  2  1

Library of Congress Cataloging-in-Publication Data

Kellerman, Faye.
    Sacred and profane.

    I. Title.
PS3561.E3864S2  1987  813'.54  87-1820
ISBN 0-87795-887-4

For my rocks of ages, past and present:

*My father, Oscar,* alav hashalom. *I miss you very much.*
*My mother, Anne.*
*My ingenious one and only, Jonathan.*
*And the three musketeers, Jesse, Rachel, and Ilana.*

Special thanks to Rabbi Gerald Werner.

# Sacred
# and
# Profane

Y ou can keep your white Christmas, thought Decker dreamily, as sunlight blanketed his prone frame. Give me December in L.A. anytime. Currier and Ives snowscapes looked swell on wrapping paper, but as far as he was concerned, icy Christmas winters were best left to penguins and polar bears.

Besides, he wasn't really sure what relevance Christmas—with or without snow—held for him any more. No tree adorned the picture window of his living room, no cards sat atop the mantle of the fireplace, no multicolored lights hung along the wood planked siding of his ranch. Hell, here it was the day of Christmas Eve and he was out camping in the foothills, isolated from civilization, playing big brother to two little boys with yarmulkes. Christmas had never been a big deal to him, but still it felt strange. Some habits were hard to shake.

Using his knapsack for a pillow, he shifted onto his back. The air was sweet and tangy, the ground rich with mulch. Throwing an arm over his eyes, he noticed that it had been cooked a deep salmon and he cursed his coloring, typical for a redhead—all burn, no tan. He should have been more generous with the sunscreen. The arm, already dully throbbing, would blossom into full-fledged pain by tonight. He propped himself onto his elbows and called out to Ginger. The Irish setter trotted over to him, plopped down by his side, and went to sleep.

Decker glanced at Sammy, who sat twenty feet away, reading

while dipping his toes into an isolated pool of rainwater. Behind him, a narrow stream carried mountain run-off from last week's rains. Earlier in the day, Decker had offered to take the boys wading, but Sammy had complained that the water was too cold. Though he wasn't weak or timid, he just wasn't keen on the outdoors. The star-studded nighttime sky, the hikes, the cookouts had left him unmoved. Though he insisted he was having the time of his life, Decker knew the kid would have been just as happy holed up anywhere as long as he had Decker's undivided attention. The boy could *talk*. Often, after his younger brother, Jacob, had fallen asleep, Sammy would start to pour his heart out, engaging Decker in conversation that sometimes lasted until the early hours of the morning. He was an overly mature kid, not surprising for a first born who'd taken on the role of man of the house.

Jacob was a different story. The eternal optimist, an enthusiastic youngster who could elicit a smile from a slab of marble. Great at amusing himself. Right now he was busy watching an ant hill, eyes glued to the nonstop action.

Decker enjoyed both of the boys, but knew if he walked out of their lives tomorrow, Jake would recover quickly. Sammy was the vulnerable one. And that worried him because his relationship with their mother was so ambiguous. He and Rina were in love but not yet lovers. Her religious values forbade intimacy outside of marriage, and marriage right now was impossible. They were in limbo until Decker officially converted.

There was an easy way out. He could reveal to Rina that he was adopted and that his biological parents were Jewish, so there was no legal reason for him to convert. But he didn't consider that a viable option. Too dishonest. He was a product of his *real* parents—the man and woman who'd nurtured him. And they had raised him a Baptist. Besides, Rina deserved a genuinely committed Jew for a husband, not a Jew by accident of birth. Anything less would make her miserable. He knew he'd have to come to Orthodoxy on his own.

He inhaled deeply, filling his lungs with the pungent, crisp air. He was making progress. His weekly sessions with Rabbi

Schulman had shown him to be a quick learner. So far, he had no trouble grasping the intellectual and legal aspects of Judaism. But Hebrew remained a roadblock. The boys loved to play teacher with him, drilling him on the *alef beis* from their first grade primers, correcting his pronunciation and handwriting. They giggled when he made a mistake and flooded him with compliments when he came up with a correct answer. It was a game with them, an ego boost to instruct a grown-up, and though he went along with their lessons good-naturedly, inside, in spite of himself, he was humiliated. Afterwards, he'd return home and take out his feelings of frustration on his horses, running them around his acreage, working up a sweat until he smelled like a man and no longer felt like a child.

He lay back down and groaned. *You're on vacation,* he admonished himself. *Take it easy and forget your obligations.* He had no trouble blanking out work, but as always, his cloudy status with Rina—and Judaism—continued to gnaw at him. Seeing life through the skewed eye of a cop, Decker found faith hard to come by.

The sun grew stronger and he took refuge under a Douglas fir. He closed his eyes and tried to concentrate on pleasant images: his daughter Cindy as a little girl, laughing carelessly as she pumped her legs to swing, himself as a boy, 'gator baiting with friends in the Everglades, Rina's touch, her breath . . . His lids grew heavy. Halfway through a jumbled dream, he felt rain on his trousers. Startled, he sat up, only to see Jacob standing over him, gleefully sprinkling his legs with dirt.

"What's that for?" he asked, wiping off his clothes.

The boy shrugged.

"You bored?"

"A little."

"Hungry?"

"A little."

Decker tousled the ebony hair that stuck out from under Jacob's *kipah* and unzipped the knapsack.

"We've got peanut butter or salami sandwiches," he announced.

"What about the chicken?"

"Finished it yesterday."

"The bagels?"

"They're gone, too. We're on our last day of vacation, Kiddo. The way we've been packing it away, it's a wonder we haven't run out of food altogether."

"I'll take peanut butter."

"Where's your brother?"

"I dunno."

Decker stood up and looked around. Ginger rose with him, coppery fur gleaming in the sunlight. Sammy was nowhere in sight.

"Wasn't he just reading over there?" Decker asked.

"He said he was going for a walk," Jake answered. "You were sleeping. He told me not to bother you, but I got bored."

"Sammy?" Decker called out, taking a few steps.

Nothing.

"When did he leave?"

"I dunno."

Decker cupped his hands and called out:

"Sammy Lazarus, are you playing a game with me?"

He waited for a response. The sounds of the woods became magnified: bird songs, the rush of water, the buzz of insects.

"Hmm. Must have wandered off." Decker took Jake's hand and started to check out the immediate area. The dog followed.

"Sammy?"

Silence.

"Sammy, can you hear me?" Decker frowned and patted the dog. "Know where Sammy is, Ginger?"

The dog's ears perked up, but her expression was blank.

"Sammy!" Jake called out.

"Okay," Decker thought out loud. "Let's take this one step at a time. He can't be very far away."

He picked up Sammy's discarded sweat jacket and held it under the dog's nose. She immediately skipped over to the area where Sammy had been sitting and parked herself.

The ground revealed a few bare footprints. Decker tried to follow them, but they were light and sporadic, disappearing altogether as the copse thickened with foliage.

"Sammy?" Decker bellowed.

*Stay organized.* He constructed an imaginary hundred-foot radius from the last footprint and decided to search that area meticulously, go over every single inch for a sign of a footprint, a torn piece of clothing . . .

Ten minutes of hunting and shouting proved to be fruitless.

"Where is he?" Jake asked nervously.

"He's somewhere around here," Decker said. Despite his anxiety, he kept his voice steady. "We'll find him, Jakey. Don't worry . . . Sammy!"

"Why doesn't he answer?"

"You know your brother. His head's in the clouds."

Decker was not given to panic—his job required a detached mind and a cool head—but images began to form in his mind. Horrible images . . .

"Sammy!" he shouted.

"Maybe he hurt himself," Jacob said. His bottom lip quivered.

"I'm sure he's fine, Kiddo," Decker answered.

But the grotesque images grew more vivid. The look of terror on Rina's face—he'd seen her like that before . . .

"Sammy, can you hear me!" he yelled.

"Sammy!" Jake echoed, then turned to Decker, wild-eyed. "Peter, what are we gonna do?"

"We're going to find your brother, that's what we're going to do." Kids, he thought. You need eyes in the back of your head. "Sammy!"

"Peter, I'm scared."

"It's going to be fine, Jakey," Decker said.

*His responsibility. His fault.*

"Did you see or hear anything unusual while I was sleeping?" he asked Jake.

The boy shook his head fiercely.

"Then he's got to be around somewhere. He's just lost." *As opposed to kidnapped.* "Sammy!"

His voice was growing hoarse.

*All those kids. Those missing kids.* He knew it all too well. Goddam dumb parents, he used to think. Yeah, they were goddam dumb. He was goddam dumb, too. Suddenly enraged, he ripped through the area like a wounded animal, trying to clear a path for himself and Jacob.

The little boy started to cry. Decker picked him up, hugged him, and continued the search as Jake clung tightly to his neck.

"Maybe we should head back, Peter" Jake suggested, sniffing. "Maybe Sammy went back to where we were."

Decker knew otherwise. Sammy should have been able to hear their calls even if he were back at the campsite.

"Sammy?" he tried once more.

He needed help, the sooner the better. Lots of people . . . Helicopters . . . There was still plenty of daylight left, but no time to waste. He gave the empty woods a final once over and headed back toward camp.

Suddenly, Ginger took off, her haunches leaping forward in a single fluid motion. The two of them raced after her and saw a small figure, shrouded by trees, standing over a thick clump of underbrush.

Decker ran over to the shadow and grabbed it firmly by the shoulders.

"Damn it, Sammy!" he said. "Didn't you hear me calling you? You scared me half to death!" He clutched him to his chest. "Why didn't you answer me?"

The boy held himself rigid. Decker saw that his eyes were glazed.

"What's *wrong* with you? What *happened*?"

"*Yuch!*" Jake spat out, staring into a pile of decayed foliage. Decker looked down.

There were two charred skeletons. Except for the right shinbone, which was buried under leaves and dirt, the first skeleton was completely exposed, a blackened armbone and fist sticking straight up as if beckoning for a hand to hoist it to its feet. The skull and the breastbone bore holes the size of a silver dollar. Shreds of flesh were clinging to the torso, petrified and discolored from exposure.

The second skeleton was partially buried, the ribcage and left legbone completely covered with dirt. A trail of leaves overflowed from the lower jaw, falling downward as if the dead mouth were vomiting detritus. Bits and pieces of charred skin stuck to the pelvis and limb bones, but unlike the first skeleton, the eye sockets and cracked skull retained dew-ladened globs of jelly that glistened in the sunlight. Brain and eye. A cloud of flies and a mass of black beetles were feasting on the leftover morsels, unperturbed by the presence of intruders.

Gently, Decker walked the boys away from the ghastly sight and swore to himself. Nothing like a vacation to remind him of work.

"Are they real, Peter?" Sammy asked at last, his troubled eyes beseeching Decker.

"Yes, they're real."

"What are we gonna do?" Jake asked.

"I think we should *bentch gomel*," Sammy said quietly.

"What's that?" Decker asked.

"It's like what you say when you don't get killed in a car crash, or like when you don't die from the chicken pox." Jacob looked up at Decker. "I don't feel so good."

"Sit down, Jakey. Catch your breath."

The boy sank into a pile of leaves.

"Go ahead and pray, Sam," Decker said, placing a broad hand on the boy's shoulder. He reached into his rear pants pocket and pulled out a pack of cigarettes. He'd been trying to cut down, but at this moment he needed a nicotine fix badly.

"And when you're done," he said, striking a match, "we'll go call the police."

## ·2

They stood like pickets in a fence: Decker, Ed Fordebrand, a homicide cop from the Foothill Division of the LAPD, and Walt Beckham, a deputy county sheriff for the Crestview National Forest Service. The woods were swarming with activity: crime technicians combing the brush for evidence, police photographers popping flashes, the deputy medical examiner barking directions for the removal of the bones. Beckham hitched up his beige uniform pants and sucked on his pipe. Fordebrand started scratching his left arm which had broken out into welts. Decker glanced at the boys. Jake was standing to one side. His color had returned and now he was fascinated by the action. But Sammy had distanced himself from the commotion and sat huddled under a massive eucalyptus.

"Nice goin', Deck," Fordebrand said, rubbing his forearm. "I thought you were on vacation."

"Fuck you."

"And a merry Christmas to you, too," Fordebrand growled.

Decker shrugged.

"Sorry," he said.

Fordebrand was six two and pure beef: the reincarnation of a Brahma bull.

"You want to take this, Sheriff?" he asked Beckham. "It's your jurisdiction."

Beckham tugged a corner of his gray mustache.

"Seems to me it's right on the border between County and Foothill."

"Closer to you," Fordebrand said.

"Detective, how 'bout you and me slicing through the shit," said Beckham. "You don't want to do this now. And I don't want to do this now. We'd both rather be home, downing a brew and singing carols to the Savior."

"How about a joint operation?" Fordebrand tried. "Cut the paperwork by half."

"Why don't you flip a coin?" suggested Decker.

"I like the man's logic," Beckham said. He won the toss and smiled. Fordebrand made a last ditch effort.

"I still think it's on your side of the border, Sheriff," he said.

"You're being a sore loser, Detective," said Beckham.

"Go home," Decker said. "We'll work it out."

Fordebrand gave Decker a dirty look.

"My replacement's coming in a half hour," Beckham said. "I'd appreciate it if you could fill him in. If any questions should come up, who do I call?"

The big bull took out his card and gave it to him.

"Edward," Beckham said, reading it and sticking out his hand, "it's been a pleasure."

Fordebrand grumbled, then pumped the deputy's hand firmly. "You can call and ask for me or call the same extension and ask for Detective Sergeant Decker here—"

"I'm not working Homicide," Decker said.

Fordebrand smiled cryptically, still digging at his forearm. The rashes and welts were manifestations of an allergic reaction that occurred whenever he dealt with corpses—inconvenient, considering his chosen profession.

"If you don't mind, I'll leave you gentlemen now," said Beckham.

"Yeah," Fordebrand said. "Merry Christmas. Merry *fucking* Christmas."

Beckham jogged away and Fordebrand turned to Decker.

"Goddam hillbilly shitheads. What the hell do they do all day? Sit up in the ranger station and jerk their chains?"

"He's right," Decker said. "The area does belong to Foothill. He might as well save himself the hassle."

"Stop being so noble."

"What's with the shit-eating grin when I said I wasn't working Homicide?"

"Well, when you get back you'll notice that we're slightly short-handed."

"We've got five homicide dicks."

"Pilkington's transferred to Harbor Division, Marriot's on vacation, Sleighton's father took sick in Canada, so he flew out to be with him for the holidays. That leaves me and Bartholemew. I just found out today that Bart broke his leg riding a bicycle."

"Shit."

"Morrison did a little rearranging. Starting December twenty-sixth, you and Dunn are working Homicide. Dunn is actually jockeying back and forth between Homicide and Sex and Juvey—"

"I don't want to hear about this, Ed. I'm still on *vacation*." Decker looked at the boys. "Such as it is."

"Rina's kids?" Fordebrand asked.

Decker nodded. "The older one found the bones. What a crappy deal! Nice weather, so I take them for a few days in the wild—unpolluted skies, unspoiled nature—and they have to be exposed to this crud."

"That's too bad." Fordebrand's right arm had begun to swell. He clawed at it and winced. "So you want this one, Deck?"

"All right. Starting the twenty-sixth. Nothing's going to go down between then and now anyway."

"Easy case," Fordebrand said. "Open and shut. Poke around a little just to say you did something. Look through a few Missing Persons files and forget about it. A week's worth of desk work—nice and clean."

"If it's so appealing, Ed, you can take the case."

"I'll be happy to, Decker, if you take the packinghouse slashings."

"Pass."

Fordebrand ran his fingers through his hair.

"Yeah, you look through a couple of Missing Persons files, then close the books, and they go down in the annals as a couple of John Does."

"Jane Does," Decker said. "They look like females to me."

"Jane Does, John Doe, who the hell cares? Nobody'll hear from 'em again." Fordebrand slapped him on the back. "I'll handle the preliminary garbage. You go off and finish your vacation. Take care of the boys."

"Sorry I had to drag you out on Christmas Eve."

"Ah, it's okay," Fordebrand said magnanimously. "I'll be back in time for the honey-glazed ham and the turkey. The ham's in the oven; the turkey's coming in from Cleveland."

Decker smiled. "Your mother-in-law?"

"Who else?"

"Have fun."

"If you get lonely tonight, Deck—"

"I'll be up here with the boys, but thanks anyway."

Fordebrand nodded.

"Yeah, you probably don't go in for Christmas anymore, do you, Rabbi?"

Decker shrugged.

"You like playing daddy, Deck?"

"They're good kids."

"What's with you and their mama anyway?"

"Beats me, Ed."

Decker called out to Jake, and jogged over to Sammy and sat down beside him. The younger boy came running and jumped onto Decker's lap.

"The police will take it from here, guys, so we can go back to the campsite now. We'd better get going. We still have to pitch the tent—"

"Peter, I want to go home," said Sammy.

Decker blew out air forcefully. "All right. Is that okay with you, Jakey?"

"Yeah, I'd like to go home, too. I'm sick of peanut butter."

Decker put his arms around the boys. "I'm awfully sorry, guys."

Sammy leaned his head on the detective's shoulder. "It wasn't your fault."

"Are you guys a little spooked?"

"Maybe a little," Sammy answered.

"How about you, Jake?"

Jacob shrugged.

"It's a normal feeling to be freaked out. You kids handled this very well." Decker helped them to their feet. "Let's go pack up. I hope you guys had a good time before all this happened."

"I did," Sammy said. "I *really really* did."

It was hard to tell whether he was convincing Decker or himself.

Decker drove them home in the jeep. The boys said nothing as they rode down winding, one-lane dirt paths with five-hundred-foot drops bouncing along bumpy mountain roads. When the four-wheeler finally exited the mountain highway and hooked onto the freeway on-ramp, Sammy let out a big sigh.

"Do you ever worry about getting killed?" he asked Decker.

"I used to when I was a uniformed policeman, but not any more, Sammy. My work is pretty safe. It's mostly pushing papers and talking to people."

"Were you ever shot?" the older boy continued.

"No."

There was a brief silence.

"I don't know what I want to be when I grow up, but I don't want to be a cop."

Decker nodded. "It can get pretty gross sometimes."

"Know what *I* want to be?" said Jake.

"What?" the big man asked.

"A pilot in the Israeli Air Force."

*"Not me,"* said Sammy. "I don't want to get killed."

"They never get killed," Jake protested.

"'Course they get killed, Yonkie. The Arabs are shooting at you. You think they don't get lucky and get a hit once in a while?"

"Well, I'm not gonna get killed!" Jake said firmly.

"Yeah! Right!"

Silence.

"I don't know what I want to do," Sammy pondered. "I'd like to get *smicha*, but I don't want to learn full time like my abba or my uncles did."

"Are all your uncles rabbis?" asked Decker.

"All except one," answered Sammy. "One of my eema's brothers lives in Jerusalem. He's a *sofer*. That's kind of interesting, I guess."

"What's that?" Decker asked.

"Uh, you know, the guy who writes the Torah and the mezuzahs," explained Sammy.

"A scribe." Decker said.

"Yeah, I think that's what they call them," said Sammy. "My other uncles, the ones married to my abba's sisters, used to teach in a yeshiva, but now they're businessmen. They live in New York."

"We've got tons of family there," Jake said, excitedly. "We've got a bubbe and a zayde and two great-grandmothers, and a whole bunch of cousins. We're not alone at all."

Then the little boy licked his lips and frowned. "But sometimes it feels like it."

"Especially when you see scary stuff like today?" said Decker.

"Aw, that doesn't bother me," Jake said mustering up bravado. "That was kinda neat . . . sort of."

"Eema's other brother, the one that's not a rabbi, sees dead bodies all the time," Sammy said. "He's a pathologist and owns cemeteries . . . Anyway, him and Eema get into fights about that all the time because he's a *kohain*—a Jewish priest—and *kohains* aren't supposed to be around corpses."

"Your uncle's not religious?" Decker asked.

Sammy nodded. "Him and Eema fight about that, too. You can bet that we don't see much of Uncle Robert."

They rode another mile in silence. Decker broke it.

"Are you interested in medicine, Sammy?" he asked.

"No way," Sammy answered. "I don't like blood."

"How about business? Like your New York uncles?"

"Borrrrring," said Sammy.

Decker smiled.

"Well, you boys have plenty of time to figure out what you want to be. Heck, it's okay to do a lot of different things in a lifetime. I used to do ranching when I was a kid in Florida. I did construction work in high school. I was a lawyer for a while, and I don't see myself as being a cop forever. You've got loads of time to experiment."

Sammy mulled that over for a while.

"You know what I'd like to be?" he said. "I think I'd like to be a journalist. Maybe write editorials that make people think."

The kid was all of eight and a half.

The grounds of Yeshivas Ohavei Torah were located on twenty acres of brush and woodland in the pocket community of Deep Canyon. It was twenty freeway minutes from the police station and fifteen minutes from Decker's ranch. The locals of Deep Canyon were working-class whites, and they and the Jews had little to do with each other, but over the past few years there had grown an uneasy, mutual tolerance.

The locals weren't the only ones who felt uncomfortable with the Jewish community. The Foothill cops were equally baffled by the enclave, imagining it a slice of old Eastern Europe that had been frozen in a time warp. Actually, the yeshiva embodied aspects of both past and present, but the cops never delved that deeply. They had nicknamed the place Jewtown, which is what Decker had called it before his personal involvement. Now, at least when Decker was around, they referred to it by its rightful name.

The lot for the yeshiva had been cut out of the mountainside. Huge boulders had been hauled away and the ground had been leveled, leaving a mesa of flat land surrounded by thick foliage, evergreens, and hillside. Set in the middle of a broad carpet of lawn was the main building—a two-story cement cube that contained most of the classrooms. On one side were smaller buildings—additional classrooms, the library, the synagogue, and the ritual bathhouse. The other side was open space for a thousand feet, then housing—a dormitory and a cluster of prefab bungalows.

Most of the yeshiva residents were college-age boys engaged in religious studies, but the place also had a high school, with secular and Jewish curricula, and an elementary school for children of the *kollel* students—married men studying Talmud full time. Private homes were provided for the *kollel* families, the two dozen rabbis who served as full-time teachers, and the headmaster—the Rosh Yeshiva. He was a meticulously dressed, distinguished man in his seventies named Rav Aaron Schulman. Rina's husband had been his protege and most brilliant student. Because of that, she and her sons had been allowed to stay on after he died.

Rina had once admitted to Decker that she was an outsider at the yeshiva. The women who lived on the grounds simply came along with their husbands or fathers. The school catered exclusively to men, and as a widow, she had no role there whatsoever. Though the residents treated her kindly—it was *demanded* of them by the Torah—she still felt like an interloper living in free housing, even though she taught math at the high school and operated the ritual bath. She knew she'd have to leave one day, but in the meantime she was grateful for the interlude that let her try to figure out what to do with the rest of her life.

Decker parked in front of the main gate, told Ginger to stay, and walked with the boys across the lawn. The place was almost empty at this time of year; most of the boys had gone home to their families. Still, a seminar was being held on the grass. A full-bearded rabbi wearing a black suit and hat sat with five pupils—*bochrim*—under an elm. The students and their teacher were engaged in animated dialogue. Decker and the kids walked down the main pathway, turned onto a dirt sidewalk that cut through the residential portion, and stopped in front of a white bungalow.

"I'd appreciate it if you boys didn't mention the bones until after I've spoken with your mother."

They nodded.

Rina opened the door at Decker's knock, her eyes widening with surprise, lips opening in a full smile.

"I didn't expect you guys back until tomorrow!"

Sammy fell into his mother's arms and embraced her tightly. He leaned his head against her breast and hid his gaze from hers. Rina cupped his face in her palms and looked at him, noticing moisture in his eyes and the tremble of his lower lip. She kissed him on his forehead and he broke away. Jake gave her a playful hug and smothered her face with kisses.

"I think they missed you," Decker said.

"Happy to be home?" she asked them as they went inside.

The boys nodded.

"I've got surprises for you both. They're on your beds."

"Oh boy!" Jake exclaimed, heading for the bedroom. Sammy lagged behind.

"Shmuel," she said, holding his arm, "is everything okay?"

He nodded.

"Something's bothering you."

"I'm fine, Eema. I'm just tired."

"Okay," said Rina, disconcerted at his evasion.

He gave his mother another hug, then trudged off to the bedroom.

"What happened?" she asked Peter as soon as they were alone.

"Could I have a cup of coffee, Rina?"

"Uh . . . sure. Of course," she said. "Sit down, Peter. You look exhausted."

He took a seat on the left side of her brown sofa, letting his head flop back against the cushion, then ran his hands over his face.

"Why are the boys upset?" she asked.

"It's complicated. But everyone's fine."

"Okay," she said. "Relax. I'll make coffee and then you can tell me what's going on."

Her house was tiny—800 square feet crammed with mementos—*tchatchkas,* she called them. Display cases full of Jewish figurines, propped photos, and sketches of Israel. The white walls were dotted with landscapes of the Judean dessert, charcoals of the Old City of Jerusalem and the Wailing Wall, and photos of the lower East Side of New York. Hanging above the sofa was a magnificently colored and elaborately scrolled Hebrew document—her wedding contract, her *ketubah.*

*That's what a Jewish marriage is, she had said. A contract. You're supposed to know what you're getting yourself into.*

*But do you ever really know, he had wondered out loud.*

*Emotionally, of course not. But a ketubah spells out the specific obligations for a husband as well as a wife. You've got to remember that back then, most societies considered women things—objects. The idea that a man was accountable to his wife was revolutionary.*

Her entire east wall was the family gallery—snapshots of her parents, and her brothers and their families, pictures of her sons as infants and toddlers clumsy in bulky diapers, and antique sienna portraits of her grandparents and great-grandparents in gilt frames. And the wedding pictures—Rina and Yitzchak under a canopy holding a shared wine glass. The groom was looking directly at the rabbi, his eyes intense and serious. He'd been a handsome young man, Decker thought, lean, with even, strong features. But Rina was the focus of the photograph—a stunningly beautiful girl with sapphire eyes and gleaming ebony hair that fell to her waist. She was dazzling as a bride. Whenever he looked at the picture, he felt a twinge in his chest.

His eyes drifted from the photo to the overflowing bookcases. She owned some secular books, but most were religious—Hebrew and Aramaic books of prayer, law, and ethics that were double and triple stacked on the shelves. She had skimmed though some of them, she had told him, but Yitzchak had known them all by heart.

Rina came back with black coffee for him and a milk-laced cup for herself. She sat down, tucked her legs under her denim skirt, and brushed midnight silk out of her eyes.

"Now," she said. "What happened?"

"Everything's okay," he started out. "Sammy went exploring in the woods and came across a couple of human skeletons—"

"*What?*"

"It scared him, of course. It scared Jake, also, but they're okay," he said.

"What'd they do?"

"They asked a lot of good questions and I answered them. Kids do well with the honest approach."

"Was it disgusting?"

"It was graphic."

"What'd they ask you, Peter?"

"They acted pretty characteristically. Jake seemed more interested in the bones per se. How did they get there? Did the bad man who dumped them still live in the city? Is he going to kill us—"

"Dear God, I'd better talk to him—"

Decker held up the palm of his hand and continued.

"He watched the police procedures, and it was good for him. Gave him a sense of resolution. He's not the one who took it to heart."

"What'd Sammy say?"

"Sammy had a more adult concept about the whole thing. He talked about death—how the rabbis approached it. I think it was a speech he'd heard in the past. It may have brought back some painful memories."

"Did he mention Yitzchak?"

"Not by name. He did tell me that Jews aren't buried in airtight coffins—that their bones disintegrate into dust. Reading between the lines, you could tell what he was thinking."

The room was silent for a moment.

"I'll see how they're doing," she said quietly.

Decker nodded. She left the room and he slowly sipped his coffee.

It had been six months since he'd first stepped onto the grounds of the yeshiva, entering an alien world governed by laws codified thirteen hundred years ago. He'd been the detective assigned to a brutal rape that had occurred outside the *mikvah*—the ritual bathhouse—and Rina had been a witness. As the investigation unfolded, it became clear that she'd been the intended victim all along. By the time the perpetrator was caught, their lives had become permanently enmeshed.

And now was the endless period of waiting. Long hours of studying that he hoped would lead to commitment. But often he wondered if this was what he really wanted. If Rina had never entered his life, he wouldn't have changed. But she had, and he felt as if he were trapped between floors in a stuck elevator. His past seemed remote, his future uncertain. Some people found uncertainty exciting. He considered it a giant headache.

He closed his eyes, attempting to rest, and opened them only when he heard Rina reenter the room.

"They seem all right," she said. "Jakey recounted everything in gory detail. He said the bodies had been burned."

She looked at him for confirmation and he nodded.

"That's repulsive," she said shuddering. "He also said you were assigned to the case."

"It's called being in the wrong place at the wrong time."

"Can't get away from work, huh?"

"Ain't that the truth," said Decker. "How's Sammy doing?"

"Quiet. He's reading a book that Yitzy used to read to him. He hadn't looked at it in years, and now it's way too easy for him. You were right about reading between the lines."

"He talked a lot about his father before he found the skeletons."

Rina was taken aback.

"He did?"

"Yes. The kid has a good memory. He told me how Yitzchak used to take him to class and he'd sit on all the rabbis' laps, about how he and his father learned together."

Her eyes misted. "What else did he say?"

"He became very emotional when he described Yitzchak's possessions—"

"What possessions?"

It had never dawned on Decker that Sammy hadn't told his mother all of this. Suddenly, he realized that he was breaking confidences.

"Uh," he stalled. "He has his father's siddur, his tallis, things like that."

Tears streamed down her cheek. She walked over to the window and stared outward.

"The day before Yitzchak's burial," she whispered, "I turned this house inside out looking for that tallis. I wanted him to be buried in it." She shook her head. "And all this time, Sammy had it . . . I'm glad he does. In retrospect, it would have been stupid to bury a treasure like that. Yitzy must have known."

Decker walked up behind her and put his hands on her shoulders. She turned to face him.

"Sammy doesn't talk to me about his father. Not that I haven't tried, but he refuses to open up. Maybe I get too emotional myself. But I'm glad he talked to you." She laughed tearfully. "You're a good guy, Peter. I'm sure you explained the corpses a lot better than I could have."

"I don't think that's true," he said. "Let's just say I'm used to talking about things like that."

She gave his hand a gentle squeeze, then pulled away.

"I was talking to Rav Schulman yesterday," she said.

"How's he doing?"

"Fine. He's impressed with you. He's says you're very sharp, that you possess a natural Talmudic mind."

Decker smiled.

"That's good to know because I sure feel like a slug sometimes, especially with the language."

"It will come, sweetie."

"Maybe. I'm too old for this, Rina."

"Nonsense," she said. "Rabbi Akiva was forty when he started learning Torah. You've got a good year's jump on him."

"And look where it got him."

"What do you mean?"

"Wasn't he one of the ten rabbis who was tortured by the Romans? The one who had his back raked open by hot iron combs?"

Rina looked at him.

"All I meant to say was that coming to religion later in life isn't necessarily a handicap," she said. "Rabbi Akiva went on to be one of the greatest sages of all time, and he was a total ignoramus when he started learning. I certainly wasn't thinking about how he died."

Decker took her hand and kissed it. "I know you meant it as encouragement," he said. "It was a morbid association."

"I guess it was in line with your day," she sympathized.

"Yeah," he said. "It goes with the territory. Cops just seem to fixate on death."

# ·3

The dental offices of Hennon and MacGrady were on Roxbury Drive, north of Wilshire, in Beverly Hills. Decker pulled his unmarked '79 Plymouth into a loading zone—the only free space he could find—and placed his police identification card on the front dash. It was late in the afternoon, almost dusk, and he was tired from battling city traffic. If the meeting with the forensic odontologist wasn't unduly long, he'd make it home before eight.

He entered the waiting room, and immediately his nostrils were assaulted by pungent, antiseptic smells that plunged him into Pavlovian anxiety. The office decor did little to comfort him. The furniture was black and gray, the table, glass and chrome, and the eggshell walls were covered by monochrome graphic art—repetitive figure-ground designs, like a black-and-white TV test pattern. It made him dizzy and hostile.

*A hell of an unfriendly way to furnish a dental office.*

He walked up to a glass window and knocked on the frosted pane. The window slid open, and the receptionist, a blonde girl no more than eighteen, gave him a practiced smile.

"Can I help you?" she beeped.

"I have a five o'clock appointment with Dr. Hennon."

"Name?"

"Decker," he said.

She scanned the appointment book.

"Yes, you do," she confirmed. "Is this your first time here, Mr. Decker?"

"I'm not a patient."

The girl was thrown off balance.

"Oh," she said, then brightened. "You're the salesman from Dent-O-Mart, right?"

"No, I'm a police sergeant."

She frowned. "Is anything wrong?"

"Why don't you tell Dr. Hennon I'm here and you can call me when she's ready to see me?"

She was still puzzled.

"She's with a patient."

"Just poke your head in, huh?"

The girl got up reluctantly and came back a moment later.

"She'll see you in a minute, Sergeant," she announced, relieved.

"Thank you."

She slid back the partition and it slammed shut. End of conversation.

Decker sat down on an unyielding ebony cushion and squirmed uncomfortably. Sorting through the magazines on the table, he settled on *Architectural Digest,* skimming through pages of mansions he'd never be able to afford. He heard a door open, and glanced upward to see a woman at the reception desk. She had to be at least his age, he thought, maybe even a couple of years older, which would put her around forty-one or two. Her face wasn't anything to write home about, but her figure was tight—a good bust and a dynamite ass neatly packaged in designer jeans. She knocked loudly on the receptionist's window, turned around, and flashed him a mouth full of ivories.

"Nice smile," Decker said, returning her grin.

"It should be," she said. "It cost me five g's."

"Well, you got your money's worth." He realized he was coming on to her inadvertently and returned his eyes to the magazine. But he could feel the heat of her gaze.

"What are you in here for?" she asked, pulling out a gold credit card.

"Business," he said.

"Interested in a little pleasure?" she asked, lowering two inches of lash.

"I'm married," Decker lied.

"So am I," she responded. "I'm on number three and he's unappreciative." She puffed out her chest and gave him a full view. "He never notices my smile. And I do hate to drink alone."

"I'm *happily* married," he said.

"Yeah, aren't all you guys with the roving eyes." She signed the credit slip, threw the card into her purse, and snapped it shut. "Suit yourself," she said, icily.

The receptionist slid open the glass panel.

"Dr. Hennon will see you now, Sergeant."

"Thanks," he said.

"Sergeant?" the toothy woman said. "You're a military man?"

"Cop."

"You don't look like a cop."

"No?"

"No. I would have said you were an architect or a producer."

Decker looked down at his outdated suit and white shirt. His striped tie was loosened and his shoes were scuffed. Nothing about his appearance suggested money or sophistication.

"Then again," the woman continued, "my second husband, Lionel, always said I was a good judge of lovers, but a *lousy* judge of character."

Decker agreed with Lionel on both counts.

Dr. Hennon's office was small but cheerful. Bright yellow walls full of posters with bold swatches of color. The room contained a cluttered desk, a corkboard full of notes and dental articles, and a Formica bridge table that held casts of teeth and jaws. Above the desk was a large, wall-mounted X-ray viewing box on which hung radiographs of teeth clipped to metal hangers.

To the left of the viewing box was a waist-up frame photograph of a man and a woman at sunset. A striking shot streaked with brilliant oranges and lavenders, the sun highlighting, almost bleaching out, the woman's face. She appeared to be in her thirties, with milky green eyes, and a head full of metallic auburn waves. Her features were sharp and her face was long, ending in a strong, dimpled chin.

Decker took out a manila folder, opened it and began to scan the forensic reports on the two Jane Does. A moment later, the woman in the photo came in and offered him a delicate, manicured hand. He stood up and held out his own.

"Annie Hennon," she said shaking his big, freckled hand.

"Pete Decker."

"Thanks for coming down to my office, Pete."

"No problem."

"I appreciate it. Most cops don't know that forensic odontology isn't a full-time job. I look at skulls maybe a dozen times a year—unless there's a disaster. We haven't had too many of those lately, thank God. If I have to take a day off from the office to meet you at the morgue, I lose a great deal of income."

"It's a pleasure to be on the good side of town for a change," he said. "That's a nice picture of you."

"Better than the real thing, huh?"

"I didn't mean it that way."

She laughed. "I'm just terrible. Thanks. It *is* a nice picture. That's my brother and me. Mom took the picture. Mom's an okay photographer."

She pulled up a chair, and they both sat down.

"Actually, my brother is the one who got me interested in forensic odontology," she said. "Him and Heinz."

"Heinz?"

"Heinz Buchholz. A little, white-haired gnome of a man who made his mark in history by identifying Hitler's jaw. When I went to dental school, he was sixty-five, maybe seventy, and he used to roam the labs asking us students if his denture set-up would pass the state licensing examination. Can you imagine that? An important man like him decked with honors, a pioneer in forensic dentistry, and he was reduced to worrying about passing the state board."

She shook her head and turned to Decker.

"You made quite an impression on Babs Terkel," she said, dryly.

"Pardon?"

"My last patient. The bleached blonde with the big boobs. She came back to my office girl and started pumping her about you."

"I thought she had a nice smile."

Hennon kissed her fingertips and spread them outward.

"My six-to-eleven porcelain fused to gold. Didn't I do a great job?"

"I'll say. She has a great set of teeth."

"*Now* she does," the dentist said emphatically. "You should have seen her when she walked through my door. Bucky Beaver." She waved her hand in the air. "Babs is all right—narcissistic as hell, but she's reliable. Keeps her appointments and pays her bills. I wish I had a thousand of those."

She walked out of the room and came back carrying two cups of black coffee.

"You want some sugar? I'm all out of cream."

"Black's fine," he said.

She noticed the forensic report.

"Been to the morgue, huh? The county one, that is, not the one out there." She jerked her head toward the waiting room. "My partner's wife and her decorator spent six months and ten thousand dollars redoing it to achieve the look of death. No accounting for taste. Anyway, what does the anthropologist say?"

"The report came in this morning. Doesn't tell me too much, although I realize there's not a hell of a lot to go on."

"What did he come up with?" she asked, sipping her coffee.

"From the bone structure, he surmises that they were both female, young—in their late teens or early twenties at most—and Caucasian. Jane Doe One looked to be about five four, five five and small-boned. She had reached ninety-five percent of her postpuberty growth. Number Two was taller, maybe five eight, and had a large frame. She'd stopped growing according to the bone plates. The bodies weren't lying in the mountains as long as I would have thought. From the skin fragments he said they probably were dumped about three months ago. They were burnt either while alive or shortly after they were shot, because their fists had curled from muscle contraction due to the heat, which could only have happened if there was still some muscle tone prior to rigor mortis. He also found a few partial fingerprints lodged in the inner folds of the finger joints, but that doesn't help unless the girls had been printed. So far, I've struck out with that. There's no record of their prints in our computer. They were shot with the same .38 caliber weapon—the bone rills match—and his guess is that the firearm was a Colt."

Decker slapped down the report.

"He said you may have a thing or two to add."

"Burnt *alive*?"

"Probably."

"That's revolting," Hennon said, sticking out her tongue.

Decker threw up his hands. "Lot of perverts out there. I've got a teenage daughter of my own. I'm constantly restraining the urge to call her and ask if she's okay."

"And they ask me how can I stand looking in mouths all day. Hey, I'd rather look at tooth decay than deal with sicko deviates who burn people alive."

She sighed and flicked on the light of the X-ray screen. Decker pulled out a notepad.

"Don't bother," she said. "I've got it all written down for you."

"I like to take notes."

"You're trying to quit smoking," she said matter-of-factly. "It gives you something to do with your hands."

"You missed your calling as a detective."

"Your teeth—smoker's stain. Probably also coffee stain," she said, staring at his mouth. "Sorry. It's an occupational hazard. Make an appointment with Kelly and I'll do a really nice polish job, gratis."

"I'll do that just as soon as I find a spare minute."

"I've heard that excuse before." She smiled impishly and covered the screen with a four-by-ten radiograph.

"This X-ray is a panoramic view of Doe One's mouth. It covers all the bony structures of the mandible and maxilla from ear to ear, thereby giving us a good overall look at jawbones and teeth. It's not great for detail, but you can see her third molars hadn't erupted. Here they are, just tooth buds in her jaw."

She pointed to four spots on the radiograph. Inside the jaw bone next to well-defined teeth were small white disks that looked like cotton balls delineated by a white circle.

"What's the circle?" he asked.

"The lining of the tooth follicle. Normal radiographic feature. You can see her third molars—the wisdom teeth—much more clearly on these radiographs." She placed several small X-rays on the screen. "These are called 'periapicals' and these are called 'bitewings'—the kind of X-rays you normally have taken by the dentist. They give much better detail than the orthopantogram. Judging from the maturation of her molars, I'd put Jane Doe One at about fifteen or sixteen."

She placed another celluloid on the screen. "This is the panoramic of Doe Two. Her third molars hadn't erupted either, but that's because they were impacted. Eventually, they would have had to be extracted. But you can see for yourself how much more differentiation there is in the tooth crown; root development had already taken place. This girl was around twenty, twenty-one at the time of her death."

She clicked off the light and looked at Decker.

"I'll tell you something else about the two girls, Pete. They may have died on the pyre together, but they didn't come from the same neighborhood."

"Why do you say that?"

Hennon walked over to the Formica table and picked up several pink plaster casts of teeth and gums.

"This is a cast of Jane Doe One's teeth. Let's call her Jean. Jean has had orthodonture; her teeth are beautifully aligned, although I betcha she hadn't been wearing her retainer as much as she should have. We've got a little slippage here. But be that as it may, her occlusion is A-1 and she's had serial extraction."

"What's that?"

"A standard procedure. In a small mouth with an otherwise normal bite, you extract specific teeth to make room in the jaw for the incoming canines or molars. It prevents overcrowding. Her first premolars have been extracted. Somebody spent money on her teeth, Pete. Orthodonture isn't cheap. And her general dental work was done by someone with integrity. The few silver fillings she does have were carved neatly. There's a tiny sliver of an overhang on number three but it happens to the best of us. Little Jean took good care of her teeth and had excellent dental care—middle class or above.

"Now take a look at the second Jane Doe. Let's call her Jan."

Decker winced and the dentist noticed it.

"Did I hit a nerve?" She grimaced. "Sorry—bad choice of words for a dentist."

"Jan's my ex-wife's name. I don't carry the torch for her, but let's call the bones Joan instead."

"Joan, it is. Poor Joanie. She never had a chance. Look at these teeth."

Decker picked up the pink casts. The first thing he noticed were the odd-looking front teeth.

"They look like pegs," he said.

"Right. Pegs notched up the center. And her first lower molars are odd-looking also. The occlusal table or biting surface is a mushy pile of oatmeal, suggesting to me Hutchinson's incisors and mulberry molars—congenital syphilis. Dollars to doughnuts Joan was born with VD. Furthermore, mom didn't do much to help her daughter's mouth, postpartum. The teeth left on the jaws are full of caries—decay. Several are broken off at the root, suggesting *severe* decay. And the little dental work she'd had done in her lifetime was strictly temporary. Trying to hold back a cracked dam with Scotch tape. You're looking at a girl who didn't have the finer things in life."

"Unfortunately," he said, "they both ended up in the same spot."

She shook her head, clearly bothered, and Decker liked that. Most of the people he worked with, himself included, had hardened their attitude so they could get the job done. You couldn't let it get to you. But once in a while he liked to be reminded that murder was something to feel badly about.

"So what do we have?" he thought out loud. "A middle-class sixteen-year-old female Caucasian about five four with a petite build, and a lower-class female Caucasian about twenty, five eight, with a big frame. Both were killed about three months ago, burned, and shot with the same .38 caliber."

"Amazing what a bag of bones will tell you. Where do you go from here, Pete?"

"Shuffle papers. I'll run a line on sixteen-year-olds reported missing for at least up to six months ago. A middle-class girl like Jean should have been reported missing, although as often as not, they're runaways. The second one will be trickier because she's older. May have been on the streets for years. I'll go with Jean first. After I get the files, I'll call the family and contact the family dentist. Then I'll send all the Missing Persons X-rays to you, and with a little bit of luck, you'll get a match."

"Long shot," Annie said.

"Yep. But sometimes long shots pan out."

"Well, let me throw this out at you—and this isn't in my report because it's not an official observation. Children with congenital syphilis are often born deaf or with hearing problems. That might narrow your search for Joanie."

"Very helpful," he said, rising. He stuck the pen in his notebook, flipped over the cover, and stuffed the notebook in his coat pocket. "Dr. Hennon—"

"Annie," she quickly said.

"Annie, thank you for your time."

He held out his hand and their eyes met.

"I've got an hour or so to kill before I meet a friend for dinner," she said. "Want to grab a drink or two?"

Jesus, Decker thought, two in one hour. He must be coming across lean and hungry. She was a fine looking woman with a very likeable disposition. If he'd met her six months ago, he would have jumped at the opportunity, but now there was Rina. Still, he ruminated, there was no harm in one drink; sit and shoot the breeze. But what would be the point? Suppose he liked her and wanted to see her again as a friend. And suppose it led to something more, like casual sex. And suppose he began to enjoy the casual sex. Then he'd have to deal with two women. He knew he was a poor juggler, which meant they'd both inevitably find out and he'd lose everything—Rina and the sex. He'd pledged from the outset to give himself a year with Rina to figure out what was going on. And it had only been four months. Most important, he loved her and she loved him even if they couldn't show it physically. It was absurd to think of other women when his heart belonged to Rina, but sexual deprivation was beginning to muddle his sensibilities.

He realized he had been silent for an awfully long time.

"Uh, thanks for the offer, but I've got to run."

"What the hell were you thinking about?" Hennon asked. "I've had pauses to size me up in bed before, but yours lasted so long you must have been up to the house and kids by now."

Decker broke into laughter.

"There's someone else . . . sort of."

"Sort of?"

"Well, we've got a few differences to work out, but so do all relationships."

"Then what *are* your plans for the evening?" she asked.

"Nothing really. I think I'll go home and pray."

"Pray? I didn't figure you for a religious man."

And Babs hadn't figured him for a cop. It was a good time for an undercover assignment.

"Well, I don't really know if you'd call me religious."

"What religion are you?" she asked.

"I'm not quite sure. I'm Jewish . . . sort of."

"Sort of?" She licked her lips and pursed them slightly. He felt a stirring below. Suddenly the months of celibacy seemed like years. Man, he was horny.

"Thanks again," he said as he moved toward the door.

"Have you always had trouble with commitments, Pete?" she asked.

"Sort of."

Back home, after working out and grooming the horses, he grabbed a bottle of Dos Equis and picked up the phone. He stood with his hip against the kitchen wall, receiver tucked under his chin, and gulped beer while listening to the ringing on the other end. His ex-wife answered.

Damn!

"Hi, Jan," Decker said. "Is Cindy around?"

"She's doing her homework."

"During Christmas vacation?"

"Well, she's working on something important."

"Can I talk to her, please?"

"You know how she doesn't like to be interrupted when she's concentrating—"

"I won't keep her long."

"It's late, Pete. It's after ten."

"It's only a quarter to."

"Well, you still should have called earlier."

"I did, Jan. No one was home."

"I was home. When did you call?"

Shit!

"I guess it was around four. Can you put Cindy on, please?"

"Four?" There was a silence. "What was I doing at four? Allen was home at four."

"Maybe it was a little earlier."

"Allen's been home since three."

"Well, no one answered the fucking phone, Jan."

There was a pause.

"You just can't help yourself, can you, Pete?" she said.

He took a deep breath.

"Can I talk to my daughter, please?"

"Hold on. I'll see how involved she is."

He heard her shriek Cindy's name. It was one of her most an-
noying habits. She'd never enter a room to tell you something.
She'd scream the message from wherever she was. Decker heard
the extension being picked up.

"Hi, Dad," Cindy said.

"Did your mother hang up?" Decker asked.

The question was immediately followed by the sound of a slamming receiver. Cindy laughed.

"What's up?" she asked.

"I just called to say hi."

"What's wrong?"

"Nothing's wrong."

"You sound upset. Did you have a fight with Rina?"

"No."

"What is it, Dad? Did you haul in another sixteen-year-old runaway who reminded you of me?"

"For your information, Cynthia, I happen to be working on a
very clean case."

"What kind of case would that be?"

"Some bones that were found in the mountains. We're trying to
identify them."

"Don't tell me. They're the bones of a sixteen-year-old girl."

He paused.

"You know me too well," he conceded.

"I'm alive, Dad. I'm alive and healthy. Here, listen real close."

He heard muffled sounds over the line.

"You know what that was, Daddy?" she went on. "That was my
heart beating."

"It's good to hear."

"I've got a really strong heart by now because I jog every day.
And you know what else, Daddy? I'm not in any trouble. I'm not
on drugs like the runaways you pick up. And I'm doing well in
school. And I'm *not* pregnant. You have nothing to worry about.

So why don't you take care of yourself instead of worrying about me?"

"I'm not worried about you, I just like to—"

"Bull, Daddy. No disrespect meant, but bull. Every time you get a case with a girl my age, you get that tightness in your voice. How are you going to cope when I go away to college?"

"I'll call you long distance."

"After you get my tuition bills, you won't be able to afford it." Decker laughed.

"Seriously, Daddy, I think I have a very good chance at getting a National Merit Scholarship. I think I did very well on the test."

"Great!"

"I mean I'd like to help you and Mom out as much as possible, but going East is just so expensive."

"Listen, honey, we told you not to worry about it. Just get the grades, and your mom and I will work out the rest."

She paused.

"You know, I've been thinking," she announced.

"Uh oh."

"Well, uh . . ."

"What?"

"Uh, you know that Eric is back east at Columbia and, uh . . ."

"Go on, Cindy. I'm not going to faint."

"Well, maybe it might be a bit more frugal if we kind of . . ."

"You two want to live together?"

"That was sort of the idea."

*Sort of,* he thought.

"Did you tell Mom?"

"God, no! At least, not yet. You know Mom. I love her dearly, but she hasn't come to grips with the fact that my age is in double digits. I thought maybe you could kind of break the idea to her . . ."

Silence.

"Dad, are you there?"

"Yeah."

"Well, you know how much *safer* I'd be living with a boy."

"Uh huh."

"And with splitting the expenses, it would be so much *cheaper*."

"Uh huh."

"So maybe you'll talk to Mom?"

"Uh uh. If you're old enough to make your own living arrangements, you're old enough to face your mother. But I'll support you, although knowing your mother, my support will work against you. If anyone asks my opinion, I'll back you up."

"I guess that's fair . . . Are you angry, Daddy?"

"No . . . Not really."

"You're worried."

"You know me. It takes me a while to adjust to something new. Don't concern yourself about me. Just take care of yourself, huh?"

"I will. You do like Eric, don't you?"

"Yeah, he's a good kid."

"It's hard to find good boys these days, Daddy."

"Well, he must be special if he hooked you. Go back to your work."

"I love you, Daddy."

"I love you, too, honey."

"Bye."

She hung up. He stared at the receiver and shook his head in confusion.

Decker sat upright in his solitary bed. It was an extra-long California king with an extra-firm mattress—good for holding a lot of bulk. But lately the only bulk it'd been holding was his own.

Four fucking months.

What the hell was he doing, surrounding himself with foreign words, strange symbols, and mystic concepts which were supposed to bring him closer to God. In his own way, Decker had always felt close to God. They'd reached an understanding based on mutual tolerance: God was tolerant of Decker's human foibles; Decker was tolerant of floods and earthquakes. Why was he doing this?

Rina, he thought. Was he just doing it to please her? At first, he didn't think so. He was very curious about Judaism. He wanted something more spiritual, something antithetical to his work. But now he wasn't so sure that Orthodoxy was the answer.

He looked down at the primer in front of him.

*Shalom, yeladim,* the first line said.

He could read it. He could actually read and understand that sentence in Hebrew. Whoopee! None of the guys at the station house could read and understand *Hello, children* in Hebrew.

He went on.

*Mi ba?,* the book continued.

Four whole months. He was going crazy. Love does have its limitations. If he was willing to accommodate her by subjecting himself to first-grade Hebrew lessons, she should damn well accommodate him a little.

*Abba ba,* he read.

But it wasn't stubbornness that was causing her to hold out. It was deep belief. He knew he could probably talk her into sex, but that wasn't what he wanted. He wanted sex with sanctification. There was something to be said for those ancient Midianite fertility rites.

*Mi ba'ah?*

She was religious. In a world full of transient morality and situational ethics, her spiritual values—which were good and just—remained absolute. How could he expect her to give up something so essential to her being just to accommodate his physical desires?

*Eema ba'ah.*

And what about *her* physical desires? It was chauvinistic to assume he was the only one suffering physically. If she could suppress her sex drive—she being much younger than he was—certainly he could show a little restraint. Give it a year, he said to himself. Priests do it for a lot longer.

He translated the Hebrew in his mind, proud that he could understand it. *Who is coming? Father is coming. Who is coming? Mother is coming.*

Well, he thought, at least *someone* is coming.

# · 4

The detective squad room of the Foothill Division was under-sized and overcrowded. The furniture could have come from a garage sale, and that made the people in the neighborhood feel right at home. The detectives rarely complained about the out-dated equipment or the makeshift desks and chairs, but the lack of elbow room got to everybody, especially when the weather was hot.

Decker was on the phone, explaining to a local dentist why a girl's X-rays were needed, when his second line rang. He put the dentist on hold.

"Decker," he said.

"Hi—"

"Rina, I'm on another call. Can you wait for a minute?"

"It's nothing important—"

"Honey, I'll be off in a second."

"Go ahead, sweetie. I'll wait."

Back to Dr. Pain. Spelled P-a-y-n-e.

"So if you could just send the X-rays you *do* have of Kristy Walkins to Dr. Anne Hennon—"

"Detective, I'm really rather choosy about to whom I send my records; they aren't junk mail to be tossed around randomly. And with the recent proliferation of lawsuits . . ."

"I realize that, Doctor, but we're talking about a homicide in-vestigation."

"If I knew for certain that the victim found was indeed Miss Walkins and the X-rays would serve as absolute proof of identification, I'd feel much better about sending them to you."

*If we knew that, we wouldn't need X-rays, schmuck!*

"Dr. Payne, I could get a subpoena and then we wouldn't have to bother with this polite conversation. Now, I'm asking you to send the X-rays on your terms. If you keep giving me a hard time, I'm going to take them on my terms. The choice is yours."

There was a long pause full of heavy breathing.

"I could round up some duplicates," Payne said, "but I guarantee you the clarity of the radiographs will leave much to be desired."

"I'm sure they'll be fine, Doctor. Thank you."

Decker gave him Hennon's address, thanked him again, gave the phone the finger, and pressed Rina's line.

"What's up?" he asked.

"Nothing really. Just called to say hi."

He smiled. "I'm glad you did."

"I . . . I guess you're busy, huh?"

"Not too busy for you."

"That's nice of you to say."

There was an awkward pause. This is leading somewhere, he thought.

"What's on your mind, Rina?"

"Why do you think something's on my mind?"

"I'm just asking."

She coughed over the phone, then cleared her throat. "I bought a gun, Peter."

*Shit!*

"You what?" he said softly.

"I bought a gun. A .38 caliber Colt six-shot Detective Special. Same one you use off duty. It's being registered now. Can you get me a conceal permit?"

"No. And you shouldn't be fooling around with a gun unless you know how to use one."

"I agree. That's why I've signed up for private lessons. At

Berry's Guns and Ammo. The teacher's name is Tom Railsback. He said he knows you."

"I know Tom," said Decker quietly. "He's a good guy. Rina, why the hell are you doing this?"

"Because I'm a nervous wreck. Because I constantly hear noises at night. Because I haven't had a good night's sleep in the six months since the violence here, and I don't want to be addicted to Valium."

"Honey, these things take time to get over. He can't hurt you now. He's locked up."

"Intellectually, I know you're right. But I can't help myself. I need something more. I need to know I can take care of myself."

"And you think a gun will take care of you?"

"Are you being sarcastic?" she asked innocently.

Decker paused, then said, "Sort of."

"Please don't be. I'm not careless, Peter. I'm not impulsive. I've thought about it a long time. I really think it's what I need."

"Then why didn't you talk to me about it?"

"Peter, I broached the subject with you a dozen times and you kept putting me off."

Decker pulled out a cigarette, lit it, and inhaled deeply. He *had* put her off. He was worried about her keeping firearms with small children around the house. He was worried it would misfire and she'd get hurt. Or maybe it was just a macho thing, feeling she should have trusted him to take care of her. Jan had never wanted a gun: she'd hated guns. But Jan had grown up in the sixties; Rina was from a different generation. Peace, love, and Woodstock had been replaced by terrorism and Rambo.

"If you're serious and you learn how to shoot properly, I'll see what I can do about getting you a permit."

"Thanks."

"But that's going to take months, Rina."

"That's okay."

"That means you can't hide the gun in your purse in the meantime."

"I won't."

"Or under a car seat—"

"The gun will be kept at home. Relax, sweetie. You sound wired."

He was wired.

"The other line is ringing," he said. "Hold on a moment."

He punched down the flashing white phone light.

"Decker," he yelled.

"Take it easy, Pete. It's only eleven o'clock in the morning."

Decker recognized the voice.

"H'lo, Annie."

"We got lucky, Sergeant. Can you make it down here by noon?"

"I'll be there. I'll even bring my own lunch."

"What a guy!" She hung up.

He connected back to Rina's line.

"Look, I've got to head on out to Beverly Hills. I'll drop by tonight. We can discuss this further then."

"I should be done with the *mikvah* around ten."

"Ten, it is."

"What's in Beverly Hills, Peter?"

"A dentist who may have identified the bones we found."

"What's his name? I can use a good dentist. My old one retired and I don't like the guy who took over his practice."

"He's a she. Her name is Annie."

"Does Annie have a last name?"

Decker smiled.

"Hennon," he said.

"Does Annie also have a red afro and a dog named Sandy?"

"Not quite. She's actually pretty. Not in your category, Rina, but her face wouldn't cause your mouth to pucker. She has nice eyes."

"Really now."

"Yes. They're green."

"Noticed the color, did you?"

"I'm a cop, Rina. I pride myself on a keen eye for detail."

"That's fine just so long as you keep your keen eye above Annie's neck."

\*    \*    \*

Decker arrived a few minutes early and was escorted into Hennon's office by the office girl, dressed in a white uniform that barely covered her ass. Chewing on bubble gum, she cracked it in her mouth, then offered Decker a stick, which he politely refused. A second later he heard Hennon yell for the girl's assistance.

The girl rolled her eyes backward. "That woman is a *terror*," she said. Her lower lip was in a sultry pout. "Dr. MacGrady is *so* much nicer."

*I'll bet he is,* thought Decker.

"You'd better go see what she wants," he said.

She left him alone with his baloney sandwich, carrot sticks, potato chips, and chocolate cupcake. He'd been over Rina's house last night while she was making lunches for the boys and she'd offered to pack him something. He had agreed under the condition that she'd go to no extra bother—give him exactly what she was making for the boys.

*Are you sure, Peter?*

*Positive.*

Hence, the kiddie lunch.

He unwrapped the sandwich. At least, it was on rye. He took a bite and in walked Hennon.

"Don't bother to get up," she said motioning him back down. "Finish swallowing."

He did and put down the sandwich.

"Want some coffee?" she asked.

"Sure."

"Kelly," she called out. "Two black coffees, one with sugar."

The receptionist ambled into the office, sulking. "It's my lunch hour, Dr. Hennon."

Hennon stared her down and a moment later Kelly brought in two styrofoam cups.

"Have a good lunch," said Hennon.

The girl mumbled and slammed the door as she left.

"I would have fired her a long time ago, but my partner has a soft spot in his heart and a hard spot somewhere else for her. Speaking of true love, how's your 'sort of' girlfriend, Pete?"

"She's fine. She just bought a gun. You own a gun, Annie?"

"No. I'd probably maim myself. Why'd she buy one? Just feeling vulnerable?"

"About six months ago, a psycho almost raped her. She's still very nervous about it. Claims she hears noises outside."

She whistled. "If I were her, I'd buy a gun, also."

"I thought you'd say that."

"You carry a picture of her?"

"Who? Rina?"

"If that's her name."

Decker dug out his wallet and showed the dentist a snapshot. Hennon frowned.

"Is this an exceptionally good photo of her?"

"Neither exceptionally good nor bad. It's what she looks like."

The dentist handed him back his wallet.

"Shall we get down to business?" she asked.

Decker said, "What do you have?"

She flipped on the viewing monitor.

"I went down to the morgue this weekend. Dr. Marvin Rothstein sent me a set of X-rays that looked promising as one of our Jane Does. This is the original full mouth set I took on Jean— twenty shots. Compare these to Dr. Rothstein's set."

She let Decker look for a minute.

"There are similarities," she said, "Same number of teeth, same teeth in the mouth have been restored, same interdental spacing, except that everything looks a little off kilter—like looking in a mirror at a funhouse. For instance, this right bitewing molar shot that I took on Jean shows the amalgam—the silver filling—covering the top of the upper molar and two sides: a typical filling for this tooth called an MOD. The angle I took it from shows a little tiny sliver of filling extending past the preparation line. It's called an overhang and it's a teeny one. Rothstein's X-rays don't show it at all."

"Meaning?"

"I'm coming to that. Take a look at this, Pete. This one is the full mouth set of Jean that I shot over the weekend," she said mounting another set of X-rays on the viewer. "Now compare this set to Dr. Rothstein's."

Decker studied the films.

"It doesn't show the sliver of filling, either."

"Exactly. And look how much more similar the two sets are. Know what I did? I angled the X-ray tube a little bit forward. Foreshortened the beam. When one compares radiographs for something as important as identification of a murder victim, one better make damn sure that the two sets of X-rays are shot from the *same* angle. Otherwise, one may miss an obvious match and feel stupid."

She breathed on her fingernails and rubbed them on her white coat.

"But the clincher is this. I called up Dr. Rothstein and asked for the patient's orthodontist. His name is Dr. Neiman and he sent me her casts. You want to compare the two?"

She showed them to Decker.

"To me, they look identical."

"Not quite. Remember I told you that the girl wasn't wearing her retainer as much as she should have. The skeleton's teeth weren't quite as aligned. But even so, I superimposed a bite plate of Jean's teeth and matched it to his patient's casts, and then I reversed the procedure and superimposed the patient's bite plate over Jean's teeth. It's the same person.

"Pete," she said, pointing to the plaster casts. "Say hello to Lindsey Bates."

# ·5

At the time of the Missing Persons report three and a half months ago, Lindsey Bates had been sixteen years and two months old, five feet four inches tall, 108 pounds, with blue eyes, blonde hair—American pie turned vulture fodder. Last seen by her mother after announcing that she was going to the Glendale Galleria to find a hot pink blouse to match her new yellow baggies. She'd planned to be back around four, and when she hadn't returned by five, Mrs. Bates began to worry. Forty-eight hours later, Lindsey was considered an official Missing Person. There were several other entries in the file—interviews with parents and friends—but nothing had proven useful.

The Glendale detective assigned to the case had been Don Oldham, an energetic, overweight man of fifty, who had reached twenty-five biggies a month ago and hung up his shield. After the Bates identification was made and the parents notified, Decker visited him in his condo that overlooked the smoggy San Gabriel mountains. Some say retirement kills the spirit, but if there existed a happier man than Oldham (*Donnie* as he insisted on being called) Decker hadn't met him. Oldham was an avid tropical fish breeder, and he reminded Decker of a mad scientist as he tested water samples and added chemicals to the fifty aerated aquariums that filled his living room. The tanks gurgled and bubbled like boiling cauldrons. It took Donnie nearly twenty minutes to get down to business.

He remembered the case. His conclusion was profound: Either an abduction or a runaway.

Did he favor one over the other, Decker asked.

Oh, probably an abduction, said Oldham. None of the girl's personal effects seemed to be missing. Her car was still in the parking lot. People don't leave without taking some memento along.

But then again, he added gleefully, she still could have been a runaway.

Decker thanked him. As he turned to leave, he saw Oldham taking off his shirt and dipping his bare arms into a tank of guppies. A caved-in patch of glossy scar tissue decorated the man's right shoulder. Decker wondered how he'd caught the bullet.

He arrived back at the squad room shortly after noon and found Marge at her desk, looking sick.

"What's wrong with you?" he asked.

"Chug-a-lugged too many beers," she answered, pushing hair out of her eyes. The blonde strands hung limply down to her shoulders. Her complexion was wan.

"You don't look hungover; you look sick. As in the flu. Why don't you go home?"

She dismissed the thought with a wave of her hand. "The aspirins'll kick in. I'll be all right."

"What are you working on now?" Decker asked.

"I just got another weeny wagger. Third one in a week. Seems this particular dude just loves to excite himself in the movie theater, preferably kiddy films. They caught him at the climax—his—buttering some little girl's popcorn at the Brave Li'l Mouse Movie."

Decker groaned.

"Mama went bonkers," Marge continued. "Started screaming in front of a full house. 'Did you see what that man just did! He ejaculated into my daughter's popcorn!' Meanwhile, the perv's just sittin' there with this smug grin plastered across his mug. No resistance to the arrest. Too damn wasted."

"I hope they got their money back," Decker said.

"Yeah, they did—and a free popcorn to boot—but Mama was none too pleased."

"Do you have any other cases—besides the wagger—that are pressing?"

"My load's pretty light. What's up?"

"We got a name to match a set of bones that we dug up."

Marge nodded approval. "Not too shabby, Pete."

"Sometimes you get lucky. A sixteen-year-old white female named Lindsey Bates. Disappeared around four months ago."

"Want me to talk to her mother?"

"If you can. I need someone with a soft touch."

"When?"

"Right now, if you feel up to it. I figured I'd take a peek at the kid's room while you interviewed Mrs. Bates."

Marge stood up. In heels, she was nearly eye level with him. Her shoulders, housed in a padded jacket, appeared immense.

She picked up her bag and said, "Let's go."

The Bateses lived in La Canada. The house was on a tree-lined street at the end of a cul-de-sac—a split level with a wood and stone facade. The lawn had been newly planted and was bisected by a stone walkway lined by manicured rose bushes bursting with dayglow colors—hot pinks, scarlet reds, and sunshine yellows—a wreath for the house of mourning. Marge gave the door a hard rap, and a moment later a wisp of a blonde appeared in the doorway.

"Mrs. Bates?" Decker asked, showing his shield.

"Come in, Sergeant . . . I'm sorry I forgot your name."

"Decker, ma'am." He handed her his card. "This is Detective Dunn."

"I'm very sorry for your loss, Mrs. Bates," Marge said, gently.

Mrs. Bates acknowledged the condolences by lowering her head. Under a different set of circumstances she might have been pretty, but sorrow had washed out her face, blurring her features. Her eyes were sunken, the blue iris faded. The cheeks sagged, the mouth was slack and pale. Her coloring was fair, as her daughter's had been, but her hair was stringy and unwashed. She seemed to wilt under the detectives' eyes and made a futile attempt to straighten her housecoat.

"Forgive my appearance," she said in a whisper.

Decker placed a hand on her small, bony shoulder.

"Mrs. Bates, I'm very sorry to intrude upon you at a time like this. Thank you for your cooperation."

The woman's eyes filled with tears.

"Please come in."

They were led to the living room sofa—white velvet, and spotless. Everything in the room was spotless. She asked them if they wanted some coffee, but they both declined.

"If it's all right with you, Mrs. Bates," Decker began, "I'd like to take a look at Lindsey's room."

"What . . . What are you looking for?" she asked.

"Nothing specific," he answered.

That was the truth. But it was more tangible than that. He was trying to get a feel for Lindsey so he could relate to her as a living entity. Her room would be a logical starting place. Rooms and luggage. Ever want to do a quick analysis of a person, find out what he packs for a weekend jaunt.

"I guess that would be okay," Mrs. Bates said hesitantly. "It's down the hall, the third door to the left. The one that's . . . that's closed."

Decker thanked her and left the two women alone.

Marge waited until Mrs. Bates spoke.

"I don't know what I could possibly tell you that I didn't already tell the police the first time around," she said.

"If you're ready," Marge said. "I'd like you to recount what happened the day of Lindsey's disappearance."

Mrs. Bates peered into her lap and Marge took advantage of the opportunity to slip out her notepad.

"It was a Saturday," she began. "I can't believe that she's actually . . ."

She paused to catch her breath, then asked imploringly.

"Is it possible they made a mistake? After all, how could they make such an important decision based on teeth?"

"They seem to be sure—"

"But it's only *teeth*!"

"I wish I could tell you differently, Mrs. Bates," Marge said, quietly. "If I had any doubts, I wouldn't be here. But we seem to be quite certain that we found your daughter. I'm so sorry. It must be so hard to accept that."

"I hope you'll never know." Mrs. Bates dropped her head in her hands and sobbed. Marge offered her a Kleenex and she blew her nose. Then she tried again.

"As I started to say, it was a Saturday . . ." She started crying again.

Marge put down her pad. "Maybe we came too soon for you to do this. It's not because we're callous. It's just that every second we let slip by is less time for us to do our job and more time for your daughter's murderer to get away. But if this is too hard on you, we can come back tomorrow."

Mrs. Bates dried her tears and shook her head no. "I'm all right."

"Sure?"

"Yes," Mrs. Bates said. "What was I saying?"

"It was Saturday," Marge answered, taking up her pad.

"Yes, Saturday," Mrs. Bates repeated. "Lindsey said she was going to the Galleria to shop, to look for a blouse . . . She'd just started driving and the mall was close to home" . . . She threw up her hands. "What else can I tell you? That was the last anyone ever heard of her . . . until now."

"Do you know if she was planning to meet someone?" Marge asked.

Mrs. Bates's face turned livid.

"The original detective asked me the same question. Don't the police ever read each other's reports?"

"I like to be thorough," Marge explained.

The woman sank back into her chair. "I'm terribly sorry for my behavior—"

"No, don't apologize. You're doing fine."

"As far as I know," Mrs. Bates said, "she wasn't going to *meet* anyone. I can give you a list of all of her friends and you can ask them if Lindsey called them."

"Thank you. That would be helpful." She continued. "Do you know the stores your daughter routinely shopped at?"

"Bullocks, Broadway, May Company, Robinson's. She liked Contempo, although I always thought they were a little on the high side."

"Did she follow a certain routine when she shopped? Park in the same place? Comb the stores in the same pattern?"

"Not that I know of. Her friends could tell you better than I can." Her facial expression became wistful. "We used to shop together years ago, but you know kids . . . They like to be with their friends . . . Lindsey loved my taste in clothes. People often mistook us for sisters."

Marge couldn't see it. But the woman had probably aged ten years since her daughter's disappearance. She consulted the notes Decker had prepared for her.

"Lindsey has a younger sister, correct?"

"Yes."

"Were they close?"

"Yes," she answered, with a defensive note to her voice. "We're a very close family."

"And she's at school now?"

"Yes. Erin's at school." As if she were reassuring herself.

"I'd like to talk to her, also."

The woman's eyes darkened.

"Why? Do you think the girls were keeping secrets from me?"

"It's routine, I assure you, Mrs. Bates."

Mrs. Bates bit her lip.

"If you think it's necessary."

Marge nodded.

"The girls are . . . were very different," Mrs. Bates mumbled.

"In what way?"

"I'm . . . I was closer to Lindsey. We shared more interests. She was the sweetest thing on two feet, Detective. And beautiful inside and out."

"And Erin?" Marge prompted.

"Erin's more of an individual. But she's a good girl also."

"I'm sure she is," Marge said. "The Glendale police interviewed Lindsey's friends. She seemed to have had a lot of them."

"What can I tell you, Detective? She was very popular."

"Did you know most of her friends?"

"Yes. Our home was their hangout." Again eyes welled up with tears. "I miss the noise."

"Did Lindsey have a boyfriend?"

She shook her head. "Her father and I discouraged her from getting too involved with anyone special. A sixteen-year-old girl doesn't need an immature boy breathing down her neck, monopolizing her attention. That's how kids get into trouble."

The irony wasn't evident to her, and Marge talked quickly to keep it that way.

"But she dated?"

"She went out in groups with her friends. We knew all her friends, Detective. They're nice kids."

"What kind of a student was she?"

"She didn't have a head for academics, but she passed her classes." She sighed. "We had tutors, but we decided against college for her . . . Her charm was her kindness and beauty. You've seen her picture. A lovelier girl never existed."

Marge agreed with her.

"She was head junior cheerleader," Mrs. Bates continued. "She had to compete with one hundred girls for that spot, but she knew she'd win. That's the type of girl she is."

Marge didn't correct her tense.

"Was she involved in other extracurricular activities besides cheerleading?"

"She was on the tennis team. What a backhand!" The woman came alive, revitalized by the memory.

"What was her weekday routine, Mrs. Bates?"

"School at 8:10. Monday, Wednesday, and Friday, tennis team

from 3:15 to 4:30. Cheerleading practice was every day from five to seven. On Wednesday and Thursday nights at eight she had patch—ice skating. Once a week, on Tuesday, piano lessons. She loved to be active. She has an incredible energy level, unlike Erin who's a—."

She fell silent. *Tension between Erin and Mom,* Marge noted in her pad. She asked,

"Did Lindsey go out on weekdays?"

"Yes. But she had to be in by ten."

Marge smiled, trying to look benign.

"Mrs. Bates, how would you describe your relationship with your daughter?"

"We were very close," she said. "My daughter was not a runaway."

"I'm sure she wasn't," Marge said quickly. She noticed Mrs. Bates was digging her nails into her hands.

*Keep her talking.*

"Do you happen to know if Lindsey kept a diary?" Marge asked.

One nail broke skin. There was blood.

"She did, didn't she?" Marge said.

"I know she kept one," Mrs. Bates admitted. "I haven't been able to find it. Everything else is the way it always was. Her clothes, her money, her records, her jewelry—and most of it isn't cheap, costume junk—sentimental mementos, her awards. But I . . . I can't seem to find her diary."

*Because she ran away from home and took it with her,* Marge thought. *That's why you haven't been able to find it.*

She asked her some wind-down questions about Lindsey. What emerged from Mrs. Bates's answers was a shell of a girl, a sweet kid who never disobeyed her mother. Marge decided to wrap up the interview since nothing enlightening was likely to come out of it.

"After the police failed to find her, did you try to locate her yourself, Mrs. Bates?" she asked. "Did you and your husband hire anyone to try and find her?"

The woman lowered her head.

"Who'd you hire, Mrs. Bates?"

"It was a reputable firm. The Marris Association."

Marge agreed they were reputable.

"And expensive," Mrs. Bates grumbled. "They wasted thousands of our dollars and came up with nothing."

"Who was the private investigator assigned to the case?"

"His name was Lee Krasdin. An older, fat man with a disgusting red face. Didn't do a damn thing! I don't think he ever left his office."

"I'd like to talk to him. Would you do me a favor? Would you ask him to release your daughter's report to me? Otherwise I'm going to have to get a subpoena—"

"Of course," she said. "I'll call him up right now."

"How about if I call him up and you write me out a release statement for your daughter's records?"

"Fine."

"And I'll need that list of your daughter's friends."

"Of course."

Marge called the Marris Agency and said someone would be there in an hour to pick up the file. She was putting the final touches on her notes when Mrs. Bates returned with a few sheets of paper.

"Here," she said, standing over the detective. She smelled slightly stale, as if her clothes hadn't been washed recently.

"This is the list and this is the release statement. Does it say what you want it to say?"

"It's fine," Marge said. "I appreciate you taking the time out to talk to me, Mrs. Bates."

"That's all right," she answered softly. "If I think of anything else, I'll let you know."

"That would be fine." Marge saw Decker standing off to the side. How long he'd been there, she didn't know. It was good that he didn't intrude. His size could sometimes be intimidating. Marge thought that this was one of the times.

She said, "Oh, Sergeant Decker's back."

"Just about done?" he asked, entering the room.

"Yes," Marge answered, winking at him. "Perfect timing."

"Did you find anything illuminating?" Mrs. Bates asked Decker. He noticed anxiety in her voice.

"Not really. It's just a teenage girl's room," he said; then added quitely, "not unlike others I've seen."

Like my own kid's, he thought.

Mrs. Bates's eyes began to swell with tears.

"I'm so sorry," Decker said.

She nodded.

"Mrs. Bates," he asked, "did your daughter ever know someone who was deaf or hard of hearing?"

The question took her by surprise.

"No. Why do you ask?"

"It may be important."

"How so?"

"I'm not really sure. But as soon as I am, I'll let you know."

"A hearing aid?" the woman asked.

Decker said yes.

"No, I don't believe so," she answered, deep in thought. "Maybe I can ask Erin . . . When does she get home? . . . Let's see, it's Wednesday . . . Thursday? . . . I think it's Thursday . . ."

She realized she'd been talking to herself and gave an apologetic smile.

"Also, I'd like to talk to your husband when it's convenient for him," Decker said. "May I call him at home tonight to arrange an appointment?"

"Certainly."

Marge flipped her notebook shut.

"You'll keep me abreast?" Mrs. Bates asked.

"Of course," replied Marge.

Mrs. Bates wrapped herself in her arms and began to knead them like dough.

"I loved my daughter," she said. "I want to catch the monster that . . . that killed her. But perhaps you can understand if I tell you that maybe I'm better off not knowing everything."

Decker flashed to his own daughter.

"I understand," he said.

"What'd you find out?" Decker asked Marge. He turned on the ignition, let the motor idle for a moment, then backed out of the driveway.

"Mom liked to shop with her daughter," answered Marge.

"The usual denial?"

Marge nodded. "Not my kid! She couldn't have run away." She rubbed her hands together. "They fix the car heater yet? Day's turned nasty."

"No, but the air-conditioning works perfectly."

"Terrific. Why don't we chill up the inside so the outside'll feel warm by comparison?"

Decker laughed. "You're looking a little better," he said.

"You talk to people with real problems, you all of a sudden don't feel so sick," she said. "What'd you find in Lindsey's room?"

Decker said, "I found an average, nice kid. Not too deep, but not angry, either. Her records were standard top forty stuff, no heavy metal or rebellious punker crap. Her clothes were a bit more adventurous than preppy, but definitely not punk, either. She was into her nails in a big way. Found at least a half dozen nail kits."

He pulled onto the freeway and floored the gas pedal. The car protested, bucked, then surged ahead.

"Girl didn't read at all. Her book shelves were filled with knick-knacks and stuffed animals. Not a single book."

"Posters?" Marge asked.

"Rock stars, a few of the top New York models. A few framed homilies—*Love conquers all . . . Money is the treasure of kings, Love is the treasure of life*. Stuff like that."

"A nice kid," Marge said.

"A nice kid," Decker said.

"Pictures of boyfriends?" Marge asked.

"Couldn't find any. Couldn't find any snapshots in her room. The family probably keeps photo albums in a different place."

"You didn't by any chance happen to come across a diary?"

Decker shook his head. "She kept one?"

"Mother says she did. She couldn't find it. She said everything else in the girl's room was left untouched."

"If Lindsey was a runaway, she traveled light," Decker said. "It didn't look like the room of an unhappy girl."

"Maybe the kid got tired of being a saint," Marge suggested.

"She wasn't a saint," said Decker. "She had her fun. I found a small stash, birth control pills and a roach clip."

"Mother didn't mention them."

"Wonder why," he said. "I discovered them inside a stuffed animal—a big turtle with a hidden zipper." Decker thought a moment. "But that doesn't change my impression of the girl. The room lacked . . . anger . . . teenage hostility. And you know what else it lacked? Individuality. There wasn't anything in there that seemed different . . . that seemed unique."

"Those are usually the types to suddenly pull up stakes," Marge said. "They keep it all inside."

"Seems strange to leave without your stash and birth control pills," Decker mentioned.

"You could pick those up anywhere. But a diary . . . That you'd take along."

"True," Decker said. "Could be she walked away with just her diary and the clothes on her back."

"I've got a list of her friends," Marge said. "They'll flesh her out. Also, someone should talk to her sister."

"How's the rest of your day holding up?" Decker asked.

"Court appearance in the afternoon."

"Give me the list of her friends," Decker said. "I'll see what I can do."

"Also, Mrs. Bates hired a private detective. Someone at the Marris Agency. I got her to sign a release. They're expecting someone down there in about an hour."

"No problem," Decker said. "Did they come up with anything?"

"According to Mrs. Bates, they came up with an enormous bill."

"Probably didn't tell her what she wanted to hear," Decker said.

"No doubt," she said. "I think *you* should interview the kid sister, Pete. I got the feeling that she and Mama don't get along so hot. Maybe she relates better to men."

"That's fine," he said. "But I want you to come with me. I don't want to be alone with a teenage girl who likes men."

"Good point," Marge agreed, then smiled to herself. "You sure as hell don't need that."

Marris was a slick operation. Lee Krasdin was even slicker. He had a face like a Toby mug and Decker didn't like him. Mrs. Bates had been right about him. He hadn't done anything.

"Is that all?" Decker said when he was done with the report.

Krasdin spread his fingers and placed them palm down on the desktop, as if he were going to hoist himself upward. The effort turned him purple.

"There was nothing left to do, Detective," he said nervously.

"You didn't think she might be a runaway?"

"From everyone we talked to, she seemed like a sweet kid. They do exist, Sergeant—sweet kids who end up in trouble."

Decker threw him a disgusted look.

"You didn't interview her sister."

"Her sister was broken up. You can't intrude upon people like that and expect cooperation."

Decker remembered the Hippocratic oath: *Above all, do no harm.* That was the only compliment you could pay an incompetent like Krasdin.

"Do you know how many runaways we process in a week?" Krasdin said defensively.

"Not as many as LAPD."

"Let me tell you," the man said indignantly. "I can spot a runaway situation with my eyes closed, and this wasn't a runaway. We talked to friends, we talked to relatives, we talked to church leaders, we talked to teachers. The kid was a random abduction, and that left us nowhere."

"Mr. Krasdin, when someone is missing, I look for them. If they don't show up at a friend's or relative's house, I look outside the neighborhood. You didn't do anything except knock on a few doors. A Fuller Brush salesman could have done better."

"If you would read the report *carefully*, Sergeant Decker, you'd notice that we did pursue a runaway assumption. We went into Hollywood and talked to the police. They hadn't seen hide nor hair of the girl."

"You talked to police to find out about runaways? That's about as worthwhile as talking to runaways to find out about the police. You want to find out about street kids, you talk to street kids."

"Assuming they'll talk to you."

"They'll talk."

"I resent your implications about the thoroughness of our investigation," the man sputtered.

"That's your prerogative. In the meantime, I'm going to keep this Xerox of the report."

"Certainly. Despite the adversarial tone of this conversation, I want you to know that I'll help you in any way I can, Sergeant. At Marris, we believe in cooperation with law enforcement."

Decker immediately took him up on it. "You interviewed Lindsey's friends. Happen to notice if anyone was hard of hearing?"

"Not that I recall. Of course, I don't routinely check for hearing aids. Why do you ask?"

"Never mind."

By the time he left Marris, it was nearly four. Decker slid into the unmarked and pulled out the list of Lindsey's friends. He had time to see one or two before heading back to the Bates's. The first one on the list was a boy named Brian Armor. After thirty minutes on the Golden State Freeway North, he swung onto 134 east—wide open lanes of asphalt that cut through the San Gabriel mountains. The air was crisp, the sky a brilliant blue; a beautiful smogless day not atypical of L.A. winters. He passed the La Crescenta city line and ten minutes later pulled the Plymouth into a circular driveway. He killed the motor.

The house was a graceful two-story colonial—a downscale replica of an antebellum mansion. During Decker's childhood, family
vacations had often included excursions into the deep South,
where majestic plantations loomed larger than life in the little
boy's eyes—the stately scrolled columns; the massive, two-story
double entrance doors; the porticoes dripping flowers, set into
acreage that expanded to the horizon. As he grew older, Decker'd
lost his lust for mansions, but he had always retained a love of
land.

He walked up to the door and pushed the bell, which chimed
resonantly. The kid who answered had a football player's build
and a very cocky expression on his face. The look was tempered a
second later when he realized he was looking up at Decker.

"Whaddaya want?" he asked, in a voice surprisingly high and
squeaky.

Decker flashed his badge.

"I'm looking for Brian Armor."

The last remnants of cockiness disappeared.

"He's not home."

"Who are you?" Decker asked.

"Listen, I don't have to talk to a cop without a lawyer." He
started to slam the door shut, but Decker was ready and caught
him off balance. The door flew back open and the boy went stumbling backward. The detective stepped inside.

"You can't come in without a search warrant," the boy said,
stunned.

The smell of marijuana was overwhelming. Decker opened his
jacket and gave the kid a view of his shoulder holster. The boy
licked his lips.

"Hey man, no trouble."

Decker made his way through the formal living room and into
the den. Four teenagers stopped talking and looked up. Bruce
Springsteen provided the background music.

Even if he had had a warrant, and even if he had been from
narcotics, it still wouldn't have been much of a bust. A lid or two

of grass—who gave a fuck? But image was all-important. He scooped up the bag and motioned Brian over.

"Where's the john?" he asked.

"Third door to the left."

Decker turned to the other teens.

"I'm a police officer," he said. "You kids stay right where you are. Understand?"

They nodded solemnly.

"C'mon, buddy," Decker said. He gave Brian a slight shove forward and prodded him down the hallway into the bathroom. When they were both inside, Decker locked the door.

The boy's hands squeezed into tight, white knuckled balls.

"You're not going to try anything stupid, are you?" Decker asked.

The boy didn't answer.

"Unclench your fists, son. I'm not about to duke it out with you." Decker smiled. "In a john of all places."

The boy's fingers slowly relaxed.

"As far as I'm concerned," Decker said, "this never existed." He dumped the contents of the bag down the toilet and gave it a flush. "I gave you a break. Now you give me one."

The kid stared, amazed.

"Whaddaya want?" he repeated, his tone of voice deferential this time.

"I'm looking for Brian Armor."

"I'm Brian."

"I want to talk to you about Lindsey Bates."

The boy stared at him.

"Lindsey? . . . This is about *Lindsey*?"

"Yep. Your bad-ass attitude lost you your stash for nothing."

"Aw, shit."

"But look at it this way. I'm not gonna bust you." Decker took out his notepad. "You wanna talk in here or you wanna go out there?"

"All my friends out there—they were friends of Lindsey's."

Decker grinned. He had just saved himself a mess of legwork. "Let's go."

The gang was waiting, stiff and grim. When they saw Brian smile, their posture loosened.

Brian cocked a thumb at Decker.

"He wants to talk about Lindsey."

"Why should we talk to you?" said a sulking brunette in torn clothing. He knew from Cindy what those rags cost.

"You're a friend of Lindsey's?" he asked.

"Maybe."

"Then maybe you give enough of a fuck about her to help me find her murderer."

She lowered her eyes.

"What's your name?" Decker asked the girl.

"Heather."

Decker consulted his list.

"Heather Hanson."

Her head jerked up.

"That's right."

The detective checked her name off.

"I'm going to read some names," he said. "Answer me if it's you."

They were all there. Decker marveled at his good fortune.

"So what do you want to know about Lindsey?" asked a big blonde with purple lips. She was Lisa O'Donnell.

"She left home at eleven A.M. Saturday morning, September tenth. Did she call any of you earlier that day?"

"She called me," Heather answered. "I was her best friend."

"And?"

"And she asked me to meet her at the Galleria at 12:30. She didn't show up."

So she had run away or had been abducted somewhere between eleven and 12:30. Amazing that no one had picked up on something so simple.

Heather went on: "I didn't think anything about it. We change our plans lots of times." She twirled her curly hair. "I mean, I didn't tell the police about her phone call the first time around."

"You're not going to get into any trouble. I'm only interested in Lindsey now. Were the two of you supposed to meet anyone else?"

"No," she said quickly.

Decker stared at her.

"Like maybe she was supposed to meet her boyfriend that her parents didn't know about and you were supposed to meet your boyfriend that your parents don't know about," Decker pushed.

The girl studied her fingernails.

"Who was her boyfriend, Heather?"

"It doesn't matter now," she said weakly. "Is she really dead?"

Decker nodded.

Heather swallowed hard and looked away.

"It matters, Heather," Decker said, "if it was her boyfriend who ripped her off."

"Hey," Brian butted in. "He wouldn't do something like that. Man, he was torn to shreds when Lindsey took off. He thought she dumped him."

"How long had they been sneaking around together?"

"They were in love!" Heather protested. "It wasn't anything raunchy."

Decker backed off.

"Okay, they were in love. Nobody's saying they weren't. How long were they going together?"

"Over a year," Lisa volunteered. "He was a nice guy, but sort of a dropout. You know, free-lance photographer, a one-day-at-a-time person."

"What's his name?"

The room was silent. Decker waited.

"Chris Truscott," Lisa blurted.

"Snitch." Brian muttered.

"Listen, jerk," the girl yelled, "if he had anything to do with

Lindsey's death, I don't want him to go unpunished." She looked to Decker for approval.

"It was okay to protect him before," the detective said. "After all, if the two of them ran away together, it's not your business. But now you *know* Lindsey has been murdered. She was probably burnt alive and suffered a lot of pain. No sense letting Chris walk away as innocent as a newborn babe if he lit the match."

Stunned silence. Decker hated this. Bullying people with misery to get what he wanted. Tears fell down Lisa's cheek.

"He lives in Venice," she said, wiping her eyes with the back of her hand. "I forget the exact address. I think it's Fourth and Rose."

"How old is he?"

"Twenty." Brian answered. "I don't know how the rest of you feel, but I feel shitty talking about Chris like he was a criminal. He was in love with Lindsey."

"Do you think she took off with him, Heather?"

"I honestly don't know."

Decker could barely hear her.

"Tell him about the gig, Heather," Lisa prompted.

"What gig?" asked Decker.

"Photography gig," Lisa answered. "See, Chris didn't get it together with Lindsey that day—"

"Why don't you let Heather tell it, since Chris made the friggin' phone call to her?" Brian interrupted.

All eyes went to Heather. She drew her knees into her chest and rolled herself up into a tight ball.

"He had this photography gig," she began in a small voice. "I think it was a wedding or a baptism. I forget. Anyway, he said that's why he didn't make it. He asked me to pass the word to Lindsey. See, he was off-limits to her. Her parents hated him even though they'd only met him once. Lindsey didn't want to upset them by telling them that she was in love with Chris, so she lied and said that she broke up with him. But she didn't. Anyway, she never showed up and I thought she'd just made other plans.

Sometimes Lindsey'd forget things if she'd get real involved with her makeup or nails."

Decker told her to go on.

"Anyway, much later that night," Heather continued, "her mom called me, all freaked out. Lindsey hadn't come home. Was she at my house? God, I got all freaked myself. I didn't know what to think. Where was Lindsey? She didn't show up at the mall, she wasn't at home . . . Maybe she really *did* take off with Chris and he just told me he didn't meet her at the Galleria to throw me off base. So I called Chris and asked him. But he swore no. I didn't think he was lying. I mean, he really, really *loved* her." She paused, then said. "God, I've thought about the whole thing over and over. What went wrong? What really happened to poor Lindsey? I've had a ton of nightmares. I just don't know what to think anymore." She buried her face in her knees and began to sob. "I don't feel so good."

Lisa threw her arms around her and rocked her back and forth.

Peter, you callous asshole, thought Decker. He comforted himself by saying he was on the right side.

When Heather seemed to have calmed down, he asked, "Have any of you had contact with Chris since Lindsey's disappearance?"

"A little. Like the first week after she split," Brian said. "He kept coming to the neighborhood, trying to find her. Then, nothing."

"Chris and I used to ride in a bike club together," answered a boy with lank dark hair and a huge Adam's apple. His voice was a rich baritone and his name was Marc. "I saw him a couple of weeks ago, first time since Lindsey disappeared. He had sold his bike to someone at the club; said he was hard up for cash. I believe it. He looked terrible, totally wiped out. Asked me if I had heard from Lindsey. 'Course I didn't." The boy's black eyes were sharp and alive. "He couldn't have killed her, Officer. I'm not saying they didn't take off together, but he couldn't rip her off. He was really wild about her."

"Any of you know his phone number by heart?"

"He's listed," Lisa said.

"Did Chris and Lindsey hang around you guys or did they have their own set of friends?"

"They hung around us sometimes," Heather said. "Sometimes, me and my boyfriend would double with them. But they tried to be alone as much as possible. I don't know much about his friends."

"Did Lindsey ever talk about knowing a deaf girl?"

"Dead?" Brian asked.

"Deaf," Lisa snapped. "Like you can't hear."

"Huh?" Brian joked.

"Get serious, Armor. This isn't the time," Marc scolded. He looked back at Decker. "She never mentioned any deaf girl to me."

"To me, either," said Heather.

"Any friend of Chris's deaf?"

Blank stares.

"So none of you heard a thing about Lindsey after she disappeared."

They all shook their heads.

"Did Lindsey ever talk, even jokingly, about running away with Chris?"

"Lindsey may have dug the guy," Marc said, "but she wasn't the type to do something like take off. She had lots of plans for the senior year."

"What kind of plans?" Decker asked.

"The prom. Varsity cheerleading." Heather said.

"She was really into cheerleading," added Lisa. "And modeling. She wanted to be a model. She certainly had the body for it."

"I'll say," Brian said, lecherously. The other kids gave him reproving looks. The boy blushed.

"Lindsey seemed to be a nice girl," Decker said. "Considerate of her parents, not wanting to hurt their feelings by going with Chris. Enthusiastic about cheerleading. Anybody want to add anything?"

"She was a doll," Lisa said. "Not real heavy on the gray matter—"

"Like *you* are?" Brian said.

"Shut up, Armor."

Suddenly Brian became enraged. *"Will you quit picking on me!"* he screamed, turning crimson.

The room fell silent. A minute passed, then Brian let out a hollow laugh.

"She was a great kid," he said in a cracked voice. "She was nice to everyone . . . Even me."

"She was real sweet," Marc said softly. "The world could use more positive people like her."

Decker had to admit it; she didn't sound like a prototypical runaway. No evidence of heavy drug use, she didn't seem to hate her parents, she had a supportive peer group and was involved in school activities. It was beginning to smell like an abduction. Which meant either the boyfriend was involved and Decker would have a substantial lead, or the boyfriend wasn't and he was up shit's creek without a paddle.

Decker folded his notepad and distributed his cards.

"If any one of you thinks of something that might help, give me a call."

Lisa squinted and mouthed the word "Decker."

"You got a daughter on the intramural track team?" she asked.

Decker nodded. "You know Cindy?"

"Not personally. I just remember this long-legged red-head named Decker who competed last year. Ran like lightning. She should go into the Olympics or something."

Despite himself, Decker swelled with parental pride.

His watch said 6:15. Hard to believe that he'd been in there for over an hour and a half. He was supposed to meet with the rabbi at eight, so he had plenty of time to fix himself dinner. But he wasn't hungry.

A nice girl disappears and turns up a corpse, murdered gruesomely. The scenario suppressed his appetite. Making matters worse, the case had little to go on.

It became all too clear to him why he had transferred out of Homicide. Any victim was better than a dead one. True, he'd seen his fair share of assholes getting blown away in sour drug deals and junkies who kacked themselves. The memories didn't keep him up at night. It was cases like this one that left the bile in his throat.

A nice girl.

He thought of his own daughter. She was safe, he assured himself. She was careful. But the words seemed empty. Careful wasn't enough.

His daughter. Alone in New York.

He took out a cigarette.

He'd call Jan the minute he got home. Cindy and Eric living together? He thought that was a fine idea.

# ·6

"**V**ery good," Rabbi Schulman said, twirling gray wisps of beard around his index finger. "You're making very good progress."

"Thank you," said Decker.

The Rosh Yeshiva closed the *chumash*—the Jewish bible. They were learning bible in the rabbi's study, a spacious, wood-paneled room that reflected the warmth of its host. The picture window revealed a tranquil evening, the foliage dappled with moonlight like early morning frost on a winter's landscape. Decker felt a spiritual calm, even though the circuitry of his nervous system was pushing overload.

"Study next week's portion and we'll go over it together. Use the English of course, but try to look at the Hebrew also. Remember what I told you about looking for the *shoresh*—the three-letter root—in the word."

"I will." Decker stared back at his open Bible and began shuffling through back pages, not quite ready to call it quits.

"And you'll be spending Shabbos weekend with us?" the rabbi asked.

"I'm planning on it. Thank your wife again for her hospitality."

"I will do that. And Zvi Adler wants to have you over for Shabbos lunch. I think it would be nice if you accepted the invitation."

"That's fine."

"Sarah Libba would have called you, but she's exquisitely shy, so Zvi asked me to invite you."

"Tell him I'd be delighted."

Schulman stood, his posture as rigid as a T-square. He sensed Decker's jumpiness and went to a liquor cabinet.

"A shot of schnapps, Peter?"

*Rotgut,* Decker thought. It was amazing the man had any lining left in his stomach. Yet, here he was in his seventies with more energy than someone half his age.

"Thank you, Rabbi. That would be nice."

The rabbi gave Decker a shot glass and raised his cup in the air.

"*L'chaim,*" he said.

"*L'chaim,*" Decker repeated.

The old man peered over the detective's shoulder and noticed the open *chumash.*

"Fascinating, isn't it"—Schulman downed the liquid fire in a single gulp—"to read about our ancestors, God's chosen people? He said to Yaakov, 'I shall remember your seed, and they shall be as numerous as the stars in the sky.' And then we learn that Yaakov's sons sold their brother, Yoseph, into slavery because they were poisoned with jealousy; that Miriam—a prophetess—was turned into a leper because she spoke ill of Moshe's wife; that Tamar, dressed as a harlot, seduced her father-in-law, Yehudah, in order to secure her rightful seed; that Shimon and Levi—brothers in spirit as well as blood—avenged the rape of their sister by wiping out a nation. Superficially, one would think we descended from a bunch of hoodlums."

The old man coughed.

"Such is not the case at all. Those men and women were righteous, Peter. On a far higher *madraga*—level of spirituality—than we are today. You must remember they were worthy enough to have been recorded in the *chumash* for posterity."

"But they were still human beings," Decker said, "with human frailties."

"This is true."

Decker closed the book.

"It's family, Rabbi," he said. "It brings out the best and worst in us. Whenever a crime is committed, the first place cops look is the family. Almost always, the perpetrator is a relative or friend. Yoseph was sold by his own brothers. No surprise. If that crime happened today, we could have saved Yaakov years of grief."

"*Chas v'chaleylah*," the rabbi frowned. He sat down and put his arm around Decker. "God forbid! *Hashem* had a bigger purpose in mind, Peter. Yoseph was *supposed* to go down to Egypt. Had he not gone, Yaakov and his sons would have been wiped out by famine. *Hashem* knew what he was doing."

Schulman took off his oversized *kipah* to smooth his white hair, then placed it back on his head.

"And of course, the Jews would have never been slaves in Egypt. And that would have been terrible, because then we wouldn't have had Passover!"

He broke into a broad grin at his own joke, then grew serious.

"Events in Jewish history have a way of coming in through the back door," he said. "Like the selling of Yoseph. Out of that came the Exodus: Moses, the Revelation, the Torah. It is said that even the messiah will not come to us openly. Why? Whenever good comes openly, the *yetzer harah*—the evil spirit—is there to destroy it."

"I don't subscribe to the concept of an evil spirit, Rabbi."

Schulman refilled Decker's cup.

"You don't come into contact with it daily?" the old man asked.

"I come into contact with a lot of bad people," Decker answered. "And most of them know darn well what they're doing is wrong. They just don't care. Ask them why they robbed or raped or killed and you'd be surprised at how creative their excuses are. It's a rare criminal who'll accept responsibility for his own actions. An evil spirit seems to me to be another way to pass the buck. The devil made me do, et cetera."

"Judaism sees it as just the opposite of what you're saying," Schulman explained. "Evil is in all of us. So is good. Man has free will to choose either. There is a very interesting *midrash* about that. Before Mount Sinai the angels asked *Hashem* to give them

the Torah instead of mankind. After all who is better equipped to
do *mitzvot*—good deeds—than an angel? *Hashem* refused. Mankind was the only acceptable recipient of the Torah because only
mankind could *elect* to honor *Hashem*. The angels were pro-
grammed only for good. It's no challenge to be good if good is
the sole component of one's makeup."

Decker took a sip of schnapps and said nothing.

Schulman asked, "Did you have a bad day, Peter?"

"A little on the rough side."

"Let me ask you something? What do policemen do when they
have a bad day?"

Decker smiled. "They get drunk and gripe to each other."

"This is what *you* do?"

"Me personally? No, not really. I've gotten drunk on individual
occasions, but I'm not a big boozer."

"I can see that," Schulman said, picking up Decker's half-full
glass. "So what do you do to cope?"

"A lot of us don't cope too well. The divorce rate among cops is
very high."

"Isn't there someone who you can talk to?"

"A shrink?" Decker said. "Yes, we have a resident shrink, but
hardly anyone uses him—or her, we've got a woman now—unless
they're after disability."

"*Es past nisht, nu?*" Schulman said. "It just isn't done if you're
truly a man."

"You've got it," Decker said.

"So what do *you* do to keep your sanity?" the old man asked
again.

"I ride my horses," Decker said. "And now I learn, also."

"Does learning help?"

"Yes, it does. It takes up a lot of my free time so I don't think
about work as much. It preoccupies me."

"Do you ever pray?"

"In addition to davening?"

"Yes," Schulman said. "Do you ever feel the need to say
*tehillim?*"

"I can't say that I have. I'd like to think that God has a reason for everything, but I don't really believe that. Some bad people have good luck, some good people are constantly behind the eight ball. What's the point?"

"A hard question and I have no satisfying answer. We aren't permitted to know the point. It would be no test of faith if we knew the point. We'd know for certain that *Hashem* exists. Even Moshe *Rabbenu*, who was permitted to understand everything else, was not allowed to know *Hakadosh Boruch Hu*'s system of reward and punishment."

"Well, maybe it takes a Moses to live with such ambiguity," said Decker. "What I see are lots of things that are unfair. Our legal system is a farce, Rabbi, confessed murderers getting off scot-free because of some technicality. If only there was divine retribution—a meteorite crashing on their heads or bolts of lightning striking them dead—then maybe I could see a purpose to all of it."

"I have a *midrash* for you." Schulman thought for a while, then said, "A quartet of great rabbis—Rabbis Akiva, Ben Zoma, Ben Azzai, and Elisha ben Abouya—went into an orchard to study the hidden recesses of the Torah. All four were very pious men, all were brilliant—tremendous Torah scholars—an absolute prerequisite for the study of Jewish mysticism."

"Okay," Decker said.

"Now the word the Gemara uses for orchard is *pardes*—a very beautiful garden. Some have taken it to mean *gan eden*—the Garden of Eden, Paradise."

"The rabbis actually went to Paradise?"

"There is debate on that. What they did was utter the ineffable name of *Hashem*—the tetragrammaton. Rashi is of the opinion that says their utterances actually brought them into contact with the *Shechinah*—the Holy Presence. Other commentators say they really weren't in heaven but the utterance of the Name made it appear to them that they were. Clear?"

Decker said yes.

"Four of our greatest rabbis in the presence of *Hashem*," Schulman said. "So what happened to them?"

His voice had taken on a singsong.

"Ben Azzai died. He leaped toward the *Shechinah* and his soul departed from his body. Ben Zoma also approached the *Shechinah*, but instead of dying, his mind was torn apart. He went crazy. What's the logical question, Peter?"

"Why did one go crazy and the other die?"

"Good. Ben Azzai had seen the *Shechinah* and couldn't return to the corporeal. What happened was he had reached such a high level of spiritual understanding that his soul no longer had need of a body. Ben Zoma, on the other hand, never reached that level. His mind became saturated with knowledge that he couldn't assimilate. When the mind can't accommodate its input, it breaks down.

"The third rabbi, Elisha ben Abouya, the Gemara tells us, 'cut down the shoots of the orchard.' What do you think that means?"

"The orchard is symbolic of heaven?" Decker asked.

"A heavenly state."

Decker thought. "He destroyed heaven."

"Meaning?"

"He destroyed *Hashem*."

"Meaning?"

Decker thought for a moment.

"You can't destroy *Hashem*," he said. "But you can reject Him."

"Exactly," said the old man. "When you reject something, it is destroyed in your eyes. Ben Abouya became an *apikorus*—a nonbeliever, an apostate. Why? Some commentaries say he'd become infatuated with Hellenistic philosophy and left the *pardes* with a dual gnostic concept—the idea that there are two gods in the universe. The core of Judaism revolves around the fact that there is only one *Hashem*."

Decker nodded.

"Others say ben Abouya fell apart when he failed to learn the secrets of the Divine's plan of reward and punishment. He couldn't understand why some evil men appear to prosper when righteous men are thrown into abject misery. Ben Abouya couldn't accommodate himself to this lacuna in his understanding of Torah. It led him to complete rejection of Judaism, to a life of immorality. From the moment of his fall from grace, Elisha ben Abouya is referred to in the Gemara as *Acher—the other—*a euphemism for an apostate."

"If a great rabbi loses faith because he can't understand God's justice system, how am I supposed to maintain mine?" Decker asked.

"Patience. We still have Rabbi Akiva left. The Gemara tells us he entered in peace, he left in peace," Schulman answered.

"Why was he spared?"

"The right question. Now the point of all of this. Rabbi Akiva was spared because he knew when to quit. He knew what not to ask. There are certain aspects of *Hakadosh Boruch Hu* that we as mortals cannot question. Yes, as frustrating as it is for rational beings, there are some things we must accept on blind faith. To not accept that is to not believe. And to not believe leads one to say that creation was a molecular accident. I look around me and I say this is impossible.

"Murder is horrible. I'm not debating that. The reason for it? It's a question I'm not going to ask. Our lives on this planet are infinitely short when measured against the hereafter. Some lives are shorter than others. To our shallow perception this may seem an injustice. But in reality it is all the will of *Hashem* and we simply cannot hope to understand His wisdom. If we try, we are destined to fail and destroy ourselves."

Decker started to say something, but shook his head instead.

"You are not satisfied," Schulman said.

"That would be little comfort to the parents of a murdered child, Rabbi," Decker said.

"Ach, a child!" Schulman said with pain in his voice.

"A teenager. A girl my daughter's age."

"And you talked with the girl's parents today?"

"Her mother."

"What did you say to her?"

"I didn't say much. I mostly listened."

"Sometimes least is best."

"What would *you* tell the parents of a murdered child, Rabbi?"

The Rosh Yeshiva became lost in thought, his posture stooped as if the discussion had added weight onto his shoulders. Several moments passed before he spoke. Then he whispered to himself, *"Hashem natan, Hashem lakach. Yehi shem Hashem mevorach."* To Decker, he said calmly "We *borrow* our children from *Hashem.* If God in His infinite wisdom took the life of *my* young child, I'd bless the fact that he was now in the hands of the perfect father."

Decker walked into the cool night air and tried to relax. His discussion with the Rosh Yeshiva, combined with the day's events, had flipped the on-switch, and he was overflowing with nervous energy. He jogged past the dorm building and through the postage-stamp lots of single-family dwellings, heading toward the parking lot, but stopped when he reached Rina's house. It was a quarter to eleven but the lights were still on. Deliberating a moment, he made a sharp left, walked up to her door, and knocked softly.

"Who is it?" he heard her say.

"It's Peter, Rina."

She unhooked the chain and opened the door.

"Hello there," she said, letting him in. "You're just the person I wanted to see."

"Why's that?"

"Someone has been having nightmares."

Decker's eyes fixed on Jacob in his Spiderman pajamas. It always amazed him how much more vulnerable kids looked in their sleepwear.

"Hey, Jakey," he said, sitting next to him. The boy's blue eyes were open and alert. "What's on your mind, big fellah?"

Jacob shrugged.

"He wanted to know whether you've captured the bad man who dumped the bones in the woods," Rina said.

*Shit*, Decker thought. *To love a kid is to live with guilt.*

"No, not yet," he said. "Jacob, that man isn't going to hurt you. He lives far, far away and isn't going to come here."

"How do you know?" the child asked.

"Because I know. He's not interested in hurting you or your eema or anybody here at the yeshiva. Jakey, you're safe."

The kid looked skeptical.

"No one is going to come in here," Decker tried again. "The windows and doors are all locked. They *can't* come in here."

"Suppose a burglar breaks a window?"

"What did I tell you I'd do?" Rina said.

The boy gave a hint of a smile.

"You'd spray his eyes with poison," he answered.

"And then what?"

"While he was rubbing his eyes and going *YOW*, you'd hit him over the head with a frying pan."

"And then what?" Rina prompted.

"You'd break a lamp over his head," he giggled.

"And?"

"After he was all knocked out, you'd tie him up with your leather belts and call the police."

"And who always makes sure you're safe?"

*"Hashem!"*

"And who always looks after you wherever you are?"

*"Hashem!"*

"And who takes care of you twenty-four hours a day, every single day of the year?"

*"HASHEM!"* Jacob shouted.

"It sounds like you're in good hands, Jake," said Decker.

The little boy turned to him.

"Are you gonna catch that bad man?" he asked, still worried.

"Of course, Jake."

"C'mon, Sweetie," Rina said. "Try and get some sleep."

"Can you walk me to my room, Peter?"

"Sure."

Jacob kissed his mother good night and led Decker into the bedroom.

"All's well," Decker said, reentering a moment later. "Have you had any problems with Sammy?"

"Fine. Sleeps like a log, eats great, plays and studies."

"And I thought it was the little one who didn't take things to heart."

"Go figure." She looked up at him. "Do you want something to eat, Peter?"

"A cup of coffee."

"At this time of night?"

"I'm restless. I'm not planning on sleeping much tonight."

"Oh?"

"I think I'll take advantage of my wide-awake mood and do some—research."

"I'm not going to ask."

"Good idea."

He sat down at the kitchen table and watched her put the tea-kettle on the burner. She wore no makeup, her hair was braided back, and she was barefoot. She could pass for seventeen.

"How'd the lesson with Rav Schulman go?"

"Fine," he said. "How long has Jake been having nightmares?"

"This is the first time." She took his hand. "Don't worry about it, Peter. It wasn't your fault. Okay?"

"Sure."

She cupped his chin in her hands and looked into his eyes.

"*Okay?*"

"Yes, okay, whatever you say." He smiled. "You're a potentially violent woman, Rina Lazarus. I'm not messing with you."

"Just don't break into my house." She smiled, then turned serious. "I just wanted him to know that I could take care of him. And I can. I want to show you something."

She left the room, and when she came back, she was carrying a box.

"Take a look inside."

The shape. The weight. He knew what it was without even opening it. *Damn*, he thought. *She really did it.* He pulled out the gun, hefted it, then flipped open the barrel.

"Where are the bullets?"

She reached inside her skirt pocket and handed him a smaller box.

"The guy who sold it to me said to keep the gun and bullets separate since I have small kids in the house."

"He's right."

"But that doesn't really make any sense. If someone breaks into your house, do you want to have to think about where the bullets are and how to load them?"

"It's the lesser of two evils. Better than Jakey thinking it's a toy and shooting off his brother's head."

"Peter, *please!*"

"I just want you to know what you've purchased."

"Well, you keep your gun loaded, don't you?"

"Rina, I'm a police officer."

"What did you do when Cindy was growing up?"

"When I wasn't wearing my gun, I kept it locked up. I never, never left a loaded gun lying in an unlocked drawer or on my nightstand. I have a great deal of respect for what it can do."

"Do you lock your gun up now?" she asked.

"No, because I live alone," he said. "But when Cindy visits me for the weekend, it's locked. When you and the kids come visit, it's locked."

She handed him his coffee and noticed the slight bulge under his jacket. He'd worn his gun while he learned Torah. For some reason, that disturbed her, but she didn't say anything. It would have seemed ludicrous to mention it in view of her recent purchase. She sat down beside him, held her gun in her hand, stared at it, then put it down.

"If you've got ambivalence about it," Decker said softly, "don't even start. There's nothing wrong with chucking the whole idea, Rina."

"No," she insisted. "I want to know how to use it. Hopefully, I'll never have to."

He picked up the Colt and sighted down the barrel.

"Let me take this home," he said. "I'll clean and oil it. Maybe even break it in for you."

"I've got a better idea. Why don't you show *me* how to clean, oil, and break in the gun?"

He frowned.

"We do such romantic things together, Rina. We talk religious philosophy and clean guns. What ever happened to midnight walks on the beach while gazing at the moonlight?"

"The beach isn't safe at night and the water is polluted."

"You're incurably sentimental."

Her lips turned upward and broke into a mysterious smile.

"You're going to be sorry for that sarcastic tone of voice." She opened a drawer and brought out a flat, rectangular package. "Something to wear for Shabbos tomorrow."

She'd bought him a tie, he thought.

"I take it all back," he said.

She stood over him as he opened the box. Inside was a flatter, black satin box. He looked at her, puzzled. "What did you do?"

"Open it," she instructed.

He lifted the lid and took out the contents.

"A watch?"

"Do you like it?"

"Rina—this is solid gold."

"Do you like it?"

He stood up and hugged her.

"Honey, it's gorgeous. But I can't accept—"

"Sure you can. You'd better. It's engraved on the back, and that makes it nonreturnable."

He flipped it over and smiled at the inscription.

"It's because I love you, Peter," she said softly. "I can't show it physically, but the feeling is still there."

"I love you, too, Rina." He gave her a suitably chaste kiss on the lips. Now he knew he'd never get to sleep tonight. "I don't know what to say."

"I see you learning in the *beis hamidresh*, Peter. You don't even know I'm there, but I see you, pouring over the *alef beis*, reading, studying. You say it all that way . . . I knew this boy, once. He was a *ba'al t'shuvah*—a nonreligious Jew who decided to live the Torah life. It lasted maybe six months. He said it was too emasculating for him. He knew too little and couldn't stand it. It takes an extremely big person to do what you're doing—learning as you do from scratch. I don't think I could. I envy your strength of character."

She gave him a bear hug.

"I'm a little choked up," Decker said.

"You're entitled."

He began to feel physically amorous. He suspected Rina was feeling the same way, because she broke away abruptly. He said, "Can you keep this for me until tomorrow? I'm not going straight home and I don't want to take it with me."

"Where're you going?" she asked.

"To find out about a possible runaway. To glamorous Hollyweird."

# ·7

He parked on a side street off Sunset, east of the Strip, took off his yarmulke and tie, and unfastened the top three buttons on his white shirt. Slipping on a couple of gold chains, he checked himself in the rearview mirror. He needed a shave and that was good, but he was still not satisfied. Mussing his hair, he pulled a lock over his forehead down to his brow, then took off his brown suit jacket and donned a cheap baggy windbreaker that didn't show the swell of his .38. He placed a pack of Marlboros and a penlight in a front pocket, opened the door of the Plymouth, and stepped outside.

The underbelly of Hollywood was a vampire leeching out the blood of the city, he thought, the sidewalk teeming with action that thrives in the shadows. He found a spot that looked good—a fine vantage point from where he could see the pimps, hookers, addicts, dealers, and everyday desperados and degenerates. But the best part about the location was the number of independent street-walkers. He needed a sucker not shackled to a pimp.

It didn't take long. The one he picked out was a skinny black girl in an electric blue tank top, denim cut-offs, and knee-length black boots. Her hair had been cornrowed, her eyelids painted blue and pink. Two red slashes highlighted her cheekbones. He gave her the eye, then quickly averted his gaze.

He'd always felt that the key to being a good undercover vice cop was thinking like a woman. You had to be coy and flirtatious.

Most bona fide johns were pretty damn shy when approaching a hooker. There was usually some resistance, and it was the whore who made the moves. Any guy who came on too strong smelled of weirdo or cop.

He pulled out a cigarette, lit it, and flashed a quick glance at Hot Pants. She cocked her head and gave him an open smile. He smiled back and returned to his smoke. He didn't turn around, but he could hear her approaching.

"Got a light?" she asked. Her voice was sultry.

Decker flipped out his matches and lit her cigarette.

"Thank you, Honey," she said.

"You're welcome."

"What you doing out here all alone, Sugar?"

He paused, then said,

"Enjoying the air."

"Nature lover, huh?"

He let his eyes drift slowly over her body. Her tight nylon top offered little support for her sagging breasts. Her crotch was bisected by sprayed-on shorts—cunt-cutters.

"I love what nature has given us," he answered trying to look hungry.

"How much do you love nature, Sugar?"

"How much does it cost to love nature?"

"I think fifty dollars will give you an awful lot of raw beauty."

"What are we talking about here?" he said exhaling a plume of smoke.

"What do you want, Honey?"

"What are my choices?"

"You tell me what you want," she said.

He wasn't about to entrap her, so he changed course abruptly.

"Listen, bitch, if you're gonna fuck with my mind, forget the whole thing. I don't need this shit."

He started to walk away, but she caught his arm.

"Sugar, Sugar, don't get so hot. Save it for when it counts." She studied his face and decided to go for it. "Suck or fuck, take your pick."

"If I want both?"

"Cost you twenty-five more."

"Let me see if I've got the bread." He reached in his coat pocket, pulled out his badge, and grabbed her arm.

"Aw Jesus," she groaned.

"C'mon, Hot Pants, just behave yourself." He turned her around, leaned her against a building, and frisked her.

"What you fuckers won't do for a free feel," she said.

"Save it," he said, cuffing her.

"Asshole," she said evenly. "Now, Sugar, just *what* do you think this is gonna do? You know I'll be back here tomorrow night. Why do you waste everyone's time?"

He propelled her into a dark, secluded alley.

"What are you doing, Sugar?" she said, suddenly concerned.

He pinned her against a wall, boring his eyes into her face. Her lids widened with fear and her mouth dropped open.

"What do you want?" she asked nervously.

"Help."

"Say what?"

"You've got a choice. You give me a little help and your ass is back on the streets in a few minutes. You jive me, you spend the night in the slammer."

"What do you want?" she repeated.

"I'm trying to locate a runaway." He pulled out Lindsey's picture and showed it to her.

She stared at it, then shook her head.

"What makes you think she's here?" she asked.

"She's not here. She's six feet under now. But she may have stopped off here before she ended up in the morgue."

"You ain't from Vice?"

"Uh uh. Homicide."

The whore looked at the picture again.

"Don't know her."

He uncuffed her, but blocked her escape.

"Where do the kids hang out?"

"Same place we do."

"C'mon."

"It's true. They're still hookers, Honey, even if the pussy's a little newer."

Decker grimaced. "Think about this—you're a new runaway without a pimp yet. Where do you go?"

"Put it that way, only one place to go."

"Where?"

"Hotel Hell."

The five-story structure was set back from Hollywood Boulevard, burnt out and condemned, peeling paint on pocked concrete, stucco shedding in clumps. The building still retained some broken windows, but most of the sashes were nothing but open holes punched into the rotting plaster. The property was surrounded by a chain-link rent-a-fence with a missing section where a gate should have been. Some of the links had been clipped, leaving the metal spurs sharp and threatening.

He entered the grounds—a jungle of tall, tangled weeds—and went inside the doorless building. The lobby flooring was cracked linoleum and dirt, and as he walked, the soles of his feet stuck to the grimy surface. It was dark and dank, reeking of urine, feces, and vomit. He waited a moment for his eyes to adjust. The moonlight shone through the empty sashes, checkerboarding the floor. Looking down the long corridor, Decker began to make out figures and shadows scurrying and darting—live pawns on a chessboard. The hallway flickered with trash-can bonfires.

A rat danced at his feet. Decker sidestepped and immediately tripped over a soft lump on the floor. He took out his penlight and shone it on a girl balled in a fetal position. A mutt was curled at her feet, whimpering. He gave her ribs a gentle prod, but she didn't move. Bending down, he turned her over and she sprawled out, arms flopping randomly. Her skin was ashen and cold to the touch. She had no pulse.

"Jesus," he whispered.

There was nothing he could do for her now. He'd take care of the body later. Standing up, he walked down the hall.

Empty eyes, vacant stares, shreds of cloth that shrouded living cadavers, muted rodent sounds. Most of the zombies were trying to get warm, rubbing together hands encased in fingerless mittens: some were crouched in corners, rocking back and forth, humming dirges. Others were sleeping fitfully. As he passed the kids, the background noises hushed. A stranger. He had to be up to something—some kind of hustle.

On the second floor he found a group huddled around a pile of burning newspaper and came toward them slowly, as one approaches a wounded animal. When he was next to them, he shone his penlight on the picture of Lindsey Bates.

They took turns looking at the snapshot, but the results were the same: dull stares and wordless shakes of the head. He moved on to the next group and came away empty again.

Slowly he combed the building, sometimes gagging on the rot around him. They looked, they cooperated passively, a few even smiled, but the story was the same. Lindsey was a nonentity in Hotel Hell.

The building turned icy, the stench stronger as the night winds died, leaving only stagnant chilled air. But noises returned as word passed that the stranger was only showing a picture. A few even came up to him, volunteered to look. *Never saw her, man.* The sounds grew boisterous—cackles, cries, retching, pissing. After canvassing all five stories, he felt fatigue begin to hood his eyes.

He'd try again next week. There'd be new kids and some old-timers returning to the fold. He put the picture away, heading for the door but stopped suddenly. It was involuntary—a psychic paralysis that froze the muscles of his calves.

He gasped as he stared at her. A moonbeam hit her smack in the face, illuminating her in deathly grays.

The girl's mouth was agape, framed by lips of orange: eyes dull and lolling. She had it all—the angle of the cheekbone, the point of the chin. But it was the hair—flaming red tresses setting off a pale, freckled face—that made his heart take off.

Cindy!

She was wearing a green sequined halter and an orange miniskirt. She caught his eye and lowered her lashes. When he didn't move, she made a funny face, swung out her hip and undid her halter, giving him a full view of voluptuous breasts. Cupping one in each hand, pinching pink nipples, she sashayed over slowly, seductively.

"Twenty-five dollars," she whispered.

He wanted to kill her.

Blinded with fury which he knew was irrational, he tried to stalk away, but she caught his arm. He turned, threw her against the wall, and slapped her hard, feeling the sting radiate through his hand. He grabbed her wrists.

"I'm a cop, you stupid fuck!"

The animal in her took over. She opened her jaws, hissed, and bit his right forearm through the jacket sleeve. He yelped and released her wrists, but she'd become wild, clawing and scratching, ripping his jacket. He managed to shield his face with his bare arm, but she continued attacking, raking the skin of his forearm. In desperation, he backhanded her, and she went flying across the hallway and into a wall.

*Oh shit,* he thought.

He started to approach her, but she scrambled to her feet and fled.

His arm was wet, crimson, and shaking. Reaching for a handkerchief and finding nothing, he took off his jacket and tried to staunch the flow.

*You stupid shithead,* he thought to himself. *To let a dumb hooker get to you like that. Your daughter is a good kid. Why the fuck do you go looking for trouble when there is none?*

He peeled back his soaked jacket. His arm was still bleeding although the scarlet stream had reduced to slow seepage. The flesh had already begun to swell and throb. He had to get out of there.

He saw her out of the corner of his eye and felt he should say something, but nothing came out. It was she who approached him, offering him a roll of bandages. He took it with a nod and began to wrap his wounds.

"You okay?" he asked.

She nodded.

"Sure?"

"Sure."

"I'm sorry I hit you like I did," he said. "I was just trying to get you off of me."

"I'm sorry I bit you like I did," she said. "I was just trying to get you off of me. You scared the hell out of me."

"Where's a twenty-four-hour pharmacy?" he asked.

"Don't know." She pulled out a cigarette. "You gonna arrest me?"

"No."

"Are you really a cop?"

"Yes."

"Whacha doing here?"

Reaching into his pocket, he pulled out Lindsey's picture. The redhead cautiously approached him to take a look.

"Don't know her," she said. "How long has she been missing?"

"She's not missing. She's dead."

The girl shuddered. He looked at her and saw a deep red palm print spread across her face.

"I slapped you pretty hard," he said. "Are you sure you're okay?"

"Are you kidding?" she shrugged. "Man, that's just a warm-up for half the kinkies I get."

He shook his head in disgust, at the perverts, at himself.

"Why'd you *stare* at me like that?"

"You reminded me of my daughter."

She let go with machine-gun laughter.

"I've heard that before."

He pulled out his wallet and flipped to Cindy's picture. The girl's eyes increased several diameters.

"God, I really do." She grinned. "No wonder you went cuckoo. Who's the black-haired girl? Your other daughter?"

He frowned.

"My girlfriend."

She giggled.

"Sorry."

"I've got to go." He straightened up and began retreating.

"Hey, Cop or whatever your name is?"

"What?"

"Give me the picture of the dead girl. I'm more likely to dig up dirt than you are."

He handed her the snapshot of Lindsey and his card.

"Decker," she said out loud. "It says here you work Juvey."

"I'm on loan to Homicide."

"Okay, Decker," she announced. "I'll see what I can do."

"Who are you?"

"I'm Kiki. But you don't contact me. I contact you."

"Fine," Decker said. "Bye, Kiki."

"Hey, don't informants get paid?"

"Only if they produce."

"Where you going?"

"To take care of my arm." He walked away, but she followed him. A fucking gosling, he thought. She'd imprinted.

"Maybe I do know where a pharmacy is."

He said nothing.

"Hey, ya know, you gotta get an antibiotic for the bite."

He spun around. "Are you infected with something?"

"Don't worry. I don't have AIDS or anything. Least not that I know of."

*Swell.*

"It's just that bites are dangerous," she went on, "even if the person isn't sick. I know that because a whole bunch of my johns bite me all the time, and if it wasn't for antibiotics, I'd be dead probably."

He resumed his pace.

"Hey, Decker, c'mon."

He kept walking.

"I'll look for this girl . . . What's her name?"

"Lindsey Bates."

"Yeah, Lindsey Bates. I got sources, you know."

He was outside of the building. Jesus, even Hollywood air felt good.

"Hey, Decker, you got a spare dime or something?"

He turned the corner and started sprinting up the quiet street, embarrassed by the hooker on his tail. Then he stopped abruptly and pulled out his wallet.

"Come here," he said, crushing a five in his fist. She held out her hand and he dropped the ball of money in her open palm. "Now don't ask me for another thing or your tail's in Juvey Hall."

"On what?"

"Soliciting."

"Bullshit. I just said—"

"Kiki, I'm a cop. You're a hooker. No one's going to listen to you. If I say you were soliciting, you're going to be busted for soliciting. Then it's Juvey Hall or foster homes or back to your old man, who's probably been raping you since you were ten."

The girl's face grew glum.

"You must have worked a lot of Juvey."

He was silent. He knew it all too well.

"I'm real sorry about your arm, Decker."

"I'm sorry about your face. Keep yourself out of trouble, huh?"

"I'm gonna find her, Decker. You'll see. I got contacts."

He slipped into the Plymouth, found a nearby pay phone, and reported the dead girl he'd found in the building to Hollywood Division.

# ·8

He awoke the next morning with an elephantine arm and cursed his stupidity at not going to an ER last night. He'd been too damn tired and now he was paying the price. Fever burned in his brain and his radial nerve shot spasmodic pain into his arm. Rousing slowly from a fitful sleep, he got up and went to the bathroom to change the dressing.

The arm was swollen a dark purple and gouged by deep red, crusty lacerations. He found some alcohol in the medicine cabinet and began to swab the wound, his flesh sizzling at each application of the astringent. The skin turned bright red and cracked open, oozing blood and pus. He washed his arm several times and took out a packet of sterile gauze, a couple of extra-strength aspirins and four leftover penicillin pills. He downed the tablets and wrapped the wound.

Once the bite had been dressed, he phoned the station and told them he'd be in later. A call to Mrs. Bates was next. Erin would be home at four, but the father wouldn't arrive until seven—after the start of Shabbos. Decker told Mrs. Bates he'd see Erin and reschedule her husband for sometime next week. The third call he made was to Chris Truscott. No one answered, so he figured he'd take a drive out to Venice and check out the boyfriend's place personally.

He slipped on a shirt gingerly, wincing at each movement of his arm. It even hurt to breathe. *Goddam it,* he told himself. *What the hell is wrong with you? So she looked like Cindy and it startled you. You've been a cop for almost twenty years. How could you let her get to you like that?*

It was time for *shacharis*. He put on a *kipah* and took out his tefillin. Kissing the two small prayer boxes, he fitted one atop his head, the seat of man's intelligence, and the other on his left bicep, the symbol of his strength. He wound the leather strap down his arm, across his hand and around his middle finger. He looked at both arms. One was encased in black as a symbol of religious devotion, the other in white thanks to a whore.

Opening the siddur, he began the morning prayers, mumbling them in English by rote, his mind darting between the holy words he was uttering and the hellish images of last night. Thirty minutes later he closed the siddur, took off the phylacteries, and slipped on his shoulder harness. It was tight, the gun weighing heavily on his sore flesh.

The phone pierced his eardrums. But the voice on the other end was balm.

"Good morning, Peter."

"Hi, Honey," he answered.

"How was Hollywood?"

"Don't ask."

"Peter, you sound bad."

"I'm just tired."

"But you're okay?"

"I'm okay."

"I had a call from Sarah Libba this morning. She invited the boys and me over for Shabbos lunch. She said you're coming."

"Yeah."

"That'll be nice, Peter."

"Yeah."

"Did you send her anything?"

Shit.

"Not yet."

"How about for Rebbitzen Schulman?"

"No."

"Do you want me to get them something for you?"

"I'll call a florist if you're too busy."

"Don't be silly. It's no bother."

"Thanks."

"Peter, are you sure you're all right?"

"Yeah. I'm really looking forward to Shabbos."

"So am I."

"I love you, Rina. Thanks again for the watch. No one has ever given me anything that beautiful."

"It's well deserved. I'll let you go now."

"See you tonight in shul."

"Bye, Peter."

She hung up. For a moment, he felt a strong urge to call her back, but resisted it and walked out the door.


Chris Truscott lived in Venice Beach. Two blocks to the south was the Oakwood ghetto, two blocks the other way was upscale Santa Monica. Truscott's apartment house was orphan property waiting to be adopted by either prospective parent, depending on economic conditions.

The building was three connected bungalows shaded by tall overgrown eucalyptus rooted in crabgrass. Judging from the fresh white stucco, the units had been recently painted, but gang graffiti already marred the walls. Vines of bougainvillea coursed through the obscene messages and exploded into a hot pink cloud when they hit the roof gutters. The air was moist and cool and tinged with brine from the ocean.

Decker entered the unlocked gate, checked for clogs, then scanned the addresses on the units. Truscott's was the rear one. He knocked on the door, but no one answered. Going around to the side of the building, he peeked inside the window. The curtain was partially drawn, allowing him a fair view.

The place was furnished but the walls and tables were bare. He was wondering how strong the locks were when a voice interrupted his thoughts.

"Who the hell are you?"

He turned around.

She was a young Latina—pretty but toughened—dressed in a housecoat and mules, with an infant in her arms.

"Police officer." He took out his badge and showed his ID.

"If you're looking for Chris, he's gone."

"When do you think he'll be back?"

"I mean gone for good. Took off a couple of days ago. I shoulda known something was up when he sold his bike. Man, he loved that thing, working on it all the time. Claimed he needed a quick buck. He paid me his last month's rent, so his taking off is no skin off my nose. I'm the manager of this place."

"Did he leave a forwarding address?"

"Not with me. Wait a sec. Hold the baby."

She handed him the infant—a boy around six months, black-eyed and toothless. Decker smiled at him and the baby proceeded to drool on his jacket. Ordinarily, he wouldn't have minded the extra weight, but his bad arm was killing him. Luckily, she returned a few minutes later and reclaimed her charge. Pulling out a ring of keys, she unlocked the door.

"Have a look."

Decker stepped inside. The place was devoid of any personal effects.

"See," she said, pulling back the curtain on the closet. "His clothes are gone."

"Do you still have his rent check?"

"Cashed it."

Damn.

"Any idea where he went?"

"Nope." She ran her finger over the dusty kitchen countertop. "I've gotta clean up this sty. I can get four fifty a month for this place cause it's so close to the beach."

Decker nodded.

"Mind if I take a look around?" he asked.

"Nope. Mind if I stick around?"

He shrugged.

"Fine with me."

He opened empty drawers, searched through bare cabinets and shelves, sorted through junk mail.

"Which post office do you use?" he asked.

"The main one on Venice Boulevard."

He picked up the phone and was surprised to find a dial tone.

"The line's still connected."

"Man's coming out tomorrow to pick up the phone."

"Mind if I use it? I want to buzz the post office and find out if he left a forwarding address there."

"Be my guest."

He called. As far as the post office was concerned, Truscott hadn't moved. He also called the DMV and ran a check through registration; no change of address listed.

"No luck, huh?" she said, after he hung up.

"No. Any idea why he split?"

"You want my personal opinion?" She leaned in close. "I think it was his girlfriend. She's *dead*."

Decker raised his brows.

"What else did you hear?"

She frowned. "Ain't that enough?"

"You ever meet his girlfriend, Ms. . . ."

The woman narrowed her eyes. "Let me see your badge again."

He pulled it out and gave her his business card also.

"Sergeant, huh?" She handed him back his shield. "My name is Alma Sanchez, and yes, I met her once. She seemed like a nice kid. Very pretty—in an Anglo way."

"He bring her here a lot?"

"I'm no snoop, but I've seen her here maybe a half dozen times."

"He have lots of friends?"

"Chris? You've got to be kidding. He was a real loner. Always hid behind the camera, if you know what I mean. He took some good shots of his girl though. Even the nudes weren't sleazy."

Nudes.

"He was going to make her a *Playboy* centerfold, he once told me. You know like that movie with Dorothy Hemingway, where the boyfriend kills the girl in the end . . ." Her eyes got animated. "You think she was ripped off, don't you?"

Decker closed the last of the empty drawers.

"What day is trash pick-up?"

"Tomorrow. Why?"

"And when did Truscott split?"

She eyed him. "You're kidding."

"They haul away the garbage yet, Ms. Sanchez?"

"You're in luck, Sergeant."

Real luck! The three units shared a common dumpster. Plenty of trash and it smelled ripe. But at least the searing pain in his arm was beginning to abate. He hoisted himself upward, vaulted in, then thought of something.

"Ms. Sanchez," he called out.

"Yes, Sergeant."

"Could you do me a favor?" He pulled out his pocket-sized siddur. "Could you hold this for me?"

She took the book.

"What is it?" she asked.

"It's a Jewish prayer book. I don't want to get it dirty."

She skimmed through the pages.

"May God be with you," she laughed. "I'll wait in the house. The kid needs his diaper changed."

It paid off. A half hour's worth of searching produced a bank deposit slip, several credit card receipts, and a newspaper classified page with seven "Apartments for Rent" ads circled in red. The manager saw him come out and greeted him with a glass of lemonade.

"Whew," she said. "You stink."

He let the remark pass and thanked her for the drink.

"You wanna take a shower or something?"

"No, thank you," he declined. "Can I have my book back?"

"Don't you think you should wash your hands first?"

She was right. He looked around and spotted a garden hose.

"I have a sink in the house," she said.

"This is fine." He flapped his wet hands in the air and when they were slightly damp finished drying them on his pants.

"Find anything?" she asked.

"Little of this, little of that. If you hear from Truscott, please give me a call."

"I will." She gave him the siddur. "You really pray outta that thing?" she asked.

"Yeah."

"Bet you feel like you need it in your occupation." She thought a moment. "Nothing meant by that. Everyone can use a little extra help from time to time, right?"

Once home, he showered quickly and changed his dressing. Although his arm was still swollen and painful, it had loosened a bit. He flexed his shoulder, winced, and dressed again. He wouldn't have time for the Bateses, the phone calls, and the doctor, so the doctor would just have to wait.

He went into the kitchen and gulped down the quart of milk standing alone in the refrigerator. Finding a box of crackers in the cupboard, he grabbed a handful and stuffed them in his mouth. Still chewing, he headed out the door and to the station.

Truscott's checking account was at Security Pacific. He called up the bank only to get a busy signal, so he tried Visa and Master-Card. Not only hadn't Truscott reported a change of address, but he was delinquent in his payments by a substantial amount of money. They had no idea where he was, and could Decker please give them a call if he located Mr. Truscott?

*Fuck you,* he thought. *Do your own detective work.*

Calling back the bank, he found out that Truscott had closed his account two weeks before and left no forwarding address. Alma Sanchez was going to be pissed.

He placed the slips in the Bates file and opened the classified ads to the "Apartments for Rent." Of the seven numbers circled, two had never heard of Truscott, but three remembered him. Although they hadn't rented to him, Decker knew he was on the right track.

*Did he give you a number where he could be reached?*

*Yes, but I threw it away.*

*Was Truscott alone?*

*Yes.*

*Has the trash been collected?*

*Yes.*

*Thank you very much.*

No one answered the two remaining numbers. It was nearly four. Time for sister Erin.

She wasn't what Decker had expected, looking older than fourteen but not because of cosmetics. On the contrary. She was deliberately understated. Her long blonde hair hung poker straight and was parted in the middle. She wore jeans, a sweatshirt, and a necklace of wooden beads. Barefoot, she sat cross-legged on her bed and twirled her hair absently. Tiny wet circles had formed under her armpits, staining her sweatshirt, and she was breathing rapidly.

Marge stood in a far corner and tried to appear preoccupied. Decker pulled up a desk chair to sit opposite her. Turning the chair around, he straddled the seat, leaning his elbows against the back. He glanced around the room.

The two sisters were opposites. Whereas Lindsey's room was a monument to conformity, Erin's room resonated with iconoclasm. Antinuclear posters were plastered to the walls, along with quotations from Thomas Jefferson, Aristotle, Thomas Mann, and Nietzsche. An erotic Aubrey Beardsley pen-and-ink was thumbtacked to her closet door. Her bookshelves were crammed with paperbacks on philosophy, art, and social sciences. A Bach organ fugue thundered from a compact disc player.

"Mind if we turn the music down?" Marge yelled out.

"Go ahead," Erin answered.

"I don't want to touch the equipment," Marge said.

Erin bounced up and turned off the system. The room fell

quiet. She plopped back onto her bed and took out a pack of cigarettes.

"Mind if I smoke?" she asked.

"If it's okay with your mom, it doesn't bother me," Decker said.

Erin plucked out a Benson and Hedges from her packet.

"I really shouldn't," she said, lighting up. "It's a filthy habit." She inhaled deeply. "Oat cell carcinoma here we come. But all of us have our vices, I suppose. It's better than boozing, or heavy doping . . . What the hell, let's be honest, huh? It's a type of dope, right?"

She tried to smile, but wasn't successful.

"Are you a little nervous, Erin?" Decker asked.

She shrugged.

"I'm ready if you are," she said.

"We're kind of starting from scratch, Erin," Decker said. "The Glendale police interviewed your mom and dad before, so I sort of knew a little bit about them. But I don't know anything about you."

"There's not much to know," she answered.

"Well for starters, you've got pretty sophisticated taste in books."

"I try," she said, embarrassed but pleased by the compliment.

"You're interested in philosophy?"

"Only as a sideline. I'm veering more toward economics." She giggled. "A little more money in it, no pun intended."

"Makes sense," Decker said, straight faced. "Ditto."

Erin smiled, then dipped her head coquettishly. The mannerism softened her face. She glanced at Marge, then back at Decker, and became serious once again.

"Lindsey and I didn't have a lot in common," she volunteered.

Decker nodded.

"We like talked different languages. I mean we both talked English, but often it was hard to discern a path of communication between the two of us. I mean I loved my sister, but our interests were diametrically opposite . . . Am I coherent?"

"Yes," Decker answered.

She looked at Marge again, then whispered to Decker.

"She was my mother's daughter. I mean, understand my mother and you'll understand Lindsey. Except . . ."

Her eyes went to Marge, then back to Decker.

"Except . . ." she said, "my mother is a bitch and Lindsey was Earth Mama. I mean, my sister was nice to everyone, even some *reeeel* turkeys—the kind that deserve to be stuffed on Thanksgiving."

"She seemed to have been very well liked."

"She was wonderful to me," Erin said, her eyes watering. "And I'm no day at the beach. She was very proud of my head, you know. She wasn't bright, but she was never, never jealous of my achievements. And another thing, I mean most older sisters would be embarrassed to ask their kid sisters to help them. Not Lindsey!"

"No?"

"Not at all!" Erin said. "I mean, I'd die if I had to ask someone *younger* than myself for help. I mean, it really kills me to ask Josh Berenson to help me with my algebra, but at least he asks me for help with his compositions so it all like balances out."

"I can see that."

"But Lindsey didn't care a fig. Just walked right up to me and said, 'Erin, I've got a little problem with the book report.'" She sighed. "Lindsey and I, we liked each other but didn't talk too much. Mostly when we did, it was she trying to set me up. I wasn't interested in the guys she'd get for me, you know. I like older men. I need someone mature."

She leaned forward.

"I've had men in their forties come on to me."

Her eyes swung from Marge to Decker, settling somewhere below Decker's belt.

"I can handle that, too," she whispered.

*Thank God for Margie.*

"Did Lindsey like older men?" Decker asked.

"Hell, no. Her boyfriend was a nothing. A nice guy but a nothing. I realize that's a value judgment."

"Did you ever meet her boyfriend?"

"Sure. She used to bring Chris around when my mom wasn't home. Mom didn't like him."

"You know why?"

"Because he was a nothing. But my definition of a nothing is different from hers. A nothing to me means empty in the skulleruno. Mom's nothing is synonymous with no money."

"Do you think it's possible that Lindsey and Chris took off together?"

"It's possible." Her voice had dropped an octave and she winked at him. "*Anything's* possible." She glanced at Marge. "Does *she* have to be here?"

"Yes."

"Why?"

"Departmental rules," he lied.

She frowned.

"So you think that Chris and your sister ran away together?" Decker asked.

"I didn't say that. I just said I thought it was possible."

"Ever see Chris get violent?"

"No."

"Did Lindsey ever tell you that Chris was violent or mean or had a bad temper?"

"No. Nothing like that. The two of them were madly in love— Hero and Leander, or something out of Bullfinch's *Mythology*. He wouldn't have hurt her."

She sounded sincere.

"Did Lindsey ever mention Chris taking nude photographs of her?"

"Yep. I've seen them. Man, she had it all." She lowered her head. "I was real jealous of her looks and her body. God just wasn't fair when He doled out the physical attributes. I used to say mean things to her to get even. It hurt her. She never said anything, but I know it hurt her."

"All sisters find something to fight about, Erin. That's normal."

She shrugged. "Yeah, I suppose you're right. Hell, I spent plenty of nights doctoring up her essays."

"I'm sure you did," Decker said. "Erin, do you think Lindsey would ever do more than just pose in the nude?"

"Like do porno?"

"Yeah, like do porno."

She shook her head. "No. I don't think she'd do it."

"Do you think Chris could have talked her into it?"

"No. He wouldn't do something like that. Nudes are one thing. Being fucked like a baboon in heat is quite another."

She gave him a suggestive smile. Decker ignored it.

"Did you know that Lindsey kept a diary?" he asked.

The girl didn't respond.

"Erin?"

"What?"

"Did you know that Lindsey kept a diary?"

"Oh?"

"Do you have it, Erin?"

Again, she didn't answer.

"Why don't you level with me?" Decker said gently.

"Yeah, I have it," she said. "I took it when it was clear Lindsey wasn't coming back. I didn't want my mother to find it. Are you gonna tell her?"

"I'm afraid I'll have to," Decker said.

The girl angrily squashed her cigarette into an ashtray and clenched her jaw.

"Oh shit! Grounded for weeks. I mean, Mom asked me if I knew where it was and I out and out lied to her. But my motivation was altruistic, you know."

"How so?"

"I knew what was in there—her and Chris. I mean, she read passages to me, the lovemaking passages. It was pretty graphic. I didn't want my mom to be mad at Lindsey, you know? 'Cause she was really a nice sister. And I kept on thinking that Lindsey would come back home, so why have Mom on her case as well as my own? Also, I didn't want Lindsey to think I was a snitch and a

snoop and be disappointed in me. Shit, I can't believe she's really
. . . gone. I keep thinking she's away at summer camp and'll be
home any day now."

She sniffed back tears.

"But she won't, will she?"

Decker shook his head.

She threw the pack of cigarettes across the room.

"Friggin' awful," she whispered.

"I'm sorry."

"What are you going to do with the diary?" she asked.

"We hope it'll help us out in our investigation."

"It won't. I know what's in there. Just a lot of very personal
stuff."

"Sometimes something very minor turns out to be very important."

The girl went over to one of her books, pulled out a false spine
and extracted a pink-vinyl-covered pocketbook trimmed in gold.

"Here," she said, giving it to Decker. "She wrote a couple of
nasty things about Mom and Dad and me. But she wasn't really
like that at all. They were written in anger and I've forgiven her. I
mean really, I know I'm not beautiful, but I'm no bag-lady either."
She looked to Decker for confirmation.

"You're a very pretty teenager, Erin," he said calmly.

She blushed. "No, really . . . What do you really think?"

"I think you're a very pretty teenager," he repeated.

"Mom's always bugging me to do more with myself. Like
Lindsey. I mean Lindsey was just much more into the superficials
than I am." The girl grew pensive. "She was also flesh and blood,
not just private thoughts scrawled on a piece of paper. Remember
that when you read this, Sergeant," she said, tapping her finger on
the diary.

"I will, Erin."

"I'm gonna miss her," Erin said to herself. At last the tears came
pouring out. "Oh God, I miss her so much already."

\*   \*   \*

A toss of the coin put Decker in the driver's seat as Marge delved into the diary. After ten minutes of reading, she chuckled out loud.

"The kid had a sense of humor," she said. "Listen to this. It's dated about a year ago. 'We made love again last night.' She's referring to Chris. 'I did something I've never done before. I opened my eyes and looked at him while he was doing it. He looked like he was going to sneeze but it never came out so I guess that's just how he looks when he's into it. I like to make love, I like the closeness to Chris, but I kept wanting to offer him a tissue when I watched him. From now on, I think I'll keep my eyes closed.'"

Decker smiled, but it was edged with sadness. Marge caught the melancholy in his eyes.

"This is very ghoulish," she said, flipping the page.

"At least we're on the side of truth and justice."

"You forgot the American way."

The Plymouth hooked onto the 210 freeway, the major thoroughfare that linked the Foothill pocket communities with intercity urban sprawl. Dusk coated the mountains, obscuring their hard edges. Marge took out a penlight to augment the dwindling light.

"Did she write about boys other than Chris?" Decker asked.

"Nope. At least not so far." She read a few more pages to herself. "Lindsey was wild about Chris. Gushing. True love."

"Get a feel for him?"

"He liked sex."

"That's the majority of the diary?"

"Oh no, not at all. Most of it is very mundane—one sentence entries. She didn't even write every day. Here—the whole weekend is summed up as 'I bought a pink blouse.' Two days later she writes, 'I got a new pair of sandals.' The next weekend it's, 'I gotta get to a beach. My tan's fading. I look like Ghostwoman.'"

Marge went back to reading. The police radio spat out calls that concerned neither of them. Decker lit a cigarette to break the monotony of the ride.

"Listen to this," Marge said. "Dated around six months ago. 'Erin came home dressed in her bag-lady getup.'"

"Aha."

"'Honestly, she's just hopeless! And she could do so much more with herself if she'd just try. God, I'm sounding like mom. How gross!'"

Decker laughed. "Insight at fifteen."

"Hey, some never achieve it in a lifetime."

"That's true. Did she write about posing for Chris in the nude?"

"Yeah. Let me find the entries . . . Ah, here's one. 'Chris took more nude pictures of me. Like always, we made love afterwards, this time doggie style. Man, he's big. I like it the best when I'm on top.'" Marge smiled. "Adventurous little thing, wasn't she."

"Can't hold back raging hormones."

She looked at him. "Is it hard being the father of a teenaged daughter?"

"It has its moments." He definitely didn't like the tenor of this conversation. "Is there anything to suggest that Chris coerced her into posing nude?"

"Not that I can tell."

Decker checked his watch and floored the accelerator. Even at high speeds, he wasn't going to make it in time for the start of the Sabbath. He wondered if Rabbi Schulman would say anything. Probably not.

"She was sensitive, Pete," Marge said. "She got her feelings hurt a lot."

"Such as?"

She skimmed a few of the back pages. "Like Heather didn't notice her new dress . . . Chris didn't call when he said he would . . . Erin was her usual sharp-tongued witch. I can sure believe that. Here's another—Brian embarrassed her in front of her English teacher."

"Brian's a jerk."

"Yeah, she knew that too. Wait a minute, let me find . . ." She turned to the back pages. "Here it is. She writes, 'Brian got drunk and threw up in his dad's car again. I know he's a loser, but I feel sorry for him. His dad is completely disgusting, always trying to put the make on girls Bri brings home. It's no wonder he scams all the time.'"

"Did she mention the dad coming onto her?"

"Not specifically."

Marge read further.

"She has her share of catty digs in here. It really pissed her off when someone looked better than her. She was vain."

"Never met a teenager who wasn't self-absorbed in some way," Decker said.

Ten minutes later Decker shot the amber light at the end of the freeway off-ramp and sped toward the station house.

"In a hurry?" Marge asked.

"A little."

She closed the diary and handed it to him.

"You take a look at it and tell me what you think," she said. "I don't find anything unusual in here. Nothing that spells an unhappy kid about to run away. And nothing to suggest that Truscott was weird. She was gaga over him—wrote about following him to the end of the universe."

Decker felt a burst of anger. Perhaps it was the lateness of the hour, or his growling stomach, or his arm beginning to awaken from its analgesic dormancy. Whatever the reason was, the case suddenly infuriated him. The waste of a young girl's life.

Through clenched teeth he said, "It's a damn shame that she fell so short of her destination."

# ·9

On his plate were thin slices of rare roast beef with horseradish sauce, three steaming hot potato pancakes smothered in applesauce, a scoop of red and white cabbage salad, and a chunk of challah. On the side was a plateful of cholent—a stew chock full of beans and beef and topped with stuffed derma. A crystal goblet full of ice water stood next to a matching wine glass brimming over with semidry rosé.

But his stomach churned.

Part of it was fever. He should have made time for the doctor yesterday. He was out of penicillin and infection was worming its way back into his system. But mostly it was Rina. She was sitting across from him and he had never seen such physical perfection. She always looked lovely on Shabbos, but not like this. He was in awe. Her hair was tied in a formal knot, outlining her magnificent bone structure. Two feathers of gold dangled from her earlobes and brushed against her creamy cheeks whenever she turned her head. Her cerulean eyes seemed deeper, more mysterious, her lips full and red. She was dressed modestly—long sleeves and a mid-calf hemline, but the rounded neck of her chemise revealed the graceful arch of her throat and the fine architecture underneath. He didn't dare let his eyes meet hers because if he did, the others at the table would know what he was thinking.

He picked up his knife and cut the meat into bite-sized pieces, knowing it would be rude to leave so much food on his plate. Taking a forkful, he began to chew with effort.

Rabbi Marcus was giving a *Dvar Torah*. This time it was a discourse on the weekly biblical portion. He wore a black suit, a white shirt, black tie, and black Borsalino. From under his shirt hung *tzitzis*—fringes. The other married men at the table were dressed identically; all had full beards.

Smoothing his mustache, Decker rubbed his naked chin self-consciously. His lack of total facial hair wasn't the only thing that set him apart from the others. His coloring was a sanguine splash amid a sea of brunettes and his navy suit looked more executive than rabbinical. Even his *kipah,* smaller and knitted, wasn't like the large black velvet ones covering the heads of the three unmarried yeshiva students.

The women's dress was more varied than that of the men, and although they wore no makeup, they sparkled with jewelry.

Marcus began to speak animatedly, his stern eyes ablaze with passion, as he brought home his point. Decker tried to listen intently, but the mixture of English and Hebrew confused him and his right arm ached. The pain increased when he noticed the cold stare of Marcus's wife, Chana, drilling into him. She was the biggest busybody he'd ever known, and he disliked her intensely. Her stony eyes marched back and forth between him and Rina—a self-appointed watchdog making sure nothing unholy transpired.

He'd made it through half his roast beef. The meat was delicious, but it sat like a stone in his belly. He sneaked a furtive glance at Rina, who met his eyes questioningly. He knew what she was thinking. *Are you okay, Peter?*

After Marcus ended his sermon, Decker returned his full attention to the food. Slowly, he cut another piece of beef, and then realized he couldn't use a knife anymore. His arm had cramped. He speared the morsel with his left hand and felt a rivulet of sweat run down his forehead. Dabbing it quickly, he pushed his plate aside. Chana noticed, but no one else did, because the children had entered the dining room from the kitchen where they'd eaten at a separate table.

Rina's boys took seats on either side of him and the table broke into *zemiros*—Sabbath songs. Sarah Libba Adler rose and began to clear dishes, and Rina, Chana, and the older girls got up to help her. Decker could feel Rina standing directly behind him, see her hand reach for his plate.

"You're not hungry?" she said softly.

He turned to look up at her and shook his head.

She piled the silverware on top of his dish and removed the plate.

"He's not used to Jewish cooking," Chana said acerbically to Rina once they were inside the kitchen.

Rina shrugged.

Chana's icy eyes narrowed. She picked up a three-tiered pastry dish and took it into the dining room.

"He's not feeling well?" Sarah Libba whispered.

"I guess he's just tired," Rina answered. "The meal was superb, as usual."

Sarah Libba looked at Decker's half-emptied plate as if it refuted Rina's compliment, but said nothing.

"Go sit down, Rina," she urged. "Chana, the girls, and I can handle it."

"Don't be silly. I know how much work it takes to prepare something like this. I want to help."

Holding a candy-dish in one hand and a nut-bowl in the other, Rina went back into the dining room and began to clear the glasses. He looks pale, she thought. But a smile spread across her lips as she noticed her boys singing loudly, curled against him. It had been ages since she'd seen them so happy.

After twenty minutes of dessert, cleanup, and singing, everyone was called back to the table for *birkas hamazon*—grace after meals. Zvi led the *bentching,* and at its conclusion, the men adjourned to the living room for Talmud and schnapps.

Decker lagged behind and caught her alone.

"When the men leave for *shiur,* make an excuse and meet me at your house," he whispered.

She nodded imperceptibly.

The children went off for the Shabbos games and activities and the women talked in the dining room while the men sat in the living room. Rina had never minded the segregation, but today it irked her. She had little patience for endless discussions of Kashruth. She didn't care which products had recently been endorsed by Agudath Israel, signifying them strictly kosher. It bored her, it peeved her, mainly it separated her from Peter.

The hour dragged on.

Finally the men announced they were leaving for the Rosh Yeshiva's afternoon lecture.

Rina looked around the room, wondering how long she should wait in order to make her leaving it appear unobtrusive. Chana was gossiping passionately. The woman knew about everyone and everything—a malevolent omnipresence. Finally Sarah suggested they go to *chumash* class.

Halfway to the study hall, Rina excused herself, claiming she had to check whether she'd locked her front door. It was feeble, she knew. She should have come up with something better and the skeptical look on Chana's face confirmed it. But it was too late now. Let the woman's tongue wag; this wasn't the first time Chana had used it against her and it wouldn't be the last.

She found him waiting by the side of her house. He looked terrible. She unhitched the deadbolt and let him inside.

"What's wrong?" she asked.

"I need sterile gauze, a bottle of aspirin, any leftover antibiotics you might have, and a sterile, *sharp* knife." He struggled with his coat, but gave up. "Help me with this, Rina."

She took off his jacket.

"Where are you hurt, Peter?"

"My right arm."

She rolled up his sleeve, unwrapped the sopping wet dressing, then brought her hand to her mouth and gasped.

The flesh had turned brown except for a protruberance of mottled green pus.

"I'm fine, just get me a knife," Decker said.

"Peter, you must go to an emergency room."

"Just get me a knife."

"Forget about Shabbos, Peter. This is life threatening. I'll even drive you if you can't drive yourself."

"I'm not going," he said loudly. "Just get me a knife."

"By not going you're committing an *avayrah*. Halachically, you have to go."

"Rina, I don't give a damn about halacha right now. I just need some relief."

"Wait here," she said. A few minutes later she reentered with a knife and a bowl full of steaming towels. "Come to the table, Peter. I'll take care of it."

"Rina, just give me the knife and get out of here."

"You can't excise the wound yet. It hasn't formed enough of a head."

He looked at her.

"Since when do you know about lancing pus pockets?"

"Come to the table," she repeated firmly.

He followed her and slumped down in the armchair, grateful for the help.

"Stick out your arm."

"What are you going to do?"

"I'm going to apply heat to bring up the head." She dipped a towel into the steaming water, then wrung out the excess. "It's going to hurt."

"Can't hurt any worse than it hurts now."

But it did. It seared his flesh.

"How'd it happen?" she asked wrapping the arm.

"I was repairing the floorboard in the barn and an old plank of jagged wood cut into my arm."

"I saw bitemarks," she said.

He paused.

"Okay, I was bitten by a dog."

"What happened, Peter?"

"I was chomped on by a whore in the line of duty. Are you happy now?"

Her eyes met his, but she said nothing. She unwrapped the first cloth, palpated the swelling, and wrapped it again in a newly heated towel.

"Where did you learn to do this?" he asked.

Rina noticed his face was drenched with sweat and mopped it with a dry towel. "Yitzchak and I moved to Israel a year after we married. To Kiryat Arba—a settlement in Hebron." She stroked his hand. "We were in hostile territory and there were no Jewish doctors handy. You learn to do things."

"You never told me you lived in Israel."

"For three years. It was a phase of my life that I've tried to forget. Except for the year of Yitzchak's death, I don't think I was ever more miserable. I was stuck behind barbed wire fencing with two small infants of my own, and in charge of the group's nursery which—*baruch Hashem*—had forty-four kids." She paused a moment. "All the men carried guns with them. It was open warfare out there."

"Including Yitzchak?"

"Yes." She took off the old towel, wrung out another, and wrapped the wound a third time.

"But you didn't?"

"The women never left the compound. We were guarded twenty-four hours a day. What would have been the purpose of learning how to shoot? Though now I wish I had."

"Why'd you live there?" he asked.

"Idealism." She shook her head. "When Yitzchak announced that we were going back to the States, I cried tears of joy, then immediately felt guilty about it. I was leaving the Holy Land and ecstatic about it."

She laughed softly.

"Then I read in the Talmud that a Jew who passes up a permissible pleasure is a fool. I was very foolish in those years."

"Why didn't you put your foot down and tell him you wanted to leave?"

"I didn't make myself clear," she said, taking off the towel. "He would have left a long time ago. I was the one who insisted we stay—always the martyr, Peter. I thought we should be religious *chalutzniks*—pioneers. Finally, he put *his* foot down. He said he couldn't live in that kind of atmosphere. When Rav Schulman invited him to join the *kollel*, he quickly accepted without consulting me. I couldn't even get mad at him. The poor guy was so miserable, and I was so oblivious to his needs because I believed in some higher purpose.

"But it all worked out in the end. Yitzchak had wanted to live and study in Jerusalem—a more beautiful and inspiring city never existed. Had we settled there, I would have never left Israel. And then I would have never met you."

She touched his skin; it was burning and taut. She told him to hold still.

His body was soaked with perspiration. Squeezing his eyes shut, he bit his lip hard, tasting the blood as it trickled into his mouth. He could feel the knife blade slicing into the swelling. A stab of pain, then skin bursting open, exploding pus that soured the room with its fetid stench.

"Good," he heard her say.

He felt faint, but male pride kept him conscious.

She began to bathe the arm in antiseptic. The pain was overwhelming and caused him to shiver. Tenderly, she dabbed his face while cleansing the open sore. Finally, she patted the wound dry.

"It looks clean, Peter. Keep the towel firmly pressed on the cut while I take a look in the medicine cabinet."

She came back with two half-empty bottles of pills and a roll of gauze.

"These are penicillin tablets from when I had strep. Take two every six hours. Take a couple of aspirin, also. They'll make you feel better and reduce the swelling and fever."

She unfurled the gauze and began to wrap the wound.

"I love you," Decker said.

"I love you, too, Peter. Promise me you'll go to a doctor after Shabbos is over."

"No argument."

"Do you want to rest here?"

"No. It would look bad."

"I don't care—"

"I do. Finish wrapping this and go on to your class. They're probably wondering what happened to you."

She nodded and worked quickly. When she was done, she helped him on with his coat.

"You go first," she said. "I want to clean up."

He looked at the pus and blood splashed over the starched white Shabbos linens on her table and frowned. The odor of decay was still powerful.

"Don't worry about it," she said calmly. "I really wish you'd go to the hospital."

"I'm all right." He hugged her as tight as he could. "I feel better already. Thanks."

"Peter, how did it happen?"

"I don't want to get into it, honey."

"Okay," she said. "I won't meddle."

"You're not meddling. I didn't mean it to sound like that. I just don't want to talk about it."

She kissed his cheek. "You'd better get going."

He kissed her back and left without another word, sucking in mouthfuls of air. Although his balance was unsteady, his pace was good. He had no intention of sitting through a lesson he didn't understand, so he entered the main yeshiva building and headed for a small classroom in the basement. It was his favorite learning spot, and he'd hidden all the English translations of the holy books there. Taking out his *chumash,* he began to learn, trying to concentrate on the text instead of his pain.

Soon he became absorbed in the material, looking up references, checking sources, attempting to translate and understand the Hebrew which still eluded him.

It seemed he'd only been at it for minutes when he found himself squinting. The daylight had turned to dusk and it wouldn't be long before the unlit room turned pitch black. He leaned back in his chair and inhaled deeply, enjoying the solitude, feeling very calm. His arm felt much better; Rina had done an excellent job. She never ceased to surprise him—so utterly feminine yet so competent. He saw firsthand how she handled crises, and her strength and willpower were scary. Maybe it was the religion; the women in the Bible were not known for their passivity—Judith lopping off the head of Holofernes, Yael driving a tent peg through the Sisera's temples. He could picture Rina doing that. After all, didn't she buy a gun?

He heard footsteps and saw Rabbi Schulman dressed in his formal Shabbos silks. Decker started to rise, but the old man motioned him to remain seated.

"How's your arm?" the old man asked.

"She told you?"

"You should have gone to a hospital. Shabbos should not be preserved at risk to human life." He sat down. "*Pekuah nefesh*— your life is more important. Halachically, you should have gone."

"Let me ask you this, Rabbi Schulman. If it had been you, what would you have done?"

The Rosh Yeshiva sighed.

"Halacha is halacha. If I were convinced it was life-threatening, I would have gone."

"You're hedging."

"What you did was unwise, Peter." The old man smiled dryly. "And on top of that, you missed my lecture."

"What language did you give it in this time?" Decker asked grinning.

"Hebrew and Yiddish. But you're a bright man. You would have picked up something."

Schulman raised his eyebrows.

"You looked tired at *shacharis* this morning. A blind person could see your exhaustion, now. Go to my house and rest."

"I want to go to *mincha*," Decker said.

The old man nodded.

"All right. Come with me. I won't waste an old man's breath to try to dissuade you."

The men rose and Decker tensed his bicep. The joint was still stiff, but there was some limited motion—progress.

*   *   *

It was Sammy's and Jacob's turn to hold the havdalah candle. They stood on top of chairs flanking Decker, at the side of the dais, and lifted the silver candle holder high in the air. The Rosh Yeshiva struck the match and held it to the wicks, and soon the multicolored strands of braided wax were aglow with bright orange flames. The light flickered over the boys' faces, and for a moment Decker flashed to the bonfires in Hotel Hell. The faces of the young squatters had been masks of death, but these boys were vibrant with life. Decker wrapped his fingers over their hands to protect them from the hot wax drippings and Sammy smiled at him. It warmed his heart.

Rav Schulman raised the silver goblet of wine and began, intoning a mellow singsong:

*"Baruch atah Adonai Elohenu, Melach Haolam borei pre hagofen."*

Blessed art Thou, Lord our God, King of the universe, who has created the fruit of the vine.

The congregation responded with a resonant "Amen."

The rabbi put down the wine cup and lifted a two-foot sculptured tower of silver. Its roof was peaked and topped by a gilt flag; gilt bells dangled from the edge of the eaves. Three of the tower's sides were embossed with Hebrew letters, the fourth held a miniature door. Inside were spices—cloves, frankincense, allspice, whole chunks of cinnamon. In a loud voice, the rabbi made the blessing over the aromatics, opened the door, and deeply inhaled their sweet/tart perfume. He passed the tower to Decker who held it to the boys' noses and his own, then returned it to the rabbi.

"Amen."

The rabbi put down the spicebox and blessed God, the creator of light, by holding his fingernails close to the flame of the candle. He then recited the rest of the *havdalah*, the prayer marking the conclusion of Sabbath. Soon the new secular work week would start and God's holy day of rest would officially be over.

Mellifluously, Schulman recited the last blessing and took a sip of wine. He poured the remaining wine into a silver dish, took the candle, and quenched the flame in it. The fire crackled and sparked until it was reduced to a stream of smoke.

"*Baruch atah Adonai hamavdil beyn kodesh lechol.*"

Blessed art Thou, Oh Lord, who hast made a distinction between sacred and profane.

# ·10

The first snapshot was a white anus being penetrated by a black penis. Decker tossed it aside, but Hollander picked it up for a second look. He was a bald man with a fringe of brown hair, a large walrus mustache, and an overhang of belly. He was smiling this morning. He liked this assignment.

"Do you think this is a boy ass or a girl ass?" he asked Decker, puffing on his meerschaum. "From this angle, I can't tell."

Decker snatched the photo out of his hands and gave him a sour look.

"Mike," he said, "we're supposed to be looking at faces, not asses." He held up several snapshots of Lindsey Bates. "*This* girl, Mike. We're looking for *this* girl."

The detective grunted unappreciatively and sucked in his gut.

"And put out the pipe," Decker snarled. "This room is cramped enough without you smogging it up."

Hollander killed the embers.

"What's eating *your* ass, Rabbi? Have a bad weekend at the Holyland?"

"I had too good a weekend," Decker complained. "I'm not ready to come back to this shit."

"Pete, there are at least a dozen guys out there just waiting for this assignment."

"And I'd be glad to give it to the drooling bastards, but the case is mine, Michael."

"All I'm sayin' is if this is gettin' to you, you've got lots of backup."

Decker picked up another photo. A blonde girl was fellating a fat man with a wart on his penis. Decker studied her face and then rejected it.

"Shit, Pete, get a load of the size of this—"

"I'm not interested."

A moment later, Marge walked in.

"You know, MacPherson offered to trade Easter weekend with me if I'd give him this assignment." She was incredulous. "Those boys are the horniest bunch of schmucks I've ever seen."

"You don't understand the male species, Marjorie," Hollander said.

"You'll explain it to me someday, Michael."

He grinned lecherously. "Just give me a date."

"Tell you what," she said. "We'll break in the twenty-first century together."

Hollander was silent and appeared to be concentrating.

"Thirteen years from now, Mike," Decker said.

Marge laughed. "Have a snapshot of Lindsey to refresh my memory?" she asked Decker.

He handed her one of their working pictures. It was Lindsey's junior high school graduation photo—a head shot of an even-featured teenager ripening to womanhood—a flirtatious smile, a gleam in the eye. There was nothing stiff and frozen about the picture. Lindsey had presence. Marge made a face.

"Pretty little thing, wasn't she," Hollander said. "Damn shame."

"She was Cindy's age," Decker said. "I asked around about her all day yesterday. Combed every mission, shelter, halfway house, and drug rehab center in the L.A.-San Fernando Valley area, and nobody had ever seen her. I even took the photo down to Skid Row and tried some of the street people. Nada. This is a last resort and it probably won't turn up anything. She was a nice kid according to everyone I've talked to. I don't think we'll find her in these archives."

"Hey, Margie," Hollander said. "Take a look at the—"

"Not interested, Michael."

Hollander grumbled and chewed on his cold pipe stem.

Marge began sorting through a pile of pornography.

"How many boxes of this garbage do we have?" she asked.

"As many as you want," Decker said, tossing photographs aside.

"You ever get hold of Mr. Bates?" Marge asked.

Decker winced and waved his hand in the air.

"That bad, huh?" Hollander said.

"One of those repressed types," said Decker "Midway through the questions, he cracked. It was *bad*. The floodgates opened and it was all downhill from that point on. God, I feel for that man. I don't think I'd do any better."

They sorted through some more photos—contorted positions designed for the camera rather than pleasure.

"Pete, what do you think of this?" Marge showed him a teenage girl masturbating.

Decker studied the photo and shook his head.

"The eyes are wrong."

Marge shrugged and attacked another pile of pictures.

"What do we do if we find her in one of these?" Hollander asked.

"They're numbered on the back, Mike," Decker answered. "If we find a match, we can look up where the photo came from and, hopefully, get a fix on who the photographer was."

"How was Saturday at the yeshiva, Pete?" Marge asked.

"Terrific."

"Your arm looks looser," she said.

"Doc says I'll be fine."

"Hey, Rabbi," Hollander said. "You never did tell us how the hell that happened."

"Would you believe I got bit by a dog? Of all the stupid things."

"Happens to the best of us," said Hollander. "I remember once getting stung by a bee. People always tell you if you don't bother it, it won't bother you. Well, I didn't do a thing and the little fucker looked me straight in the eye and stuck its stinger into my arm. Really pissed me off."

"Ernst got stung by a bee," Marge said. "Blew up like a blimp."

"How is he?" Decker asked, shuffling photos.

"Beats me. Haven't seen the sucker for two weeks."

Decker looked up. "You're kidding. I thought you two were tight."

"Appearances are deceiving," Marge said.

"What happened?" Decker asked.

"It was mutual. I think I was too much woman for him."

"I'll say," Hollander snickered. "You outweighed him by a hundred pounds. Take a look at this, Pete."

Another blonde girl, not more than fifteen, was performing cunnilingus on a gaping vagina. Decker studied the snapshot closely.

"I'd say no, but it's close. What do you think, Margie?"

She scrutinized the picture.

"Too close to call. My gut instinct is no, but I'd check it out."

"This photo reminds me of a joke," Hollander said. "What's the difference between pussy and parsley?"

"Not everyone eats parsley," Marge said. "That's old, Mike. Even older than you."

"Okay. How about this one?" said Hollander. "What's the difference between pussy and parsley?"

"What?" Decker asked.

"Parsley leaves a good aftertaste."

Decker smiled, but Marge frowned.

"You've been munching the wrong carpet, Mike," she said.

"You sound jealous, Margie," Hollander said, grinning. "Maybe it's your recent loss of male companionship. For a small fee, I can accommodate your needs sooner than the twenty-first century."

"Don't make me ill," she answered, looking ill.

"Give me the snapshot, Mike," Decker said. "We'll start a close-call pile over here." He turned to Marge. "You want me to spread the word around that you're available?"

"Thanks, but I just met someone."

"Jesus, you don't waste any time, do you girl," Mike said.

"When you're hot, you're hot," Decker said.

"Who's the lucky guy, Margie?" Hollander asked.

"Carroll."

Hollander looked at her. "A girl?"

"Watch your mouth, Mike. Two r's, two l's. He's six six and weighs a hard two ninety."

"Carroll's a great name," Hollander said quickly.

"What instrument does he play?" Decker asked.

"He's tone deaf," Marge said glumly.

"That's a departure," said Decker, discarding another photo.

"Yeah, well, I haven't done too well with the musicians in my life. I figured it was time for a change. The only trouble is now I don't have anyone to play my flute with."

"What a shame!" Hollander said, holding back a smile. Marge was a terrible musician, but that didn't stop her from performing in public, usually with her musician boyfriends. No one had the heart to tell her the truth.

"But it's good for me," she continued. "I'll work on some solo pieces and let you guys know when I'm ready."

Decker stifled a groan.

"Great, Marge," he said.

"How's Rina?" Marge asked.

"Fine."

"You two going to do something soon?" Mike asked. "You're obviously smitten by the lass. Or is it smote? You should know about that, Rabbi. Didn't the Jews smote the Egyptians or something like that?"

Decker shrugged. The digs were good-natured and he let them pass. After all, his transformation over the past months had to seem strange to his colleagues. No doubt they attributed his metamorphosis to Rina; he loved her and was changing to please her.

But Decker knew it was deeper than that. Religion had given him a spark of renewed faith, and though it hadn't blossomed into fire—maybe he was too cynical for it to ever get that bright—it was still better than complete darkness.

His thoughts were interrupted when a young detective with a pencil-line mustache stuck his head in the room.

"You've got a call, Pete."

"Okay, George."

The mustache turned upward into a grin.

"Want me to take over for a while, Rabbi?" George asked. "All those immoral photographs must be very unsettling to the spirit."

"That won't be necessary," answered Decker. He picked up a receiver on an empty desk. A shrill young voice broke through.

"Ya know, you guys have a lot of nerve. I musta called this number a hundred times over the weekend and nobody answered. What if I had something important to tell you? I don't think you give a shit who gets ripped off just as long as it don't happen on your precious weekend—"

"Who is this?" Decker yelled into the receiver.

"It's your *informant*, Decker."

"Got something you want to tell me, Kiki?"

"Not over the phone."

"I'm not meeting with you unless you tell me what this is about."

There was a pause.

"Well . . ." she teased.

Decker checked his watch. "I've got a shitload of work, Kiki, so either put up or shut up."

"I didn't find out anything about the girl, but I'm still trying."

"At least you're honest."

"Yeah, that and ten cents—excuse me—twenty cents won't get me a fucking phone call. I do have a name for you. A photographer who shoots porno. Lots of young ones and runaways."

Decker grabbed a scrap of paper.

"Go on."

"He runs a legit operation, also. You know—weddings, graduation, confirmations—"

"Name, Kiki."

"Cecil Pode. His place is in Culver City. Is that worth anything, Decker?"

"Could be."

"Man, I'm busted. Have a heart."

"What do you want?"

"A sawbuck would sure feel fine."

"Get me some names of pimps who specialize in runaways and we may be able to work something out."

"By what time?"

"Two."

"Okay," she said. "Meet me at the Teriyaki Dog on Sunset and Vermont. It's across the street from the kiddy hospital. I should be able to dig up some names by then. How's your arm, Decker?"

"Fine. I'll see you at two."

"Did you go to a doctor?" she persisted. "Like I told you, bites can be dangerous—"

"Kiki, I've got to go."

He hung up and went back to the photos.

"Any luck?" he asked.

"Nope," Marge answered. "What I'd like to know is why I can go through an entire box in the same time it takes Hollander to go through three pictures."

"I'm a careful observer with an eye for detail," Hollander retorted. "Get off my back, lady."

Decker started in on the next box.

"Jesus," Hollander exclaimed. "Have these young women no shame? She's got jism up her nose."

"A picture that grosses *you* out?" Marge said to Hollander. "This I've got to see."

She held the snapshot.

"Ugh! She's covered in cum."

Decker took a peek and his eyes widened. He grabbed the photo out of Dunn's hand.

"What is it, Pete?"

"Got any more pictures of this one, Mike?"

"Yeah," Hollander said. "Tons. She's a busy little beaver, 'scuse the pun."

"What is it?" Dunn repeated.

"Her teeth!" Decker exclaimed. "Look at her front teeth! They're *pegs!*"

"Here's some others," Hollander said.

Decker shuffled excitedly through the pile. None of the others showed her teeth, but he did find one that looked promising. She was performing fellatio, and it showed a complete side view of her face.

"I've got to make a couple of phone calls," Decker said. "Margie, contact Vice and reference these photos. Mike, keep looking for Lindsey Bates."

"Will do," Hollander said, grinning and saluting.

Decker rushed out of the room and nearly collided with George.

"Got another phone call, Pete."

Decker punched down the line.

"This is Mrs. Grover. I got a message on my machine to call a Detective Sergeant Decker at the Foothill police station?"

The woman sounded elderly.

"Thanks for calling back, Mrs. Grover," he said. "This is Sergeant Decker. I'm calling about that one bedroom you had advertised in the *Santa Monica Express.*"

"I'm sorry, Sergeant, It's been rented."

"Could you tell me the name of the person you rented it to?"

"Uh, am I allowed to do that?"

"Yes, ma'am, you are."

"I guess it's all right, then. After all, you are the police."

Decker waited.

"His name is Christopher Truscott."

Bingo!

"Is Mr. Truscott in right now?"

"I believe he is."

"Thank you, Mrs. Grover. I want to stop by and talk to him and I'd appreciate it if you didn't mention our little conversation."

"Is he in trouble, Sergeant? I don't want any troublemakers—"

"No, no. It's nothing like that. But I want to surprise him with my visit."

"Well . . . All right."

"I'll stop by and introduce myself, ma'am."

"That would be lovely."

"Good-bye."

Decker clapped his hands together, rubbed them vigorously, and let go with a broad smile. Leads! He was getting some leads! He called Annie Hennon.

"Hello, Pete. What's up?"

"Have you got a spare lunch hour?"

"Personal or business?"

"The latter."

"Either way, it's fine."

"Then I'll see you at noon, Annie."

"Hey, what say I send out for some Chinese food?"

He paused. "I keep kosher."

"Pizza?" she tried. "Plain cheese pizza?"

"Strictly kosher."

"I thought you weren't sure you were Jewish."

"I'm still not sure, but I'm working on it. I've got a sack lunch anyway."

"Fine," she said. "I'll pick up some cottage cheese. It's a good time to start my diet."

Her figure didn't need it, he thought.

"See you at noon," he said.

His next call let Freddy at the Police Photo Lab know he was sending up a few snapshots to enlarge. Marge came up to his desk.

"The photos of Pegteeth were clipped from a defunct rag called *Erotic Ecstasy*. These are at least a year old, and naturally, the editor has cut town. But this is a list of photographers the magazine hired."

Decker took the list and scanned the contents. Cecil Pode's name jumped out at him. He felt that surge of excitement, the hunting instinct. But instead of prey, he ferreted out resolution—order in an otherwise disintegrating world.

"This guy," Decker said pointing to Pode's name. "I want to find out more about him. He's a legit photographer, but one of my ears on the street tells me he has a sideline specializing in the younger trade."

Marge checked off the name. "I'll see what I can dig up," she said.

"Good," Decker answered. "Mike, run these photos up to Freddy. I've called him and left instructions, so all you have to do is give them to him."

"Sure. Where are you going?"

"To talk to Lindsey Bates's boyfriend."

Truscott had moved up in the world. Apparently being remiss on debts paid off. His new residence was in a thirty-unit building in a fashionable part of Santa Monica—new construction made of cheap, brown stucco that wouldn't wear well. But each unit had a balcony and the front was abloom with flowers. The complex contained a pool, a hot tub, a recreation room, a small but well-equipped gym, and plenty of BMWs in the subterranean parking lot. Decker found the manager's unit and knocked on the door.

"Who is it?"

He recognized the voice.

"It's the police, Mrs. Grover."

He heard a series of clicks and snaps, locks being unhinged. The door opened. Mrs. Grover was in her seventies, with thin blue hair.

"Sergeant Decker?" she asked tentatively.

Decker showed the woman his ID.

"Won't you come in, please."

She whistled her S's. Dentures.

"Thank you," Decker said, "but I'm fine out here. Which unit is Mr. Truscott's?"

"Number thirteen. The second one on the left. He's still there, Sergeant. Would you like to come in for a cup of coffee first?"

"I'd love to, Mrs. Grover, but I'm a bit pressed for time."

The old woman accepted his excuse as if she'd heard it plenty of times before. Decker noticed the change in her expression.

"But if you don't mind, I could use a glass of water," he said.

She perked up. "Certainly."

"I'll wait here," Decker said. "I want to keep my eye on the apartment."

"I understand," she said.

She came back with a frosted tumbler. Decker took the water and thanked her.

"Mrs. Grover, how much does Mr. Truscott pay for his apartment?"

"Six fifty a month. If it wasn't for rent control, it would bring a lot more."

"What kind of security deposit did he give you for the unit?"

"The boy's in trouble, isn't he?"

"No."

*Not yet.*

"Did he give you a first and last month's rent?"

"Yes. And a one month's damage deposit."

Almost two grand. No wonder Chrissie boy wasn't paying his bills. Decker finished his water, thanked her, and left.

Truscott answered the door with resignation.

"I knew you'd be coming. It was only a matter of time."

He was a good-looking boy with a dark complexion, thick curly hair, and big gray eyes. His face was lean—almost emaciated—with a sharp jawline, and his expression was unmistakably sad. The lower lip curved downward as if frozen in a tragedy mask. He was taller than average, with a good build, and Decker thought that he and Lindsey would have made a striking couple.

The place had been transformed into a shrine—curtains drawn and walls covered with black cloth. A black sheet blanketed the lone mattress on the floor. Three ebony plastic parsons tables held a dozen or so lit candles. There were no other furnishings.

Truscott motioned to the floor and sat down. Decker followed suit.

"Where'd you get the money to afford this place, Chris?"

The boy was taken aback.

"I . . . I don't know what you mean?"

"Photography must be hauling in *beaucoup* bucks."

"You kidding?"

"I've been checking into you, Chris. You aren't paying your bills; you leave a dump near the ghetto in Venice after paying your landlady with rubber. Then I find you playing yuppie in Santa Monica. What's the story?"

The boy looked down.

"Ain't no story. I'm busted. Flat, stone cold broke. This is all borrowed time. Ain't got more than fifteen bucks to my name and I haven't had a gig since . . ."

He shook his head.

"I wanted to do something nice for myself, you know. To escape the pain. Say 'Fuck it' to the world and go out in style. It didn't work. What does it matter anyway? You're here about her, right?"

"Where were you between eleven A.M. and twelve-thirty P.M. on the day of Lindsey's disappearance?"

"Working."

"Can anyone verify your presence?"

"Only about two hundred people." He looked at Decker. "If you want a confession, I'll give you a confession. I'm dead as far as I'm concerned anyway."

"I want the truth, Chris. Not convenience."

"The truth is I didn't kill her physically. But I'm responsible for her death. If I would have showed up like we planned, this never would have happened."

His lip began to tremble.

"Tell me about your gig, Chris," Decker said.

"I was photographing a wedding. Came through at the last minute, and I thought the bread was too good to pass up. If I had only known . . ."

The boy was aching.

"Who hired you for the job?"

"The lady's name was Bernell. Margaret Bernell. Her daughter got married. I showed up at the church around nine-thirty, maybe ten, and left around three in the afternoon."

"Do you have her phone number?"

The boy went and got it.

"I'm going to call her now, Chris."

"I don't have a phone."

"Come with me to the manager's unit. We'll borrow her phone."

"I'll come, but I ain't gonna split on you. Don't have anywhere to go."

"Come on, Chris."

His alibi checked. Mrs. Bernell had only nice things to say about him and the quality of his work. Decker walked him back to his apartment.

"You keep close by," the detective said. "I might need you."

The boy shrugged.

"I want to find Lindsey's killer," Decker said.

"Don't matter none to me," Truscott said. "Nothing will bring her back to life."

"Well, later on, after the numbness wears off, you may want to see the bastard strung up by his balls. So stick around."

Truscott nodded.

"Chris, were any of your friends deaf or hard of hearing?"

Truscott shook his head.

"Lindsey know anybody deaf or hard of hearing?"

"Not that I know of."

"Ever seen this girl?" Decker showed him a head shot of the female with the peg teeth.

He glanced at it and shook his head.

"Look carefully."

Truscott took the picture and examined it closely.

"Don't know her. What does this have to do with Lindsey?"

"I'm not sure."

*But I hope something*, he thought.

\*   \*   \*

By the time he got back to the station, a manila envelope was waiting on his desk. Dependable Freddy! Decker broke open the gummed seal, pulled out the enlargement, and grinned.

*The man is on fire, he's so hot.*

He headed for Captain Morrison's "office" on the other side of the building. Morrison and the station's day watch commander, Roy Ordik, shared a pint-sized cubicle—barely enough room for the two desks, two chairs, a computer on a stand, and a filing cabinet. At least Morrison was thin and could squeeze through the cracks, but Ordik was fat. Decker rarely saw them in the office at the same time. Maybe that was the secret.

Morrison raised his head when Decker entered.

"What's up, Pete?"

Decker placed the original porno photo and the enlargement on the captain's desk. Morrison looked at the obscene portrait and the enlargement and waited for the explanation.

Decker said, "This is a blowup—the ear of this pegtoothed girl. She's wearing a hearing aid." He pointed to a tiny nub behind the ear lobe.

"Go on."

"I'm hoping this is the Jane Doe found with Bates. That skeleton had the same peg teeth. The dentist said that people with this kind of teeth often have hearing problems."

"How many people have teeth like that?"

"I don't know. I'm taking the photos over to Dr. Hennon this afternoon. I'll see what she says."

The captain nodded approval.

"Check out the boyfriend?"

"Yeah, his alibi panned out. I'm going to drive by his place again, just to make sure he hasn't decided to split. If he stays put, I see no reason to consider him a suspect. He seemed to have been broken up by her death."

"Good," Morrison said. "Keep it up."

Decker rushed out of the office and bumped shoulders with Marge.

"Gotten a whiff of a scent, Peter?" she asked, smiling.

"Just call me bloodhound."

"Cecil Pode," Marge said, reading off of a page. "He's fifty-two—a self-employed photographer with a studio in Culver City. Stable little bugger. Same business for over twenty years. Ran him through NCIC. No wants, no warrants, no priors."

Decker frowned.

"Yeah, it would have been nice if he'd have come back a scumbag," she said.

"He's a scumbag," Decker said. "Nice guys don't snap Polaroids of young girls smothered in spunk."

"Well, then he's a legally clean scumbag," she answered. "I'll dig a little deeper. Talk to a few of my ears. I'll see what I come up with. Hollander will do the same."

Decker nodded.

"What's with the tooth lady in the porno shots?" Marge asked.

"I'm going to see the dentist about her now. Want to come?"

"Gonna have to pass," said Marge. "I've got a court date with a weeny wagger."

Decker pulled out the porno photo and laid it in front of Hennon. The peg-toothed girl had brought a man to ejaculation and his penis was spurting into her mouth. She was covered with semen. But Hennon zeroed right in on the teeth without glancing at the action. A real pro.

She smiled broadly. "These look like Hutchinson's incisors to me. What an eye!"

"Take a gander at this, Annie." He showed her the blowup of the ear and the hearing device.

"You don't miss a trick, do you?"

He grinned. "What do you think?"

"There's potential here. I want to fool around with the photos and compare them to the x-rays of Doe Two's skull and teeth. I've got a darkroom. Give me about twenty minutes."

"Fine," he said. "I'll eat my lunch."

She left, and he opened his paper sack and pulled out foil-wrapped packages. Rina had prepared him a piece of cold poached salmon, cucumbers in sour cream smothered with fresh dill, and a square of noodle kugel with raisins, pineapple, and pecans. No doubt about it, if they ever married, he'd turn into a blimp. Reaching into the bag again, he took out a Bert-and-Ernie thermos. He'd asked her before not to pack it, but she was insistent that it was the only way to keep drinks cold. If he wanted an adult thermos, go out and buy one. But of course he never got around to it, and she kept using the kiddie one.

He unscrewed the top and poured the liquid into the white plastic top. It looked like carbonated apple juice, but to his surprise it turned out to be beer—Dos Equis. He laughed. Before knowing him, Rina had never bought a six-pack. Although he never drank while on duty, he felt impelled to take a sip. A toast in her honor. He ate heartily and took another swig of beer at the end of the meal. He had just finished a cigarette when Hennon reappeared.

"You have the luck of the Irish, Pete."

"It's a match?"

"I wouldn't swear in court based on what you've given me, but let me show you something. I've superimposed Jean's craniofacial skeleton onto the picture you gave me. Look how everything lines up. The eye sockets, the antrum or maxillary air sinus, the nasal sinus, and of course, the upper teeth. A case could be made for positive identification just based on photography, but I'm conservative. Go ahead and find out the identity of this girl. Then we'll get the dental records, if she has them, and confirm what we already think."

"Super. That's what I wanted to hear."

"Good."

"Good."

They stared at each other. For some reason, he couldn't avert his eyes. She licked her lips. He felt a wave of heat and knew he'd had enough.

"Whew," he said, wiping his forehead with a napkin. "Is it hot in here or is it my imagination?"

"I feel fine," she said with an impish grin.

"I'd better leave." Decker picked up the empty sack with the Bert-and-Ernie thermos inside.

He headed for the door.

"Pete," said Hennon, "do you want your pictures back?"

He laughed.

"Yes, I do, thank you."

"Anytime, Sergeant."

After checking out Truscott again, Decker headed for the Teriyaki Dog. It was a ramshackle fast-food stand on Sunset across the street from Children's Hospital. This part of Hollywood wasn't hooker turf and Decker suspected that was why Kiki had picked out the spot; she didn't want to be seen with a cop in front of her peers. But if that was her rationale, the girl wasn't too bright. The stand was open and visible from the boulevard.

She was wolfing down a concoction of hot dog, chili, and chinese vegetables, and the mixture of smells was potent. He sat down beside her at a splintered picnic table. Placing his elbows on the table top, he noticed it was sticky with crusted food. He raised his coat sleeve and grimaced.

"Wanna bite?" she offered.

"No thanks," he frowned. "One arm is enough."

She looked puzzled, then broke into a laugh and punched him on the shoulder—his good one.

"You're a kidder, huh?"

"What do you have for me?" he asked.

"Slow down," she said, talking with her mouth full. "What's the hurry?"

"I'm busy, Kiki. Put up—"

"Or shut up, I know." She stopped eating, wiped her hands on a napkin, and took out a small scrap of paper. "These two guys specialize in young meat and they're both bad dudes."

Decker looked at the names: Wilmington Johnson. Clementine.

"Clementine have a last name?" he asked.

"Just Clementine," she answered licking her fingers.

*As in 'Oh my darlin'.'*

"Black? White?" he asked.

"Both are niggers. Clementine is pretty light from what I hear. I've never seen him."

She picked up her food and took another bite. "Can you get me a Coke?"

He handed her a twenty. "Buy your own."

"You're a real big-timer, Decker," she pouted. Then she broke into a smile. "So I did all right, huh?"

"Not bad. Where'd you get the names from?"

"Here and there. You check out Pode yet?"

"No. Tell me about him."

"Don't know anything other than what I told you," she said. "Just that he takes fuck pictures on the side—young kids—boys as well as girls. Lots of chickenhawks out there."

Decker pulled out the snapshot of Doe two—Joan.

"Ever seen this girl, Kiki?"

The adolescent's eyes widened.

"Yeah."

It was Decker's turn to grin.

"Who is she?"

"Countess Dracula. They call her that because of her teeth. She's kinky, Decker, real kinky."

"Tell me about her."

"I don't know anything really. Just talk on the streets. They say stay away from her. I haven't heard about her in a while."

"That's cause she's dead, Kiki. You don't have to be worried about her anymore. C'mon. What do you know?"

"Dead?"

"Yes."

"This have to do with the girl you were asking about?"

"What do you know about the Countess?"

Kiki sighed.

"Man, I'm really thirsty. And hungry, too. I dunno if they can change a twenty."

"What do you want?"

"Make it a number six this time, with lots of cheese and garlic. And a large Coke."

He got up and returned with her order. It smelled toxic. She bit into the hot dog, chewed, then wiped her mouth and took a sip of soda.

"What can I tell you? She's a weirdo. Or *was* a weirdo. She's really dead, huh?"

*Probably,* he thought.

"Yes," he answered.

"You know, I hear Clementine knew her before she got real weird. I bet he could tell you a bunch about her."

"You're stalling," he said.

"Decker, I don't *know* anything for sure. She was bad and did weird things, or so they say."

"What weird things?"

"Just weird things."

"Like what?"

The girl brought her face close to his. Her breath stank.

"They say she snared dupes, ya know? Maybe some illegals who she threatened to expose to Immigration. She'd do kinky things with them—make 'em fuck dogs or eat dead rats. They say she cut up animals and drank their blood."

*A real sweetheart,* he thought. What could that have to do with Lindsey?

Kiki pulled away from him, sweating profusely.

"I talk too much."

"What else?"

"I don't know anything more."

"And Clementine was her pimp?"

"I dunno. Maybe they had a thing goin'."

"Did she photograph her parties?"

"Shit, I dunno."

"I'm a pervert," he said. "Where do I get ahold of kinky films?"

"I dunno."

"C'mon!"

"I *dunno!*" She sniffed and wiped her nose with the back of her hand. "Honest."

"Then ask around for me, huh?"

"Uh uh," she said, quickly. "I got my own ass to think about." Decker was silent. Kiki bit her lip.

"How much will you give me?" she asked.

"You get me any kind of still or celluloid that links the Countess and Lindsey Bates and I'll do more than get you money, I'll get you off the streets, Kiki. I'll get you into the best halfway house in the city and make sure you're taken care of until you reach legal age. If you've got a habit, I'll get you into a top-notch rehab program. No cold turkey, something with compassion. I'm in Juvey, I have a lot of favors owed to me, and I know how to pull strings."

"And if I don't find anything, I stay out here peddling my ass. That the idea, Decker?"

The detective chewed on his mustache, pulled out a cigarette, and lit it.

"I need something to bargain with in order to strike deals," he said. "I'm sorry but that's the way it works. If I took you off the streets now, maybe they could find a home for you, maybe not. But if I take you off after you've *produced* and tell my buddies, 'Hey, guys, this little gal has come through at risk to herself and we need to pay her back, otherwise our credibility with teenage informants is diddlysquat,' then we've got something. They still won't give a shit about you, but they'll do it."

She folded her arms and scrunched her body into a tight ball.

"You guys are a bunch of creeps, you know that?"

He said nothing.

"Give me a cigarette."

He handed her a Marlboro and lit it for her.

"I start nosing around where I don't belong, and bad people are gonna get suspicious."

He took a deep drag on his smoke and patted her shoulder.

"Listen, you've got rules, I've got rules," he said. "First thing you have to do is stay alive."

He stood up. She looked skinny and her chin was smeared with sauce.

"No matter what you come up with, I'll see what I can do about getting your ass out of here. But no promises."

She tried to look tough, but her face crumpled. She started to cry. He sat back down, and she threw her arms around him, hugging him hard while sobbing on his shoulder.

"You must get a lot of this crybaby shit," she sniffed.

"It's happened before."

"I'll do what I can, Decker."

"Good. But don't get yourself killed for it." He broke away. "Take your time, Kiki. You poke around too quickly, someone's ears will perk up. So don't rush it."

She nodded and wiped her tears with a dirty napkin.

"I've got to go," he said. "You keep in touch."

"Yeah."

He tousled her hair and slipped her a five from his own pocket. *Kids,* he thought. Inside, they were all just kids.

# ·12

$C$ecil Pode's work address led Decker to a block-long shopping center off Venice Boulevard in Culver City. The studio, sandwiched between a shoe store and a take-out pizza shop, was fronted by two large windows that displayed blowups of stiff poses and pasted-on smiles: a family dressed in Sunday finest, a bride silhouetted by backlighting, a bar mitzvah boy, a confirmation girl. In the distance, propped on an easel, was a sixteen-by-twenty photo of a pair of hands with matching wedding rings resting against a background of flowers.

No cum or beaver shots here.

Decker walked inside, and as he stepped over the threshold, a bell jingled. The room was empty, but a voice from the back told him he'd be out in a second. Decker said okay and sat down on a couch. In front of him was a coffee table covered with albums containing sample photos. He picked one up. More proofs of brides, grooms, bar mitzvah boys, nice families.

Restless, he stood up and walked around, his eyes finally focusing on a cork bulletin board full of tacked-on business cards—a professional baby-sitter, two shyster lawyers promising cheap fees (*se habla español*), CPA's, interior designers, a licensed marriage and family counselor (flashing on his sessions with Jan, he knew what *that* was worth). One card caught his attention. It bore the same last name as the studio's owner. *Dustin Pode, Vice President/Executive First Brokerage House. Member SPIC/The quality dis-*

*count broker: investments, tax shelters, real estate, and retirement funds.*

Decker pocketed the card, and a moment later a man came out of the back room. He looked older than fifty-two, stoop-shouldered, with coarse black hair streaked with steel encircling a large bald spot, and a matching swatch of brillo under his small, round nose. He was overweight, with loose jowls and thin lips. The dark eyes managed to be weary and alert at the same time.

"How may I help you, sir?"

"Police," Decker said taking out his badge.

Pode smiled unctuously.

"How can I be of service, Sergeant?" he asked.

"Tell me about *Erotic Ecstasy*," Decker said.

The smile didn't waver.

"I don't know what you're talking about."

Decker took out the picture of the Countess and laid it on the countertop.

"This is your handiwork. Shall we hang it in the window next to the confirmation girl?"

"Never saw her in my life," the photographer said.

"Cut the bullshit, Pode."

"All right, all right."

He went over to the front door, turned the *open* sign to *closed,* and locked the door. For a fat man, his gait was surprisingly graceful.

"I had some gambling debts, so I moonlighted to keep from going under. But I'll tell you this much. It was all legit stuff. All the chickies I shot were over eighteen, so the most you can accuse me of is bad taste. I'm not proud of it, but it kept my head above water, and we all gotta make a living, right?"

"Who's the girl?" Decker said, pointing to the Countess again.

"Beats me. I don't remember photographing her."

"How could you forget these teeth?"

"I'm saying I don't know her."

Bastard was hiding something. Decker showed him Lindsey Bates.

"How about this one?" he asked.

Pode barely glanced at the photo. Decker thought he saw a flicker of recognition in the wary eyes, but it faded so quickly it was hard to be sure.

"Nope. No way!" Pode shook his head emphatically. "This girl isn't more than sixteen, and like I told you, I only did legit stuff."

"Right, Pode. You're Joe Citizen." Decker shoved the photo under his nose. "Take another look."

"I don't know her," Pode insisted.

"Who peddles the kiddy stuff?" Decker pressed.

"I don't know."

"I'm getting really pissed off, Cecil," Decker said.

Pode began to breathe heavily.

"Try a pimp named Johnson—Wilmington Johnson. He goes in for young girls."

"Who else?"

"That's it."

He hadn't mentioned Clementine, which meant that Clementine was the biggie and Johnson was a throwaway.

"Where does Johnson hang out?"

"Hollywood. Where else?"

"*Where* in Hollywood, Pode?"

"Golden Dreams Motel. Sunset near Highland. He gets the runaways and the little kids, sells 'em on the street."

"And photographs them?"

"Maybe," Pode said. His mustache quivered.

"How's your son, Cecil?"

The question threw him.

"Which one?"

"Dustin. How's he doing in the investment business?"

"Uh, fine. Fine enough that he doesn't come around here borrowing money. Bought himself a Porsche and a condo in the Marina. Boy has a nose for a deal."

"So why don't you invest with him? This place sure could use an overhaul."

"I've got a couple of bucks in his projects," said Pode guardedly.

"Tell me about the Countess."

The man's eyes darted about.

"Uh . . . who?"

"The Countess. People say you know her."

"Then people are full of it. Look, what do you want? If you're going to batter me with questions, I want to call a—"

"Where does Dustin work?"

Pode broke into a smile. "I know what you're trying to do. You're trying to *confuse* me."

"Where does he work?"

"Century City, in a big high-rise on Avenue of the Stars. Got some spare cash you want invested, Sergeant?"

"Johnson," Decker said. "How well do you know him?"

"I don't know him at all. I've just heard rumors that Johnson specializes in tender meat."

"Who'd you hear these rumors from?"

"This person, that person." Pode shrugged. "Long time ago. The old memory isn't what it used to be."

"With a few well-placed kicks, I bet we can dredge it up. What do you think?"

"Are you threatening me with physical abuse, Sergeant?"

"Me? Perish the thought! Course I could put out the word that you're my snitch. There's no telling what could happen."

Pode's fat face turned ashen.

"You got something you want to tell me, Pode?"

"No," he said, quietly.

"Good. Thanks for your time." Decker smiled. "You can keep these photos. I've got copies. And you want to know something else? I think you've got copies, too." He paused, then said, "Point of information. This little vampire-toothed lady smothered in cum—she's the Countess."

"Are you ready for this?" Marge said to Decker. "Pode's a widower. His wife died, burnt in a fire about fifteen years back."

Decker's eyes widened.

"Pode's house had a history of calls to the Fire Department,"

Marge explained. "Apparently, Pode's wife—her name was Ida— used to imbibe spirits, then smoke in bed and set it on fire. Usu- ally she escaped unharmed except for a little smoke inhalation and bad sunburn. One time the Fire Department found her uncon- scious and revived her. The last time, she was charred to a crisp, identified through dental records. Sound familiar?"

"Did they check out arson?"

"Yep. The fire was clean. Pode's insurance on her life was noth- ing to write home about, either. A ten-thousand double indemnity with hubby as the sole beneficiary. Pode was paid with no ques- tions asked."

"Anyone else die in the fire?"

"Nope."

They were silent for a moment.

"Let's not jump to conclusions," Marge said. "Just because Lindsey was burnt to death doesn't mean Pode's our guy."

"I'm aware of that."

Marge said, "But it is a coincidence."

Decker said, "I'm not a big believer in coincidences."

The year Decker worked as a lawyer for his ex-father-in-law had been a total bust except for Jack Cohen's dirty jokes. Lawyers told even bluer jokes than cops and no one could tell them better than Jack. Despite the end of his marriage to Jan, he and Jack had somehow remained friends. Decker made a quick phone call to him and explained the situation. Cohen agreed to let Decker use his name as a cover, then began to pump him about his newest, *young* girlfriend. Decker swore to himself. Cindy was a great kid, but discretion was not her forte. He hemmed and hawed, dodging the personal questions as best he could, and finally ended the con- versation with a vague promise to bring Rina by the office one of these days. Jack sounded delighted, confirming what Decker had thought all along. Jan's old man was an incorrigible lecher.

Decker knew from experience that discount brokers didn't place a premium on image, and Executive First was no exception. It was bare bones: four walls, two metal tables, a few unoccupied folding chairs, and a disheveled-looking bleached blonde wearing a polyester stretch top that didn't give where it should have. If you want glitz, go to any full-service brokerage house. The big desks, the high tech electronic ticker tape, and the busty young secretary all cost extra, and those hidden expenses were passed on to the client in the form of higher trading fees.

The blonde was seated at one of the tables taking a call from a switchboard. She motioned Decker onto a folding chair as she spoke into a headphone mike in a soft, modulated voice. She put the caller on hold.

"Harry?" she shouted. "Oh Haaaarry!"

She turned to Decker and said, "Must be in the little boy's room." Punching back the button, she took the caller's name and number, then hung up the receiver. Another light started blinking. She debated answering the call, but instead turned to Decker.

"You want to see Harry?" she asked.

"Actually, I'm interested in seeing Dustin Pode."

"Dustin isn't in and I'm not sure when— Ah, here's Harry."

Harry was Harrison Smithson. He was in his fifties, with a full head of thick white hair and pale blue eyes rimmed in red. He wore a white shirt with the sleeves rolled up to the elbows and a pair of navy gabardine slacks that had seen better days. He sat down at the other table.

"Have a seat," he said to Decker.

His phone rang. Smithson picked it up, greeted the person on the other end, and began rummaging through the piles of papers in front of him.

"I've got the confirmation order right here, Mr. Amati. Yes, I have the check also, but I'm holding it because the settlement date hasn't been established yet. . . . Yes, it should be by next week. . . . If the issue is cancelled, you'll be the first to know. Yes, yes, thank you."

He looked back at Decker.

"What can I do for you?"

"I'm looking for investments that are speculative in nature but have a higher rate of return on the upside. A friend of mine tuned me into Dustin Pode. I thought I'd come down here and check him out personally."

"Which of Mr. Pode's investments interest you?" Smithson asked matter-of-factly.

"Well, what kind of prospectuses do you have to offer me?" Decker hedged. His year with Jack doing wills and estate trusts had been good for something. You learn the lingo.

"Well, I don't know if Mr. Pode ever got around to any formal prospectuses."

"What did he file with the SEC?"

Smithson hesitated. "They're not exactly public offerings."

The phone rang again. The receptionist answered it.

"It's Grunz, Harry."

"Take a message," Smithson said wearily. He turned his attention back to Decker. "It would be best to have Mr. Pode call you directly, Mr. . . . ."

"Cohen," Decker said. "Jack Cohen." He handed Smithson one of his father-in-law's business cards.

Smithson inspected it briefly.

"All right, Mr. Cohen. I'll have Mr. Pode call you."

Decker was about to stand up, but paused.

"My friend told me that Mr. Pode had done very well in movie production limited partnerships. Does he still do that?"

"Yes," Smithson answered. "Occasionally. But he and my son, Cameron, are also involved in a real estate syndication which, to my mind, is going to really take off. It's speculative, of course, and I wouldn't recommend putting your life savings into it. But as far as potential for an upside profit—you're talking sky's the limit."

"Sounds like my type of deal," Decker said smiling. "A little cash and a lot of stomach acid."

The outer door burst open and a young man flew in. He stomped up to Smithson's desk, completely unaware, it seemed, of Decker's presence.

"Where are Cumberlaine's certificates?" he demanded of Smithson.

The older man turned pink and lowered his voice.

"The securities are still being registered, Cameron. The order was only placed a couple of weeks ago."

"The guy wants his certificates," Cameron said, loudly. "I told him I'd have them for him." He started pacing. "This isn't some penny-ante bimbo, Harry, we're talking big stakes. Somebody who can inject a little class, not to mention a lot of money, into this firm. The man's connected!"

Smithson cleared his throat and turned to Decker. "This is the senior vice-president of Executive First," he said, "Cameron Smithson. This is Mr. Cohen, an interested investor."

"Hello," Cameron said, shaking Decker's hand. "I'll leave you two alone in a minute."

Decker regarded Smithson's son. He wasn't particularly small, but his overall appearance suggested delicacy. His complexion was baby-smooth, almost translucent, with a hint of peach fuzz above a narrow pink upper lip. His hair was blonde and fine and combed to cover a patch of denuded scalp. His eyes were watery blue, his nose thin with surprisingly wide nostrils. His blue cashmere blazer was perfectly tailored, his charcoal slacks, razor pressed. A red silk tie hung against a backdrop of white sea island cotton, the collar of the shirt secured by a gold pin. His hands were slender with uncalloused palms, fingernails filed and shaped and coated with clear polish.

*Not a man used to getting his hands dirty.*

Cameron glared at his father. "I *need* those certificates, Harry."

"I can't get them now," Smithson said, embarrassed. "Can't get blood from a turnip, Cam."

"Then what the hell do I tell Cumberlaine?" His expression suddenly shifted. "Never mind! I'll think of something. Blame it on the SEC or, better yet, blame it on the post office."

He stormed out of the office. The room was eerily quiet—the stifling calm after the cessation of freak tornado. Smithson cleared his throat.

"You'll have to forgive Cameron," he said sheepishly. "He gets a bit overexcited when he can't make good on his word. He takes his work very seriously."

Decker nodded. He was making excuses for his son. It sounded like something he was used to doing.

"I'll have Mr. Pode call you," Smithson said, trying not to appear nonplussed.

"That would be fine."

"I hope I've been of service to you, Mr. Cohen."

"You have," answered Decker. "I'm glad I made it over here."

The men rose. Smithson held out his hand and Decker took it.

There was more action outside the Golden Dreams Motel than inside. The proprietor, a middle-aged Armenian, complained animatedly to Decker that the prostitutes and pimps had driven away all his legit business. Decker listened with half an ear, and when the man paused for air, stuck in his question. Who, of the half dozen pimps outside, was Wilmington Johnson? The owner pointed out a tall, emaciated black with a full Afro, wearing purple stretch pants, a gold lamé V-neck shirt, and a black velvet jacket. Around his neck were plaits of gold chains and on his arms were two babes of fifteen or sixteen—both white.

The man had *arrived*.

He went up to Johnson and told the girls to beat it.

"Say what, white boy?" Johnson asked, staring out into the street.

"You Johnson?" Decker asked.

The black turned around and gave him a quick once-over.

"Well, that all *depends* on what you *want*, man."

"Oh," Decker said meekly. Then he spun around and gave the pimp a short, hard punch in the solar plexus. Johnson folded over like a loose strand of licorice and began panting, teary-eyed. His whores stared at the detective, one with animosity, the other with admiration.

"Jesus," Decker said helping him up. "I'm so sorry. I just lost my balance for a second. Jesus." He brushed off the pimp's coat. "I'm really sorry."

Johnson stared at him with evil eyes.

"I'm looking for Wilmington Johnson," Decker said, smiling.

"Who the fuck are you?" Johnson spat.

Decker took out his badge.

"Police."

Johnson muttered to himself. Pulling out a pair of glasses, he stared at the shield, then looked at Decker. "Yeah, you're po-lice all right. What you want?" He was about to remove the spectacles, but Decker held his arm and showed him the picture of the Countess.

"Yeah," Johnson nodded. "I seen the bitch."

"Was she one of yours?"

Johnson laughed, showing off horse-sized teeth.

"No way. Ain't got that kind of animal in my stable. Try a dude named Clementine."

"Where does he hang out?"

"Here and there."

Decker scowled at him.

"Where is 'here and there'?"

"The Strip, the Boulevard, the back alleys," said Johnson. "Catch him when you can."

"What do *you* know about the Countess?"

"She was bad-assed. Kinky."

"Know this one?" Decker showed him Lindsey.

Johnson took a long look.

"A nice one," Johnson nodded. "Fresh meat. Could get a lotta *mileage* from her. But the angel hasn't crossed my path."

"You sell pictures of your girls, Johnson?"

The pimp laughed.

"Say what?"

"Sell pictures of them with their johns."

"Shit, no. Who needs the extra hassle? I ain't greedy."

"Some people say you do."

"Who?"

"Cecil Pode."

Johnson sputtered out guffaws.

"Ole Cecil. How's the fat boy doing?"

"What do you know about Cecil?"

"Fat old fart. Used to slip me a few extra bucks if I'd let him shoot some of my girls in the raw. After a while he got in my face, man. Tried to steal some of my cuties. But my girls are loyal. I told him to take a hike. Musta been two years ago."

Decker put away his notebook.

"You stay put," Decker said. "I may come back for you."

"Hey, Mr. Po-liceman, where the fuck should I be goin' to? My livelihood is right out here." The pimp's eyes narrowed and shifted to the hookers. "Interested?"

Decker gave him either a hard pat or a light slap on the face. "No."

The cop who walked into the interrogation room was no more than a kid.

"You're Vice in these parts?" Decker asked.

"Yup."

The cop's name was Beauchamps—all-American surfer boy with peroxide hair, movie idol eyes, and the deep tan that a redhead could never attain. Decker felt tired and old. And whenever he felt tired and old, he also felt pissed. The kid gave him an aw shucks grin.

"Welcome to Hollywood PD. Want a cup of coffee?"

"Pass," Decker said.

"How long of a shift have you been on?"

"I didn't have a mustache when it started."

Beauchamps laughed, then said, "I've seen you before."

"I was here last Sunday asking about a runaway."

"That's right. You spoke with Martell."

"Yeah," Decker said. "I've got some new developments. A kinky one that goes by the name of Countess Dracula." He showed Beauchamps the picture.

"Don't know her personally," said the Vice cop, "but I'll circulate it."

"How about a pimp named Clementine?"

"Him I know."

"Where does he hang out?"

"All over. His main squeeze lives in a pink duplex on Genesee, off of Hollywood Boulevard. Her name matches the house. Get this—Pinky Lovebite."

Decker nodded. "Where can I get hold of kinky films, real nasty stuff?"

Beauchamps grinned boyishly. "If I knew that, Decker, I'd have a hell of a bust."

"Ever hear of a photographer named Cecil Pode?"

"Nope."

"Thanks."

"Stop by again," Beauchamps said. "I'll buy you dinner."

# ·13

"The murdered girl?" the Rabbi asked. "Have you found the culprit?"

Decker took another drag on his cigarette and shook his head. Schulman looked upset.

"Have you talked to the parents at all?"

"Not since the initial interviews," Decker answered. "I figured I'd call them when I had something worthwhile to tell them."

The Rabbi crushed out the butt of his handrolled cigarette.

"I'm sure something will break open soon for you, Peter."

"I appreciate the optimism, Rabbi. This is one of those cases that's wrapped in layers. And as I peel them off, I know I'm going to find a rotten core. It stinks."

"Are there ever good cases?" Schulman asked. "That was not meant rhetorically. I'm wondering if there are any cases from which you walk away feeling good?"

"Not really," Decker said. "But most are very straightforward. A wife shoots her husband because he had a lover. A husband shoots his wife because she nagged him. Mama picked on the son-in-law at the wrong time. This one is not like that, though."

The Rosh Yeshiva was clearly troubled.

Decker cursed his stupidity. He shouldn't have told Schulman about his work. The old man had been insulated from the depravity of the outside world and was not equipped to deal with it.

"Don't worry, Rabbi," Decker said. "We'll solve the case."

\*   \*   \*

He had told Rina that he'd stop by after his session with Schulman. As he approached her door, he could hear voices inside her house—a foreign tongue—Hungarian.

Her parents! Shit!

Reluctantly, he knocked. Rina swung open the door and stared at him, looking haggard. She was holding Jacob and was struggling under his weight, the boy's feet dangling down to her shins. He was dressed in pajama bottoms but was barechested, his swollen eyes evidence that he'd been crying.

Her parents were standing around the doorway, looking their usual stiff selves. Her mother, Mrs. Elias, though wrinkled around the eyes and lips, was still a very pretty woman. Rina resembled her except that she'd inherited her father's baby-smooth complexion, ending up with the best of both worlds. Mr. Elias was shorter than his wife, with a solid frame packed with muscle. He appeared agitated, his round face flushed and wet with perspiration.

"What's wrong?" Decker asked.

"Come in," Rina said, wearily.

"You didn't ask who it was?" her mother scolded her in a heavy accent. "It could have been anyone."

"I saw him through the peephole," Rina said tensely.

"C'mere, Jake," Decker said, forcing himself to breathe regularly. "Give your mama's arms a rest."

As Decker reached out to take Jacob, the boy screamed, kicked, and buried his face in his mother's neck.

"He's had another nightmare," Rina explained. "I don't think he's fully awake. He woke up soaked with sweat, and everytime I try to put a shirt on him he screams. If I try putting him back to sleep, he screams. If someone tries to take him, he screams. I just don't know what to do."

"Sit down with him, Ginny," suggested her father. "You'll sprain your back."

"I've tried that already, Papa," Rina answered.

"Remember what happened when you carried Sammy too much as a baby," her mother warned.

"So *what* do you want me to do?"

"Give him to me," her father said. As soon as he touched Jacob's shoulders, the boy emitted a high-pitched wail.

"Forget it, Papa," Rina said. "He just won't go to anyone else."

"Let him sleep with you, Ginny," the mother suggested. "Just for the night."

"Oh, that would be wonderful," Rina said, sarcastically.

"For one night it won't kill you. I did it with you," her mother said. "You sleep on your own now, don't you?"

"Mother, I am not going to let him sleep with me. You know all the trouble I had with the boys doing that after Yitzchak, *alav hasholom*, died."

"He's falling asleep," her father announced. "Try putting him down."

"Everytime I try putting him to bed he screams," Rina said, exasperatedly.

"Try again," her mother insisted.

"At least let me wait until he's deep asleep."

"And until your back breaks," her mother muttered. "Just let him sleep with you."

"Rina, maybe I should come back at another time," Decker said.

"Well, that's to be expected," Mrs. Elias said acidly.

"What was *that* supposed to mean?" Rina said, forcing control into her voice.

"After all, we know the reason behind Yonkel's nightmares—"

"It wasn't anyone's fault," Rina defended.

"Nothing like this ever happened when we had the children," her mother insisted.

"It was one of those unfortunate things, Mrs. Elias," Decker answered, supressing his anger. "He'll survive."

"There is a big difference between survival and happiness, Detective," Mrs. Elias shot back. "I *survived* in the camps."

"Mother, that's not fair!" Rina exclaimed.

"I think I'd better leave, Rina," Decker said.

"As I was saying, that is to be expected," her mother said. "Don't pay any attention to her—"

"That is what you call me, Ginny?" said her mother, with her eyes watering. *"Her?"*

Decker balled his fingers into a fist and headed for the door. Jacob shouted out his name.

Decker turned. "C'mere, fellah," he said, holding out his arms. This time, Jacob leaped.

"Let's talk in bed, okay?"

Jacob nodded. Decker carried him into the bedroom, relieved. As he cooed the youngster back into sleep, he heard hostile mutterings outside. Gently, he brushed black locks off Jacob's forehead and tucked him into bed, the boy's bony shoulders peeking out from the edge of the comforter. As soon as Jacob drifted off, Decker rose from the bed, acid pouring into his gut, his head throbbing in anticipation of the showdown.

Rina and her mother were deep in battle. Her father tried unsuccessfully to arbitrate, attempting to comfort both women and managing to comfort neither. Mrs. Elias cried something to her daughter in Hungarian. Rina came back with a reply. Decker sighed inwardly. It wasn't enough that he had to struggle with Hebrew, Yiddish, and Aramaic. Now he had to cope with Hungarian. He'd fallen in love with a walking UN.

The discussion increased in volume, and the women began gesticulating wildly with their hands. Then Mrs. Elias spotted Decker, pointed to him, and shouted something to her daughter. Her tone was virulent. Turning crimson, Rina shot back at her and pointed to the door, sobbing. Her mother stalked away. Confused, Mr. Elias alternated between calling out to his wife and consoling his daughter. Spousal obligation won out over filial love. Mr. Elias kissed Rina a hurried good-bye and ran after his wife. Decker waited for Rina to calm down, then asked,

"What'd she say to you?" he asked.

"Nothing."

"C'mon. I'm a big boy. What'd she say?"

Rina wiped her face with a Kleenex and looked up at him with puffy eyes.

"She said—and I quote—'I lived through the camps only to see the day that my daughter would marry a *shaigetz* and a Cossack as well!'"

He broke into laughter.

"Well, I'm glad *you* find her amusing because I don't."

But the corners of her mouth had turned upward.

"Here I am, Chmelnicki on a pogrom, killing the men, raping the women, and plundering the spoils." His laughter turned bitter. "I've been called a lot of things, Rina, but Cossack is a first."

"It's not funny."

"Let's be charitable and assume your mother had an off night."

"She said some horrible things to you."

Decker shrugged. "I'm the big, bad goy who's kidnapping her daughter. We'll work it out in time."

"You're not a goy, you're a *ger*—a convert. Or at least you will be soon."

"But she sees me as a goy."

"I am not going to *marry* a goy!"

"No," Decker said. "You're not. You're going to marry a Jew. You're going to sleep with a Jew. You're going to have children with a Jew. But let's face facts, honey. You fell in love with a Gentile."

She said nothing and stared vacantly out the living room window. Shaking his head disgustedly, he swore to himself, knowing he'd just added a tributary to her already overflowing river of guilt.

"Rina, I'm running off at the mouth. I'm very tired. Forget I said that."

Remaining motionless, she spoke without looking at him.

"Every morning after I wake up, I take out my siddur and daven *shemoneh esreih.* And afterwards, every single morning, I pray to *Hashem* for understanding and forgiveness of my transgressions . . . Sometimes, I pray for the strength to do what I should have done a long time ago—send you away until you've become a Jew."

She turned to him.

"But I must not have the proper *kavanah*—intent—when I

pray, because I never have the fortitude to say goodbye." She brushed a tear off her cheek. "Do you hate me for feeling that way?"

"No." He ran his fingers through his hair. "We both have misgivings."

"Do you not want to convert?" she asked.

He shook his head. "That's not what I meant. But it isn't easy to throw away nearly forty years of conditioning, especially when your own parents are very vocal about their disapproval." He smiled sadly. "We're getting it from both ends."

"You told your parents you're converting?"

"Sure. It's no secret. I wrote them a letter." He grimaced. "I wrote to my mother and told her I fell in love with an Orthodox Jew and I was converting to her faith. You know what she wrote back?"

"What?"

"She wrote, 'You got singed in the fire the first time around, Peter. This time you'll burn.' She wasn't nuts about Jan being Jewish, and Jan wasn't all that Jewish. But at least I didn't convert. This was too much for her."

He shrugged and Rina took his hand.

"That was an awful thing to say," she said indignantly.

"Aah, I couldn't even blame her. How do you tell your parents that you reject their values but you don't reject them? I hurt them, Rina. I spat in their faces."

"No you didn't."

Decker said nothing. She threw her arms around his waist, leaned her head on his chest, and gave him a bear hug.

"I love you, Kiddo," he said softly.

"I love you, too," she answered. "I've been so wrapped up in my own guilt, I've never considered the other side."

He smiled and kissed her forehead.

"Have you spoken to your parents since the letter?" she asked.

"Yeah. I called them about a week ago. They were civil. Said if we were ever down their way to stop by—as if they were talking to a casual acquaintance."

He tightened his embrace.

"Rina, we have a lot going against us: meeting under such lousy circumstances, the difference in our ages and backgrounds. We can try and say screw it all—we're our own people and love is all that matters—but you know as well as I that the baggage our parents loaded on our backs is with us forever. Let's both try to be tolerant of them—and tolerant with each other."

She nodded.

"I love you," he said. "Kiss me."

She gave him a peck on the cheek.

"No." He cupped her chin in his hands. "I mean really kiss me."

He lowered his mouth onto hers, and at once he felt the passion she'd been holding back, her lips parting and her breath warm and sweet. She threw her arms around his neck, almost a chokehold, and latched onto his mouth like a suckling baby to a breast. Not wanting to get excited, he tried to break away, but she brought his mouth back to hers, greedily taking what had been denied her for so long.

She pulled him down to the floor and fell on top of him, smothering his face with kisses. Her hands tugged at his shirt, jerking the tail out of his pants, fumbling with the buttons. Decker was caught between his own fever and the guilt he knew she'd feel if they continued. The fire won out. He tore at his shirt, popping a button as it opened, then yanked at the zipper of her dress. He'd opened it half-way when Jacob cried out—a piercing screech like the whistle of a tea kettle.

"Oh God!" Rina wept, covering her face in her hands. "Life is so damn frustrating!"

"Tell me about it," Decker groaned.

"I've got to get out of here," she said, panting. "I'm going nuts. I need to escape to a desert island."

"Just take me with you."

Jacob began to howl.

She chomped on her thumbnail, trying to steady her shaking hands. "I can't deal with this, Peter."

Decker stood up, buttoned his shirt, and tucked it into his

pants. "You sit and dream of rum and coconuts. I'll see what's wrong with Jake."

When he came out, she had regained her composure.

"Is he okay?" Rina asked.

"Yes," said Decker. "For the time being."

"It's going to be a long night."

"Would you like me to stay—"

"No," Rina answered quickly. "No, that won't do at all." She took Decker's hands, squeezed them, then let them go.

"Now I know why there are such strict separation laws in Judaism," she said.

"I hate every one of them," Decker answered. "I don't suppose you'd want to continue where we'd left off."

She shook her head. "If it's any consolation, I've become very tired, Peter. I'd probably be terrible."

He could deal with that, but didn't push it. The moment had been lost.

# · 14

The alley was a tunnel of black and smelled like a setup. Decker unhitched his gun and took out a penlight. Shining it on the lumpy asphalt, he inched his way toward the rear of the third building on his left, nostrils flaring at the odor of rotting garbage and excrement. He stopped. There was something wrong, and as much as he wanted a handle on this case, this wasn't the way to get one. Turning back, he froze suddenly at the sound of a hiss.

"Son of a bitch," the hoarse voice croaked.

Decker spun around in the direction of the whisper and saw nothing but boxes and dented trash cans.

"Clementine?"

"I said no pieces, Cop."

"It's my security blanket."

"That wasn't the deal, Cop."

Decker said, "I've got the cash, Clementine." He began to sweat. Killing the penlight, he backed up against a wall. The conversation was taking place in the dark. No sense being in the spotlight.

"Throw over the green," the raspy voice instructed. "Across the alley, second building on your right."

"First you tell me what you know about the Countess."

"First you toss over the bread."

They were at a standstill. No one so far had known the Countess's true identity, and all roads pointed to Clementine. This powwow had been arranged via the pimp's number one lady. Info for cash—$200 in twenties.

He played the scenario in his head. Once he forked over the money, the pimp couldn't escape without coming into his line of vision. And he did have his piece . . .

He shone his penlight across the alley and pitched the envelope of cash where Clementine had instructed.

"It better be good for what we're paying you, Clementine."

The pimp made no move to pick up the package.

Silence. Decker turned off the light. In the distance he saw the glowing orange tip of a cigarette.

"Name was Kate Armbruster. A mud duck from Klamath Falls, Oregon," the voice whispered. "Picked her up when she was fourteen. She wasn't even fresh then—a had-out piece of shit. But she worked her tail off. Got a lot of action from her. Then she got weird."

"What happened?" the detective asked.

"Met up with a dude called the Blade—skinny, crazy cracker into knives and pain. Permanent pain, if you can dig what I'm saying. Boogying with the high beams on—smoking lots of Jim Jones. I know they offed animals—big dogs. Get the poor motherfuckers tightroped on water and watch them rip each other apart. They say Katie just loved the puppies. Cut 'em up live and offer 'em to old six sixty-six himself. Some say they got more sofist-to-cated in their taste."

"Meaning?"

"Only one step up from animals, Cop. You put two and two together."

"Who is this Blade?"

"Don't know his real name. Dude must be in his twenties, average height, and skinny, like I said. Brown hair and maybe brown eyes. Can't tell you much more. All white meat looks alike."

"Where did they hang out, Clementine?"

"Don't know."

Decker illuminated the money with his penlight, aimed his .38, and shot off the tip of the envelope. The alley reverberated with the echo of the blast and filled with the smell of gunpowder. He reloaded the chamber and shut off the light.

"If that's the best you can do, I'm going to blow your wad to bits, Clementine. Where did they hang out?"

A cackle came from the garbage cans.

"You are a fuckin' A, Decker," said a hollow whisper. "An A number one fuckin' felon. Don't you know it's against the law to shoot money in America?" He laughed again. "Shoot it until it ain't nothing but a pile of green Swiss cheese. My answer's the same. Don't know where they did their shit, don't know who their stooges was, don't know 'cause I didn't want to know, Cop. I wasn't into that shit, so I closed my eyes."

"Did they film their cult rituals?" Decker asked.

"Yeah."

"Who has the films?"

"Don't know who their customers be."

"Who deals in snuffs around these parts?"

"Lots of people."

"Names."

Silence.

Decker waited.

"Talk says the main distributor is a fat fuck named Cecil Pode." Clementine coughed—a dry, hacking sound. "Works out of his studio in Culver City."

"Who gives Pode the films?"

"Don't know."

"Who does Pode sell the films to?"

"Used to sell 'em to the Countess. Like I tole you, don't know who her customers be."

"Let me get this straight. The Countess made films with the Blade. Then Cecil would buy them from the producer and sell the finished product back to her?"

"That way she be paid off twice. Once as the star, the other when the goods be delivered. She knew who all the weirdos be and have an easy time unloading the shit at the price she wanted."

"Then why bother using Cecil as a distributor? Why not sell directly to the customers?"

"Rumor has it that Cecil does the filming as well as the distributing."

"Are the films videotaped?"

"No way! Good old-fashioned 16 mm half-inch film. Keeps it cheap and rare. Videotape's too easy to pirate."

"Who paid Pode for his camera work?"

"Don't know."

"The Countess?"

"Don't know."

Decker felt frustration growing inside. He lit a cigarette and took a deep drag.

"Why was the Countess whacked?"

Clementine didn't answer. Decker repeated the question.

"Sometimes people get carried away," said Clementine softly.

"Where could I find the Blade?"

"Tole you before, man. Don't know."

"Cecil know him?"

"Don't know."

"Ever know a girl named Lindsay Bates?"

"Nope."

"Are you sure—"

"I said I don't know the chick," Clementine interrupted. "You got enough for your money. I see you, Decker. Got your piece in your right hand and your smoke in your left. I got cat's eyes, Cop—see things coming in as well as out. I didn't trust you anymore than you trusted me, so that means, my man, that I got my piece too. You get cute, you be dead. Now get the hell out of here while you still got your balls in one piece."

"Stick around, Clementine. I just might need you again."

"Fuck you. Get out of here."

Decker backed out of the black void and into the silvery mist of the street lights. Suddenly he felt hot. Mopping his forehead with the back of his hand, he stood for a moment to catch his breath, then took off his jacket. By the time he reached the Plymouth, he was drenched in sweat.

Pode lived in a frame house in Mar Vista. The neighborhood was predominantly white working class, but over the past few years, a slow trickle of immigrant Latinos had worked their way into the cheaper homes. Pode's place was badly in need of a paint job and the lawn was a tangle of weeds. The porch steps were crumbling and the flagstone walkway was as much dirt as it was rock. If Pode had money, he obviously wasn't spending it on hearth and home.

The house was dark, the curtains drawn. After determining that no one was home, Decker went back to the car and waited. It was not the time to play hot dog and attempt a break-in. He knew Cecil was trapped. Marge was at the shop, he was here, and all good homing pigeons return to roost.

He sipped a container of black coffee, listening to the staccato voices of the dispatchers reporting crimes—burglaries, robberies, GTAs. The *yetzer harah* is alive and well. More than well. God-damn robust.

Devil worship, living sacrifices, pain flicks. How the hell did Lindsey figure in? Suppose she and the Countess had been snuffed in a film. How had the Countess gotten hold of her in the first place? Pulled her into a car at gunpoint in front of a busy shopping center? Stranger things had been known to happen, but he didn't like it. And why was the Countess killed along with her? Maybe Lindsey Bates had a secret life as a satanic cultist and had been involved from the start.

No. It didn't make sense.

The hours passed. Decker's hopes for a quick catch began to fade. He'd come on too strong with Pode and Pode'd split town along with his goods.

Decker radioed Marge.

"Anything?" he asked her.

"Dead."

"I think Pode might have taken an extended vacation."

"So now what do we do?"

"There's his son, Dustin, the stockbroker and film maker."

"Why do you think he's dirty, Pete?"

"I don't think he's one way or the other, but I still want to feel him out. We've returned each other's calls but haven't been able to connect."

"Doing the old Jack Cohen alias again?" Marge asked.

"Jack loves intrigue."

She asked: "How long do you want to hang around?"

"You can go home, Marge. He's more likely to show up here than at his studio."

"Unless he has business to clear up here."

There was a pause.

"How about another hour?" Marge suggested.

"Okay."

At 4 A.M. they called it quits.

It came to him—a flash of insight as he was pulling up into the driveway of his ranch. He shifted into reverse and headed for Santa Monica, arriving at the apartment complex a half hour before dawn. The chill and wetness of the night had seeped into the nape of his neck, and he pulled up the collar on his jacket. Stopping in front of number thirteen, he knocked hard on the door. Five minutes later, Truscott answered in his underwear and swayed drowsily, using the doorhandle for balance.

"What's goin' on?" he muttered.

"You remember me, Chris?"

The boy nodded sleepily.

"Come in." He yawned and opened the door wide.

Neither one bothered to sit.

"What's goin' on?" the boy repeated.

"The gig you got on the day of Lindsey's disappearance—you said it was a wedding."

"Yeah."

"You said you got it at the last minute."

"Yeah."

"Who was the original photographer supposed to be?"

"A guy I know."

"What's his name?"

"Cecil Pode. He's a—"

"Shit!" Decker slammed his fist into a waiting palm. "Did Pode know you were supposed to meet Lindsey?"

The boy's face was the picture of confusion. He rubbed his eyes. "What are you gettin' at?" he asked.

"Did Pode ever meet Lindsey?"

"Couple times. I used to develop my pictures at his studio. He saw some of the shots I took of her and asked me to bring her around. He said he wanted to snap a couple of shots of her for his window display. Made a point of telling me how photogenic she was. I don't think he ever did it, though."

"Did Pode ever see the nudes you took of Lindsey?"

"I guess. I don't remember."

"How'd you meet Pode?"

"On the beach. He hung around the Venice boardwalk a lot."

"Did you tell Pode before the day of the gig that you had a date with Lindsey on the day of her disappearance?"

"I might have. I don't fuckin' remember." Panic seized the boy. "What is it?"

"I'm not sure."

"What the hell do you mean you're not sure?" Truscott's voice cracked. "What's Cecil got to do with Lindsey? Did he do anything to her?"

Decker was silent. Truscott grabbed his shoulders. He had an alarmingly tight grip for a man his size.

"Did he do anything to her?" he shouted.

"He might have," Decker said quietly. "He might have told her to come with him to meet you. And then he might have abducted her."

The boy's scream came out a strangled, sucking gasp. Then he collapsed into Decker's arms.

Decker slept in the station's dormitory from 6:30 to 8:30 A.M. Bleary eyed at 9 A.M., he placed a call to the information operator in Klamath Falls. There were three Armbrusters. The second one was the winner. Kate had left home seven years ago and hadn't been heard from since. Decker explained the situation, expecting to hear emotional upheaval on the other side, but the mother's only comment was good riddance to bad rubbish. She gladly supplied the name of Kate's dentist and made it a point to tell him not to bother to ship the body home. Katie was trash, and a Christian funeral for her would be sacrilegious *and* a waste of hard earned money.

Decker reminded himself that Katie had been born with congenital syphilis. The indignation of the hypocrites.

Katie's dentist had only X-rays of current patients at his fingertips. It would be a couple of days before he could find her radiographs. He did remember working on her once or twice. The Armbrusters really couldn't afford too much. If he found the X-rays, he'd be glad to send them down. A shame about Katie, he said to Decker. She was a wild kid, but that was no reason to die.

Morrison sat across his desk, eyes fixed on Decker's face.

"You want to tell me what the hell is going on, Pete? You've requested two search warrants and a tail on some stockbroker named Dustin Pode."

"The warrants are for his father's home and studio. Cecil Pode is a snuff film distributor. I'm betting he's involved in Lindsey Bates's abduction and death. After I questioned him, I think he cut town. I want to see if he left anything incriminating behind."

"Who says he's a snuff distributor—the pimp you talked to?"

"He and another source."

"Who?"

Decker rubbed his eyes and supressed a yawn.

"A hooker. Her street name's Kiki. She seems on the up-and-up."

Morrison thought for a moment, then said, "Let's do it this way. We'll try for search warrants for Pode's house and studio based on what you found out from Truscott. Unlikely we'll get them without *something* concrete. A still or a film or at least someone who saw Bates and Pode together the day of her disappearance."

"Dunn is going to comb the Galleria and ask around at all the stores. Maybe we'll get lucky."

"Maybe," the Captain said.

"What about the tail?" Decker said.

"Dustin Pode is a private citizen who isn't residing or working in our jurisdiction. He hasn't been implicated—"

"Not yet."

"Maybe not at all."

"You don't have any real evidence on Cecil Pode; you have *nothing* on Dustin Pode. A tail is out of the question. Takes up too much manpower."

"I have a gut feeling that Dustin Pode is involved."

"You're a good intuitive cop, Pete, but I can't authorize men based on your hunches."

"At least send Hollander out to talk to Dustin Pode about his father. Maybe Dustin will implicate Daddy in something naughty," Decker said. "Mike's got a light load this morning."

"*You* can talk to Dustin Pode," said Morrison. "I've no problem with that."

Decker stalled a moment. He didn't want to tell Morrison about his Jack Cohen alias just yet. "Let Hollander handle it. He's good with these broker types. He loves to play dumb."

"Fine. Hollander goes out for a one-shot deal. But scratch any idea about a tail." Morrison lit a cigarette. "You've done a good job, Pete. Taken a dead case and breathed some life into it. Just don't go overboard. And don't do anything dumb-ass with this Dustin Pode. I don't want a citizen's harassment complaint slapped on this division. God knows LAPD gets enough fabricated shit from the papers. Let's not give them something real to work with."

Decker nodded.

"Now what is this about getting another juvey into the Donaldson halfway house?"

"I owe someone a favor."

Morrison didn't press it.

"Okay," he said. "Start the paperwork."

"Thanks, Captain."

"When are you taking the lieutenant's exam?"

"I thought maybe next year."

"Why not this year?"

"I haven't had a hell of a lot of time to study."

"You're a *lawyer*, Pete. After the bar, the exam should be a snap."

Decker shrugged. He didn't have time to study because the yeshiva courses were occupying all his free time—or lack thereof. But he couldn't tell the captain that.

Morrison looked disapproving, but said nothing. He stood up and walked away without a word. Decker rubbed his eyes.

Man, he was tired.

The phone rang.

"Decker."

"It's the illustrious Patsy Lee Newford, better known as the redheaded superspy."

"Patsy Lee Newford?"

"Hey Decker, that's a *boss* name in Indiana." She laughed, sounding like a soprano jackhammer.

"What do you have for me, Kiki?"

"Pode took a hike."

"Know where he went?"

"Uh uh. But he was one of the major distributors of snuff films 'round these parts."

"Yeah," Decker said. "I found that out."

*A little too late.*

"Have any other names of snuff men?" he asked.

"Nope. I'll see what I can do."

"Lie low, Kiki. This is getting messy. You've done enough. I'm working on paying you back like we discussed."

She was silent.

"You there?" he asked.

"Yeah. I can't believe you're coming through."

"Call me back in a week," he said. "It should be all set up."

"Okay. I'll see what I can dig up in the meantime."

"No!" Decker said, more loudly than he'd intended to. "Just cool it. We'll find Pode ourselves. Don't do any more."

She was silent again.

"Kiki, if you keep poking around, you're gonna get whacked. Is that straightforward enough?"

"Hey, I did all right so far. I can take care of myself."

"Honey, I'm sure you can," Decker said, backing off. "How 'bout you doing me a favor and just keep your nose clean until I can get you into this program?"

A long pause on the other end of the line.

"What's it like?" she asked in a tiny voice.

"It's a really good place, Kiki. Lots of trees and grass and a swimming pool. The people are good—strict but honest. You'll do real well there."

"Will you visit me?"

Decker hesitated, then said, "No. But you'll make loads of friends, Honey. Good friends."

"What if I don't make it, you know? I mean what if—"

"Kiki, let's take it one day at a time."

"It's just that I'm not so sure it's what I want. I mean I want to get off of the streets you know, but I'm real independent like."

"You'll do fine."

"I mean I got a couple of quirks you know."

"Everyone has quirks."

"Do they have TVs there?"

"Yes."

"Do they watch Wally George?"

Decker smiled. "I'm sure you'll get TV privileges."

"I dunno . . . I just dunno if I'm ready. Maybe I'm better off working for you."

"Kiki, if you want to help me out, keep yourself out of trouble until I contact you, okay?"

"How will you know where to find me?"

"Still got my card?"

"Uh huh."

"Then come by the station house in a week. You need bread in the meantime?"

"I'm okay."

"Then come by in a week."

She was silent for a long time.

"I'm a little nervous, you know."

"That's okay, Kiki. Everyone gets nervous occasionally. Even big, macho cops who pack iron. You come by in a week. Deal?"

"Deal," she said, then hung up the phone.

Decker placed the receiver back in the cradle and leaned back in his chair. He felt good. Marge came over to him with a hot cup of coffee.

"Drink," she said.

"Thanks."

"How much sleep did you get last night, Rabbi?"

"'Bout two hours."

"Taking the morning off?"

"Not until I find Pode."

"Good luck," she said. "I'm off to the Galleria." She zipped up her shoulder bag and looked at the leather shredding around the seams. "Maybe I'll look at purses as long as I'm there. This one is shot. Literally. An old gun I used to carry accidentally discharged and blew a hole out the bottom. It's patched up with electrical tape. Think it's time for a new one?"

"I'd say that's reasonable."

"Can I pick you up anything as long as I'm out?"

*Sleep, a steak, and sex,* he thought. *In that order.*

"No thanks," he said.

"Anything?" Decker asked hopefully.

"Nothing," Hollander answered.

Angrily, Decker crumpled a piece of scratch paper and threw it in the garbage. Marge hadn't come up with anything at the Galleria either. If he didn't come through with some hard evidence, Lindsey would remain an open file. He felt he owed her more.

"What's ole Dustin like?" Decker asked.

"A sleazebag," said Hollander taking off his jacket. He pulled up a chair and sat down, his widespread buttocks overflowing the seat. "Wouldn't trust him to clip my hangnail."

"What'd you ask him?"

"Well, first thing I do is try to develop the old rapport. Told him his jacket was pretty sharp. Next thing I know, I'm getting a goddam fashion lecture on where to buy clothes. He knows this fart and that putz who'll give him fifty percent off on all Italian silk imports. The upshot of the whole thing is the guy loves to play teacher. So I'll play the dupe. Maybe we'll get lucky and he'll talk himself into a corner. But no dice."

"You wouldn't put it past him to make snuffs?" Decker asked.

"Hell, no. I wouldn't put it past him. Guy has radar eyes. Always trying to size you up then figure out his angle."

"What did he tell you about his dad?"

"Hasn't talked to Daddy in months. They aren't as close as they used to be."

"Maybe we can pull out phone bills that says he has."

"So what?"

"Well, if it were to show lots of calls between the two of them, at least we'd establish Dustin as a liar."

"Then what?"

Decker shrugged. "I don't know."

"We'd prove what I already instinctively know," said Hollander. "The guy's an asshole."

"What did Dustin think about Daddy's sideline in porno stills?" he asked.

"Dustin got pissed at that one—claimed that Daddy is just a downhome country photographer. If Daddy ever did anything nasty like that, it was just to feed his poor li'l chilluns!"

"How dare we besmirch Daddy's blemishless image!" Decker mocked.

"You'd better believe it. Guy was ready to call in the ACLU. I calmed him down. I asked him what kind of car he drove. Guy chewed my ear off on the marvels of the Mercedes."

Mike scratched his nose, thought a moment, then said, "The guy plainly likes his father. He didn't say much about his mother."

"You asked him about the fire?"

"Yep. He said this. Mom got drunk a lot. She was very careless about drinking and smoking in bed. More than once he had to pull her out of smoldering bedcovers. Most of the time he'd gotten her out before any real damage was done. Once in awhile, the room was really smoking and he had to call the FD. The day she died he wasn't home.

"He spoke about his mother in a real detached way, Pete. I don't know. Maybe it was because she died so long ago."

"Or maybe he was real pissed off at her for setting the house on fire," Decker suggested.

"Yeah," Hollander nodded. "I didn't detect much love lost."

"What about Pode's limited partnership movies?" Decker wanted to know.

"Pode and this partner of his," Hollander began. "What the hell was his name?"

"Cameron Smithson."

"That's the one," Hollander said. "They invested in low-budget flicks. Grade B horror movies and teenage jiggle films. I asked if it was possible to see them. I wanted to make sure they were what he said they were."

"That was smart."

"He showed me the videos—as much as I wanted to see. And what I saw wasn't porno: just a lot of healthy looking babes showing off their boobs and buns. Standard R fare. Pode also let me look at the books. Some of those turkeys even netted him some pocket money."

"Numbers can be fudged."

"Yeah, no doubt the sleaze has at least four sets of books: one for his accountant, one for the backers, one for the IRS, and one for himself."

Hollander scratched his nose again.

"I can't put my finger on why I hated him so much. Yeah, he talked down to me, but I was feeding into his image of me as the dumb cop. He wasn't an ornery bastard. He was cooperative, polite. He seemed so . . . so goddam oily. Even his looks—Pode's a good-looking guy if you like the male model type. I could see him getting laid by a lot of Marina airheads. But to me, the guy sizes up as a grease ball."

"Did he have the kind of good looks that could sway an impressionable young girl?"

"Definitely."

He went over the play in his mind. Act One: Lindsey meets Chris, who introduces her to fellow photographer Cecil Pode. Act Two: Cecil sees Lindsey as much more than a would-be model for *Playboy*. Act Three: Cecil introduces her to his son, Dustin. Act Four: Dustin seduces her and convinces her to star in his skin flicks. Act Five: Lindsey dies, maybe because she didn't like what she was doing and Dustin had a low tolerance for recalcitrant actresses; maybe because she starred in a snuff; maybe because she was in the wrong fire at the wrong time—like Dustin's mother.

A whole lot of maybes.

Why would she bother to make arrangements to meet Chris at the Galleria if she was going to run away with Dustin? Did Lindsey ask Cecil to get Chris out of the way so she could run away with Dustin and throw suspicion on Chris? Poor Chris. Decker could still feel the boy in his arms, cradling him like a baby as he sobbed. And what gasping sobs—like a dying man fighting for air.

He needed the Podes. Cecil was gone. Dustin was all he had.

# ·15

Discretion was the word of the hour. Hollander's interview with Dustin Pode had been a double-edged sword. Decker hoped it would smoke out Dustin and make him do something foolish, but he also knew that it had heightened Pode's awareness of cops. The tail would have to be close to invisible.

He debated over which car to use. Although it had a police radio, the unmarked was a terrible vehicle for a tail, a giveaway to anyone perceptive about cop cars. His personal vehicles were a red '69 Porsche 911, which he'd rebuilt, and a Jeep. Neither blended inconspicuously in street traffic. Finally, he settled on Rina's '77 bronze Volvo station wagon and gave her the Plymouth. He carried his beeper and had asked Marge to buzz him if anything important came up. He hoped all his bases were covered.

So far, the only place Pode had gone to was work. Decker parked a couple of stalls down from the broker's white Mercedes 450 SL on level C of the underground garage. The place was dank, the air loaded with exhaust fumes, and he felt a headache coming on. He sat in his car for an hour, then wanting to stretch his legs, climbed the stairs to the fifth floor. The hallways were empty and soundless except for an occasional inner door closing or a ding from the elevator bell. He leaned against the wall and waited. Another hour passed. At 11:15, Dustin finally came out of his office. From a corner, Decker had a good chance to memorize his face as he waited for the elevator.

Mike was right. The younger Pode was a good-looking man. Five eleven, one seventy or eighty, and well built. An iron pumper, his chest swelled under his shirt, big shoulders. Coiffed dark hair with a full mustache. A deep sunlamp tan. His face was lean with a sloped nose and deep-set dark eyes under dark brows.

Tall, dark, and handsome with little resemblance to his father. As soon as Dustin stepped inside the elevator, Decker rushed down the stairwell to his car. He pulled out of the space a couple of seconds after the Mercedes.

Pode's destination was Beverly Hills—lunch at La Ragazzina Boutique, a one-room Italian restaurant jammed with a mixture of businessmen, entertainment hangers-on, and women shoppers with acute ennuitis just dying for a little attention. It was a good place in which to observe Pode because everyone was either self-absorbed or wanted to be noticed. Decker found a spot at the end of the tiny bar and ordered a club soda.

Pode sat in a dark red booth in the corner opposite the bar. Five minutes later Cameron Smithson joined him with two other suits. The four of them talked animatedly for a while, until Cameron pulled out a briefcase. Within moments, the table was covered with papers.

Decker glanced at his watch. Half a day shot. Maybe Morrison was right. This *was* a waste of manpower. He got up and found a pay phone occupied by a lady with the hands of a fifty-year-old but the face of a woman twenty years younger. Good lift. Her hair was as orange as his, but her color came from a bottle. Rechecking his watch, he grew impatient with the woman's blabbering and glanced over to Pode's table.

The pile of papers had grown.

Finally, she hung up. Turning around, the woman smiled at him and reached for his hair. Instinctively, he backed away.

She let out a chuckle.

"It's natural, isn't it?"

"Yes."

"Lucky boy." She turned around and caught the headwaiter's eye.

"Tony!" she purred huskily, spreading out her arms widely and embracing the tuxedoed Hispanic.

The hug didn't help her get a table any faster. Smiling all the way, ole Tony led her to the bar.

Decker dialed the station and Marge told him there had been no new developments—the warrants hadn't been approved yet, the X-rays from Oregon hadn't arrived. She had decided to put the case in abeyance for the moment and work on another that had just come over the line.

Swell!

Yesterday, the case had been hot, but now a definite chill was settling in. Goddam it, Lindsey deserved more.

An hour later Pode left the restaurant. Decker followed him to the Rox-San building, five blocks from where he'd eaten. More waiting. He pulled out his lunch—a chunk of kosher salami with crackers and nothing to drink. He'd made his own brown bag today. The garlic lingered on his breath and he became irritable.

If nothing came of this, he'd have to go back to Hollywood, and a return to scuzzville didn't thrill him. Lately the crap was beginning to get to him. The dichotomy—one minute he was a spiritual being, praying, seeking a higher order in his life; the next, knee deep in scum and shit. He was living in two worlds, not sure which part of his life was real and which was an undercover assignment.

Pode left an hour later and returned to Executive First. He was there for another twenty minutes, then came out with a gym bag. Decker followed him to the Sports Connection.

More cooling of the heels outside the health club.

At least the view was good. He stared at the leotard-clad women going in and out of the gym. Good bodies, but too sharp-edged, too muscular for his taste. He liked his women softer, with curves—like Rina.

He was in a pisser of a mood—angry with himself. Time was a precious commodity, and he'd blown a whole day and ended up with nothing more tangible than air. Yeah, maybe Cecil had contacted his son, maybe Dustin did set him up somewhere and slip him a little bread. But if anything had happened, it'd probably taken place already and the two weren't going to do him any favors and meet in front of his eyes.

He'd finish out the day, and if nothing panned out, he'd try a last ditch stake at Pode's studio tonight. If all of his efforts failed, he'd have to try a different approach.

On impulse, he opened the glove compartment in Rina's car. It contained maps and scribbled scraps of paper—grocery lists and reminders to herself—written half in Hebrew, half in English. He smiled at her penmanship, visualizing her delicate hand dashing off a note, at the look of intensity on her face as she wrote. Once, he'd seen her topless—just for a moment. It had been an accident. Jacob had spilled ketchup on her blouse and she'd changed in the bathroom, closing but not locking the door. He'd had to use the bathroom, had opened the door and there she was. She'd covered herself in the same instant he'd closed the door, but he'd seen her. It demonstrated to him once and for all that she wasn't a china doll, but was made of flesh—like him. They both had been embarrassed when she'd emerged and neither one had ever mentioned it. But now, engulfed in loneliness, the recollection helped ease the pain.

He had the luck of the Irish, Hennon had said. Ironic for a Jew who'd been raised Baptist. Cecil Pode showed up at his studio a little after midnight. Shrouded in the lacy shadows of an elm, Decker saw his fat face looking greasy and white under the artificial lighting of the street lamp. The photographer was fumbling with his keys trying to unlock the studio. He threw a furtive glance over his shoulder, then managed to open the door.

*How to proceed,* Decker thought. *Catch him on his way out. No sense gangbusting your way in with no warrant. Any incriminating evidence will be inadmissible without proper search and seizure.*

Fifteen minutes later Pode came out with a canvas bag slung over his shoulder. He was about to lock up when Decker made his move, his footsteps soundless.

"Police, Mr. Pode." Decker stuck his foot in the door.

Pode gasped, then saw who it was and exhaled loudly. "You scared the shit out of me. What the hell is this?"

"I'd like to talk with you for a moment, Cecil," Decker said.

"What about? It's after midnight, for Chrissakes. Can't it wait until the morning?"

"No."

"You got a warrant?"

"No," Decker answered. "Last I heard you don't need one for talking."

Pode paused. Decker could feel the fat man's brain straining in indecision.

"Come in," Pode said, shutting the door behind them.

Out of the corner of his eye, Decker caught the glint of steel. Instincts took over. He pounced on Pode as the gun cracked out cordite that sprayed black onto his jacket. The revolver flew out of Pode's hand and skittered across the linoleum.

"You *motherfucker!*" Decker yelled, pinning the squirming hulk to the floor. Underneath the fat was a layer of muscle. It was a bitch trying to contain him and find the handcuffs at the same time. Pode bucked up forcibly, throwing Decker off balance, and made a crawl toward the gun. Decker grabbed the back of his shirt and slammed his face against the ground.

"I don't believe it!" he said, clamping on the metal bracelets. He took a deep breath. "You tried to shoot me, you stupid ass! You're under arrest!"

"Oh Christ!" the man began to blubber.

"You have the right to remain silent. If you give up this right, anything you say may be used against you in a court of law—"

"Oh Jesus Fucking Christ!"

"You have the right to legal counsel during questioning—"

"I can get you what you want, Decker."

"If you can't afford an attorney—"

"I can get it for you right now, but it's not on me. I gotta make a phone call."

"One will be appointed to you by a court of law before questioning—"

"I can get the film, Decker! The film you want."

"Do you understand your rights, Pode?"

"I know where it is."

"DO YOU FUCKING UNDERSTAND THE RIGHTS I JUST READ TO YOU?"

The fat man nodded.

"Say yes, Pode," Decker said. "Say: yes, I understand my rights."

"Yes, I understand my rights. I can get you what you want, but I gotta have a deal."

"If you wish to waive your right to—"

"Yeah, I wish to waive everything so long as I get a deal—"

Decker hoisted the man to his feet and pushed him against the wall, leaning hard into the small of his back. "You motherfucking son of a bitch, you are in deep shit. You know what you just did? You tried to whack an officer of the law with no provocation whatsoever after he properly identified himself. That's a fucking no-no." Decker gave him a roundhouse punch to the left kidney. Pode let out a gush of air and moaned. "Now I've got to see some good faith before I talk deal. Where's the film, Pode?"

"I don't know the address."

Decker rammed his knee into the right kidney. Pode screamed.

"I swear I don't know the address," he sputtered. "But I can take you there. I just know the place. We changed the location after you started poking around."

"This place you're talking about. What is it? A warehouse for your shit?"

"Screening room for the pervs. They're showing the movie you want."

"Which movie's that?" Decker said.

Pode was silent. Decker yanked his hair.

"Remember what I said about good faith and deals?"

Pode nodded.

"What film are we talking about?" Decker asked.

"That girl, the blonde one you showed me—Lindsey Bates."

Decker felt sick. "Go on."

"The film was custom-ordered by a very rich man," Pode said, panting. "He didn't want her specifically. Just someone with her kind of looks—someone pert and fresh."

"What's the perv's name?" Decker asked.

"Don't know."

Decker bashed Pode's face into the wall. His nose and lips began to bleed.

"Jesus Christ!" Pode cried. "I *don't* know. Arrest the son of a bitch and you'll find out."

"Take me there," Decker said.

"I gotta make a call first."

"Bull fucking shit! You just take me there." Decker unhitched his .38 and stuck it in a roll of adipose below the photographer's rib cage. "I'm taking your bag also. Later you can show me what you've got inside."

Pode nodded.

"No funny business, Cecil."

"Right."

"Let's go."

Decker walked him out to the Plymouth, seating him in the passenger side, and secured his feet with an extra set of cuffs. Tossing Pode's bag in the back, he climbed into the driver side and started the engine.

"It's near here," Pode said weakly. "In Venice."

"That how you met Chris Truscott?" Decker asked, turning on the siren and flooring the gas pedal. "You remember him don't you? Free-lance photographer who once lived in Venice."

Pode didn't say anything.

"He said you met him on the boardwalk. Did you meet Lindsey there, too?"

Pode lowered his head.

"We know you kidnapped Lindsey. We know you killed her—"

"I didn't kill her."

"Who did?"

Pode remained silent.

"Good faith, Cecil."

"She was iced in the film," Pode said.

"Who'd you deliver her to?"

"I don't know."

"You're going to fry, Pode."

"I swear I don't know. I left her in a designated spot, locked in this room, doped up. I don't know who took over the show from there. My contacts are by phone, Decker. I never see 'em face-to-face."

"Try convincing a jury of that."

"It's the truth!" Pode implored.

"How far are we to the place, Pode?"

"It's close," he responded in a cracked voice. "Turn left on Pacific."

Decker slowed the car and killed the siren.

"This isn't just Venice, this is the Oakwood ghetto," Decker said. "You wouldn't be trying to set me up, would you, Cecil?"

"I swear this is where they show the films."

"Who's they?"

"I *don't* know!"

"Yeah, right," Decker sneered. "Contacts by phone and all that crap. Why the hell would a rich perv come out here?"

"They all do, Decker. There's a bunch of 'em and they all love to slum. See some sicko films and get all heated up by them. Then they go out trawling for young meat on the streets and act out the fantasy. They're the ones who're sick, not me!"

Decker wanted to puke.

"Turn here," Pode said. "It's on Brooks right before Electric. The garage apartment in the back. Slow . . . that's the house."

It was a tan one-story cube with security bars on the windows and doors. It wasn't unusual to find prisonlike houses here, because the neighborhood was bad—tiny stucco cells or government housing units spray painted with graffiti. Even the streets and sidewalks were tattooed. This was gang heartland and life was expendable. A jaunt from the front door to the driveway could prove fatal if it was a night for busting.

He drove by and saw a faint illumination on top of the garage.

Parking a half block down, he called in for immediate back-up, giving firm instructions to approach without lights or sirens.

"Who's in there, Cecil?"

"Just the perv and a projectionist."

"Who's the projectionist?"

"I just call him Joe."

"What's he armed with?"

"He isn't armed."

*Guy must have a machine gun,* Decker thought.

"Mr. Rich Perv have a bodyguard?"

"Not that I know of."

*Figure at least one guard.*

Two cruisers arrived in less than a minute.

"Stay put, Cecil. Don't try anything dumb."

Decker got out of the Plymouth and briefed the four uniforms. They conferred, and radioed in to their superior. A minute later a bull-necked black cop named Lessing came back to Decker.

"Ordered to go in and take it," he said. "I'll lead."

"It's your territory," Decker said.

"You want in?" Lessing asked.

"You bet," he answered. "Place is probably guarded and armed."

"Let the insider do the talking," suggested a six-foot female who reminded him of Marge. Her partner was toting a shotgun.

"Good idea," agreed Decker. "Pode will get us inside and we'll make the bust. I need that film. It's material evidence for a homicide I'm working on."

"Let's go," Lessing said.

"Fourteen-L-six's here," the woman said, as another black-and-white pulled up.

"We can use all the help we can get," Decker said.

Two more uniforms came up, also carrying shotguns.

"I'll go get our card key," Decker said. He went back to the Plymouth, uncuffed Pode's hands and feet, and pulled him out of the car.

"You've got to get us inside, Cecil. The place is a barbed-wire camp."

Pode nodded. "I'll tell you what to do."

Decker laughed and pushed the fat man forward. "You've got a nutty sense of humor, my man. You're coming with us. But don't worry. You said no one's armed."

They walked the half block, and Pode led the seven officers up the outside stairs to the garage apartment. They took their positions. The entire rear of the structure was a mesh of steel wires and bars. Sitar music was coming from the inside.

"Get us inside," Decker whispered to Pode.

The fat man was bathed in his own sweat.

"I lied," he whispered back. "They have guns."

"How many?"

"Projectionist and bodyguard. They have Uzis."

"Get us inside, Cecil."

"They'll shoot me," he sobbed. "They shoot first and ask questions later."

"Get the door open and we'll protect you," said Lessing.

Looking like a condemned man, Pode gave a signaled knock. They heard a series of knocks and clicks, and then a voice from inside said, "Who is it?"

"Pode. I got another one who was insistent."

"Show started."

"He already paid me big for the viewing," Pode said shakily. "For Chrissakes, just open the door."

Locks began to snap open. Everyone stepped aside. The minute the door showed light, Lessing kicked it open and yelled, "Police! Freeze!" Instantaneously, he pitched backward as if blown away by torrential wind, his stomach gushing a scarlet river.

Pandemonium broke out. Bursts of machine guns. Blasts of shotguns. The pops of the .38s. Screams, blood splattering all over the walls and floors. The exchange of gunfire lasted less than a minute, but its aftermath left a slaughterhouse. Pode was a crumpled pile at the foot of a free-standing movie screen. Another man was sprawled over a puddle of blood at the base of the projector, a hole ripped through his chest, his left arm blown off and propelled five feet to his left. Still another person had exploded into chunks on the south wall of the room. One man was still alive, hunched into a corner, sobbing.

Miraculously, the movie was left intact and kept on rolling.

Decker saw Lindsey's face and was stunned into immobility. She was still alive, but barely, having been sliced in the chest, stomach, and genitals. A red-robed man in white face accented with black lines for whiskers, eyebrows, and mouth was drinking her blood. The Countess, also in a red robe, was smearing it over her face. The painted man took a .38 and shot the girl in the breastbone and forehead. She jerked at each bullet, released her bowels and died. Decker saw the Countess pour clear liquid over her from a metal canister and light a match. Lindsey began to melt, the skin crackling and charring against the sound of a deep, resonant chant.

"Jesus Christ!" someone groaned.

"Someone turn that shit off!" the female cop barked. "Jesus!"

"Holy Mother of God," another cop whispered, shaking his head in disbelief.

The film stopped. Decker threw up.

# $\cdot 16$

He finished the paperwork at 5 A.M. and went home to catch up on sleep. At first there were no dreams, just blackness. But they came later—the images, smells, sounds. He tossed, ripped the sheets, soaked them in sweat. By ten he knew sleep was impossible. Resolution was the best revenge.

He showered, shaved, dressed, and davened hurriedly. Today the prayers held little meaning—words without content. And for the first time in over three months, he ate breakfast at a nonkosher restaurant. Nothing definable as *traif*—no ham or bacon—but he didn't give a flying fuck if the eggs were fried in lard or the bread was baked with animal shortening. He wolfed down three over easy, four pieces of toast, double hash browns, a large orange juice, and three cups of coffee. Afterwards, stomach full, he felt much better and was surprised that his conscience didn't bother him.

Off to the station.

At his desk, he cleaned up the last bits of paperwork, checked his watch, and headed for the viewing room.

The captain shut off the projector and flicked on the lights. Neither he nor Decker spoke. It hadn't been any easier for Decker the second time around. If anything, it had been harder to witness Lindsey's destruction. The scene would be fixed in his memory forever. A curse. But he had to concentrate now on what needed to be done.

The end of the film was the giveaway that Clementine had been right. Something had gone awry. The last few seconds showed a look of horror on the Countess's face and the widening eyes of the painted man. A moment later the Countess clutched her breast and the film ended. Although Decker saw no firearm, no blast of gunfire, and no blood, he knew what had happened. She had been shot. The terror in her eyes was no act.

"Who's the man in the film?" Morrison asked Decker.

"I don't know. I think it's the Countess's accomplice. He goes by the street name Blade, but no one I've talked to knows a thing about him. Only this pimp Clementine."

"Then find Clementine and squeeze him," Morrison said. "Although I doubt if he could make a positive ID based on that film. The guy was painted like an Indian."

"Captain?"

"What?"

"I think the guy's dead."

Morrison sighed heavily.

"It goes like this," said Decker. "The Countess was whacked at the end of the movie. A last minute thing, not part of the script. The guy looked just as surprised as she did. Both of them were probably ripped off and burnt just like the Bates girl, then dumped in the mountains."

"So there should be another bag of bones up there."

"I think so," Decker said.

Morrison digested that.

"Was Pode the film maker?"

"He distributed. He kidnapped Lindsey. But I doubt if he was the brains. Probably a minnow and we're missing the big catch. Goddam nuisance, Pode dying last night." Decker paused. "When's the burial for Officer Lessing?"

"Three o'clock."

"Kids?"

"Two."

"I'll try to make it over," Decker said, looking at his watch. The room was silent.

"Who's the man we brought in last night?" Decker asked. "He had no ID on him."

"They've IDed him. Armand Arlington. As in Arlington Steel."

"Son of a bitch!" Decker exclaimed. "Has he been booked yet?"

Morrison threw his cigarette across the room and swore. "He was charged with possession of marijuana."

"*What!*"

"Sucker's got connections with the right people," Morrison spat out.

"We found at least half a pound of crack," Decker said. "Not to mention all the illegal ammo."

"I wasn't in on the plea bargaining," Morrison said. "But I will say this: Pacific questioned him about the films. Apparently they had nothing to connect him to the murder of Lindsey Bates."

"That's a load of crap!" Decker said. "Cecil Pode said the film was custom-ordered by him."

"Did he mention Arlington by name?"

"Dammit, no."

"So we're nowhere, Pete. Pode's dead, and as far as the books go, it isn't against the law to like revolting films."

"It's against the law to withhold evidence crucial to a murder conviction. We need to know his contact."

"Pacific Division was told that further investigations are now being conducted by a special pornography task force—"

"Give me a fucking break!" Decker said. "Pornography task force? A judge from the old boy's network beating his meat to dirty pictures."

"You're right," agreed the captain. "It's a whitewash. It's shit. But the fact still remains that Arlington's ass is covered by legal eagles. No one can get close to him."

"There are ways," Decker said.

Morrison frowned. "Don't fuck with legal channels, Sergeant. You'll do more harm than good."

"Marijuana," Decker muttered. "Was it a felony possession, at least?"

"Misdemeanor," Morrison said.

"Shit!" Decker lit a cigarette. "I knew I shouldn't have gone to bed this morning."

"There wouldn't have been anything you could have done," Morrison said. "Let Arlington rest and concentrate on finding Clementine."

"Did they ID the other sleaze buckets who were blown away?" asked Decker. "Paper didn't mention their names."

"Hard to ID hamburger, but we finally got a fix on them. The projectionist was a part-time grip named Sylvester Tork. His yellow sheet was longer than the Nile. The other guy was a roofer named Alvin Peppers. Alvin was released from San Quentin three months ago after serving time for assault and a plea-bargained involuntary manslaughter."

"Who hired them?"

"We don't know."

"If someone would lean on Arlington—"

"Don't you think we fucking *tried*?" Morrison exploded. "Jesus, Pete, you're not the only one who feels like shit about the whole thing. I saw the fucking film! I'm a parent! Get down off your high horse before you fall off and get your ass broken."

Decker felt his anger grow. "Well, maybe I, as an individual citizen, can do some things that you, as a police captain, can't."

"You're on your own if you do, Pete. I won't back you up."

"Consider me duly warned."

Morrison gave him a hard stare. "Speaking of warning, you tailed Dustin Pode yesterday. I told you not to do it."

"Who told you?"

"No one," Morrison answered. "Everybody was so busy covering your ass I figured you must be out playing hot dog. I made an educated guess."

The detective said nothing.

"We'll let it pass this time," said Morrison, "but don't fuck around with my orders again."

"Yes, sir."

"Now what did you find out about Dustin Pode?"

"Nothing."

"He's been notified about his father's death. You can question him about Cecil if you want."

Decker cleared his throat and told Morrison about his Jack Cohen alias. As he talked, he could see the captain's expression waver between admiration and disapproval.

"What do you hope to find out?" Morrison asked.

"If Dustin's making sicko films on the side, maybe I could get him to strike a deal with me as an interested investor. He does legit film syndications, which would make it awfully easy to launder some dirty stuff. I'd like to keep my cover and let Hollander continue with the interviewing."

"You leaned on Cecil Pode," Morrison said. "What if he described you to Dustin? You're a pretty noticeable guy. Your cover would be worthless."

Decker groaned inwardly. How could he be so fucking dumb!

"Yeah, that's true," he said. "Look at it this way, Captain. If Dustin makes me for a cop, then we're back to square one. If he doesn't, we've got an advantage. I'll get a better feel after I meet with them."

In the end Morrison agreed it was best for Decker to stay undercover.

The mountain air was biting. Decker buttoned up his overcoat as he watched the teams dig up the hillside. Hard to believe that a month ago he'd camped in this graveyard with Jake and Sammy. The day had been bright and warm, not like today, which was overcast.

The ground became pocked with potholes—aborted digs—but Decker was sure the bones were there. It just didn't make sense to dump the girls out here and leave the guy at another location.

Unless the killer was smart.

"Sergeant Decker!" one of the lab men shouted.

"Yeah?"

"We've found something—a foot bone."

"Attached to anything?"

"No, just a foot bone."

He walked over, bent down, and saw the burnt remains of a foot.

"Wait a minute, wait a minute . . . I think we struck gold," the man said, digging deeper into a mesa of hard-packed soil.

Gradually, the entire remains were exposed. The skeleton appeared to be large—a male. Had to be the Blade. Decker was reassured. Most of the time killers weren't that smart.

Mrs. Bates was in the front yard pruning roses. She raised her head when Decker got out of the car but made no attempt to rise from her squat. He went over to the flower bed and knelt beside her.

"Hello," she said softly. "What do you want, Sergeant?"

"I was in the neighborhood. I thought I'd stop by and see how you're doing."

She snipped off a rose hip and shrugged.

"I like those red ones," Decker said. "Olympiads, aren't they?"

She nodded.

"My mother has a bed of them," he said. "She's a big gardener."

Mrs. Bates said nothing.

"She says it's her therapy," Decker continued. "Claims the world wouldn't need shrinks if everyone would just grow things instead."

"I can understand that," Mrs. Bates whispered.

He watched her trim the bushes for a minute.

She asked, "Does your mother live out here?"

"No. Florida."

"There's plenty of sunshine over there also."

"That's true," he said. "But Gainsville also has a lot of humidity. You can't beat L.A. for weather. I've tried to tell my mom that, but she and my dad are settled where they are."

"It's hard to . . . adjust . . . to new things," Mrs. Bates said in a cracked voice. "What . . ." She swallowed back tears. "What brought you out to Los Angeles?"

"My ex-wife's family and a job in a law firm. I thought I wanted to be a lawyer. I'd been a cop in Florida for eight years and I'd convinced myself that it was time for a change."

"You didn't like law?" She blushed. "I don't mean to pry—"

"You're not prying," Decker said, smiling. "No, I didn't like law. Not the kind I was practicing anyway. But I'm glad I moved. It's worked out well for me here."

She pricked her finger on a thorn, said "ouch," stuck the finger in her mouth, and sucked.

"I'm distracting you," Decker said.

"No," she protested. "Really, I'm fine. I should have worn gloves."

"How's Erin?" Decker asked.

"She's . . . fine. More subdued. More serious." She faced him. "Have you . . . learned anything new?"

His throat became dry. The police had reported the ordeal of last night to the press as a drug bust—an officer-involved shooting during the raid on a rock house. Decker had insisted upon it. The thought of the Bateses waking up to front-page headlines that splashed out the gory death of their daughter nauseated him.

But he could break it to her now. Tell her gently. Ease the shock of the horrible news to come. She'd have to know eventually. That was originally why he'd come out to visit her. But now, seeing her like this . . . To tell her what he knew, what he'd seen . . . He couldn't do it.

He cursed his cowardice.

"Just bits now," he answered. "But don't you worry, Mrs. Bates. I'm going to nail the bastard."

"My husband would like that. Justice and all that kind of thing. I don't think much about justice. It drives me crazy when I think of how unfair it all is, so I don't think about it. I just want to pick up the pieces and go on. But my husband . . . he's consumed with the idea of revenge." She went back to snipping. "I suppose I shouldn't tell you this, but he's trying to solve this thing himself."

"What has he come up with?"

"Nothing. He's fixated on the idea that Chris . . . Did I tell you about Chris?"

The boy's sobs echoed in Decker's head. "I know who he is," he said.

"My husband seems convinced that Chris is guilty."

"What do you think?"

"I think my husband needs someone to blame and Chris is convenient. I never liked the boy, but . . ."

"You don't think Chris had anything to do with it?"

"No. And I think my husband is driving the boy crazy. He calls him all the time, writes him letters, follows him all weekend and on his lunch hours. I can't seem to convince him that this is all wrong. He's obsessed, Sergeant. My husband is going insane."

Decker placed a hand on her shoulder.

"I'm sorry," he said.

She continued her gardening. Neither spoke for a while. Then Decker stood up.

"I'll keep in touch," he said. "Take care, Mrs. Bates."

She snipped off a longstemmed Olympiad rosebud. Without looking up, she handed it to him.

Praying didn't cut it. He slipped the pocket siddur back in his jacket and took off to a house of refuge he'd used in the past.

It had once been a topless joint, but for the last five years it was a cop's bar. He waved to a few of the off-duty uniforms sitting at a corner table laughing, then seated himself on a stool at the far end of the counter. A two-year hiatus since he'd last been here, and he'd come back to the same damn bartender polishing the same damn glasses. He acknowledged Decker with a nod.

"What'll it be, Pete?" he asked.

"Double scotch straight up." Decker took out a cigarette. He was smoking too much, he was going to drink too much, and he didn't give a shit. "How's it going, Pat?"

"Nothin' much has changed since you been in here last."

Decker looked around. The walls had been repainted a dark red and the linoleum was new. The honey oak tables and chairs were the same, a little more worn. Same plastic light fixtures hanging from the ceiling. The pool table had been refelted—red this time. Country music wailed from a corner jukebox—Bocefus moaning about an attitude adjustment. The place was still a bar.

Decker took a sip, then a healthy swig of his scotch. He glanced up at the TV set—a soccer game from Mexico. He'd never liked soccer much, but after watching Rina's boys play, he'd developed an appreciation for it. He leaned against the bar and listened to the TV announcer rattle off a blow-by-blow of the previous quarter. Decker understood it all, his Spanish as fluent as ever. He had first learned the language as a beat cop in Miami in order to decipher all the bullshit the Cubans gave him. Man, could they bullshit!

His glass was empty and he ordered another.

He'd joined the LAPD after his brief fling as a lawyer, and they'd sent him straight to East L.A. A goddam mistake. Latinos didn't trust a white boy who understood their tongue. He'd always be a spy, and try as he would, he could never ingratiate himself. The hell with 'em.

He drank the booze and set down the empty glass.

Ed Fordebrand materialized. He was wearing a red-and-green plaid sports shirt, brown slacks, polished oxfords, and a tan leather jacket.

"What the hell are you doing here, Deck?"

"What the fuck does it look like?"

"You and Rina had a—"

"No." Decker ordered a third scotch.

"The bones in the mountains turned out messy, huh, Rabbi?"

"I'm not a fucking rabbi," Decker snapped. He took a gulp of whiskey and finally began to feel a glow. He slapped Fordebrand on the back. "Let me buy you one, Ed."

"Won't turn it down."

"How's Annette?"

"Getting old and crotchety. On my ass, day and night." Fordebrand ordered a bourbon and Seven. "But we're used to each other. I'm not saying divorce hasn't crossed my mind. Or hers for that matter. Seems we just never got around to it. Linda's almost out of the house. She's the last of them. We'll see what happens then."

Pat wiped the counter and placed the bourbon in front of Fordebrand.

"Drink up," Decker said. "I'll buy you another."

"One a day is my ration. I run into problems if I don't stick to it." Fordebrand eyed Decker. "You never were much of a boozer, were you, Pete?"

Decker shook his head and ordered another. "Usually I work instead. Now I'm here to avoid work. And nothing waiting for me at home except piles of horseshit."

"What about Rina?"

"What about her?" Decker's expression soured. "Why bother talking to them, you know? All they do is get all worried and start prying, and pretty soon you're telling things they can't handle, and then all you've got is a hysterical woman on your hands."

Fordebrand paused a moment, then said, "I only met her a couple of times, but Rina never seemed to be the hysterical type."

"They're all hysterical, Ed. Just give 'em time. Jan wasn't *that* hysterical at first either, but later . . ." He laughed. "A fucking Camille! Everything was such a big goddam deal."

He drank up and ordered a Dos Equis chaser. Fordebrand watched him down the suds.

"Let me drive you home," he said.

"I'm not drunk," Decker protested. "Not nearly drunk enough. You gonna drink with me or you gonna be my mother?"

"I'm not going to do either one. I've got to go."

Decker nodded. "Regards to Annette."

Fordebrand left. And then the girls started to filter in. Decker drank a fourth, fifth, and sixth double as he watched them play their mating rituals with the uniform boys. He liked to observe, watch the boobs fall out of the loosely draped tops, see the nipples jutting against the fabric, the long shapely legs poking out from the miniskirts, the tight asses scrunched into jeans, hair loose, free and brassy—all of them heavily made-up and smelling of too much perfume.

Through a boozy haze, he saw a babe approach him. A tall one with a full head of platinum curls. Gold hoops dangled from her ears and her eyes were painted purple. She wore a gray, deliberately torn T-shirt that fell off one shoulder, and sprayed-on jeans that outlined her ass and crotch. Smiling, she took a seat next to him.

"Buy me a drink?"

He signaled Pat over.

"What's your pleasure?" Decker asked.

"Gin and tonic."

Pat nodded.

"Give me another scotch, will ya?"

"I haven't seen you here before," she started out.

Decker lit a cigarette.

"I haven't been here in a long time."

"Are you a cop?"

He laughed.

"Sometimes they call me that."

"Don't tell me," the woman said cocking her head to one side. "You look like a detective."

Decker smiled.

She gently bit her lower lip. "And I'd say you work in Robbery or maybe GTA."

"Juvey and Sex Crimes," he corrected her.

The girl wrinkled her nose. "Sex Crimes! I hear it's the worst! All those disgusting rapists."

"Rapists are disgusting . . . What's your name?"

"Nadine. What's yours?"

"Pete."

"Nice to meet you, Pete." She stuck out her hand and he took it. It was warm and soft. She pulled it away and took a sip of her tonic.

"So what brings you here, Pete?"

"Atmosphere."

"Are you married?"

He hesitated a moment.

"No."

Nadine laughed.

"Oh yes you are. I can spot 'em."

He chuckled.

"All right, I am."

"S'okay," she said. "I'm just interested in a fun night anyway."

His eyes scanned her body. One word and he had company for the evening. A warm woman in his bed. He felt hot. What did he owe to Rina anyway? What did he owe to anyone? Man, he was roasting. He could feel the smoke rising, enveloping him. It was fucking *burning* him!

"Shit!" The girl jumped up. "Your jacket's on fire."

He bolted off the stool and pounded on his right jacket pocket. A cigarette ember had spat fire onto his threads.

"Holy fucking shit!" he yelled, smothering the flames with his bare palm. It left a blackened hole in the tweed and had burnt the first pages of his pocket siddur. Decker stuffed the ruined prayer book in his other pocket. The girl was giggling.

"You okay?" she said, holding her hand over her mouth.

"Yeah."

"C'mon," she chirped. "Let's get outta here before you burn the place down."

"I'm going home," he said disgustedly. "Maybe some other time, okay?"

The girl stopped laughing.

"C'mon," she said, tugging at his jacket sleeve. He jerked away violently, and she stepped backward, frightened. Without a word, he slapped some bills on the countertop, turned around, and left.

As he drove home, the images grew stronger. The smoky stench of his jacket polluted the car, made it stifling. He threw open the windows and allowed a blast of cold air to hit his face, but still he sweated profusely. The images became real—fire, the stink of rotting flesh. Long buried memories surfaced. Nam. Tracers lighting up the sky. Blood and bursts of rocket fire. Dismembered bodies.

Stopthebleedingtreatemforshockgetemtoachopper. He shook his head fiercely. His mind segued to the ravaged young faces at Hotel Hell. And to Lindsey, her flesh darkening, oozing, cooking in the flames. He closed his eyes for a moment, but the nightmare stayed.

A horn honked, reminding him that the car was drifting into oncoming traffic. He jerked the wheel around and nearly side-swiped the vehicle on his right. Flooring the gas pedal, he raced over to the yeshiva, managing to get there unharmed.

It was nearly midnight, the place calm and peaceful. He banged loudly on her door, the knocks echoing in the quiet.

"Who's there?" he heard her say, startled.

He had scared her.

"Peter," he whispered. But she didn't hear him and repeated her question, her voice small and frightened.

"It's Peter," he said again.

She unbolted the door.

"You scared— What's wrong?"

He stepped inside and began to pace.

"I burned it," he said, wiping off sweat with a jacket sleeve.

"It's all right," she soothed him. "Calm down and tell me what happened."

He grabbed at his hair and pulled it.

"You don't understand. I burned it with my goddam cigarette." He took out the siddur and threw it on the floor.

She bent down and picked it up. An angel, he thought. Under her open robe he could see a diaphanous white nightgown. He could make out the outline of her body, but nothing more.

"Sit down, honey," she said quietly. "Let me get dressed. Then we can talk."

He grabbed her arm.

"You've got to believe me! It was an accident! I didn't mean it!"

She leaned over to stroke his clenched hand and recoiled involuntarily. His breath.

"I know you didn't. It's okay, Peter. You're okay."

"I didn't fucking mean to do it! It was an *accident*! I didn't mean to burn *it* or *her* or *anyone!*" The sweat began to drip off of his forehead and nose. "I'm so fucking sorry."

"It's okay." She brought him to her breast and embraced him. He threw his arms around her neck and nuzzled against her ear.

"Hold me, Rina," he said, kissing her cheek, her neck. He pulled her nightgown off her shoulder and exposed the delicate white skin, kissing it, licking it, gently biting the sweet smelling flesh.

"Love me, baby," he said softly. "Please love me tonight."

Even before he was fully awake, he knew he was going to be sick. His main concern was making it to the bathroom. Upon opening his eyes, he realized to his horror that he wasn't in his bedroom. He looked around without moving his head. The room was faintly familiar, but her fragrance was pervasive. Rina's bedroom.

He had no memory of how he got there.

He was stripped down to his underwear, tucked under smooth soft sheets that urged him to go back to sleep. But his stomach lurched, letting him know that if he didn't find a toilet soon, he'd upchuck in the bed. The house was quiet. Hopefully, no one was home and he could make a dash for the bathroom without being seen.

Forcing his body upright, his head spinning, he stood on his feet, buckled, but didn't fall. On the second try, his feet were able to hold his weight and he staggered to the bathroom and knelt over the toilet. His guts caved in and afterwards he felt much better. On the bathroom counter were a hand towel, an electric shaver, and a bottle of aspirin. After downing two tablets and rinsing out his mouth, he washed his face and neck and shaved. Back in the bedroom, he found a set of tefillin and a siddur resting on the dresser. His clothes had been neatly draped over the back of an easy chair. On top of them were his gun and holster, and a note from Rina.

*Coffee's on the stove. Juice is in the refrigerator. Key's in the door. Lock up and leave it in the mailbox when you leave.*

He picked up the phylacteries but put them back down. Empty words. No sense being a hypocrite.

He poured himself a cup of coffee. What the hell had happened between them last night? He remembered the feel of her skin, remembered that he'd kissed her, but beyond that it was a blank. Not even a blur—a blank.

He had wanted her so much. And now to think they might have made love and he had no memory of it.

Life wasn't fucking fair!

He checked his watch. It was close to ten. Morrison had told him to take a day off, but he was too keyed up. Might as well proceed.

Clementine had disappeared, no one Decker talked to had ever heard of the Blade, he couldn't find Kiki, and nobody recognized the painted dude in the red robe.

A total bust.

He slumped in his chair and rubbed his bloodshot eyes. Marge approached him.

"Not going too well, Rabbi?"

"It's going shitty, Marge."

"Well, I've got some good news."

Decker perked up.

"It has nothing to do with the case," she said. "Marriot and Bartholomew have returned to their posts. We're back in Juvey and Sex Crimes."

Decker tossed her a dirty look.

"Well, at least our victims can talk," she pointed out.

"This case is eating at me."

"No one's stealing it from you, Pete. No one wants it. Stop being so hard on yourself. You took two bags of bones, identified them, and solved the Bates murder—"

"I don't know who killed the Countess."

"You know how Lindsey Bates was killed. Who gives a damn how the Countess bit it? She deserved to die."

"I have to find out who's behind it all. We can't let this happen again."

Marge sighed. "You're right. So what's your next step?"

"Damned if I know." He snapped a pencil in two.

"By the way, Pete. Dr. Hennon called. She says Armbruster and the Countess are a match, just as we thought."

Decker bolted out of his chair. "I just had a brainstorm. I've got to go down to the morgue and borrow a skull."

"Who do the teeth belong to?" Hennon asked over the phone.

"I'm betting it's the guy in the snuff film I told you about," Decker said.

"But you don't know the man's true identity?"

"No idea."

"So how am I supposed to match him up with the teeth?"

"I'm cutting a few stills out of the movie and I'm going to bring them over to you. Remember the photographic match you did on Armbruster before you got definitive results with the teeth X-rays? How you lined up the cranium with the photo—"

"I don't like to give an opinion based on photographic matches alone. It's too easy to make a mistake."

"I just want to see if the bones I found in the foothills match this creep in the movie. I'd like to see if I'm on the right track. Please, Annie."

"I don't know when I can do it. I'm booked solid."

"I've got the skull. I'll send it by, along with the stills. We'll pay you extra for your time."

"That's not the point. The living before the dead, Pete." She paused. "I'll work it in somehow."

"You're a doll. I owe you one."

"How about dinner?" Hennon suggested. "Just between friends? Or is that against your dietary laws?"

He should have kiboshed the invitation immediately, but something held him back. Goddam it, he wanted to go out on a normal date and eat normal food with a nice-looking woman. What was wrong with that? Just between friends.

"There are exceptions," he said calmly. "Maybe we can work something out."

He felt guilty as soon as he hung up the phone.

"Have a seat," Rina said. "We're just starting dinner."

"I'm not hungry," said Decker. "I just came over to say thanks."

"Please." She pulled out a chair at the kitchen table.

Decker sat down. She handed him a yarmulke and he put it on without a word.

She placed a steaming bowl of creamy fish chowder in front of him. The soup was thick with chunks of white halibut, bits of diced potatos, and lots of onions. In the middle of the table were slices of thick-crusted garlic bread, buttery and full of cheese. Rina poured him a bottle of chilled Dos Equis.

"I'm really not hungry," he repeated.

"Don't eat," she said, quietly.

He stared at the soup, smelling its rich aroma. He *was* hungry. He was *starved*. But he refused to eat. He was acting like an asshole and didn't know why. He was the one who'd shown up drunk as a skunk, acting like a lunatic. Why was he mad at Rina? And why the hell hadn't he told Annie no?

Times like this reminded him that his divorce was a two-way street. He could hear Jan's voice. *You're self-destructive, Peter.* Her favorite word—*self-destructive*. She'd used it the day he'd quit the law practice; she'd used it the day she'd kicked him out of the house.

The boys slurped the last of their chowder and gave him sidelong glances. Quiet. He was making everyone uncomfortable. He stood up.

"I've really got to go, Rina."

"Boys, I want to talk to Peter alone for a minute," Rina said. "Please go to your room."

"We didn't *bentch* yet, Eema," Sammy said.

"The *avayrah*'s on me," Rina answered.

The boys left quickly.

Decker said nothing. Any remark would come out trite or stupid.

"Peter, what upset you so last night?"

He rubbed his chin and realized what a lousy job her electric shaver had done on him this morning. For some odd reason, it embarrassed him to be scruffy in front of her.

"Sometimes my work gets to me," he answered.

"Are you still working on the bones?" she asked.

"Yes. I don't want to talk about it."

"At least will you sit down while *I'm* talking to you?"

He sat back down.

"I'm acting like a jerk, Rina. I do that when I'm under pressure. I'm sorry."

She patted his hand. "It's okay. I'm sorry you had a bad day . . . or night. I wish I could help you. If you'd tell me about it, maybe—"

"Just drop it, Rina."

He was hurting her. He saw it in her eyes. She said nothing.

"I won't barge in on you like that again," he said. "It was an exception."

"It's all right."

"Thanks for taking in a stray dog."

"You're not a stray dog, Peter. You're the man I love."

*Tell her you love her, damn it.*

He smiled weakly and was silent.

*Withholding son of a bitch. Why are you doing this to her?* He ran his fingers through his hair.

"What happened between us last night, Rina?"

She stared at him for clarification.

"I had a blackout," he said. "Did we make love?"

She shook her head.

"You groped around a little, then passed out on the living room floor. I was scared to death. At first I thought you had a heart attack, but, *baruch Hashem,* you started snoring."

He rolled his eyes.

"How'd I get into the bedroom?"

"I'm not as weak as you think I am," she said, quietly.

"You *carried* me?"

"Dragged you."

"You should have left me on the floor to sleep it off," he reprimanded her. "Why risk straining your back?"

Her patience suddenly snapped.

"Peter, for goodness sake, what if the boys would have seen you like *that?*"

He looked down.

"You slept on the couch?"

She nodded. "It's comfortable. I've slept on it many times when I've had company."

"Okay. I'll go now."

"Wait, I almost forgot." She opened a drawer and pulled out a pocket siddur, not unlike the one he had burned. But this one was covered with silverplate and studded with blue stones. She handed it to him and he thumbed through the pages.

"It's beautiful. Thank you very much. I'll try to take better care of this one."

"Don't put it in a glass case and treat it like an object of art. *Use* it, Peter. Use it until it falls apart. It will help you—"

"I don't need any help, Rina."

"That's ridiculous. Everyone needs help."

*You're going to start an argument unless you shut your mouth,* he warned himself.

He stood up and placed the siddur in his pocket.

"Thanks," he repeated.

Walking out to his car, he stopped a few feet away from the unmarked. The guilt trip wasn't over yet. The Rosh Yeshiva was standing against the car, holding a volume of Talmud and reading in the dark with the aid of a penlight.

Shit!

"H'lo, Rabbi," Decker said. "I assume you'd like to talk to me?"

"Take me for a ride, Peter," the old man answered, turning off the light.

Decker opened the door for him, then went around and settled in the driver's seat. He drove out of the grounds and onto the mountain road, the Rosh Yeshiva sitting impassively beside him. The silence was suffocating. The rabbi took out a silver case and pulled out two handmade cigarettes. He lit the first one, gave it to Decker, and lit the second one for himself. The man's profile was as chiseled and intense as a Rodin sculpture.

They rode on, smoking wordlessly until the old man finally spoke:

"You slept at Rina Miriam's house," he said, quietly.

The old guy had eyes behind his head.

"She slept on the couch," answered Decker.

The Rosh Yeshiva's voice hardened. "Do you think for one moment I had assumed that you had slept *with* her?"

Decker said nothing.

"And because you didn't, do you expect praise?"

The detective remained silent.

"If you were just a gentile converting to please the woman he loved, I would have *never* started with you, Peter. *Never*! But that's not the case. You're a biological Jew who has had his heritage ripped away from him by a quirk of fate. I checked into your adoption, Peter. Your birth mother had arranged for you to go to a Jewish family, but there was a bureaucratic snafu and you were placed in the wrong agency."

"It was the right agency," Decker said harshly. "I have terrific parents."

"I'm sure you do," Schulman answered. "And they did a wonderful job raising you. But that's not the point."

Decker waited for the old man to continue.

"Four months ago you came to me, saying you were interested in finding out about Judaism. Yes, Rina was the catalyst, but you told me it went deeper than that, and I believed you. Now I wonder about your sincerity, if maybe you weren't snowing me just to get to Rina."

"That's not true."

"Perhaps. But even if that were the case, I wouldn't have acted any differently. I was anxious for you to discover your roots, even if it meant hardening my ears to gossip. After all, to the world, you have not officially converted and you are still a gentile. I say nothing as you openly court a religious woman on the yeshiva's premises. But your actions of last night! You've gone too far!"

"Look, Rabbi. I'm sorry if I embarrassed you by sleeping over Rina's house. It won't happen again. I told her that, too. Sometimes my work affects me and makes me do impulsive things."

Schulman's face remained stony.

"You're not the only person with enormous responsibilities, Peter. You're not the only person who has come into contact with the worst elements of human nature. And you're not the only person to have suffered pain. The dilemma you face is how best to cope with adversity, and you need help, my friend. You need guidance and you need comfort."

The old man's eyes turned to fire. He took out a pocket siddur and slapped it on Decker's chest.

"*This* is where you find *comfort*! *This* is where you find *guidance*! You open your heart; you beseech *Hashem* to give you the strength and understanding to make it through another day, for He alone can give you peace. *Hakadosh Baruch Hu! Hashem*. Not a woman who will pat you on the hand and say 'there, there,' comforting you as she would a child who's skinned a knee."

"I tried praying—"

"You didn't try hard enough!"

"Sometimes you need more!"

"And you expect to find relief for your soul in the arms of a woman? Or worse, from a bottle?"

The words tore through Decker. Rina had betrayed him. He had come to her for solace and she had turned his pain into a matter for public scrutiny.

"She told you," he said bitterly.

"She's conscious of the reputation of our institution."

"Well, now I know where her loyalties lie."

"Loyalties!" The old man blew smoke out the window. "You have no faith in *Hashem*. You can't possibly have faith in human beings—even those you love. Do you honestly think that Rina Miriam called me up and told me you arrived at her house drunk? She phoned and told me that you had come to her, agitated and sick, and she was going to put you up for the night. I told her it was inappropriate for her to do so and I'd come get you. And do you know what she said?"

Decker didn't speak.

"She said, 'Absolutely not. He's going to stay here. If my decision has shamed you, I'll move from the premises, but he's sick, he's sleeping, and I don't want him moved!' Do you know what she was really saying?" Schulman said fiercely. "'I'd rather shame myself than shame him before your eyes, Rav Schulman.'

"At that instant . . ." Schulman held up his index finger. "At that instant I knew you were drunk, for it's no shame to see a sick person, is it? In fact, it's a good deed to care for the sick, and she of all people wouldn't deny me an opportunity to fulfill a *mitzvah*."

The rabbi crushed his cigarette with his bare hand and threw it in the ashtray.

"Rina erred by getting involved with you in the first place. No matter how nice and understanding you were during that horrible time, the bottom line is you were a gentile. That's it! Until you became a Torah Jew, she should have refused to see you. But she chose differently, and now she pays for her decision. I hear and see things, Peter. She puts up with daily ridicule, constant pressure from her parents and friends. She does it because she loves you and because she believed you when you told her you wanted to convert. Last night you placed her in a compromising situation. Her ethics were bound to be scrutinized by prying eyes. She chose your honor over hers. She's an *eishes chayil*—a woman of valor. She's too good for you."

Decker swallowed back a dry lump in his throat.

"I never said she wasn't."

His answer didn't seem to please the rabbi. He asked to be taken back. Decker turned the car around and headed toward the yeshiva in silence. He pulled the Plymouth into the parking area and shut the motor. They sat in the dark for a moment, listening to the nighttime sounds. The sky was clear, moonbeams peeking through the branches of oak and eucalyptus.

The rabbi turned to face him.

"You can either wallow in self-pity or you can do better." His voice had softened. He placed a firm hand on Decker's shoulder and said, "The choice is yours, my friend."

## ·18

"**Y**ou're not working today?" Rina asked as she opened the door.

"I took the day off." Decker stepped inside.

He looked angry, she thought. His jaw was clenched and his pulse throbbed in the veins at his temples. She tried to make eye contact, but he was averting his gaze.

"What's wrong?" she asked.

"Why did you tell Rabbi Schulman I was here the other night?"

"I had to."

"You *had* to?" he mocked. "Some little gremlin picked up your finger and forced you to dial his number?"

"Peter, I'm a single woman living on the grounds of a yeshiva. I have a responsibility to uphold a certain standard of conduct."

"What happened two nights ago was strictly between you and me, Rina. It wasn't anybody else's damn business."

"It is if I'm living under a certain set of rules—"

"Funny you should mention that. I seem to remember a certain scramble on the floor where rules didn't count too much."

She blushed a deep rose.

"That was a rotten thing to say."

"Did I go and report *you* to the rabbi? Little Rina Lazarus was a very naughty little girl today—"

"Stop it!"

"How the hell do you think I feel, Rina?"

"I didn't say anything—"

"Is this what I have to look forward to if we marry, Rina? Every little transgression or imperfection on my part gets related to the holy man so he can impart his divine judgment on my character?"

She stared at him coldly.

"I won't even dignify that with an answer."

"Humor me. Dignify it."

She spoke through tight lips.

"What we do after we're married as husband and wife in our own place is no one's business but our own. But this wasn't the same situation—"

"All you had to do was wake me up in a couple of hours and tell me to leave. Nothing happened. No one would have been the wiser."

"We're not children sneaking behind the backs of our parents, Peter. I had nothing to hide by letting you stay here. I just wanted Rav Schulman to know that."

"What other things do you tell the great rabbi about me?"

She became furious.

"Nothing."

"After all, he must have a hotline to God—"

"Every single Jew has a hotline to *Hashem,* anytime they want. All they have to do is open up a siddur and say *tehillim.* Rabbi Schulman is respected because he is a *tzaddik* and a *talmid hacham*—a pious and learned man—and not because he's of divine descent. We don't have popes, remember?"

"Well, some Jews obviously believe they're more worthy—"

He was interrupted by the phone.

"Don't answer it!" he ordered.

"This is still *my* house," Rina retorted angrily. "I can answer my phone, thank you." She jerked up the receiver, said hello, then wordlessly held out the receiver to him. He took it, and as he listened, his face became etched in pain. He said that he'd be right down and hung up.

"Bad news?" she asked anxiously.

"Do I ever get *good* news?" he answered caustically.

Something had deepened his horrible mood, hurting him. "What's happened?" Rina asked.

"One of my informants, a sixteen-year-old girl who looks like my daughter, is in the hospital, beaten to a bloody pulp. Indirectly it was my fault. She was feeding me information, and when the case began to get complicated, I told her to back off. She didn't listen, and I think someone got to her. Now she's hanging on by a thread and I'm pissed off."

"Peter, you can't be responsible—"

"Don't give me your pep rally routine. Life is not sugar and spice. Life sucks. This *place* sucks. I *hate* it. I hate the holier than thou attitude around here. I hate the self-righteousness! I hate the our-way-is-right-and-your-way-is-wrong pigheadedness. The goddam absolutes. You can believe in your little rules and rituals, but let me tell you something, in the real world there're no blacks and white—only goddam muddy grays!"

He picked up a cup from her kitchen table and flung it across the room. He'd always had a good arm and a crackerjack aim. The brass had given up trying to lull him over to SWAT. It hit her wedding picture smack in the center, shattered the glass, knocked it to the floor.

She stared at the blank spot in the wall, then looked at Decker, holding back tears.

"How long have you wanted to do that?"

"A long time."

"I know you've been under terrible stress, Peter, and I'm trying to be understanding—"

"Rina the angel. Or is it Rina the martyr taking abuse from her friends who don't at all approve of her big, dumb goy—"

"Stop it, Peter!"

"You want to tell them something interesting, Rina? The next time they razz you about me being a *shaigetz,* you tell them I'm Jewish. That'll shut them up."

She stared at him blankly.

"It's true, you know," he said. "I'm Jewish, Rina. Just like you."

"I don't understand—"

"I'm adopted. My biological parents were Jewish. Understand now?"

She couldn't answer him.

"I've known about it since I was eighteen," he went on. "I knew I was technically Jewish the first time I stepped foot on the grounds here."

"Why didn't you *tell* me?"

"I had my reasons."

Tears welled up in her eyes.

"How could you keep that from me? Didn't you *trust* me?"

"It wasn't a matter of trust. I didn't tell you because I wanted to find out what being *your* kind of a Jew is like, so I could either accept it or reject it. You know what, Rina? I reject it! I reject all your phony baloney customs and laws because they were made by rabbis who dwelt in ivory towers and never had to deal with the day by day crap of living. Like Schulman. Give him a month on the streets, seeing the garbage I see, putting up with scum and mud and shit that fills you up until your eyes turn brown. Give him one month of it and I guarantee you, the man's iron-clad faith will be cleaved as wide as the Red Sea."

He tried to stare her down, but she held his gaze with rage burning in her eyes. He'd never seen her like that.

"You're so far off base, Peter, you're not even in the ballpark," she said. "Rav Schulman was in Auschwitz for three years. He lost his entire family. His wife was made sterile by Nazi butchery. His children were executed in front of his eyes—shot in the head. He was forced to dig their graves with his bare hands."

Decker continued to look at her, but his eyes were no longer confrontational. A sour taste filled his mouth, a putrid stench clogged his nostrils. He felt nauseated. Lowering his head, he swallowed back a dry heave and walked to the door.

"I'm not a saint, Rina," he said quietly. "And I don't want to live with one, either."

Her skull was a headdress of bandages, and what showed of her face was raw and ripped and poked with plastic tubing. Her eyes were closed when Decker walked in, so he pulled up a chair at her bedside. A cockpit of panels and dials monitored her vital signs. Green fluorescent lines jumped about on a screen and he heard beeps at irregular intervals. Techno-medicine. Decker wondered if any of it really helped in the long run.

Noticing her damp forehead, he took a tissue and dabbed the sweaty skin gently. She opened her eyes.

"Hi, Kiki," he said softly.

Her lips turned upward. Her mouth tried to form a word, but instead she coughed feebly.

"Don't talk. You'll have plenty of time to talk."

She nodded.

"Go to sleep."

Again she nodded. Her eyes closed and moments later she drifted off.

Decker walked outside the room and lit up. Immediately, two nurses and an orderly told him there was no smoking. He extinguished the cigarette.

A young woman approached him—a hooker who was trying to hide it. Her skirt was of modest length, but too tight. Her blouse was buttoned up to her neck but was still sheer enough to see her bare breasts and nipples. Her crimson-nailed feet were stuffed into open-toed sandals with fuck-me heels. She was long-limbed, with a horsy face—big teeth, thick lips, and large hard eyes saturated with hate.

"Are you the cop friend of Kiki's?" she asked. Her voice was low and breathy. In the dark it would have been sexy.

"Who are you?" Decker asked flatly.

"I'm Lilah, a friend of Kiki's. Like her *best* friend."

Like her lover, he thought. The protective posture, the defiance. *Dare you to say anything against her, pig.*

"Are you Decker?"

He nodded.

"I'm the one who called you down," she said. "I did it for Kiki. I knew she'd want to see you. God only knows why she singled you out. You're just another cop—not even that good looking."

"Do you know what happened to her, Lilah?"

"I have an idea."

Decker waited.

"She had a bunch of these johns," she said. "Real rich kinky types who pay well but toss her around . . . A bite here, a kick there . . . This time . . . I don't know. Someone went overboard."

Decker was taken aback.

"A john?"

The girl nodded.

"She was beaten up by a *john* that she's serviced before?"

"Yeah, but none of them ever went this crazy."

"She was *turning tricks*?"

"I know you told her not to, but—"

Decker clenched his fists. "For Chrissakes!"

"She just didn't know if she could handle another bad foster home."

"This wasn't a *bad* foster home," Decker said, struggling to keep his voice low. "All she had to do was keep her nose clean—"

"She wasn't gonna go to that place, Decker. She told me that."

"For God's sake, why not?"

"The street may not be much, but to her at least it's home."

"*Home*? What kind of shit are you feeding me, Babe? She was smacked around and now she's on the critical list. Home! Wake up and smell the roses."

Lilah turned fierce. "She told me you did Juvey, Dick."

"I do."

"So *you* wake up and smell the roses—or the fucking garbage. Yeah, she was smacked around. What the hell do you think her father did to her? And the hairball never paid her for it, either."

Decker ran his hands down his face. "I don't *believe* this. I busted my ass . . . Who are these scumbags?"

"They ride by in Jeeps, four-wheelers. They could buy anything or anyone, but they love to slum in Hollywood. I tried one of them once, a fat old fucker named Maurice. Musta been about sixty-five. The money was great, but I got some pride."

Decker said nothing.

Lilah shrugged philosophically. "Actually, the sucker didn't like me. I guess I was too old for him. What an asshole! He broke my fucking tooth!"

"Do you know which one did this to her?" Decker asked.

"No," she said quietly.

"Can you tell me anything more about these assholes?" Decker asked.

"No."

"Think, Lilah!"

"Look," Lilah said. "I don't know anymore. I'm tired. Leave me alone."

"Don't you want this bastard to *pay* for what he did to Kiki?"

"Cut the justice speech, cop. Assholes out there are big fat zits. Squeeze one, a dozen more pop up. I love Kiki, but I only got so much energy inside and I got to save it for when it counts. I was a white knight once. I just don't give a shit anymore."

Suddenly a high-pitched noise emanated from Kiki's room. A monotone. A flat monotone. To correspond with flat vital signs. The lights outside the doorway flashed bright blue. He was shoved out of the way by a team of two nurses and a doctor. Decker made himself scarce, walking down the hallway, not wanting to know, but forced to stay until there was closure.

Fifteen minutes passed. The look in Lilah's eyes said everything. Shit!

The girl fell into Decker's open arms. He held her as she sobbed pitifully. After she composed herself, Decker pulled away and said:

"You know who her parents are?"

"She hates her parents."

"We've got to send the body to somewhere, Lilah."

The girl wiped tears and running mascara off her cheek with her fingers. "She's from Indianapolis. Her real name is Patsy Lee Norford. I think her father's name is Mick or Mike."

"I'll find him," Decker said.

"You're a nice guy," Lilah said. She whipped out a compact and began to fix her melted face. "Kiki said you were a nice guy. I frankly didn't think they existed anymore."

"If Kiki thought so highly of me, why the hell didn't she listen to me and just stay out of trouble for a week?"

Lilah broke into wicked laughter—a mixture of irony and bitterness.

"She was a dumb-ass," she said, starting to cry. "And you're a dumb-ass, also . . . I mean, don't you *get* it?"

Decker waited for her to explain.

"She was fucking in *love* with you, for Chrissakes! She didn't want to go to that halfway house because she knew she'd never see you again. I mean, you *told* her on the phone you wouldn't visit her! She figured at least on the streets she could be your stoolie, and then she could be with you."

She clicked the compact closed and stuffed it in her purse. "You men are real stupid shits. I don't care who the hell you are—john, cop, asshole father of five fucking kids—you're all shit for brains."

She spat at him and walked away.

# ·19

H e trudged into the station house and was greeted by Marge's smiling face.

"Cheer up, Rabbi," she said. "The warrants for Cecil Pode just came through."

"It's a little after the fact," he said, gulping down some aspirin.

"You look horrible, Pete."

"Not as horrible as I feel. Look, I'll meet you out at Pode's place in about an hour."

She wrinkled her forehead.

"Hey, isn't this your day off?" she asked.

Decker just laughed.

Cindy approached the principal's office with trepidation. The receptionist in the outer office told her to go inside immediately.

The young girl's face was anxious as she opened the door.

"Hi, Cindy," Decker said.

"What is this, Daddy? Where's Mr. Richardson?"

"He's off campus. His secretary was kind enough to let me use his office—with a little prodding from my badge."

"What's wrong?"

"Nothing. I just wanted to say hi. I haven't been able to get hold of you for a while."

The girl was confused.

"Why did you pull me out of class?"

"I was in the neighborhood," he said, sheepishly.

Cindy sat next to her father.

"You look terrible, Daddy. What happened?"

"I'm fine, Beautiful." He kissed his daughter's forehead, then hugged her fiercely. "I love you, Baby. Take good care of yourself for Papa, huh?"

She hugged him back.

"You want to talk about it?" she asked.

He laid his hand against her cheek.

"Cynthia, parents are supposed to console kids, not the other way around."

"But we're both adults now, Daddy."

He laughed.

"Never. You'll always be my baby whether you like it or not. When you're seventy and I'm ninety-three you'll still be my princess. I shouldn't have dragged you out of class. I've been doing a lot of impulsive things lately . . . This time, it turned out nice."

"I love you, Daddy."

"I love you, too, Cynthia. Go back."

"Are you sure—"

"I'm fine, honey. Go back to class."

He watched her leave. Dear God, he thought. It was hard to let go.

"For a photographer, he sure didn't have many personal snapshots," Marge said to Decker as they finished combing Pode's bedroom. "No baby or graduation pictures of Dustin, no hidden pictures of his wife. You'd think a widower would have one honored picture of his dead wife."

"Maybe he wasn't a sentimentalist," Decker said, closing the last bureau drawer.

"But it's weird." Marge scanned the room then said, "Look at the walls. Those square white patches. Pete, there were pictures hanging up there."

"So someone cleared them away. Maybe they were valuable. Besides, we're not interested in family photos, and I don't think Pode hung his porn on his bedroom walls."

Marge thought about that and said nothing. She sat down on an empty double bed. "We've been through this place twice and haven't come up with anything," she said. "Want to move on to the studio?"

"Yeah," Decker said, resigning himself to finding nothing.

"Hungry, Pete?"

"A little. We'll stop by McDonalds on the way over."

"Hey, I know you by now, Rabbi. I brought my lunch. Just stop by a 7-Eleven and let me pick up something to drink."

"I didn't bring my lunch, Marge," he said quickly. "Let's pick me up a Big Mac."

She gave him a funny look.

"You've been bringing kosher lunches for the last four months and now it's McDonalds?"

"I don't want to talk about it, Marge," he said brusquely. "Let's just do the job so we can go home."


The back room of Pode's studio was a mess—cramped and packed with props. In the center was a professional camera perched atop a tripod. On the north side was the sitting area—a bench, a few chairs, and boxes of photographic accoutrements. Strewn on the floor were parasols, fake flower bouquets, neckties, jackets, false collars, and yards of velvets. The dressing stalls were open, the curtains crumpled heaps on the floor. He didn't see any file cabinet. Not here, not at the house.

"Either someone tossed the place or Cecil was an unbelievable slob," Decker said.

"Move the tripod over to the side," Marge said as she began kicking junk into a corner. "We need a little elbow room."

Decker hefted the tripod, folded the legs, then leaned the apparatus against the wall. He turned around and walked across the room. He pivoted and retraced his steps. Did it a third time.

"Getting some exercise?" Marge asked, bemused. She knew he was up to something.

Decker stood at the room's center and bounced on the balls of his feet. The flooring underneath was springy. He bent down and felt the linoleum tiles.

"We've got a trapdoor here," he said. "Get me something to pry it open with."

After a minute of searching Marge found a screwdriver.

"This isn't heavy enough," Decker complained. "I can't get any leverage. The damn thing's not budging."

"Maybe it's locked," Marge said.

"I knew there was a reason for having you here."

Marge slugged him. Hard.

"Spring lock," he said. "Where the hell is the release button?"

Marge searched the walls. Nothing except light switches, and that wouldn't make sense. Accidentally flip the wrong switch and up flies the tripod. But she tried all of them anyway. Nothing.

"Try the ceiling fan," she suggested.

Decker pulled the cord. The fan turned on. Another pull, the fan turned off.

"Leave it on," Marge said. "Get some air in the place."

He tugged on the cord and walked inside the dressing rooms. The walls were bare.

"We could saw the door open," he suggested.

"Where's your spirit of detection?" she said.

"I'm tired."

"Let's be logical," she said. "If that's Pode's hiding place, he'd have to be able to get into it quickly. It wouldn't make sense to move the camera, run out to the waiting room, push a button and run back into this room. His enemies would get him by then. The button has to be close by. It also has to be wired through the floor and maybe through the wall and ceiling. So the button has to be on the floor, wall, or ceiling. We've scoured the walls and ceiling. That leaves us to crawl around on our hands and knees, big fellah."

The button was under a loose corner tile. Marge depressed it and the trap door sprung open. The area underneath was pitch black.

"Got a flashlight?" he asked.

"Wait a sec. I'll get one from the trunk."

Decker stuck his hand inside the dark hole. He shouted hello, and from the sound of the echo, knew the space was deep. Marge came back a minute later, bent down next to him and shined the light into the darkness.

"How the hell do we get down there?" she wondered out loud. "I don't see any sort of ladder."

"How many feet to the bottom?" Decker asked, squinting over the edge, trying to make out the dimensions.

"It looks too deep to jump," Marge said. "Wonder how he got down here."

Decker stuck his head in the hole and felt under the edge. "There are hooks screwed in here. Bet he had a rope ladder and it latched onto the hardware. Get the rope out of the trunk of the car."

"Now you're Tarzan?"

"Got any better ideas?"

"I'll fetch the rope," she said, laughing.

She returned and handed him a hemp cord. Tying it securely onto the hooks, he slid down, hands burning against the coarse fiber.

The drop was about fifteen feet and the hole was cool and dank. He turned on the high beam and looked around.

The room was a six-by-eight cell of almost-empty metal shelving. Scattered film canisters and video cassettes had been dumped onto the ground. Several yards of loose celluloid streamed across the floor.

Bingo. Cecil's warehouse.

Two empty nylon bags fell from above.

"I'm coming down," Marge said. A moment later she dropped onto the floor.

"The good news is this was his gold mine," Decker said. "The bad news is he's already stripped it of any real evidence."

"Here's a filing cabinet," Marge said, opening the top drawer.

"Empty?"

"Scraps," Marge said, scanning them. "A few memos, his water and gas bills, a magazine subscription offer." She began to stuff an empty tote. "I'll take 'em, but I don't suspect we'll find much."

"Get a load of this, Marge," Decker said, pointing to a typewriter-sized machine in the corner. "A humidifier. The fucker had the place humidified to protect his films from burning and cracking when the weather got hot and dry. Like it was some archive."

"The shelves are categorized, Pete. Look at the labels. This one is BD 1000–1789. This one's SM 1000–1124. SN 1000–1006, GaySM 1000–1122, BE 1000–1148, Kiddie 1000–1219—"

"They're inventory numbers of the films."

"God, this is sickening, Pete. Amputee SM 1000–1021. Here's another abbreviation. RET? And SCHIZO?"

"Porno with a nutcase?" Decker tried. "The night of the shootout, Pode's confiscated bag contained ten films—six sado-masochisms, and four bondage-and-disciplines. We know he dealt in at least one snuff—"

"That's what SN probably stands for—snuff," Marge said.

"Yeah," Decker nodded. "The numbers only go up to six, indicating he didn't have too many of 'em floating around, and that would make sense . . . Goddam, if only we could find his books."

"Maybe Dustin has 'em."

"How the hell are we going to get to Dustin?" Decker said. "If the guy's in on it, he's going to be careful to the point of paranoia."

"Then forget about Dustin. Concentrate on the other one. The broker's son."

Decker nodded. "Cameron Smithson."

"After all," Marge went on, "the father said they do their ventures together. Besides, he impressed you as a weirdo."

"I've got an appointment with the two of them next week," Decker said. "Jack Cohen is going to learn about film limited partnerships."

"Ignore Dustin," Marge said. "Zero in on Cameron. It'll throw Pode off the track just in case he's suspicious."

"Okay." Decker thought for a moment. "You want to poke around a little for me?"

"What do you have in mind?"

"Armand Arlington."

"Peter . . ."

"Don't tell me you're intimidated."

"I like my job," she said.

"One of my ears was beaten to death by an old rich guy she used to service," Decker said. "She died today."

"I'm sorry."

"I am, too. And I'm very pissed. A hooker I talked to said there's a bunch of them out there who trawl the area looking for young streetwalkers to pounce on. You want to hear something funny? Cecil Pode said the same thing. And so did Hollywood PD. I called up a Vice dick named Beauchamps. He said there's a group of men who called themselves the Loving Grandpas—"

"That's sick."

"They have stooges in Jeeps who do the soliciting so they can't get busted. Hollywood has tried using undercover women, but they never take the bait. Beauchamps thinks someone is tipping them off."

"So what do you want me to do?"

"Talk to the ladies of the night. They'll open up more to a woman than a man. I know one of the pervs goes by the name Maurice. I think Arlington's involved. I know it's a long shot, but I'd love to stick him with the death of my ears, Kiki. A murder would be too big for protection. If he wasn't the actual murderer, try to find out who it was. And try to get someone to implicate Arlington in this group."

"You're not hot for job security, are you?"

"My ex used to say I was self-destructive."

"That's a good adjective."

"Will you do it?"

She sighed. "All right."

"Thanks."

They collected flotsam and jetsam, filling a bag and a half. Marge zipped up the sack and said:

"You go up first. I'll tie the bags and you pull them up. Then drop the rope back and reel me in."

Decker looked upward at the dangling cord and rubbed his hands together, grateful for the callouses, for the years of ranch work that had kept his body trim and muscular. But his arms, though strong and well defined, weren't used to hoisting his own bulk. He felt his deltoids tighten, his pectorals strain, as he stretched toward the top. Man, he was hot. Goddam stupid to forget to take off his jacket before going down. He reached the top drenched in perspiration and knew his chest would be sore tomorrow.

"How we doing up there?" Marge shouted.

"Piece of cake," he answered as he rolled his shoulders in their sockets. Again, he rubbed his hands together. Up came the bags, then Marge. The reeling in left him winded. The woman was no lightweight.

They picked up the canvas bags, locked the door, and left the studio. They had gone a block when the explosion occurred. Decker immediately hit the ground, but Marge turned around and stared in disbelief, mouth agape. The front window of Pode's studio had blown away. Glass shards had turned the sidewalk into a deadly obstacle course, eddies of ripped photographs flying through the air like a snowstorm. The front door had burst into a pile of splinters. They heard screams. Someone could be hurt.

"You believe in God, Rabbi?" Marge asked.

Decker rose quickly and brushed off his clothes. "We'd better call an ambulance," he replied, shaking.

He entered the study and took the chair opposite the Rosh Yeshiva. Schulman closed the tractate of Talmud he was studying and opened the Bible without uttering a word, then noticed Decker was empty handed.

"Where's your *chumash*?" the old man asked.

"I didn't bring it."

The rabbi closed the leatherbound book and waited.

"I ate *traif* today," Decker said.

"What did you eat?" Schulman asked.

"A Big Mac."

"Was it good?"

Decker broke into a smile.

"Actually, it was terrible. The meat wasn't tainted or anything like that, but it didn't go down well."

"Hmmm," said Schulman. "If you were going to eat *traif*, why didn't you splurge on delicacies—lobster, shrimp, filet mignon?"

Decker shrugged.

"I could never figure it out," Schulman said, pondering. "When *bochrim* go astray, they sin in the most mundane ways. Instead of committing adultery with a beautiful woman, they have sex with the ugliest *zonah* around. Instead of dining in the finest restaurant in L.A., they go to Taco Bell. Such lack of imagination. It defies logic. Why did you aim so low, Peter?"

"I don't know. I guess if you want to debase yourself, you don't do it in high style."

The old man smiled.

"So, my friend, I enjoy talking to you, but this is not a confessional. I am a teacher. If you want to learn, I will teach you. If you want to ruminate upon the meaning of life," Schulman pointed upward. "Talk to Him."

"I nearly got blown up today, Rabbi. A bomb went off and I was saved by seconds. I thought it might be a good time to pause for reflection. I sat for two hours tonight and prayed, Rabbi. I prayed and meditated and contemplated and came up with this. Today notwithstanding, there are times when I feel God is omnipresent. I feel Him everywhere I go, in everything I do. And there are times I think there's nothing in the skies but an ozone layer. I'm not an agnostic. I'm not waiting for God to come down and prove His existence to me, because sometimes I just know He's out there. I can't explain why I feel so strongly one minute and like a total atheist the next. In short, sometimes I have doubts."

The old man looked at him impassively and extended his hand across the desktop.

"Join the club, Peter."

# ·20

"**I** know it's late," Decker said. "I won't stay long."

Rina stood at the threshold of the open door, then stepped aside and let him in.

"Did you learn with Rav Schulman tonight?"

"A little."

She stood with her arms folded across her chest with that *look* in her eyes. Decker had seen it umpteen times in Jan. What was it? Hostility? Contempt? Injury? Probably a little of all three.

"Do you have any coffee handy?" he asked.

"I'll make some."

"Don't bother."

Defiance suddenly vanished from her face. Replacing it was sadness. His heart sank. He could deal with her anger, but not with her melancholy. He felt like a total ass.

"It's no bother," she said softly. "Would you like something to eat?"

The muscles of his throat tightened. He answered her with a shake of the head. As she started to the kitchen, he called out her name. His voice cracked.

"What is it?" she asked.

"Forget about the coffee," he said. "Come sit down."

She did as he requested.

"I brought you a peace offering." He held out a flat, square package wrapped in gold embossed paper, but she didn't take it.

"Go on," he urged. "It's not much, but it's a start."

Slowly she extended her hand.

"Open it."

Methodically picking apart the paper, she exposed a sterling silver picture frame.

"Thank you," she said, barely audible.

He took the frame from her.

"Should be the right size. Where's the picture, Rina?"

Walking over to her kitchen, she pulled out a drawer and handed him the wedding photo. Decker slid it between the backing and the glass, clamped the closure pins shut, and hung it on its old spot on the wall.

"Much better," he said. "Actually, I think the picture looks nicer in this frame. You notice it more."

She said nothing.

"I'll go now."

Tears spilled over her lower lashes and down her cheeks.

"I'm sorry for this morning, Rina," he said softly. "I acted like a madman."

"I never knew the picture bothered you, Peter." She pulled out a tissue and wiped her eyes. "Of course, I don't know too much about you, do I?"

The anger was back.

"What do you want to know?" he asked calmly.

"Come back next week. I'll have a questionnaire made up."

"I don't blame you for sniping at me, Rina, but it really isn't getting us anywhere."

"Why did you come here tonight?"

"To apologize."

"Well, you've done that."

"You say you want me to talk to you. Now I'm trying, but it doesn't appear to do any good."

"Maybe I'm too angry." She lowered her head. "Maybe I'm too hurt."

"I should have told you about my adoption. But believe me, Rina, it wasn't stubbornness that held me back. I didn't want to misrepresent myself to you. Call myself Jewish when I really didn't know what it meant."

"I'm not stupid, Peter. I know how hard it is to live this kind of life. I mean it's not hard for me—I love it. But for someone not brought up like this, there are restrictions—"

"A lot of restrictions."

"You don't believe in any of it, do you?"

"I don't know," he confessed. "I think some of the laws are nonsense."

"Such as?"

"The separation of sexes. Women are considered chattels—"

"That's not true."

"Honey, your *ketubah* is nothing more than a sales receipt. Your husband bought you."

"It's not that simple."

He waited for clarification.

"I don't want to get into a religious discourse right now, Peter. Why don't you talk to Rav Schulman about it? He could explain it better than I could."

"Yes, the good *rav* does seem to have an answer for everything. And when there's no answer, he tells me to take it on blind faith. That's not the answer I'm looking for."

"What are you looking for? A neat little solution? You won't find it."

"Then why bother concocting religion, Rina? Why not say things are just random? Sometimes they work out well, sometimes they don't."

"Because that's a very bleak outlook on life. I don't believe we are just some random Darwinian mutation . . . that in a million years we'll be giant brains resting on vestigial bodies. I don't believe that at all. Judaism is more than just a series of blind beliefs, Peter—or a concoction. It's history. The *chumash* isn't cute little fables; it's a family chronicle of my ancestors—*your* ancestors. When I immerse myself in the mikvah, I think: this is what Sarah, Rivkah, Rachel, and Leah did thousands of years ago. Torah is timeless.

"I don't understand why my husband died at twenty-eight of a brain tumor. I don't understand why I miscarried three times. I could curse the world and reject God, but then what is my alternative? To believe in a world that is ruled by laws solely conceived by *human beings*? Laws that can be altered at the whim of a crazy man? That's what happened in Nazi Germany, Peter. The country had a constitution. It had laws. You saw how seriously the people took them."

He had no answer.

"Torah law is irrevocable, Peter, because it is *divine*. That's not to say Judaism is a static religion; it isn't at all. But the Ten Commandments are the Ten Commandments. They aren't going to change just because some guru goes on a talk show and says it's okay to commit adultery. I believe in Torah because its truths are absolute."

"I've always envied the faith you have in your religion," Decker said.

"It's your religion, too."

He shook his head. "Maybe it will be, but it isn't now. Look at it through my eyes, Rina. My Jewish parents dumped me. My Baptist parents raised me, loved me."

She faced him, took his hand. "Are you resentful?"

"Not really. My mother was a kid—fifteen. I couldn't—can't—blame her for what she did. It isn't resentment that holds me back from Judaism, Rina. It's belief. I'm not even sure I believe in God; I certainly don't believe in structured religion. I'd like to feel the same way you do about Judaism, but I can't. At least I can't right now."

"That's going to cause problems for us."

"I know," he said wearily. "So where do we go from here?"

"I don't know."

"Swell."

"I know what I *should* do," she said quietly. "I should tell you to leave me."

"Is that what you want?"

"Not leave forever, but maybe for a year or longer if you need it. Study Torah. Learn what it is to be a Torah Jew. See if you don't change your mind. I love you. I'll wait for you."

"A year?"

"It's not that long. Rabbi Akiva left his wife for twenty-four years to study Torah."

"A *year?*" He shook his head. "Honey, perhaps this is a very unspiritual thing to say, but I would find it extremely difficult to remain celibate for an entire year."

She lowered her head.

"I know. I thought of that, but I don't know what else we can do."

"I love you, Rina. I'm not going to find anyone I'd love more. That I know. And I know you feel the same way about me."

"I do."

He sighed, then blurted out, "Let's get married. We'll work it out over time."

"Peter, if you were a Torah Jew, I'd marry you tomorrow. But feeling as you do about Orthodoxy, it would be suicide for us to marry. We've both been married before. You know that marriage doesn't reduce differences, it magnifies them."

"I can accept you as being religious," said Decker. "I wouldn't interfere. All you have to do is accept me for what I am."

"It wouldn't work."

"It could if you'd let it."

"No, it couldn't."

"Damn it, Rina," he said sharply. "If you loved me, you could find a way!"

Burying her face in her hands, she started to cry. Decker pulled her into his arms and let her sob on his shoulder.

*Shit!*

"I'd do anything for you, Honey, you know that. But I can't help the way I feel."

Her response was to cry harder while hugging him tightly. Acid churned in his belly and his temples began to throb. He started to take masochistic pleasure in how lousy he felt. Everything in his life was going rotten, and he marveled at his reverse Midas touch.

"Honey, I love you. I want to marry you. I just don't think I'll ever be the type of religious person you want me to be. If you can live with that, there's no problem."

She said nothing.

"But you can't live with that, can you?"

"I'd never give up this life—"

"I'm not asking you to give it up. I'm asking you to respect me for what I am."

She didn't answer.

They sat in silence, neither one sure what to say. The tension increased. Finally Decker couldn't take it.

"How're Jakey's nightmares?" he asked.

"They're still pretty frequent," said Rina quietly.

"Maybe you should take him to see someone," suggested Decker.

Rina flashed him a look of hostility.

"I know what's best for my child, thank you," she said.

"I'd better go home," Decker said. "We don't seem to be getting anywhere."

"We're not going to get anywhere if you leave every time things aren't going great."

Decker clenched his jaw and took out a cigarette. He stuffed it between his lips, lit it, and inhaled deeply.

"You want me to say the obvious? I'll say the obvious," he said, blowing out a plume of smoke. "We've reached an impasse. I think it might be best if we saw other people."

Her eyes filled.

"What do you think?" he asked.

"I don't like it."

The room was quiet for a minute. Rina broke it.

"If you and I were to . . . to maybe stop seeing each other, would you still learn with the rabbi?" Rina asked.

"No," Decker answered.

"You mean you're not interested in this kind of life at all?"

"No," he answered. "I'm not—at least, not now."

"So if you stopped seeing me, you'd stop being religious?"

"Yes."

"But if we were to marry, would you be religious to please me?"

"Probably in the beginning. Then, quite honestly, I could see myself giving it up. But I'd never interfere with your beliefs."

"It would be a very hypocritical example for the boys. How could I espouse religion to them if I go ahead and marry an irreligious man?"

"I suppose there's a grain of truth to that."

She sat motionless.

"I think I'm meeting you half way, Rina. *I'm* willing to let you live your life. If you just wouldn't be so rigid—"

"I have no choice!" she exclaimed. "I'm not going to be a hypocrite. I want my husband to be religious. What is so wrong with that?"

"Nothing. But that's not me." Decker sighed. "Look, we're both really confused at the moment. Maybe we need a little time to ourselves, a temporary breather from each other—"

"I don't want to see anyone else," she answered.

"Maybe I don't want to either," he said. "But I want to keep the option open . . . just in case . . . So we both know the score."

She stared at the wall and didn't answer. Decker waited a few more minutes. When she remained silent, he got up and left.

"Somebody didn't like us poking around," Marge said to Decker.

It was nine o'clock Friday morning. She was sitting on his desk, sipping coffee. Decker had his feet propped up on his desk, hands behind neck, and eyes on the ceiling.

"Or somebody may have wanted to destroy evidence," she added.

"Then why place a bomb in the front part of the studio?" he asked. "Place it in the underground room. I think it was a warning. Anyone seriously wanting us out of the way could have done so by now. I've got a call in to Culver City PD. We should know more as soon as they dissect the remains of the bomb."

"Watch your ass, Pete."

"I intend to."

Mike Hollander walked up to Decker and placed a manila envelope on his desk. The return address was from a Dr. Arnold Meisner.

"As requested, Rabbi," Hollander said. "Fresh off the press."

"Please quit calling me rabbi."

Hollander looked at him. "Go get a night's sleep, Pete."

"Who the hell is Arnold Meisner?" Marge asked.

"A doctor who used to work under Dustin Pode's pediatrician," Hollander said. "When the old man died, Meisner took over the practice. He was kind enough to dig up those records for us."

"How'd you find out Pode's pediatrician?" Decker asked.

"I asked Dustin," Hollander answered.

Decker laughed.

"The direct approach," he said.

"Don't know any other kind," said Hollander. "Dusty Pooh was so busy defending his father—calling the raid entrapment—I think the question was a relief. Something he could answer truthfully."

"What do you want with his medical charts?" Marge asked Decker.

"I'm a sucker for theoretical models," he said. "I'm looking for bed-wetting. It usually goes along with fire-starting . . . and cruelty to animals."

"The old psychopathic triad," Hollander said.

"The old psychopathic triad," repeated Decker, flipping through pages. Marge peered over his shoulder.

"I don't like to have someone reading over me," Decker said curtly.

"*Excuse* me." Marge backed away.

Decker laughed. "Sorry. I've been a real son of a bitch lately and I make no excuses for it. My life is going shitty."

"Not that I'm trying to meddle, but—"

"Then don't."

"Geez," Marge said. "I'll give you a pair of tweezers to take the hair out of your ass, Pete."

He smiled and concentrated on the page in front of him.

"Any bed-wetting?" Marge asked.

"Not so far." Decker read for a while. When he finished, he reread the chart again. "No bed-wetting," he announced at last.

"Oh well," said Marge. "Everything's always perfect in theory."

"No bed-wetting, but you know what I see here?"

"What?" inquired Hollander.

"A hell of a lot of cuts and burns in weird places. And a whole lot of broken bones."

"Child abuse," Marge said.

"Yep," said Decker. "Only twenty years ago no one talked about it, much less reported it. Poor Dustin was getting whopped for years and the old doc didn't make one damn notation on it." He turned a page. "Will you look at this? Burns on the buttocks. Mom claimed he sat on the stove."

"We haven't heard that one since—" Marge looked at her watch "—oh, since maybe two hours ago."

"Look over here," Decker said. "Lacerations of the hard palate when the kid was three. Mom said he fell with a spoon in his mouth. The doc records not one, not two, but three semicircular cuts in the region. Looks like Dustin fell with three spoons in his mouth."

"Jesus, what a bitch!" Hollander said.

"Yep," said Decker, closing the chart. "Psychos don't come out of nowhere."

Friday blurred into Saturday. Shabbos was just another day of the week.

Mary Hollander opened the door and gave Decker a startled look.

"Pete! I haven't seen you for ages. Thought you'd dropped out of all the shenanigans."

Decker smiled.

"Guess not. How's it going, Mary?"

"Fine. They're all in the back room hooting and hollering. Sounds like a good game."

Decker stepped inside.

"Bring you a beer?" she asked.

"Sure."

He walked through an immaculate living room full of knick-knacks collected over the course of a thirty-year marriage and into the den. It was crowded. Hollander sat on the edge of an ottoman, munching popcorn and shouting at the TV. Marge was parked on the red Naugahyde loveseat, next to a behemoth of a man he didn't recognize. Fordebrand and MacPherson filled the matching sofa and Marriot reclined on the Barcalounger. They fell silent when he walked in the door.

"What's the score?" Decker asked.

"What are *you* doing here?" Fordebrand asked puzzled.

"Oh boy," Marge groaned.

MacPherson started singing: "Oh it's crying time again . . ." He was from Robbery—a black man with a sizeable paunch who loved Shakespeare and had a lousy voice.

"Shut up," Decker said grumpily.

"Want a hot. . . ?" Hollander paused. Decker could smell the wood burning. "Want something to eat?"

"Hot dog's fine," Decker answered.

"They're not kosh—"

"Hot dog's fine," Decker repeated.

Hollander grunted as he rose from the ottoman and went into the kitchen.

"You just missed a hell of a play, Rab—Deck," Fordebrand said.

"Does he really give a damn about football?" MacPherson mused. "When the cloth of passion's gown hath been rent—"

"Knock it off, Paul," Marge said. "Pete, this is Carroll."

Decker shook hands with the behemoth, noticing that the man's paw was twice as big as his own. Marge had described him as big, but it didn't do him justice. The guy was a barn.

Hollander brought Decker a hot dog and a cold beer and sat back down on the ottoman.

"What did I miss?" he asked.

"Pete was just going to tell us his sob story," MacPherson said.

"Knock it off," said Fordebrand.

"Hey, he's among friends."

"There's nothing to tell," Decker said mildly.

"Peter! Come on!" MacPherson pressed.

"Why the fuck should he tell a loser like you?" Fordebrand asked.

"Because one loser can *relate* to another." MacPherson's eyes gleamed. "Besides, if he and Rina are really kaput, I wouldn't mind giving her a try."

Decker laughed.

"Well," MacPherson said, "I've had black women, white women, spics, and chinks. Never tried a Jew. Certainly not an *orthodox* Jew. Certainly never one who looked like Rina. Those big blue eyes and pouting lips. That nice tight—"

"You're pushing it, Paul," Decker warned.

"Can we watch the fucking game?" Hollander asked, annoyed by all the noise.

"I have to make a phone call," Decker said to Hollander. "I'll use the kitchen phone."

"I thought she didn't answer the phone on Saturdays," Mac-Pherson said.

Decker ignored him and left the room.

"Poor guy," Marriot said sympathetically. He was a wiry, bespectacled man who never spoke hastily.

"I'll say." Hollander turned to MacPherson. "Rina was one piece of ass."

"Think she was really any good?" MacPherson asked. "I mean being like a nun and all."

"Probably dynamite," Hollander answered, "I mean, the man had to be hooked on something else besides God, right?"

"Mind you the only thing I did was superimpose the X-rays of the skull over the painted boy's face," Hennon said over the phone. "But as an off-the-cuff opinion, I'd say the boy in the film matches the skull you dug up."

"Thanks for doing this on your weekend, Annie."

"I'm still waiting for a dinner, big man."

"How about tonight?"

There was silence over the line.

"You're serious?" she asked.

"If you are."

"You're on," Hennon said. "Anywhere specific you want to go?"

"You choose. I'll pick you up at seven."

"Great."

She gave him her address in Santa Monica and Decker hung up the phone. He turned around and saw Marge.

"Eavesdropping on me?"

"I just came in to use the phone," she said.

"It's all yours."

She looked down and kicked the floor absently.

"Of course I couldn't help but overhear a *little*."

"Hennon says the skull that we dug up in the mountains matches the painted man in the snuff film."

"Just as you figured."

"Yup."

"So who's the painted boy?"

"The Blade," Decker answered. "Whoever he is. Find out what happened to Clementine?"

"No."

"Damn. I'm so pissed at myself. I should have pulled him for a composite when I had the chance."

"He'll show up eventually unless he's running from something."

"My informants tell me no one is after him as far as they know," he said.

"Then he'll turn up." Marge paused, then asked: "What happened with Rina?"

"Cultural differences," he said.

"I thought you liked being Jewish?"

"It seemed like a good idea at the time. I wasn't aware of how involved it got. Now I am. Judaism is a hands-on religion. It takes over your life. There are dietary restrictions, sexual restrictions, drinking restrictions, clothing restrictions . . . You know you're not even allowed to wear a garment made of wool and linen."

"Why?"

"I don't know. No one does. It's just a law."

He paused a moment, then said, "Over there, I'm an alien. But I've been a stranger in a strange land before, and I consider myself very adaptable. But adaptation is empty unless you believe in what you're doing. I know that and so does Rina."

"I think about God once in a while," Marge said.

"You do?"

"Yeah, I think about the size of His penis."

Decker burst into laughter.

"Must be a humdinger, don't you think?" she said.

"That's blasphemous."

"Yeah, it is," she said. "I was raised an Episcopalian, but I stopped going to church the day I sprouted pubic hairs. I don't believe in it at all. But every once in a while, when I'm all alone in bed—a rare occasion if I can help it—I get to thinking, what if I'm *wrong*? What if all that crap they fed me at Sunday school turns out to be *right*? Then I get real spooked."

"Rina has it made," Marge went on. "Even with all the restrictions. If she's wrong and there's no one up there, she'll be dead anyway and won't know the difference. But if she's right . . . man, she's hit the jackpot."

"Do you want to come in for a nightcap?" Hennon asked, flicking on the lights to the apartment.

"Sure," Decker replied.

Her condo was comfortable, full of soft colors, a pillowy sofa and plants sprouting from terra-cotta pots.

"Have a seat," Hennon said. "What can I get you?"

"Coffee's fine," Decker answered.

"Take off your jacket. Make yourself comfortable."

She disappeared into the kitchen.

He removed his jacket and holster and stretched. Looking

around, he saw the bathroom. A few minutes later he came out to find her pointing his .38 at one of her Boston ferns.

"What the hell are you doing?" he said irritatedly.

She lowered the gun.

"I just wanted to see what it felt like being behind one of these." She smiled. "God, you feel so invincible."

He didn't smile back. Walking over to her, he gingerly took the revolver from her hands.

"It's loaded, Annie. You shouldn't be fooling around with a loaded gun," he said, placing the gun back in the shoulder harness.

"Sorry," she shrugged. "Coffee's ready."

He sank into a brown chair, irked. Not only had she done something dumb, she'd violated his personal property.

Returning with a tray, she set it on the coffee table.

"Cream or sugar?" she asked.

"Black."

"That's right," she said. Handing him a mug, she parked herself across the table.

"You use your gun a lot?" she asked.

"As little as possible."

"It gives you a sense of power, doesn't it?"

"Not really." He forced a smile. "Can we change the subject?" She frowned.

"Okay. What's the weirdest case you ever were on?"

"I don't mean to be rude, Annie, but I don't want to talk about my work. If you want to talk about dentistry—"

"God, no."

"So you understand—"

"Yeah, but my work is so damn boring."

"So's mine. Believe me."

"The bones case is boring?"

"The bones case is frustrating!" He lit a cigarette. "Do you have an ashtray handy?"

"Not really. I'm allergic to cigarette smoke."

"You didn't say anything at the restaurant."

"I was trying to be polite."

Decker stared at his smoke.

"Where can I throw this?"

"Toss it down the sink."

He got up, did it, and came back.

"So what happened with your girlfriend?" she asked.

"I don't want to talk about that either." He sipped his coffee. "So you like to ski and play tennis."

"We exhausted that over dinner, Pete."

Decker smiled.

"Yeah, we did."

"Come to think of it, I did most of the talking."

"Yeah, you did."

"So I'm getting a little tired of hearing myself blabbing."

"I'm a little quiet tonight," he said.

"True. And it makes it mighty hard to get some snappy banter going." She chuckled. "Most of the men I date . . . you can't shut them up. Always chewing your ear off about the latest hustle they have going. Trying to dress up their essentially lackluster lives. Now I get hold of a cop who works in the blood and guts of the city—who does something *primal*—and he doesn't like to talk."

He shrugged.

She shrugged.

"Wanna fuck?" she asked.

Decker burst into laughter.

"No, I don't wanna fuck."

"What kind of a girl do you think I am?" she mocked, crossing herself. "Jesus, it was just a thought. And not that unusual a question. Where have you been for the last fifteen years, Kiddo?"

"I like you," Decker smiled. "You make me laugh."

"I like you, too," she answered. "You make me horny."

"Thanks."

*"Thanks?"*

"Yes, thanks. Would you have preferred my ripping off your clothes in mad lust?"

"That sounds good."

"You try to be a gentleman . . ." He laughed. "Famine to feast."

"Pardon?"

"Never mind."

"You've got your ex-friend on your mind, don't you?"

"She's left her watermark."

"Then this was for nothing." She seemed hurt.

"It wasn't for nothing. I had a nice time with you. You're great company and a lovely woman."

"Sure. Let's go out for a beer sometimes," she said sarcastically.

"Not in the bars I frequent. You'd have ten guys on your tail the minute you walked in the door."

She smiled.

"Trying to redeem yourself, Pete?"

"How am I doing so far?"

"Not bad. Keep going."

He rubbed his eyes. "In all seriousness, tomorrow I'm going to kick myself for being such an ass tonight. I must be crazy to let you slide through my fingers."

"So do something about it. Make the plunge."

"I can't. I'm too confused. Give me about a month or so."

She folded her arms across her chest and looked him over.

"I'll think about it."

"Thanks for the consideration," he said. He hoped he was being disarming. Luckily, the awkward situation took care of itself. His beeper went off.

"Phone's over in the kitchen," she said.

It was Marge.

"What's up?" he asked.

"I found Clementine."

"I'll be right down," he said eagerly.

"Hold on, Kiddo. He ain't going anywhere. He's in the county jail."

# ·21

On Monday morning Decker watched Clementine pick up his personal belongings at the grilled window of the county jail. Seen in the light, the clean-shaven, bespectacled man was the color of a paper bag, with blue eyes, a bald spot, a weak chin, and a close cropped Afro. Thin, short, and slight, he could easily have been mistaken for a *café au lait* Mr. Peepers. Not very intimidating. No wonder he liked doing business in the shadows.

He eyed Decker, and the two of them walked out of the receiving area into a grassy courtyard. Clementine looked up at Decker's face and then at the bulge in the detective's jacket.

"Sergeant," he said, acknowledging Decker.

"You beat the rap, huh?"

"The lady dropped the charges."

"She was in a coma for two days."

Clementine smiled.

"The incident between the lady and me was purely a business matter, Sergeant. Nothing personal."

"Have to keep 'em in line, right?" Decker pulled out a cigarette, lit it, and offered it to the pimp.

"The lady don't mind," Clementine said, taking the smoke. "She depends on my good will for her livelihood."

Decker gave him an impassive stare and got a grin of porcelain caps in return. Teeth again. He noticed them all the time now.

"What do you want?" Clementine asked.

"Recognize this guy?" Decker showed him the picture of the painted man in the film.

Clementine took off his glasses, squinted, then replaced them on his nose.

"Dude's got on a shitload of warpaint. How the hell should I know who he be?"

He'd dipped into his pimp persona.

"Take a good look," Decker pressed. "Look at the build, at any distinguishing marks that might remind you of someone."

The pimp shrugged.

"Clementine, is this the Blade?" asked Decker.

"Don't know, Cop. Can't tell with all the camouflage."

"Look at these other stills. Could these be the Blade?"

Clementine quickly sorted through the photographs.

"Can't help you, Decker."

He handed back the pictures.

"What did the Blade look like?" Decker urged. "C'mon, you've seen the dude."

"I tole you what he look like, Cop. A white dude. Just a basic white dude."

"Short, tall—"

"Everyone looks tall to me."

"How was he built? What kind of threads did he wear?"

"Dude was skinny. I tole you that. I know I tole you that. Hey, I'm no fuckin' fashion consultant. I'm a free man. I gotta go, so if you'll excuse me—"

Decker grabbed his bony arm.

"I want you to come down to the station and do a composite for the police artist."

The pimp swung out a hip and sneered at Decker.

"Now *why* would I wanna do that, Cop?"

"Community service. And if you don't, I'm going hunting for you, Clementine. Your whores'll be marked. Your 'livelihood' will wind up in jail and your spare cash'll be pissed away for bail money. And if you don't think I'm serious, you ask anyone I've ever worked with how determined I can be."

The pimp snarled and spat a chunk of brown saliva on the ground. Mr. Peepers was trying to save face.

"*Perhaps* I could work it into my busy *schedule.*"

"*Perhaps* you could work it in right now."

"Find anything in the crap we picked up from Pode's studio?" Marge asked Decker.

He looked up from his desk, took a sip of lukewarm black coffee, and shook his head.

"No such luck. The films left behind were legit, the junk papers were random numbers or meaningless scribbles. Nothing illuminating or incriminating."

He leaned back in his chair.

"How'd the interviews go this morning, Margie?"

"I must have hit every dirty bookstore and porn studio in Hollywood. A few had heard of Cecil Pode, but none admitted doing business with him."

"If you believe that, you'll believe anything."

"My sentiments exactly," she agreed. "But you can only roust so much before the ACLU gets on your ass."

"How about Dustin Pode? Anything new on him?"

"Far as I know, Joe Broker's clean as a whistle," she said. "When's your appointment with him and Cameron—and the inimitable Jack Cohen?"

"Three. Drinks at the Century Plaza." Decker rubbed his eyes. "Did you find out anything about the Blade?"

"The name sounded familiar to a few of 'em. Nothing beyond that. What about Clementine?"

"He's giving a composite of the Blade to Henderson right now. I hope to have a face to match the name in a few minutes."

"Good," she nodded. "You know, I tried to call you yesterday. Now that you're eating like a normal person, I wanted to invite you over to a Sunday barbecue at Carroll's, but you weren't home."

"What the hell was I doing yesterday?" He wrinkled his forehead. "Oh yeah, I took Rina's kids out on the horses."

She gave him a funny look.

"You're back together again?"

"No, I don't think we've said a dozen words to each other. She's called here twice, but I keep putting off calling her back. But why take it out on the kids, we'd arranged this outing weeks ago."

"You break up with the woman, but keep the kids?" She shook her head in amazement. "You're a sucker, Decker."

He shrugged. "What can I tell you? There's an attachment."

His phone rang. He picked up the receiver, listened while jotting down notes, thanked the party on the other end, and hung up.

"That was Colin MacGruder of the Culver City PD bomb squad."

"And?"

"Homemade number. Could have picked up the components anywhere. I forgot to ask him how the damn thing was detonated."

Decker started to redial, but put down the phone when he saw the police artist walking his way, Clementine behind him. Decker and Marge met him halfway across the room.

"What do you have, Larry?" Marge asked.

He handed her the composite of the Blade.

"Holy shit!" she said.

Decker grabbed the picture. "This is the *Blade*?" he asked Clementine.

"As best I remember," the pimp answered. "Like I tole you all you white boys look alike."

"That's Dustin Pode!" Marge exclaimed.

"Goddam if it isn't," agreed Decker.

"Then who the hell is the boy in the movie?" she asked.

"I'll see that question and raise you one better: Whose bones are lying in the morgue?"

Decker sat at the table in the Century Plaza Bar and played with the swizzle stick in his glass of club soda. Dustin was on his third whiskey sour, Cameron was nursing a gin and tonic. Things were

going smoothly; Pode hadn't made him as a cop. Neither of them
had batted an eyelash when he ordered plain soda. Probably
thought he was an alkie on the wagon. Pode began his initial
pitch:

"The initial investment will most likely net a fifteen-and-a-half
percent return on a buy-in at five thousand K per unit. That in
itself is a handsome return. But the big pay-off, Mr. Cohen, is the
capital appreciation."

Dustin Pode straightened his Countess Mara tie, smoothed his
cashmere blazer, and handed Decker a four-page glossy. The color
photos included pictures of ruddy men with white hair and flabby
chins dressed in gray flannel suits, and several views of spanking
new structures—apartment buildings, condos, motels. Next to the
photos were profit/loss statements, earnings for the two previous
years, and projected earnings for the next fiscal year.

"You can see here, Mr. Cohen, average time of investment hold-
ings is about five years, and figuring the rate of return based on
projected earnings, you should be able to walk away with a long-
term gain of at least twenty-five percent per year."

"Guaranteed," Smithson Junior added.

Dustin chuckled nervously at the statement.

"Nothing is guaranteed," he corrected. "But this is as close to a
sure thing as anything around."

Dustin sipped his sour. Nothing but ice left in it now. Decker
smiled encouragingly and Pode continued:

"Of course, you, Mr. Cohen—being the sophisticated investor
that you are—don't have to be reminded about the inherent risks
in any syndication—"

"I like risks," Decker interrupted.

"No gain without some pain, right Mr. Cohen?" said Cameron.

Pode flinched and produced a sickly smile.

Decker tried not to stare at Pode, but it was hard. He couldn't
imagine this unctuous salesman—when you got down to it that's
all brokers were—associating with someone like the Countess. But
then again, the repressed ones were usually the kinkiest.

It was easier to imagine violence in Cameron. There was something dead about his eyes.

"You know," said Decker. "I thought I might like to take a stab at something even riskier, but with a higher potential upside."

Pode finished his drink and waited for Decker to go on. Cameron wasn't as patient.

"Such as?" he asked.

"I hear you boys have done well on film deals."

Cameron cleared his throat. "We've had a *great* deal of success in the past—"

"But we don't do film syndication anymore unless something spectacular comes along," Pode broke in. "The movie industry is too risky, what with inflated budgets and the unpredictable tastes of the public. More important, the new tax laws have minimized the amount of loss now deductible on initial investment. It used to be that even if you invested a portion in a film, the total loss allowable to be deducted was the sum total of the amount of the invested—"

"I'm sure Mr. Cohen doesn't want to be bored by details," Cameron interrupted.

Pode stiffened. His hand squeezed his glass and his knuckles whitened.

"The upshot is," Cameron said, "film doesn't bring in the money it once did. However, once in a while a good limited partnership presents itself. We'll be happy to let you know when one does."

Decker picked up the P/L statement, the three prospectuses, and a stack of graphs and charts.

"Do that." He stood up. "I have to be getting back. Thanks for your time. I'll rethink what we've talked about and let you know just as soon as I've come to a decision."

Smithson and Pode stood up and extended their hands. Decker took Smithson's first.

"Nice to talk with you, Mr. Cohen," Cameron said flatly.

Decker offered his hand to Pode.

"Thank you, Mr. Cohen. It was a pleasure talking to you, and I hope the future portends a mutually advantageous business relationship for us."

Decker smiled. "I'm sure it will."

He sat in the darkness of his bedroom and felt like a widower. He mourned the lost relationship with Rina; he mourned the staleness of the Bates-Armbruster case.

If Dustin was the Blade, then who was the painted-face kid in the movie? An understudy who'd stepped in at the last moment?

Had Dustin pulled his father into porno or vice versa?

Just what was Dustin's involvement?

How could he tap into Dustin without scaring him off?

The hell with it.

He turned on the light and stared at the siddur resting on his nightstand. He shouldn't leave it out like that. He should put it away on a shelf so he wouldn't spill coffee on it. For no reason, he picked it up and began reading the praises of God. Without his realizing it, he had said *maariv*—the evening prayers. He turned off the light and stared at the blackness that surrounded him. He had been moved by the words. Solitude always brought out his religious nature. Strange that the only time Marge thought about God was when she was alone in bed. Perhaps God was best seen in the dark. He closed his eyes and scrunched up the pillow.

Wisps of conversation kept drifting into his consciousness.

*It's family, Rabbi. Cops always look in the family.*

*All you white boys look alike.*

*Just a white boy.*

*How's your son, Cecil?*

*Which one?*

*WHICH ONE?*

He bolted up in the darkness.

There had been no personal photos in Cecil Pode's house. It was time to construct a family portrait.

# ·22

"I need all of his tax forms, not just the 1040s," Decker said to the voice on the other end. "Yes, ma'am, state as well as federal for the last thirty years—"

The voice grew shrill.

"I realize it's a hell of a lot of information," he said, peeved, "so instead of arguing about it, why don't you program it into the computer and quit wasting time? This is a homicide investigation . . . Oh, and any army records you can dig up."

A curt reply, then a click.

"Fuck you," he said, slamming down the receiver. He picked it up again and dialed the county assessor's office.

"This is Detective Sergeant Peter Decker of LAPD Homicide. Has Ms. Crandell returned from her morning break?"

He sipped his coffee as the woman put him on hold.

"This is Ms. Crandell," a birdlike voice tweeted.

"This is Detective Sergeant Decker of LAPD—"

"Yes, Sergeant. I have the information you asked about."

God bless the competent few. They may not inherit the earth, but they make it an easier place in which to live.

"Great," he said, grabbing a pencil.

"Mr. Cecil Pode acquired the house on Beethoven Street twenty-two years ago in joint tenancy with his wife, Ida. Ten years ago—let's see, that was 1977—it was reevaluated for tax purposes after major capital improvements were made and . . ." she paused

". . . and the ownership was changed from joint tenancy to sole ownership."

"What kind of capital improvements?" Decker asked.

"I don't know."

"So Cecil Pode's lived in that residence for the past twenty-two years?"

"I don't know where he actually lived. But he did pay his property tax for those years."

"Thank you."

Decker hung up and Marge walked over. "Rina called again," she said to him.

"I'll get back to her."

"You're not being nice."

"I said I'll call her. What do you have, Marge?"

"We struck out, Peter. I couldn't find out any of Pode's film investors. Confidential."

"Damn." Decker lit a cigarette. So he'd die of lung cancer. He had no one to live for anyway. "Did you ever get a chance to talk to the streetwalkers in Hollywood about the Grandpas?"

She pointed her thumbs downward. "Their lips were zipped. A couple of young ones—their ID says eighteen but their faces say at least a couple of years younger—got very nervous when I mentioned Maurice. But they denied knowing anyone by that name. I got the impression that these old farts were paying them lots of money, maybe scaring them also."

"Did you tell them about Kiki?"

"They knew about her. 'Aw, too bad. She was a nice kid, but kinda dumb. I take care of myself better than she did.' I'm sorry I couldn't do better—"

"No, no." He crushed his cigarette out in an ashtray. "I really don't like working Homicide. I've got to finish the case just to be rid of it and this division." He looked at her. "I'm going to talk to Arlington."

"Don't chance it without departmental okay, Pete."

"A cop died during that shoot-out."

"Yes, I know. The whole department knows. But Arlington didn't pull the trigger."

"He was there. Someone's got to crack his nuts."

"Patience. The timing's wrong. If anyone comes within a mile of him, he screams harrassment and makes a phone call. You get dressed down. What's the point?"

The phone rang.

"Decker," he said.

"Is *Detective* Sergeant Peter Decker there?"

He stared at the receiver and shook his head. "This is Sergeant Decker."

"This is Ms. Lotta from the Hall of Records. You asked about the Podes' marriage, birth, and death certificates?"

"I sure did. What do you have for me?"

She cleared her throat.

"Mr. Cecil Pode married Miss Ida Brubaker in Fresno, California, on June 21, 1955. Mrs. Ida Pode's death certificate was signed on May 17, 1977. Cause of death was indeterminate because she was burnt up so badly. She was identified through dental records."

"Any names of surviving kin?"

"If there are, I don't have any. All I deal with is certificates. I have no access to obituaries, Sergeant."

"Do you have the name of the dentist who made the identification?" Decker asked.

"No. The death certificate was signed by the ME."

"That's fine, Ms. Lotta. What about the birth certificates?"

"There's a registration of birth for a Dustin Pode, but I didn't find any other children born to them. That doesn't mean there are no other children. It only means Dustin Pode was the only child born in L.A. County."

"Thank you."

He put down the receiver, scribbled a few notes, and dialed Parker Center—Police Statistics.

"Casey? Pete. Can you get an obit for me? Yeah . . . Ida Pode—Peter-Ocean-David-Edward—died May 17, 1977 in a fire. I know she was survived by her husband and son, I want to find out if there were any other children in the family. . . . Yeah. Thanks, I'll hold."

He tucked the receiver under his chin, rubbed his hands together, and waited.

"Margie, did the original fire report say where Ida Pode died?"

"I think they found the body—or what was left of it—in bed."

"Sure?"

"No. I'll look it up again."

Casey came back on the line.

"The woman left behind her husband and two sons—Dustin, 22, and Earl, 17."

Bingo!

"Thanks, Casey." Decker hung up.

"What did he say?" Marge asked.

"Dustin has a little brother, Earl."

"Aha. So whose bones are in deep freeze?"

"Either Dustin's or Earl's. And the living Dustin is either Dustin or Earl. What I need are their respective sets of dental X-rays to make a positive ID, and to do that, I need the family dentist."

Decker lit a cigarette and ruminated.

"Jesus, seems I've been talking to a lot of tooth jockeys these past couple of weeks. Might as well make an appointment for a cleaning."

"Bowl 'em over with your grin."

Decker laughed.

"Problem is, Marge, if I call up the living Dustin and ask for his family dentist, he's going to get suspicious if he's really Earl. I have to do it on the sly without his catching on."

"You know," Marge said "the 1040s sometimes list the name of the accountant who prepared the tax forms. You could probably get the name of Pode's insurance carrier from him. If Pode had dental insurance, we could trace the dentist from insurance records."

"Good point, except their 1040s are in transit."

"The medical charts!" Marge shouted.

"Of course!"

He opened his file, pulled out Dustin Pode's folder, and took out the chart. Ten minutes later he plunked the medical files back into the folder and closed the drawer.

"No such luck?"

"You'd think a pediatrician would have at least listed the kid's dentist."

Decker knitted his brow and thought. "How about this? Cecil lived in the same house for the past twenty-two years. I bet the boys went to the local high school. And I bet they filled out health forms. Maybe I'll check it out while I'm waiting for the tax records to come in."

"Okay," Marge said. "And while you're at it, take a look at the yearbooks and get a picture of Earl."

His phone rang again. MacGruder from Culver City PD.

"Thanks for returning my call," Decker said.

"No problem, Sergeant. The bomb wasn't triggered by a timing device. It was detonated by a remote-control unit—a BSR. One of those fourteen-button jobs that can turn on your jacuzzi by phone while you're still at the office."

"Long range of operation?"

"Miles."

"Which means the button could have been pushed from almost anywhere."

"Yep."

"Thanks."

"Anytime."

"Now what?" Marge asked.

"Bomb was set off by a long-range remote-control unit," Decker said. "The person could have been anywhere when he pulled the trigger."

"I don't think the person was just anywhere, Pete."

"Neither do I," he said. "Someone was watching the place and didn't want us to get hurt." He thought a moment. "The whole thing's ridiculous, Marge. If you want to destroy evidence you don't do it in broad daylight. Besides, nothing incriminating was left. If you want to scare off a cop you don't do it by nearly blowing his head off. Way too unpredictable and way too messy. And it attracts too much attention."

"Maybe Dustin blew it up for insurance?"

"Cecil rented the place. There wasn't more than a couple of grands' worth of photographic equipment in there. You don't blow up buildings to collect two g's."

"But someone was trying to prove a point."

"Right. Someone was struttin' his stuff."

Sitting in the registrar's office of Mar Vista High, Decker tried not to stare at the dowdy, graying lady with thin, cotton candy hair. But she was so full of nervous energy, he couldn't help sneaking in sidelong glances.

"Can I get you some coffee in the meantime, Sergeant?" she said, jumping out of her seat.

"No, thank you," he answered. She sounded like Aunt Bea in the old Andy Griffith show. "While I'm waiting, I'd like to look through some yearbooks. Where do you keep them?"

"Last year's is right in my desk," she said, pulling out a drawer.

"I need the ones from 1969 through 1978."

"Oh dear," the woman said, touching her cheek. She coughed, scratched her head, and rose from her seat. "Just a moment and I'll see what I can do."

Ten minutes later, she returned and said sweetly, "They haven't forgotten about you, Sergeant. It takes a long time to find old records, especially health records. If you had asked for transcripts, it would have been easier. We have almost immediate access to transcripts, but you don't need those, do you?"

"Not right now."

She put an armful of annuals down in front of him. "Here you go."

"Thank you."

He went through Dustin's first. The caption under the graduation picture stated that he was a member of the student council, the Spanish club, the honors club, the scholastic achievement organization, and the B-string football team. The portrait was stiff and unsmiling, but the handsome features shone through the somber pose.

He looked through the '78 album—the year of Earl's graduation—but not a trace of the younger brother could be found. Probably dropped out. He tried the '77 yearbook. Nothing. But he was listed in the '76 album, and much to his surprise, the picture of Earl was almost a duplicate of his older brother's.

For starts, the physical resemblance was remarkable. Earl's features were a little softer and less brooding, but the faces could have been Xeroxes. What was even more noteworthy were the activities that the younger brother had chosen—student council, the scholastic achievement organization, Spanish club, and the B-string football team. The group picture showed him squatting in the front row, padded heavily and looking absurdly beefy under a thin face.

The brothers seemed to have followed the identical trail to a point. What had happened?

Nineteen seventy-seven was the year of the fire, the year of their mother's death. And in '77 Earl'd dropped out of school.

Decker stared at the team picture. Some of the boys had tried to look scary and menacing, often ending up looking tentative and scared.

And one looked unusually familiar.

Quickly Decker flipped the pages back to the eleventh-grade class roster.

Baby-faced Cameron Smithson.

The detective looked at the '78 album. Smithson had graduated, but no honors were listed under his name. His only distinction was his position as a tailback, second string on the B football team. Closing the book, Decker frowned.

The hyperactive woman had come back smiling, with sheets of paper in her hand.

"Here are the records, Sergeant," she said, rocking on her toes. "I told you we'd find them."

He scanned through the health charts noting their illnesses—

lots of flu, infections, colds, broken bones from falls. He knew some of those falls were manufactured—the results of abuse rather than accidents. Then he found what he was looking for. In fourth grade Dustin had lost a front tooth in a fight during recess. Next to the entry was the name of a dentist. Using the school phone, he made a call and arranged to see the man.

Onward and upward . . .

An hour later Decker left the office of David Bachman, DDS. The dentist, an elderly blue-eyed leprechaun of a man, remembered both boys as being polite and slightly troubled. ("I'm no headshrinker, but I've seen an awful lot of people and have gotten to know human nature pretty damned well.") Bachman said it would take a couple of days to dig up the records, but when he did, he'd send a copy over to Anne Hennon, whom he knew. ("A great looking gal with a fine pair of gams.")

As Decker got into his car his beeper went off. He called in from his car radio, and a moment later Marge's voice was patched through the line.

"I'm over at Cecil Pode's home," she said. "The place was torched this morning."

"I'll be right down."

"You can come down, Pete, but there's nothing left except ashes. Mike and I are sifting through the rubble."

"Arson?"

"Yeah. Incendiary material all over the place—rags and newspapers soaked with gasoline."

"Have they determined the hot spots?"

"Three. In the bedroom, the kitchen—stove blew up—and the living room."

"Anyone talk to Dustin Pode?"

"Someone from Culver City PD. Seems he was at work all morning. Security guard at his office says he checked in about six, around the same time as the fire."

"Was the place insured?" he asked.

"Underinsured, Pete. Fact of the matter is Dustin had the place up for sale and had a prospective buyer. Guy who talked to Dustin said he sounded real pissed. Anything else?"

"Yeah. Check around and see if any fire starters have been spending a lot of cash lately."

"Will do," she said. "Are you going back to the station?"

"Probably," said Decker. "Marge, when Mike's done with Pode's house, have him call Arnold Meisner and ask him to find Earl Pode's medical records. Tell Mike to impress upon the doc that this is a homicide investigation and we need the chart ASAP."

"What do you think you're gonna find besides more evidence of child abuse?"

"I want to see if Earl was a bed wetter."

"You don't give up, do you?"

"I'm a closet theorist. We all have our weaknesses."

"Okay," she said. "Check in with you later."

He placed the mike back on the receiver, gripped the wheel, and pondered his dilemma. Dammit, he needed something more—a break! If he wanted to do right by Lindsey—maybe even by Kiki—it was time to put his butt on the line.

The executive offices of Arlington Steel were on the fifteenth floor of a downtown building that looked like a monolith carved from Swiss cheese. Odd holes and balconies robbed the structure of any smoothness of line. Decker took the elevator up. The receiving office was manned by a receptionist who had her nose buried in a donut and coffee. She was chunky, with big knockers and a permanently confused look branded on her face. He approached the desk.

"Excuse me, ma'am."

The woman looked up.

"I'd like to see Mr. Arlington."

She started flipping through the appointment calendar.

"He's not expecting me, but this . . ." He leaned in close. "This is a personal matter. I think he'd like to talk to me."

"You can't see Mr. Arlington without an appointment," she said.

"But I have to see him. He'll be very disappointed if he doesn't see me."

The baffled look deepened.

"Uh, let me buzz Ms. Scott, Mr. Arlington's personal secretary—"

"Is she through that door?"

"Yes, all the offices are. But you can't—"

"That's okay."

"Wait a minute," the plump woman protested, hurrying after Decker as he sprinted down the hallway.

The corridor ended in a pair of twelve-foot rosewood double doors with a pair of brass name plaques affixed to them: Armand Arlington, Chairman of the Board, and directly under it in smaller letters, Ms. Monique Scott, Executive Secretary. He swung one door open, almost clipping the receptionist, and marched into the interior office. A statuesque blonde stood up and glared at both of them.

"He just stormed past me, Ms. Scott. I—"

"I'll handle it, Jeanine. Go back to your desk."

Decker locked eyes with Scott. *The stuff of which dreams are made, Mama.* She was in her late twenties, with wide-set gray eyes and full, bee-stung lips. Decker smiled. She didn't. Her eyes hardened into cold, metal dimes.

"How can I help you, sir?"

"I'd like to see Mr. Arlington," he said.

"He's not here."

"Then I'll wait in his office."

"The adjoining door is locked and I'm not about to buzz you in."

She sauntered to the front of her desk and placed her hands on her hips.

"Listen, sir, I don't know who you think you are storming your way in like this, but Mr. Arlington doesn't see *anyone* without an appointment. If you don't leave, I'm going to call Security."

Decker flashed her his badge and Ms. Scott sighed.

"What seems to be the trouble, Officer?"

"It's personal, ma'am."

She dialed a number and spoke into the receiver in a carefully modulated voice.

"Mr. Arlington won't be available for another three hours," she told him.

"I'll wait." Decker held up a folder he was carrying. "I'll just do a little work in the meantime."

He sat down in a brocade wingback.

"I'd prefer that you wait outside in the receiving office. The chairs are quite comfortable out there. I'll have Jeanine bring you coffee if you'd like."

"It's a lot quieter in here," Decker answered without budging.

"It's impossible for me to concentrate with you here."

"I'll be real quiet."

She glared at him, but returned to her desk chair and lit a cigarette.

"Oh, you smoke," he said. "Then you don't mind if I do?"

"I only have one ashtray. There are several outside."

"I like to share." Decker lit up, walked over to the desk, lit a match, and tossed it in the crystal dish. Standing over her shoulder, he peered at her paperwork.

"Officer, I find it difficult to work with you breathing down my neck."

"Oh, sorry." He backed away. "I was just curious about what you do. People ask me all the time about my work."

She didn't answer. Walking back to his chair, he took off his jacket.

"I work in Sex Crimes, you know."

She looked up at him. When he had caught her eye, he un- hitched his gun and opened the barrel, dumping the bullets into his palm.

"I had this rape case once that was unbelievable," he said. His cigarette dangled from his lips and dropped ash as he spoke.

Her eyes fixed on the gun for a moment, then quickly focused down to her desktop. "I'm very busy—"

The first bullet clunked into the chamber.

"Seems these two convicts had just gotten out of the slammer and picked up this whore . . ." He sighted down the revolver and aimed it toward the window.

"Do you have to do that?" the secretary asked nervously.

"Do what?"

"Point that thing?"

He laughed, lowered the gun, and plunked two more bullets into the barrel. "Hey, you're safe. I'm an A-one shot. Only pick off what I'm aiming at and I'm not aiming at you."

The woman didn't appear consoled.

"Where was I?" He puffed out a cloud of smoke from his cigarette, finished reloading, and snapped the chamber shut. "Oh, yeah . . . these two hardtimers bought this bimbo and brought her to a hotel room—not too far from here actually, around Fifth and Main. Anyway, they took turns doing a number on her with a coat hanger and a bar of soap—"

"Officer, I'm really not interested—"

"Then, one of them gets the bright idea of calling up a bunch of their buddies for a little party. Ten minutes later, about fifteen of them show up—"

"Officer—"

"And do their thing 'til the poor hooker passes out. When she comes to, she's got six guys still going at her in every conceivable orifice. Blood's spurting like a geyser—"

"Please!"

"Know what happened?" He smiled. "They pierced through the vagina into the abdominal wall—"

"Let me try and get hold of Mr. Arlington again."

"That's a terrific idea, Ms. Scott," he said, smiling. He stared at the beautiful face, now coated with a sickly green pallor. He almost felt sorry for her.

Five minutes later Arlington stomped in. Decker remembered him from the film bust as being a small man cowering in the corner, hiding from the spray of human remains. But on his own turf he seemed larger, augmented by power and anger. His black eyes spat fire, his mouth quivered with fury, lips almost white from tension. The only thing that softened him was his nose—veiny, bulbous, a product of too much ninety proof.

"You're in big trouble, Detective," he bellowed. "I'm going to call up your superior right now and—"

"I'm not here in an official capacity, Mr. Arlington. Why don't we have a little chat in your suite?"

"Get out of here!"

"Mr. Arlington, there are things I'd like to say to you, and I don't want to say them in front of your secretary."

"Call Security, Monique," Arlington ordered.

Decker ripped the phone away from her hands.

"You've got a wife and six kids," Decker said quickly. "I'm sure they know about Monique here. I don't think they're aware of any of your other peculiarities. I'd be happy to tell them about it if you'd like. After all, I was there when you were arrested, Charlie."

The rage subsided as Arlington weighed the options. Perfectly composed, he unlocked the door to the inner office and stood aside for Decker to enter.

His suite was rich, dark, and austere, and smelled of leather and good tobacco. The desk was nine feet wide, traditional, and intricately carved, with a leather top upon which sat a marble desk set and crystal inkwell. The walls were oxblood embossed leather alternating with floor-to-ceiling bookshelves with gold mesh doors. The oils were Flemish and mostly unfamiliar to Decker, but he knew they weren't dimestore copies. The artists he did recognize were a Hals over the marble mantlepiece and a Vermeer on the opposite side of the room. Decker sat in a leather armchair and propped his feet on an ottoman. Next to him was a mounted globe, which he spun idly, watching the countries pass under the tips of his fingers.

Arlington sat behind his desk.

"Who is your superior?"

Decker flipped him a card.

"Call this extension. Ask for Captain Morrison. He'll deny sending me here and I'll catch hell, if that's what you want."

Arlington picked up the phone, but put it down. Wordlessly, he opened his drawer and took out a wad of cash.

"How much?"

"I'm not interested in money. I need information."

"As I told the police before, the screenings were arranged by Cecil Pode. He's dead. That's all I can say."

"Pode distributed, but he isn't the type of scum you'd work with directly. You'd deal with someone more respectable than a two-bit bagman—someone with at least a *veneer* of respectability."

Arlington pursed his lips.

"I have nothing else to say."

"Then maybe I'll ring up your little woman. I also have this friend over at the *Times*—"

"I'll sue your ass off. I'll ruin you."

"I'm sure you will." He stood up and trudged over to the Hals with his hands in his pocket. "I was at the Rijksmuseum in Amsterdam in 1970. Unbelievable—a place like that buried in the midst of all that decadence. Back then Dam Square was triple-stacked with dropouts. I've heard they've cleaned it up since then." He glared at Arlington. "It's good to do housecleaning and take out the garbage, don't you think?"

"I'm not interested in a travelogue, Decker. If you have nothing further to say, leave and we'll both get on with our business."

"You know," said Decker, "I figure, what the hell! Time for a career change. I've been thinking of doing something more spiritual anyway. Jesus, you work on the street and see shit pile up day after day—burnt out runaways, hookers, pimps, murderers, rapists, burglars, robbers. And kinky rich scumbags with influence buying their way out of retribution." He raised his eyebrows. "I'm sick of this job. I'd like to get away from it all. Maybe you'd be doing me a favor, Armand. Let's put it this way. If I don't hear from you by, let say . . ." Decker glanced at his watch, "this time tomorrow, you make your move and I'll make mine."

"Get the hell out of here!"

"Thank you for your time, sir."

# ·23

Decker decided to ride bareback. He threw a woolen blanket over the black stallion and mounted the rippling back. The horse protested by lurching forward and breaking into a gallop around the pen. Decker dug his heels into its haunches; the animal neighed, stopped, and reared. He tightened the reins and pulled backward, but again the horse rebelled, sprinting wildly, racing toward the fence. Decker jerked tightly to the left, forcing the horse to turn to avoid collision. The stallion sprinted, slowed down to a canter, then down to a trot, panting from the sudden burst of activity.

The horse was a beauty, too thickset for show, but light on his feet and full of spirit. Decker loved breaking in the animals, but once they were tame, he felt guilty. Afterwards, they never seemed quite as spunky, always carrying themselves with an air of wounded pride. On a rare occasion a horse would defy his best efforts. He'd curse his failure, but couldn't help admiring the animal's tenacity. Way to go, he'd think. Some fires just can't be put out.

He exercised the horse for an hour, changing directions with a simple pull of the reins, picking up speed with the slightest increase of heel pressure on the hindquarters.

Cut another notch for Cowboy Pete. Why he's just a good ole boy, herding them dogies, riding the wilds of Lake Okeechobee, Florida.

Florida cowboys. A proud tradition. His uncle had ranched all his life, took over the place from his grandfather. As a kid, Decker would spend summers on the central plains of the state, hanging out with the ranch hands, laughing at the western hot shots who'd wilt in the humidity of the swamp's heat.

*Them boys never had to deal with 'gators, skeeters, and swamps*, the hands would say. *They mighten be big men in Texas, but out here, they's pussies.*

*Eat shit, Waylon and Willie.*

If things didn't work out with Arlington, he could always go back and ride with Uncle Wilbert, or even back to Dad and the store.

Uncle Wilbert and Dad. Just your typical down-home millionaires. One day, while herding near Orlando, Uncle Wilbert had discovered Disney scouts sniffing land. Dad had been reluctant at first, but at last agreed to fund Wilbert's real estate ventures.

Mucho moolah, and in the end, it didn't make any difference. Dad went back to his hardware store in Gainesville, Uncle Wilbert continued to ride, and all the money was still sitting in the bank collecting interest. No fancy stocks and bonds, just plain old cash clogging up the bank. Millions accumulating for a rainy day.

Lack of sleep was catching up with him. He dismounted and led the horse back into the stable, with Ginger nipping at his heels. He patted the setter's head and offered both animals water—dog and horse, drinking a toast together. Taking out the combs and brush, he began to methodically groom the horse. An hour later he headed for a hot shower.

He turned the pages and sat upright as he read the climax of the novel. Bam! The cops just blew away the society lady. A righteous shooting but strong stuff for fiction, he thought. The author hadn't crapped out the ending because the woman was delicate, and he liked that. But he felt sorry for the cops. All the paperwork. Then there'd be the visit from Internal Affairs. And since the family had money, no doubt there was going to be a hell of a lawsuit.

The superiors breathing down their backs. Not to mention the bad press!

The doorbell rang. Ten pages from the end. He glanced at the clock—11:30. He'd been reading for three hours straight.

Who the hell could that be?

Reluctantly he put the book down and got out of bed. He threw a robe over his nude body and went over to the front door. To his astonishment, it was Rina.

"What's wrong?" he asked.

"Can I come in?"

"Yeah . . . Sure." He stepped out of the way. "Is everything all right?"

"Fine."

Her eyes ran down his body, arousing and embarrassing him at the same time. She turned away and sat down in a buckskin chair, folding her hands tightly in her lap. Decker took a seat opposite her and waited for her to speak. But she didn't.

"What's going on?" he asked.

"You didn't return my calls. I wanted to come when I was sure to catch you home."

"I was going to return them—"

"But you never got around to it."

"I've been swamped with work, Rina."

She said nothing.

"Who's taking care of the kids?" he asked.

"They're at my parents for the night."

Decker ran his fingers through his hair. "Look, let me get dressed—"

"Don't bother. I'll make it quick. I'm leaving for New York tomorrow night. I just wanted to say good-bye."

"How long are you going to be gone?"

"I'm moving there."

Decker's mouth dropped open.

She shrugged.

"Bye," she said.

"You're *moving*?"

"Yes."

*"Permanently?"*

She nodded.

"You're leaving the yeshiva?"

"It was a womb for me, Peter—nurturant, protective. It served its purpose. Now I have to get on with my life."

"Just like *that*? You're picking up your kids and moving to New York?"

Again she nodded.

Decker was dumbfounded.

"What do the boys think about it?" he managed to choke out.

"They're very excited."

"What are you going to do there?" Decker got up and began to pace. His heart clopped against his chest and his head began to throb. "I mean have you thought about what the hell you're going to do there?"

"My husband's parents have found me an apartment very close to them," she answered calmly. "I've always gotten along very well with my in-laws. Much, much better than with my own parents. They're delighted to have me come out, and especially happy to get a chance to really know their grandchildren. I'm also very close to one of Yitzchak's sisters. She's found me a job."

Decker began to panic.

"What kind of a job?" he asked.

"A bookkeeper in her husband's factory."

"What kind of a factory?" he asked. As if he gave a shit!

"He's a wholesale furrier. He makes furs for the major department stores."

"What do you know about bookkeeping?" he said, challenging her. *Why am I asking her stupid questions?*

"I'm a math teacher, remember?"

"That's not the same as bookkeeping!" *How can she be so fucking calm!*

"I'm sure I can figure it out," she said. "Peter, there is nothing here for me anymore. My house is a nightmare of lost love and what should have been. If I stay in this town any longer, I'll rot."

He walked over to the living room window and peered into the darkness outside.

"Isn't this what you wanted?" she asked, joining him at the window. "Freedom?"

"I never said I wanted to . . ." He was flustered. "I just wanted a little elbow room, damn it! The yeshiva is so goddam stultifying. I had no *idea* you were going to pick up and leave me."

"I'm not leaving you."

"What do you call *this*?"

"I'm giving you the distance you wanted. That is what you wanted, wasn't it? Distance. A *breather* from each other, as you called it."

He shook his head no.

"Then what do you want?"

"I don't know," he whispered to himself.

"What?"

"I don't know," he yelled. He ran his hands over his face. "God, I don't believe this. How could you just leave me like this! Is that the extent of your feelings for me?"

"What do you *want* out of me?"

"I want you to fight for us, damn it. Not just . . . give up and move away."

"It would have helped if you'd returned my phone calls."

He looked at her. "You're doing this out of spite, aren't you."

"I don't know what you're talking about."

"You're pissed off at me for not being what you wanted me to be. So instead of being honest and admitting it, you're gonna bust my balls by leaving me. Congratulations, Rina. They're busted."

Encircling him from behind, she slipped her arms around his waist and leaned her head against his back.

"I'm not punishing you, Peter. Neither one of us can help what we believe. I'm just trying to rectify a bad situation. I figure if we're apart, maybe we can think better."

Her voice had started to waver from its cool, collected tone. She moved her hand upward and tucked it under his open robe. He felt her playing with his nipple, brushing it lightly with her finger-

tips. Immediately, he found himself growing erect and not wanting to be. He pushed her hand away.

"Don't do that."

"I want to sleep with you tonight," she blurted out.

He turned to her and laughed bitterly. "Really now? Is this the
final fuck before the dramatic exit?"

He couldn't have slapped her harder had he done it with his
hand. She recoiled and turned to leave. He grabbed her arm.

"I'm sorry."

She jerked around, trying to hide her tear-stained face from
him. He gathered her into his arms and hugged her tightly as she
squirmed to break free of his grip. "I'm really sorry, Rina. I know
what that admission means to you. It just took me by surprise,
that's all."

Relaxing in his hold, she sobbed in his arms. When she calmed
down, she said, "You're partially right."

Decker waited for her to go on.

"I *am* a little angry with you."

"A little?"

"A lot." She wiped her eyes. "So maybe there's a little bit of I'll-
show-you in my decision. But most . . . most of it was made after
honestly considering the alternatives. Peter, what do you want
from me? Do you want me to stay here and watch you take out
other women knowing what you're going to *do* with them?"

"I guess it would be hard on you to see that," he said.

"Yes."

He smiled and said, "I could be discreet."

She socked him.

He cleared his throat. "If you were to make good on your . . .
suggestion, shall we say, there'd be no reason for me to date other
women, would there be?"

"I am not going to stick around here and have a sexual, unmarried relationship with you."

"How about a sexual, married relationship?"

"Have you changed your feelings toward religion?"

"Not really."

"Then we've had this discussion before."

"Yes, we have." He suddenly became choked with emotion. "Rina, please don't leave me."

"I'm only leaving you physically, Peter," she said. "I'm not leaving to find someone else. I'm utterly in love with you and nothing is going to change that. If you turn religious, I'll be waiting. If you don't, so be it. It's my problem, not yours. That's how I can rationalize . . . sleeping with you. I've been thinking of it for a long time."

"You have?"

She nodded.

"You know it would have helped me along if you would have mentioned that there was a possibility."

She reddened like a boiled lobster.

"It wasn't something I was comfortable talking to you about. I was afraid that if you knew I was wavering, that would be it. I'd give in."

"Would that have been so terrible?"

"Of course not! Emotionally, it would have been wonderful, but morally . . . Peter, premarital sex isn't that big a deal in Judaism, but it's something that religious women just don't do."

"So why now?"

"I don't know. Maybe it's because I'm leaving, but I think it's because I've finally decided that you're the only man in my life, period. If we do get married, you'll be my husband anyway. If we don't, I'm still not going to marry someone else, so it's not like I'm being unfaithful to a future husband. Besides, I'm sick of postponing gratification indefinitely. I'm sick of being righteous all the time."

"I didn't want it to be like this," he said softly. "Believe it or not, I had this idealized image in my mind of what it was going to be like, and it wasn't under this set of circumstances. Love you and poof, you're gone."

"I *have* to go. We both need time to ourselves."

He cupped her chin. "If you need time away from me, then go. But don't think you'll escape my clutches. If you settle in New

York, I'll follow you. If you move to Israel, I'll follow you there. We're *basheert*."

"I know that."

"Good," he said, kissing her forehead. "You're all packed up?"

"The van left the yeshiva this morning." Her eyes swelled with tears. "Amazing how little time it took them to pack everything."

"You've left your imprint, my dear. Believe me." He gently eased the kerchief off her head and a wave of jet black hair rolled down her back. "Do your parents know you're here?"

"Yes."

Decker raised his brows. "What did they say?"

"They were stunned. They didn't say anything. We left it at that."

"You're taking the red-eye out tomorrow night?"

She nodded.

"I'll drive you to the air—."

"No," she interrupted. "My parents will drive me . . . I don't do well with airport good-byes, Peter. I'd rather you didn't drive me."

"Okay."

"So I guess this is it."

There was an awkward silence. She smiled. He smiled.

"I'm very nervous," she said.

"So am I."

"Don't expect too much. It's been almost three years—"

"The mechanics haven't changed, Rina."

"Well, that's comforting."

He burst into laughter, scooped her into his arms, and carried her into the bedroom, kicking shut the door behind him.

# ·24

**W**aking. That delicious stage of limbo between sleep and full arousal. The senses working but not consciously coding. Decker's body was drugged with exhaustion from all night lovemaking, his mind groggy from words and confessions. He turned to his side and hugged his pillow as if it were a lover.

His mouth had been hopelessly manic last night. He had talked, confided . . . babbled. What had he told her? It made no difference. There was still so much more left unsaid. So much more for the future.

He opened his eyes. She was gone, as he knew she would be. But she had been no phantom, no dream. The room was a testament to what had passed between them, the air still redolent of musk and sweat, the sheets still damp with their juices.

He shut his eyes. *Pardes,* he thought. *Me and Ben Azzai. Neither of us wants to go back.*

Promises between passion. Vows between tears. What words of hope had filled their hearts? He had agreed to continue studying with the rabbi. No guarantees about the outcome. If something clicked, she'd meet him halfway. In a sense, she had done that last night.

In the end, it was left up to destiny. *Basheert.*

Marge caught him as he exited from the unmarked.

"Where the hell have you been?" she said.

"Sorry."

"It's two-thirty, for chrissakes!"

"I got hung up." He tucked his tie under his shirt collar and started to make a knot.

"Hung up?" she said skeptically. "You look like a piece of trash that the wind just blew in and smell like a whale's testicle. I sure hope she was worth it, Pete, 'cause you're in hot water right now."

He'd misjudged the length and the tie came out too short. "What's wrong?" he asked, undoing it.

"Let me do that," Marge said disgustedly. "Armand Arlington's in one of the interview rooms waiting to talk to you. Morrison feels he's about to drop a dime, and the good captain is pretty damn pissed—at you and *me*—that Mr. Megabucks had to cool his heels for the past hour. I'm supposed to know where you are, remember?"

"Well, how was I to know he was here?"

"Try answering your phone or your beeper. What'd you do? Turn them both off?"

Decker gave her a helpless smile and shrugged.

Marge looped the tie and pushed the knot to his chin.

"What did you do to Arlington, Pete? The man didn't come forward because he wanted to clear his conscience."

"I just talked to the guy. Jesus! You can't even talk to someone anymore without someone jumping down your throat."

"Yeah, you talked to him with a gun up his ass," she said.

"If I had had a gun up his ass, Marge, I'd have fired it. Then he'd look like what he is—a pile of shit."

Decker walked into the interview room and unfolded the lone chair leaning against the wall. The place was cramped when occupied by only two people; with five it had become vacuum-packed. The others were squeezed around a metal bridge table, stuffing butts into an overflowing aluminum ashtray. He sandwiched the chair between Morrison and the wall.

*Not exactly the executive suite.*

"So good of you to show up, Sergeant," Arlington sneered from the opposite side of the table. "That is your *current* rank, isn't it?"

Decker ignored the comment but zeroed in on the man. Arlington was dressed expensively and conservatively—Italian silk navy suit, fine white cotton shirt, navy-and-maroon silk striped tie. His feet were ensconsced in crocodile loafers, and a maroon hand-kerchief blossomed from his breast pocket.

His face was suffused with contempt.

*Of what?* thought Decker. *The surroundings? The police? The indignity of it all?*

He became enraged.

*The guy's a first-class scumbag and* he's *contemptuous?* Decker's eyes drifted to Arlington's left, to his lawyer. A white-haired Modigliani, strictly high power. The guy reeked of self-confidence—the kind that had come from years of being kept on retainer. Opening his Mark Cross briefcase, Mr. Long Face took out a pile of papers, a fine-point felt-tip pen, a notepad, and a Sony tape recorder. Not to be outdone, Morrison brought out his own cassette deck. He pushed the pause button and waited.

The last man at the table was George Birdwell, the deputy DA, a bespectacled black Berkeley grad in his late twenties. *Good,* Decker thought. *We're in fine hands.* Birdwell was as conscientious as anyone Decker had ever met and was as sharp as a cactus needle.

Arlington's lawyer spoke up in a deep voice. "Let's begin now."

"Go ahead," Morrison said, turning on the tape recorder.

"My client has a few remarks he'd like to offer in the hope they may aid in your investigation of the Bates-Armbruster case. Mr. Arlington has come here of his own volition—against legal advice—and in good faith, in order to advance the course of justice. Furthermore, it is agreed upon by all parties present that any information disclosed in said statement may not be used against Mr. Arlington should there be any further legal proceedings pertaining to this matter." He looked at Arlington. "You may begin."

The steel man read from a prepared statement:

"I first came into contact with Cameron Smithson through a

mutual acquaintance on or about July fifteenth of last year. After a brief discussion of security investments, Mr. Smithson offered to show me explicit, illegal, pornographic material for the disclosed sum of five thousand dollars per viewing. I accepted the invitation in the hope of gathering information that could lead to his arrest, since the thought of viewing such filth for pleasurable purposes was personally sickening. During the course of my investigation, I came into contact with Cecil Pode and his son, Earl, who appeared to be business partners with Mr. Smithson. I was about to delve further into this highly organized network of illicit activity when the police invaded the premises of 791 Brooks Ave. in Venice. I state this in order to aid in your ongoing police investigations and to put an end to the perversion that is so widespread in our society."

He tossed the sheet of paper toward Decker.

"End of statement."

"How did Cameron Smithson arrange the filming?" the captain asked.

"End of statement!" Arlington boomed, rising out of the chair.

"Where did Smithson get the films, Arlington?" Decker prodded. "Did he finance them and hire Cecil to do the camera work?"

"You heard my client, gentlemen. Now if you'll excuse us . . ."

The captain pushed the stop button on the cassette player.

"What I just read was for the record," Arlington scowled, brushing a piece of lint off of his lapel. "Now this is *off* the record." He glowered at Decker. "If you ever, ever show your face around my homes or any of my offices again and try to roust me, I'll personally cut off your balls, have them pickled, then eat them with my chef's salad for lunch. I hope you understand what I'm saying, Sergeant?"

"Are you threatening my man, Arlington?" Morrison snapped.

"Just a statement of fact." Arlington opened the door. "Good day."

The two of them walked out.

"Asshole," Decker muttered, then smiled at Morrison. "But we've got something."

"Besides," Birdwell said excitedly, "it's all bluff. He knows he could be subpoenaed as a material witness to the raid. We all know that Arlington's involvement goes deeper than a marijuana charge. Why else would his mouthpiece be so insistent upon immunity?"

"Immunity for anything connected with Cameron Smithson," Decker said. "But not for everything. If we can connect him to other illicit activities, he's an open target."

"Like what?" Morrison asked.

"Soliciting minors for immoral purposes. Assault. Murder. Minor things like that."

"You're trying to link him to the Loving Grandpas?" Morrison asked.

"Yes," Decker answered. "Who told you about them?"

"Someone called me from Hollywood and said Dunn had been questioning hookers about them. I figured she was there at your behest."

"Loving Grandpas?" Birdwell asked.

"A club of old, rich pervs who beat up runaways," Decker said.

"Jesus," Birdwell said. "And Arlington's connected with them?"

"Maybe," answered Decker.

"Maybe not," Morrison answered.

"If he is, this could be big," Birdwell said, licking his lips.

"If it turns out that way, you'll be the first to know," Morrison said. "Thanks for coming down today, George."

"No problem."

After the prosecutor left, Morrison shut the door and looked at Decker.

"You're being dunked in the cesspool, Pete," Morrison said. "I've got a notice of transfer sitting on my desk. Guess who it's for?"

"Oh shit!"

"Someone thinks you went overboard and wants you off the case," Morrison said.

"Jesus Christ, all I did was goose the asshole," Decker said.

"Yeah, well now the asshole just fucked you over."

"Who's got a hard-on for me?"

"I don't know."

"Well, Arlington's got someone in the Department."

"I have a feeling it's more than one person," the captain said. "The transfer notice was sent by Hollenbeck Division. Ostensibly they need a Spanish-speaking detective of your rank."

Decker swore under his breath.

"I'm not going," he said.

"You fucked up."

"Fuck this noise." Decker took out his shield and gun and threw them on the table.

"Cut the dramatics, Pete. You know you fucked up. You're damn lucky your ass is still in one piece." Morrison pushed the rewind button on the tape recorder. "Yeah, we *knew* Arlington was holding back, but you *can't* harass him. You *can't* threaten him. Damn it, Pete. You know that!"

"Sometimes you've got to bend the rules a little. Goddam it, I saw . . . *you* saw what happened to that poor kid, and goddam it, I don't want it to happen again if I can help it."

"Let me ask you this, Sergeant? What the hell would you have done if he'd called your bluff and slapped you and the Department with a multimillion dollar harassment or defamation of character suit? You'd be ruined as a career cop, and you'd probably also get disbarred. What would you have done?"

"I don't know."

"Don't you think you should have thought about that?"

"You've got to follow your own dictates once in a while."

"What would you have done?" Morrison pressed.

"I don't know, for Chrissakes! But I know one thing, Captain. If I didn't do anything, I wouldn't have been able to live with myself. No job is worth that."

"I've got no room in this department for puffed-up crusaders, Decker."

*You've got the ball,* Decker thought. *You goddam serve.* He stayed silent.

"Why didn't you let me know what the hell you were doing?" Morrison asked.

"You already told me that Arlington was off-limits. If I get fucked over, why bring you down with me?"

"Let's hear it for loyalty," Morrison said sardonically. "Why didn't you tell me you were looking for a connection between Arlington and the Loving Grandpas?"

"I should have."

"Yes, you should have."

Decker threw up his hands. "I was wrong. For what it's worth, I haven't gotten past first base with it."

Neither one spoke for a moment.

"I'm not going back to East L.A.," Decker said. "Especially not under these circumstances."

"So you'll quit the force and then what? Law? You hate law. What are you going to do?"

"You could keep me here if you wanted to," Decker said. "My Spanish is needed here as much as there."

"Why should I? You've been a bad team player lately."

"Look, Captain. You're the one who put me in Homicide."

Morrison reflected on that.

"Take your badge and piece and get back to work," he said. "I'll see what I can do about the transfer. Maybe you'll quit acting like a schmuck once you're back with Juvey."

"Kids bring out the best in me."

"Snotnose remarks are unbecoming in a veteran like you, Pete."

Decker suddenly felt old. His mind flashed to Rina's smooth, naked, *young* body. He wondered if he looked the way he felt.

He flipped through the stacks of 1040s and 540s on his desk. Cecil Pode had earned about the same amount of money each year of his life, with no sudden windfalls. The last couple of years, the photo business had experienced a slight decline in income. If Pode was making side money in the porno business, he was either stuffing it in a bank in the Cayman Islands or pissing it away. The man had admitted a gambling problem. Might be how he got involved in the first place. But one thing was certain; he wasn't reporting the dirty income.

Pode's army record gave no further insights into his personality. He'd spent a hitch in Korea and had been discharged honorably.

Decker pushed away the papers just as Marge bounced in.

"You hit a winner!" she announced, pulling up a chair. "Ida Pode's remains were not found in bed. She was found inside the room at the threshold of her bedroom door."

"And no arson was suspected?" Decker asked.

"Nope. The Fire Department figures she fell asleep while smoking."

"Then why didn't she die in bed?" Decker wondered out loud.

"Maybe she was awakened by the smoke, tried to get out, and before she could, she was overcome by fumes," said Marge.

"Or?" Decker said.

"Somebody set her bed on fire and prevented her from leaving the room," she answered. "What would be the motive for murder?"

"My intuition says insurance money," he replied. "But we're only talking ten g's here."

"Ten thousand dollars bought a lot more back then," she said. "And desperate gamblers have been known to do it for a lot less."

"I've got another motive, Margie," he said. "Hatred."

The phone rang.

"Decker."

"Detective? This is Dr. Bachman, family dentist for the Podes."

"How are you, Doctor?"

"Fine. It took me a while to find the X-rays. Earl hadn't come in for quite a while. Must be ten years since his last appointment. Dustin was in here three years ago. If you want me to, I'll send copies to Dr. Hennon, but you might want to run the originals over to her place and then give them back to me—save us all a little time and inconvenience."

"I'll be right over." He hung up the phone.

Mike Hollander strolled up to the desk and handed Decker a manila envelope stamped: *Dr. Meisner—Confidential Records.*

"Earl's pediatric records," he said. "Can this man get the lead out or what?"

"Amazing what you can do when you work, Mike," Marge said.

"Thanks," Decker said, ripping them open. He flipped over the cover sheet and began to read.

"Anything new?" inquired Marge.

Decker didn't answer.

"Pete?" asked Marge.

"Huh?"

"Anything new?"

"Decker, the woman's talking to you," Mike said, slapping his back.

"Uh . . . sorry. At least now I know why L.A. County had no record of Earl's birth. He was born in Fresno."

"A scenic spot to dump your load," Hollander said.

"If you like armpits," Marge said. "Weren't the Podes married in Fresno?"

"Yep," Decker answered. "Ten to one old Ida went home to Mama to foal."

He read further, then said, "Earl broke his arm when he was eighteen months and was treated for burns at ages two and three. Jaw fracture at three also. Contusions and head injuries from a so-called fall at four, broken rib at four and a half . . ."

"Goddam, that stuff makes me sick," Hollander exclaimed. "I've seen it over and over, and I never get used to it."

Marge placed her hand on his shoulder. "You may be a horny old slob, but you've got a heart, Mike."

Hollander threw her a dirty look.

"Burnt hands at seven," Decker said. "Aha! Enuresis at nine. That's bed-wetting. The doctor prescribed To . . . Tofin . . . I can't read this."

"Tofranil," Marge said.

"Yeah, that's it. Okay, okay. Here we go. He upped the dosage at age eleven." Decker looked up. "The kid was still pissing in his pants at age eleven. The first time the Fire Department was called over to the Podes' house was a year before. I think little Earl was a pyrophile. Let's hear it for the headshrinkers."

He read on, frowned, then began flipping back to the beginning pages.

"What's wrong," Marge wanted to know.

"Hmmm."

"What is it?"

"You know, the burnt hands at seven were the last recorded abuses," Decker noted. "Dustin's chart had physical abuse into his teens."

"You're talking about the old lady like she was rational or something," Mike said.

Decker smiled. "You're right." He folded up the chart and tucked it under his arm. "I'll double-check the records over lunch."

Hennon stood in front of the viewing monitor, compared the sets of radiographs, and shook her head in amazement.

"I want you to promise me one thing, Pete."

"What's that, Annie?"

"If I'm ever found dead under mysterious circumstances, you'll be the detective on the case."

"A promise I hope I never have keep," he chuckled. "Which one belongs to the bones?"

"Earl . . ." She stared at the screen. "His teeth had shifted and changed a bit over time—a few new amalgams—but there's enough similarity to some of the older restorations and a very distinctive old hairline fracture of the mid-mandible for me to say a definite match."

She turned off the light switch and picked up a plaster replica of Earl's skull. "Alas, poor Pode. I didn't know him, Pete. Nor did I want to."

The detective smiled.

"Got time for some coffee?" she asked.

"Thanks, but I've got to get these back to Bachman before he closes up shop."

She nodded.

"How's it going with your lady?" She made a face. "I don't mean to be nosy—"

"It's okay. I'd say it's going . . ." He searched for the right word. "Well, let's just say we have an understanding—a very nice understanding. She's moving away to New York."

"For good?" Hennon asked, surprised.

"For the time being."

"What are you going to do in the meantime?"

"I don't know. We've left it open. But some chains are permanent even if they are invisible."

He shrugged, and she broke into a warm, wide smile. "You've got my number. A beer with a pal doesn't seem like a bad way to spend an evening. Give us a call sometimes."

"I will," said Decker.

Hennon handed him the packet of X-rays. "Good luck, Pete." They shook hands. Hers was firm and confident.

"Peter!" the boys cried simultaneously.

He hugged them both, smiled at Rina's parents, and looked around.

"Where's your eema?" he asked.

"Buying some books and junk at the gift shop," Jake answered.

The airport wasn't busy, but their flight was going to be crowded. The area around the departure gate was full. The adjacent plane was going to Madison, Wisconsin, and the passengers were mostly blonde and blue-eyed. The travelers to New York were a salad of ethnicities—a little black, a little Italian, a little Puerto Rican, some Irish or German, several Jews including some wearing knitted yarmulkes and dressed in ordinary street clothes and others with side curls, wearing long black coats and black hats and speaking Yiddish. Decker sat down and the boys took seats on either side.

"You know any of those men?" Decker asked pointing to the black-garbed Jews.

Jacob shook his head.

"They're Chasidim," Sammy said. "Fanatics!"

Decker laughed, but stopped quickly when he realized the boy was serious.

"I've got something for you guys," he said, reaching into a paper bag.

"What?" Jake asked.

"A couple of Go-Bots. I didn't have time to wrap them. One's a bad guy, the other's a good one. You boys decide who wants who."

"We can switch off," Jacob said, tearing the plastic bubble over the toy. He started pulling on the die-cast metal pieces, changing the figure from a bulldozer into a pocket-sized robot.

"Excited about going?" Decker asked.

"Yeah!" Sammy exclaimed, holding his unopened toy in his hand. "I *love* my *bubbe* and *zaydah*."

Decker glanced at Rina's parents. They pretended not to hear, but the wounded look shone in their eyes.

"You have lots of relatives in New York, don't you?" Decker said quietly.

"Tons!" said Sammy. "My abba's two sisters live there. Tante Esther has five kids; the oldest one just turned eighteen and got his driver's license! Tante Shayna has four kids, and my cousin Reuven and I are only two days apart."

"And Shimon and I are only two months apart," Jake said.

"I look exactly like Reuven," Sammy continued. "People used to always mistake us for twins 'cause I look like my abba and he looks like Tante Shayna, and my abba and she looked alike. And you know what else?"

"What?"

"I have great-grandparents there! They are *so* old—like seventy-three or four."

"That's great," said Decker.

"And they're not even senile or anything."

Decker laughed. His own parents were close to that age. "You should have a good time."

"Eema said we're going to go to a big school," Jake said. "And there'll be lots of people, so we won't have to worry about bad guys dumping bodies and Eema being alone."

The younger boy quieted suddenly and leaned his head on Decker's shoulder.

"I'll miss you, Peter. I'll miss the horses. I don't think they have horses in Borough Park."

The thought of horses roaming the wilds of Brooklyn made Decker smile.

"I'll miss you, too," said Sammy in a small voice.

"I'll miss you guys like anything. More than you could know. But I'm also very happy 'cause I know you'll be having lots of fun being with your abba's family."

Decker hugged them and gave them each a big kiss.

"Take care of yourselves."

They hugged and kissed him back.

"Aren't you gonna wait for Eema?" Jake asked.

"I'll meet her at the newsstand." Decker got up and nodded to Rina's parents.

"It was nice that you came down," Mr. Elias said.

"Couldn't let the kids leave without saying good-bye."

Her mother looked at him, then turned away.

"Good-bye, Mrs. Elias."

"Good-bye," she said formally.

Decker tousled the boys' hair and headed toward the gift shop, saddened. He knew he'd miss the boys tremendously, but at least they seemed excited about the move. It was some consolation.

He found Rina paging through a paperback with a lurid cover. She was wearing a muted pink cable-knit sweater, a full, pleated gray wool skirt, and gray suede boots. Her hair was tucked into a knitted angora tam. Her face was soft and serene even under the harsh fluorescent lighting.

He walked over to her and took the book out of her hand. She jumped.

"Peter! What are you doing here? I told you not to come!"

"I wanted to see the boys off." He looked at the cover of the paperback. "*The Jackknife Slasher—The True Account of a Woman's Plunge into Terror.* Sure you want to read this?"

She began to cry uncontrollably. Decker put the book back, escorted her out of the airport gift shop and into an isolated corner. He hugged her fiercely.

"I knew . . . this . . . would happen," she said between sobs.

He rocked her, kissed a delicate earlobe jeweled with a single diamond stud.

"Don't go," he whispered.

She didn't answer. He knew she would leave. It was best for both of them. But every condemned man can still pray for an eleventh-hour reprieve.

"I love you," he said. "We'll work it out if you stay."

She still said nothing. Her tear-streaked face leaned against his shirt, looking as lost and forlorn as a wet puppy.

He sighed and gave up. "I'm a phone call away, Honey," he said. "You ring, I take the next flight out."

She nodded and brought his mouth down to her own.

A sweet kiss.

A flight number was announced over the loudspeaker.

"That's my flight," she said, wiping tears off her face. "Oh my God, Peter. What am I going to do without you?"

He smiled. "You'll do real well without me."

*Too well*, he thought.

"I don't think so," she said, breaking away. She took a deep breath. "Walk me to the gate?"

Decker hesitated. "I've already said bye to the boys. I don't think your parents are too anxious to see me again."

"I'll miss you terribly," she said.

"I'll miss you terribly, too," he said. "You write, you hear? Or better yet, call . . . collect."

"That won't be necessary, Peter," she answered. "I have a feeling we're going to rack up enormous phone bills."

"I'll pay for them all."

"We'll split them down the middle," she said.

"Liberated woman."

"Hardly." Her lip began to tremble.

"You know, Rina," he said. "If I'm going to keep studying with Rabbi Schulman, I figured I should take on a Jewish name. What do you think?"

"I think it's a *great* idea," she said, breaking into a dazzling smile.

"Schulman suggested Pinchas. I guess that was as close an approximation to Peter that he could find. Then I discovered that Pinchas is Phineas in English—as in Phineas Fogg. I vetoed that one."

"It doesn't suit you, either," she said. "Pinchas was a religious zealot."

"No, that's not me," he said. "I like Akiva. What do you think?"

"I *love* it!"

The loud speaker announced the final flight call.

"I've got to go." She kissed his lips softly. "Take care of yourself."

The tears had come back, but that didn't stop her. She pivoted and walked toward the gate. She had a lovely sway, a graceful step.

"I love you, Rina," he called out.

"I love you too, Akiva," she shouted, turning her head to look at him as she strode toward her family.

By the time Decker got back to the car, he noticed his cheeks were wet. *Goddam smog,* he thought, rubbing his stinging eyes. *Even at night, it doesn't leave you alone.*

# ·25

Decker revved the Porsche up to ninety and flew on the empty stretch of freeway. The speed and wind gave him an illusion of infinite freedom, youth, and immortality. It had been months since he'd last burned rubber, and after seeing Rina off, he needed to rid himself of the emotion that had swelled inside and cut loose. The abandon lasted only a few minutes; his beeper went off, and his rearview mirror reflected a cruiser flashing him its blues. Pulling the Porsche onto the shoulder, he took out his badge disgustedly, got out of the car, and handed it to the uniform. The officer examined it carefully, then handed it back to him.

"What'd you clock me at?" Decker asked.

"Ninety-two." The officer eyed the car. "Nice set of wheels."

"Thanks. Put her together myself from bits and pieces over the years," said Decker. "She sure can race."

"I've got a '68 'Vette myself. Blown and supercharged. It's one hell of a fast motherfucker."

"A land jet."

"You've got it, Sarge." He smiled at Decker. "Take it easy."

"I just got beeped," Decker said. "I'm working Homicide. Mind if I use your radio?" He gave the cop his unit number and a moment later was patched through to Foothill.

"A break?" the patrolman asked after Decker hung up.

"Not sure, but I can hope," Decker said. He got into his car and left behind a cloud of exhaust.

\*    \*    \*

Marge was waiting for him at his desk.

"What's so urgent at . . ." Decker checked his watch, "11:36 P.M.?"

"Did you take your No-Doz tonight?"

"What do you have?"

She slapped some papers into his hands—warrants.

"That was fast," he said.

"Arlington's statement carries clout with a certain judge. Morrison called up and voilà!"

Decker read the documents—search warrants for Executive First and Cameron Smithson's condo, and an arrest warrant for Smithson Junior himself.

"Nothing for Dustin?" he asked.

"We don't have anything on him. Let's be grateful for what we've got." Marge put on her coat. "A couple of West L.A. detectives are searching Junior's house. We'll take Executive First."

Decker pocketed the papers.

"Let's go catch a bastard," he said.

Forty minutes later, the detectives turned onto Avenue of the Stars. The Century City thoroughfare was an empty ribbon of glistening blacktop bordered by steelgridded buildings that shimmered in the cool, overcast air. Marge pulled the unmarked into a loading zone in front of a postmodern edifice of chrome and glass—no doubt someone's architectural statement, she thought. *Cold cold cold!*

They walked up the black brick pathway to double glass doors. The entrance hall was brightly lit by a ceiling of fluorescent tubing and a security guard sat reading *Sports Illustrated* in a booth to the right of a bank of six elevators.

Decker knocked and the guard looked up—a middle-aged man with thick, fleshy features and a cue-ball head. Placing his hand on his gun, the guard swaggered over to them. They showed him their badges through the glass.

"What is it?" he asked them, opening the locked door.

"We have a search warrant for suite 581 of this building," Marge informed him. "Your superior should have notified you of our arrival."

"No one called me," said the bald man, shrugging.

"Why don't you call in?" suggested Decker.

As the watchman phoned, they waited on a bench in front of the elevators. Decker placed his elbows on his knees and rested his head in his palms. Until now he hadn't fully realized how much of his life Rina, the boys, and the yeshiva had taken up. Now, with long stretches of time suddenly at his disposal, he felt aimless instead of liberated. Sudden anger welled up inside his chest. Rina had no right to desert him. Or maybe it was the other way around. Hadn't he suggested they take a breather from each other? But a breather didn't mean her *leaving* him and moving away.

Fuck it all! Well, better hostility than depression. At least anger pumped him up for work. Depression left him a zombie.

"What do you think we'll find?" Marge asked.

"I'm not naive enough to think that the asshole left his books out in plain view, but maybe we can locate something incriminating against the whole shitload of scum."

"You okay, Pete?"

"Fine."

The guard put down the receiver and motioned them over.

"Yep," he said to them, "you're all cleared. Someone should have called, but you know how messages get screwed up. I think half our operators are on something." The man scrunched his eyes and rubbed his egghead. "They talk kind of slurred and giggle all the time."

"Can you take us up now?" Marge asked impatiently.

"Oh yeah. Sure, Detective. Right away."

He unlocked an elevator, rode with them up to the fifth floor, took out a passkey, and walked them to the suite. Muffled voices could be heard through the walls. Decker put his index finger to his lips and motioned them into the corner of the hallway, far enough away from the suite not to be heard, but close enough to keep an eye on the door.

"When did they come up here?" Marge whispered to the guard.

"They must've entered before I came on duty because they didn't come after I got here. I came on duty at ten P.M."

"Maybe they never went home from work," Decker suggested in a hushed voice. "Go back to your station. Use the stairwell and be very quiet about it."

The guard nodded and disappeared. Decker drew his gun.

"Expecting trouble?" Marge asked, taking out her own.

"Not really," he answered. "I checked gun registration, and nothing was ever issued to any of the Podes or Smithsons. But Cecil pulled a .38 on me and I'm not taking any more chances with these pricks.

"If Cameron Smithson is in there, the case is duck soup. We go in and make the arrest. If he isn't, then we'll have to do a number on whoever is in there."

"Namely Smithson Senior or Pode or both," Marge said.

"Just what we were going to do anyway. Any last minute things you want to go over?"

She shook her head. "How about yourself?"

"I'm clear. Let's go."

They went back to the office. Decker pounded on the door and stepped aside.

"Police," he yelled. "Open up."

Harrison Smithson responded by partially opening the door and sticking out his head. Flushed and panting, he looked over-wrought.

"What's going on?"

"Police officers," Marge said. She opened her wallet and showed him the badge. "Open up."

The broker paused.

"We have a search warrant, Mr. Smithson," she added. "You have no choice."

Decker pushed the door open.

Dustin Pode was stooped over, brushing off the knees of his trousers. The room was in complete disarray. Filing cabinet drawers were pulled out, boxes stuffed with papers were piled on the desks and chairs. A paper shredder was going full force in the corner. Marge ran over and shut it off.

"What the hell is going on?" Pode asked.

"Planning on going somewhere, gentlemen?" Decker asked, putting his gun away.

"Who are you?" Pode spat at Decker. "Sure as hell your real name isn't Jack Cohen."

The detective pulled out his badge and ID, and as Pode read, a look of horrified recognition swept across his face.

"You're the cop who murdered my father."

Decker stuffed the badge back in his jacket and said, "We have a search warrant for this premise and an arrest warrant for Cameron Smithson."

"Cameron isn't here," Harrison said quickly.

"Where is he?" Marge asked.

"I don't know," his father answered. "Just what the hell do you think you're doing barging in on citizens like this?"

The feigned outrage did little to conceal the obvious fright that was overtaking Smithson. Decker bore into him.

"Unless you want an obstruction charge tacked onto whatever else we find, I suggest you let us get on with our work."

"Call Cahill and Jarrett," Pode said softly to Smithson. "And don't say anything until someone gets here."

"Dustin, I think—"

"Harrison, just do as I say!"

Decker walked around the room, tangled his leg in the switchboard cord, tripped, and ripped it out of the wall.

"Goddam!" he swore. "I sure am clumsy."

He searched his pockets and pulled out some change.

"Here. There must be a pay phone in the building somewhere. The call's on me."

"Generous," Pode said, glaring at the open palm. "Keep your change. I don't want anything from you." He turned his attention to Smithson. "Use the phone in the lobby, Harry."

"I think I need some air, Pete," Marge said. "I'll walk you down, Mr. Smithson."

"A phone call to my lawyer is confidential, Detective," Smithson said, trying to remain calm.

"Yeah, but a phone call to your son warning him off could get you in a lot of trouble," Marge replied. "I'm only thinking of your welfare."

"Make the call, Harrison," Pode ordered.

As they left, Marge gave Decker a surreptitious wink. God bless Marjorie, he thought. If only he and the woman he loved were as attuned to each other as the two of them were.

He started sorting through the piles of papers while trying to size up Pode. Out of the corner of his eye he watched the stockbroker methodically remove a box from a chair, pick up a copy of *Forbes* that was lying around, and bury himself in the magazine. He looked nervous but still in control. *Well, let's see if something can't be done about that.*

"You know, Pode," he began. "I've been checking into you."

"Do tell."

"I've been checking into you like the way I checked into your father." Decker pulled out a ledger and opened it. "Like I checked into your mother, like I checked into your brother . . ."

Pode didn't react.

"Tell me something, Dustin. Did Earl ever stop wetting his bed?"

Pode's only response was fingers gripping the edges of the magazine.

"He didn't?" Decker pressed.

A small laugh emanated from behind the periodical.

"I guess not, huh?"

Silence.

"Hey, there's nothing to be embarrassed about. A lot of boys are bed wetters. I'm just curious if Earl ever licked the problem."

"Why don't you ask him?"

"I would if I could find him," said Decker. "Heard from him lately?"

Silence.

Decker had asked the morgue to hold off notifying Pode about his brother's death. Just now Pode had responded acerbically, without fear or trepidation. Either Dustin didn't know that Earl had died or he didn't care.

"Where's Cameron?" Decker asked.

"I don't have to answer your questions," Pode said. "Just do what you have to do and get out of here."

"You're right," Decker agreed. "You don't have to answer my questions, but I can still ask 'em. For instance, how come your mama had such a hard time opening her bedroom door to escape that fire she died in?"

Pode slammed down the magazine. His face had turned white. "I don't have to listen to this!"

Decker ignored him. "Now sometimes people can't turn door handles because they're just too damn hot to touch," he went on. "But that's usually the case when the fire starts on the outside, not on the inside. And if Mama did grab a red hot handle, some of her flesh would have seared onto the metal. That didn't happen. Now how could she not have had enough strength to turn a door handle and get the hell out of there?"

"I'm going to take a walk," Pode said.

"I don't think so."

"And how do you propose to stop me?"

"How about I'm delaying you for questioning? Material witness to a triple homicide."

"Is that official?"

"If you want it to be."

Pode said nothing, turned around, and started straightening some papers.

"Don't touch anything," Decker commanded.

Clenching his jaw, Pode went back to *Forbes*. Decker scanned a ledger, put it aside, and ripped open another box.

"Now I know that your mother was drunk that day. In fact she was a chronic alcoholic. And chronic lushes have a keen sense of survival." He dumped the contents of the carton on the floor and began to sort through the scattered papers. "See, what I figure is maybe Mama was trying to get out from the inside and someone was holding the door from the outside."

Carefully, Pode placed the magazine on the floor and went to the water cooler. Beads of perspiration had formed on his forehead.

"As long as you're up, how about you getting me a drink?" Decker asked.

"Get it yourself!"

"C'mon. Don't be sore."

"Fuck off!"

Decker got up, kicked another box and, walked over to the cooler. Dustin walked away, but Decker dogged his heels.

"Did you ever see that special with Farrah Fawcett that was on the boob tube a couple of years back? 'The Burning Bed,' I think it was."

Dustin sat back down in his chair and didn't answer. Decker stood behind him, peering down over his shoulders.

"I remember when the real case hit the papers," he said. "Francine Hughes murdered her husband by burning him to death after putting up with years of physical abuse."

"Are you insinuating anything?" Pode croaked out.

"Nah," he said, dismissing the thought as absurd. "Want to know what I found out about you?"

"I'm not particularly interested in what you found out," Dustin said. He had interlaced his fingers, but the hands were still shaking.

"I looked at your medical records and found out you were an abused kid," Decker said. "Damn shame no one reported it back then. Your mother used to get drunk a lot and whop the shit out of you. You want to know what else I found out?"

Dustin didn't respond.

"Earl was an abused child also. But when he reached five, something amazing happened. His pediatric records stopped showing signs of physical abuse. Now yours were full of them clear up through your teens."

Pode began to breathe heavily.

"Now this is just speculation—"

"I'm not interested," uttered Pode weakly. But Decker went on.

"When Earl was seven, he was hauled into the doctor for treatment of burns on his hands. At first I thought this was abuse also, but then I started thinking. Burns for abuse are usually on places where people don't see them—the back, the stomach, the butt. Burns on the hands indicate a kid playing with fire.

"See, that's why I asked you about the bed-wetting. Fire-starting and bed-wetting, along with cruelty to animals, are a triad you find in a lot of psychopathic teenagers. I'm wondering if Earl ever tortured anything living—like bugs or pets . . . or people?"

Pode refused to answer. Decker began to circle him—a vulture ready to swoop.

"Let's get a little more hypothetical," he said. "For some reason Earl stopped getting beat up by your mother. Now I, being a curious kind of guy, think to myself, why? Maybe Earl was a weird kid who played with fire to scare Mama off, huh? What do you think about that?"

"You have a vivid imagination."

"Earl started setting fire to Mama's bed as she slept off her stupors. And she was a bright lady who got the message real fast. Of course she never *told* anyone that sonny boy was trying to burn her. Then she'd have had to admit what she was doing to you both. So she just covered her ass and said she fell asleep while smoking. And besides, she knew you'd rescue her. You were the good boy—"

"Lies—"

"Mama knew the score," Decker said, talking over him. "Kicking the shit out of Earl just wasn't worth getting barbecued for. Besides, there was always little old Dustin to kick around. She began laying off Earl. But that just made it worse for you, didn't it, Dustin?"

"Filthy lies!"

"Earl thought he was helping both of you. He didn't realize that Mama was still picking on you when he wasn't looking. And you were too ashamed to tell him."

Decker crouched in front of him, almost nose to nose.

"Let's go back to May 1977," he said.

Dustin gasped out, "No."

"Mama was alone in her bed," Decker said. "Earl had run away from home by then. There was no record of him in high school in '77. Now I don't know what the catalyst was but the idea hit you. Mama was sleeping one off, and you took a match—"

"No!" Pode yelled. "I mean, this is preposterous!"

"You set her bed on fire. Maybe you suddenly grew yourself a set of balls—"

"You don't understand a thing!" Dustin blurted out. "My father . . ." He didn't finish.

"She didn't stay asleep like a good girl, did she, Pode? She tried to get out. No one was there to help her. Maybe someone even hindered her a little . . ."

"No!"

"No one blames you," Decker said gently. "Man, I'd be pretty damn pissed if someone binged on hooch and then beat the crap out of me. And you must have been pretty pissed at her, Dustin. I mean, to go to all the trouble to take down the personal pictures in your dad's house and destroy them after he died. But even that wasn't enough. You had to burn down the whole house even if it meant losing money on resale. Now that's an angry kid."

Dustin shook his head feebly.

"You also blew up Daddy's studio, didn't you?"

"No!" Pode gasped. "That's not true! I mean, none of it is true."

"It's all true," Decker continued. "I've seen child abuse thousands of times, Dustin. I'm just moonlighting in Homicide. I usually work Juvenile, and you'd be amazed at how many cases I've worked on that tell your story."

Sweat dripped down Pode's nose onto his shirt.

"You hot, Buddy?" Decker asked.

"No."

"Want a handkerchief?"

"NO!"

"Okay. Just take it easy." Decker walked away. *Don't crack him before you read him his rights.* He poked around another box and found a ledger that looked promising—erasure marks, write-overs, numbers that didn't add up. "Who does your books, Dustin?"

Pode said nothing.

"Someone's been fudging, huh? Skimming off the top. Trying to bleed a little out of legit profits to finance turkey films and shoddy real estate deals."

"Shut up!"

"Nah, it wasn't you. You're too smart. But Cameron . . ." Decker paused. "He's a dumbshit, isn't he? Earl's best friend whom you've always hated. But Earl liked him. Actually they were two of a kind. Weird kids. Neighbors used to say the two of them were inseparable."

"I'm not going to say another word, Decker."

"I'm not saying that Earl didn't love you. In fact, he worshipped you, emulated everything you did. If you were in Spanish Club, so was Earl, if you were on the football team, so was Earl. So you couldn't figure out why Earl would keep seeing this creep whom you hated. Little did you know how similar they were."

Pode said nothing, but his body was trembling.

"Let's go back to that fateful day in May. You killed your mother—"

"No!"

"Earl had left home, but he was still in contact with you—and with Cameron. You told Earl what happened. I mean if anyone could understand, it had to be Earl. But then Earl did a dumb thing. He told Cameron."

"I need some air," Pode said, suddenly gasping.

Decker turned the air conditioner on full blast.

"Want to get it off your chest?" Decker urged.

"Fuck off!"

"Now Weirdo Cameron had you by the balls. He started black-mailing not only you but your father as well. Cameron would make sadistic porno films—snuffs—and force your father to film them and use his old porno contacts to peddle them. If your father refused, Cameron threatened to tell the police how you murdered your mother—"

"No!"

"Ever see one of the films, Dustin? Ever see the look of abject terror on the girl's face as she's being sliced and tortured. Ever see flesh burn? Too bad the films couldn't have featured the putrid smell of sizzling skin—"

"NO, NO, NO!" Pode screamed. "They were all staged, damn it! It was ketchup and Karo syrup . . ."

He sunk to his knees.

"Tell me about it, Dustin?"

"NO!"

"Then I'll keep talking." Decker glanced at his watch. "Wonder what's keeping Detective Dunn and Mr. Smithson?"

He smiled, knowing the number she must be playing on Senior. Damn, she was good.

"Before I keep going, let me just read you your rights, just for the hell of it."

Pode said nothing as Decker Mirandized him.

"Sure you don't want to talk about it?"

Pode didn't answer.

"Where were we?" Decker pulled Dustin back onto the chair and leaned over his shoulder. "Oh yeah. Cameron made films, Earl and the Countess starred in them, and the proceeds went to pay off Cammy Boy's sour investments. Damn son of a bitch always fancied himself as a bigwig producer *artiste,* didn't he. Kissed up to assholes like Armand Arlington when they all thought he was a piece of shit."

Pode let out a low moan.

"When you protested, Cameron would threaten to blow the lid on you and your father. At first your dad was genuinely coerced, but then he started enjoying the extra revenue—helped pay off his gambling debts to the loan sharks. But the only problem was, the more money he had, the more he blew. See, Dustin, I know everything—"

Pode bolted up and began to pace.

"You don't know a *damn* thing!" he shouted. "She would have killed us all! She was getting worse. She was *paranoid* when she was drunk. Thought everyone was out to get her. She was coming after us with knives! She once cut up Dad so badly . . ."

He leaned against a wall and started to weep. Decker let the sobs continue for a minute, then walked over to him and gently placed his hand on his shoulder.

"I understand," he said softly. "Look, Dustin, none of this is your fault. It's Cameron's. He was the one who murdered. He murdered the Countess, didn't he?"

Dustin sniffed and nodded his head.

"Did he tell you why he did it? He did it for money, didn't he?"

Again Dustin nodded, as he dried his eyes on his shirt sleeve. The man had turned pathetic.

"She wanted a bigger piece of the pie, huh?" Decker asked.

"That's what Cameron told me," Dustin said in a weak voice. "He threatened to expose me if I told anyone."

"Threatened you with what?"

"You know."

"Your mother?"

Dustin nodded.

"Cameron's evil, Dustin, a psychopath. He's the one who talked your brother into killing Lindsey—"

"My brother never killed anyone. I told you it was all *staged!*"

"I saw the film, Dustin. The girl died. Your brother and the Countess killed her. Then Cameron went ahead and used the same gun that killed Lindsey Bates to murder the Countess and your brother."

Either Pode didn't hear him or Decker's timing was off, because the broker didn't react.

"Did you understand what I said, Dustin?"

The tear-stained face looked up.

"Earl's dead, Dustin."

Pode shook his head no.

"He was positively identified by dental records, Dustin. Cameron killed him—"

"No!" Pode screamed, drool slipping out of the corners of his mouth. "*No!*" He lunged at Decker, who sidestepped the attack, and went stumbling onto his knees.

"Cameron killed your brother. I know about it. Tell me where he is."

"No, no, no!" He was wailing now. Decker let him cry it out, then helped him off his knees and back onto the chair.

"He *couldn't* have killed Earl," Pode argued desperately. "He told me Earl had left town. I just got a postcard from Mexico."

"Cameron must have had it mailed. Earl's dead, Dustin. I saw his skull this afternoon, complete with the midline lower jaw fracture."

"Dear God!" The man's shoulders heaved with sobs. "He was all I had. I don't believe you. I don't believe any of this nightmare."

"It's all true. Cameron killed your brother for the same reason he killed the Countess. They were trying to extort more bread from him, and Cammy Boy couldn't afford 'em any longer. So he whacked 'em. I've got the ledgers, Dustin. They'll tell me the whole story."

Dustin shook his head like a child denying a sinful thought.

"Help me find the bastard, Dustin. Tell me where he is."

"I don't know," Pode said weakly. "I don't know."

"We all know that Cameron wasn't just working with your father and brother. There had to be someone bigger. Who else was involved?"

"I don't know anything. I tried to keep out of it."

"Maybe for names, we could strike a deal with the district attorney."

"I don't know anything." Pode's body was shaking, jerking loosely as if he were having a seizure. "I swear it!"

"Did Cameron take off?" Decker asked.

Numbly, Pode nodded.

"When?"

"Few hours ago. One of his contacts . . ." Pode blew his nose and started crying again. "When can I see him?"

"Who?"

"My brother. When can I pick him up?"

"I'll see to it that the body's immediately released, but you've got to help me out, Dustin."

Pode began to weep uncontrollably. Decker shook him.

"Help me, dammit. Help yourself, for God's sake!" he yelled. "Where is Cameron?"

"I don't know!" Dustin screamed back. "I swear it! A contact tipped him off over the phone that the cops were closing in. He didn't even bother to pack. Just took off."

"Where?"

"I don't know."

"Would his father know where he is?"

"I don't know. Harry didn't tell me if he did."

If Smithson Senior knew anything, Marge would find out.

"Why didn't Cameron take off as soon as the cops started to investigate."

"He claims he had protection."

*Arlington!*

"Was Harrison Smithson involved in the film business?" Decker asked.

"Not as far as I know. He knew something wasn't right, but never asked questions. When Cameron told him to start packing, Harrison did as told. That was part of the problem. Harrison spoiled the kid rotten. His only child. Let the son of a bitch have everything he ever wanted."

"Why didn't you take off after Cameron called?" Decker asked.

"Someone had to clean house," Pode said flatly.

"Do you know who the contact was?" Decker asked.

Pode shook his head.

"C'mon, Dustin! Save your ass and tell me a name!"

"I don't know anything, Sergeant. I swear I don't know!"

"I hope you know something for your own sake. Something you can bargain with. Tell me anything you know that might help your case, Dustin. These ledgers are full of incriminating evidence. You admitted knowing about the snuff films—"

"They told me they were staged!"

"But you knew about them."

Pode said nothing.

"Dammit, Dustin. Who made the fucking call to Cameron?"

"I don't know."

"Who were his contacts?"

"I don't know."

"Big shots?" Decker asked.

"He claimed they were." Pode looked at Decker and beseeched. "What do you *want* from me? I don't *know* anything."

Decker sighed. He'd have to get Arlington another way.

"All right. Let's take it slow. What time did Cameron take off?"

"The call came at about ten tonight. He left right afterwards."

After banking hours, Decker thought. If Cameron was going to hole up somewhere, he'd have to get hold of some money.

"Did Cameron have cash on hand?"

"You kidding? The son of a bitch was always in the hole."

"Did he have any kind of nest egg?"

Dustin looked sick.

"We had a . . ."

"Slush fund?" Decker tried.

"More like an emergency fund. At the Security Pacific here in Century City."

"How much is in there?"

"About twenty thousand."

"Can he withdraw from it without your consent?"

"He needs all three signatures, and he can only withdraw the money at this branch."

"How is Cameron at forging signatures?"

Pode's face turned a bilious green.

"God!" He bowed his head in utter defeat. "I know what you're thinking. That he'll probably come by tomorrow morning and try to pick it up." He buried his face in his hands and began to cry again. "Oh Jesus Christ, what happened to my life?"

It was close to five by the time Decker finished all the paperwork. His back and shoulders ached and his head was exploding.

Popping a couple of aspirins in his mouth, he swallowed them dry, stretched, and walked over to the coffee urn. Some kind soul had the decency to brew up a fresh batch.

He poured himself a cup of black coffee and went back to his desk, troubled. Dustin Pode had burned his house down because he hated his mother. But he didn't harbor overt animosity toward his father. So why would he blow up Cecil's studio? And why the sudden switch from arson to detonators? Dustin insisted he hadn't done it. Maybe he was telling the truth.

He walked over to Marge. She was catnapping at her desk and he shook her shoulders gently. She awoke abruptly and confused.

"What time is it?" She bolted upward.

"About five."

"Why the hell did you wake me up?" she asked, irritatedly. "We've still got three hours before we have to be at the bank."

"Take a ride with me," Decker said.

"Where?"

"To the beach."

"*What?*" she said, laughing. But she was already reaching for her coat.

"Let's go visit another angry young man," he said. "I'll explain on the way over."

Truscott opened the door, rubbed his eyes, and broke into a vacant grin.

"I was expecting you," he giggled. "I was. I was. I was."

The kid had changed. The depression was gone. He was dancing around in a tiny circle, clapping his hands and stomping his feet as if doing a hora.

Decker looked around. The place had changed, too. The black sheets had been removed, and in their place were photos of Lindsey, hundreds of them, papering the walls. The floor was a garbage dump—heaps of empty styrofoam hamburger containers, empty Coke cups, cigarette butts, half-eaten doughnuts and cookies, quart containers with melted ice cream oozing out, cupcake wrappers.

*Twinkie defense,* thought Decker.

"You shouldn't have blown up the studio," Decker said gently.

"We had to," Chris said, looking at the walls. "Didn't we, Lindsey? I told you we'd get the sucker, and we did, Babydoll." He burst into applause and shouted, "Yea!"

"Chris, someone could have gotten hurt," Marge said.

"Uh uh, no way. No way, Jose!" Truscott shook his head vehemently. "I made sure. I saw you guys go in, I waited for you guys to go out. I waited till everyone was far away. I made sure. I don't want to hurt anybody except the fucker who hurt us. Right, Babydoll?"

He was talking to the wall again.

Marge looked at Decker. He shrugged.

"We're going to call Santa Monica police now, Chris," Decker said. "You're going to be arrested. Do you have a lawyer?"

"Nope."

"They'll give you one," Decker said. "Don't say anymore until you've talked with your lawyer. All right?"

Truscott smiled angelically. "May I use the bathroom?" he asked politely. "I'd like to wash up before I go."

"No," Marge said. "Stay right here."

"I have to make pee-pee," Truscott babbled out.

"Make in your pants," she said softly.

He did and smiled as his pants leg became saturated with urine.

"Suicidal," Marge whispered to Decker. "I don't want him alone in there."

They waited in silence until the police arrived. The detectives gave their statements as Chris was lead out whistling "Somewhere Over the Rainbow." Decker watched as they stuffed him in a blue and white cruiser. Involuntarily, he found himself planning the kid's defense. A psych. eval.; the kid was obviously distressed—no, *distraught*. Much better word. Bring in a few of Lindsey's friends as character witnesses. Mention that Lindsey's father had been feeding Chris's bottomless pit of guilt. The kid had no priors—Decker had checked that out when he'd suspected him in Lindsey's death. No one had been injured in the blast. Even with a mediocre lawyer, Chris should get off with probation.

Decker rubbed his arms, remembering how he had held Chris, rocked him as he wept. A pitiful, broken kid, consumed with guilt. He made a mental note to call up Chris's PD. The young man needed psychiatric counseling and his lawyer could request it. Decker hoped to God that the court would follow the recommendation. The last thing he needed was another body on his conscience.

# ·26

"Think Cammy Boy will show?" Decker asked Marge over the radio.

"Who knows?" she answered. "But we've got nothing else to lose. Daddy doesn't know where he is; Mommy doesn't know where he is; Pode doesn't know where he is; and Cameron doesn't have any other friends."

"If he doesn't turn up," said Decker, "maybe the papers we seized last night will tell us something."

"Hope springs eternal."

The bank had opened fifteen minutes ago. Decker readjusted his stance and scanned the twenty-story building. He was situated behind a pillar with a view of the back exit. Marge was watching the front. Behind him, across a large, paved courtyard was Century City Shopping Center. The outdoor mall was a conglomeration of department stores, trendy boutiques, and alfresco sandwich shops. Around noon, the walkways were often filled with popcorn, cookie, and candy vendors, flower stands, and espresso machines on pushcarts. Decker's ex-wife often shopped there with Cindy. Decker found the place overly cute.

He looked in front of him, then over his shoulder. People were mulling around, skittering about like moths on a lightbulb. Then what was he, he thought. A hawk? Was there a purpose to all of this? He looked at the sky. *Damn it,* he swore. *If You're out there, why don't You ever show Your face. Make it all so much easier.*

He was still angry at Rina. She had finally given herself over to him completely only to withdraw literally from his grasp. He ached inside and out and felt it was all her fault.

Aw, screw it! Maybe it wasn't Rina at all. Just lack of sleep or a decent meal. Maybe it was age.

He saw Cameron and snapped himself out of his funk.

"Go in and take him, Pete," said a voice on the radio.

Decker began his cautious approach, and when he was close enough, called out his name. Smithson turned around.

"He's got a gun!" someone shouted into the wireless.

Decker hit the ground as Cameron let go with two shots and headed in the direction of the mall. Decker and a half dozen cops took off after him, dodging screaming shoppers.

Smithson stopped, took aim, fired again, and ducked into the Broadway, knocking down mannequins and upsetting racks of spring fashions. Bright-hued fabrics spilled onto the floor, dripping color like paint off an artist's palette. Decker tripped over an anorexic dummy modeling a string bikini and red plastic sunglasses. The head split open, revealing a skull as empty as the expression frozen on its face. He regained his footing, heard the crack of a bullet whizzing past him, and fell back onto the floor. As soon as he saw Smithson take off, he got up and followed. His quarry sprinted up the escalator, pushing women behind him as he approached the second, then the third level.

Shrieks were accompanied by shattering glass. Smithson was in the China Department. The police approached slowly, avoiding the shards of broken crystal and china. An eerie calm hung in the air, the sound of shallow breathing.

Then a lead crystal ship's decanter shot out of nowhere and smashed into a cop. The heavy mass of solid glass bounced off his face and blood poured out of his nose. Gouges etched his cheeks and face. He clutched at his eyes.

"Call an ambulance," Decker shouted.

Another officer ministered to the wounded man as Decker rushed after Cameron, who had sped back down the escalator to the first floor, into Men's Wear.

"He's at the tie counter!" Decker shouted. "Dammit it, clear everyone out of there!"

"Freeze, fucker!" a policeman yelled.

Smithson grabbed the first person he could reach—an elderly gray-haired woman with thick glasses that made her eyes look bulging—and placed a gun to her temple.

"Step back or she's dead," he said between gasps of air. "You understand?"

"No one make a move," the commanding officer yelled. "Everyone back off!"

The woman began to hyperventilate, and her eyes rolled backward.

"Just do what he says," the commander ordered. "Just do what he says."

"All right!" Cameron screamed. "You dogs have *two* minutes to clear out before I do something desperate." He fired into the air. "I mean it!"

The commander was a man named Pearson, tall and thin, with a hard mouth, penetrating dark eyes, and a leathery face full of creases. He crept along the floor over to Decker.

"No time for SWAT. I've heard you're a crack shot." He handed him an FAL-Paratrooper. "Take him out."

Decker took the rifle.

*The man deserved to die.*

*It was up to him.*

*Arlington would be lost.*

*But the fucker deserved to die.*

Suddenly Decker felt the enormity of playing judge, jury, and executioner. With a steady hand and a clear eye, he brought Smithson's skull into sight. His index finger gripped the trigger and began to exert pressure while his hand drifted a fraction of an inch.

The blast.

Cameron Smithson stared at the gushing stump that had once been his right hand. Within moments he was down on the floor being read his rights while cops tried frantically to staunch the flow of blood. Decker wondered if he'd bleed to death. He looked at the hostage. She was splattered with blood, screaming hysterically, limbs jerking spastically. Marge gripped her shoulders and the woman slumped into her arms.

Getting up from the floor, Decker brushed off his knees.

"Everything all right?" he yelled.

"She's okay," Marge shouted back.

Pearson walked over and Decker handed him back the rifle. The commander was rigid with fury.

"Did you miss or was that on purpose, Sergeant?"

Decker didn't answer. Pearson repeated the question.

"I aimed for his head, Commander," Decker said.

Pearson stared at him. "You aimed for his head, but managed to blow off his hand?"

"I aimed for his head," Decker repeated.

"You have a rep as an ace with a gun. What the hell happened?"

"I don't know."

"You don't know," Pearson muttered. "You don't know, huh?"

Decker was silent.

"Were you in 'Nam, Sergeant?"

"Yes."

"How many gooks did you kill?"

"Point blank, three."

"Three gooks?"

"Yes, sir."

"And when you blasted them, did you ask if they were good gooks or bad gooks?"

"No, sir."

"Did you try to *incapacitate* them before you wasted them?"

"No, sir."

"You just blew their fucking heads off, right?"

"Right."

"And why was that?"

"Because if I didn't kill them, they would have killed me."

"Very good, Sergeant," Pearson mocked. "Very good. You know, Decker, we fought a fucking war out there and we're fighting a fucking war here. You didn't incapacitate the enemy out there; you don't do it here. If you don't believe me, look up the procedure on how to handle a hostage situation."

"I aimed for his head," Decker reiterated.

"I *bet* you did." Pearson poked Decker's chest. "Your captain will hear about this. In the meantime, do some target practice."

"Yes, sir."

Pearson walked away and Decker exhaled out loud. Marge came over to him.

"How's the old lady?" Decker asked her.

"So far, so good. Tough gal. No signs of shock or heart attack. Paramedics will take good care of her."

"That's good."

"Are you in deep shit?" she asked.

"Nah, I don't think so. Hell, I shot him. My aim was just a little off."

"Pete, if you'd have aimed for his head, he would have been ready for the meat wagon."

"If I missed, it was an unconscious thing."

Marge chuckled.

"Just who do you think you're shittin', big buddy?"

Decker shrugged. "Let's just say I passed the buck to a Higher Source. Besides, I want Arlington and all the other fuckers like him. Can't get any names from a dead man."

"Go out and get a breath of fresh air, Pete. You're white."

Suddenly feeling dizzy, he knew she was right.

# ·27

He'd closed a lot of cases, but this one had all the ingredients for sensationalism—pornography, murder, and big names.

From his hospital bed, Cameron Smithson accused Arlington, providing proof of his involvement in the snuff films. Arlington, surrounded by loving wife and children looking teary-eyed into the cameras, maintained his innocence and pointed his finger at others. Prominent people were brought in for questioning, prominent people were arrested.

With every new accusation, out swarmed a new flock of vultures pestering him at the station house or, worse, at his ranch. The ubiquitous microphones shoved in his face. It made him weary, he told Rina. They spoke daily, mostly in the late hours of the evening when both households were quiet.

The more attention he got, the more he retreated. He took to sneaking into the station through the back door. He avoided going home to the ranch at dinnertime, opting instead for long walks in the hills that surrounded the yeshiva. In the beginning Rabbi Schulman had joined him, but as the furor faded, Decker found himself hiking greater distances in solitude.

Sometimes he'd take a book with him as he walked, sometimes a camera, more often than not he'd explore empty-handed and talk to himself. Maybe he was talking to Someone Else.

Mrs. Bates greeted Decker warmly. It was late afternoon and the day had been gorgeous—spring temperatures that had begun to climb into summer heat. He suggested they take a walk. She thought that was a fine idea.

They began their journey in silence, inhaling clear air, talking in sunshine. He heard her breathing, and it sounded a little winded. He slowed his pace, and she smiled at him and said thank you. Their trek took them past rows of well-tended houses to La Canada Boulevard. Ten minutes later they were in front of a convenience store. She declined Decker's offer of a drink, so he bought a pint of orange juice for himself. Another five minutes and they were at the edge of a municipal park. Mrs. Bates suggested they sit on a bench under an elm.

Decker drank half his juice and wiped his mouth with a napkin. He said: "County Hospital called me this morning. Smithson's dead."

She said nothing at first, then asked, "How'd he die?"

"Pneumonia." He took another swallow of juice.

"I thought he had blood poisoning or something like that," she said without emotion.

"He did. Apparently the infection from the hand wound wasn't responding to any of the safer antibiotics, so they gave him a real strong one. It killed the infection, but it also wiped out his immune system. He contracted pneumonia about a week ago and died late last evening."

"Good. I hope he suffered."

"I think he did." Decker looked up at the sky, then down at his lap. "How's your husband doing?"

"We've separated," she answered.

"I'm sorry," he said.

She shrugged.

"We have little tolerance for each other's faults now," she said. Decker nodded.

"Financially, it won't be easy for either one of us." She hesitated, then said, "He lost his job, you know."

"I didn't," Decker said.

"Yes." She shook her head sadly. "In a way, he has it much worse than I. A woman is allowed to grieve—although no one wants to be with her while she's doing it. A man has to pull himself together. Snap himself out of it." She sighed. "We're both living on savings—exhausting them. It's a good thing Erin is bright. She's going to need scholarships." She faced Decker. "I told her that, and you know what she said?"

"What?"

"'Don't worry about it, Mom.' I do believe that's the first time we talked civilly since she's reached her teens."

"That's nice."

"Yes, it is." She took a deep breath. "I know I have to look for work eventually. But most employers don't think a museum docent has marketable skills. I suppose they're right."

"I'm sure you'll find something."

"I feel a little tired, Sergeant. Perhaps it would be best if we headed back."

When they reached her doorstep, Decker held out his hand. She took it and squeezed it tightly.

"Thank you for everything," she said. "Thank Detective Dunn, also. She was out here the other week. It seems very strange that I should find comfort from the police."

"Call me from time to time," Decker said. "Let me know how you're doing."

"I will."

He left the house and drove to his ranch. The sun was beginning to set—striations of pinks and rusts cutting into a darkening expanse of teal sky. Standing on his back porch, he faced east, peering into the advancing dimness. Feeling at peace, he took out a siddur and said his evening prayers.